THE FINAL LAP

Topsy,

Abby & I welcome you to our world.

May the journey be interesting & exciting.

Ian

February 2023

THE FINAL LAP

IAN LAXTON

GUIDE BOOK PUBLICATIONS

First edition published in 2023
by Guide Book Publications
73 Greenside Road
Greenside
Johannesburg 2193
South Africa
www.guidebooks.co.za

ISBN: 978-0-6399825-3-3

© Ian Laxton, 2023

All rights reserved. No part of this publication may be reproduced, stored in or introduced into a retrieval system, or transmitted, in any form, or by any means (electronic, mechanical, digital, photocopying, recording or otherwise) without the prior written permission of the publisher. Any person who performs any unauthorised act in relation to this publication may be liable to criminal prosecution and civil claims for damages.

This is a work of fiction. Unless otherwise indicated, all the names, characters, dates, businesses, places, events and incidents in this book are either the product of the author's imagination or used in a fictitious manner. Any resemblance to actual persons, living or dead, or actual events is purely coincidental.

Cover design by mr design
Typeset by Triple M Design
Cover image by iStock/MichaelSvoboda
Back cover image by iStock/LeArchitecto
Printed and bound by Kadimah Print, Cape Town

*This story is inspired by two amazing women,
in their own way, world class.
You know who you are.
For my special friends, Lucy, Noopy and Benji*

'Instead, they called her a name. They called her "a genius". And even though it really didn't explain anything, everybody considered it a satisfactory explanation. And that way, nobody had to try to understand.'

Louis Sachar, *Someday Angeline*

PROLOGUE

2009

The whole thing seemed to be well planned. The famous kid, the wealthy parents, the known routine. Predictable. Risky, but manageable. 'Surprise is on our side,' the main guy said. The other two guys agreed.

It was a normal Tuesday. School finished at two-thirty and the moms were parked outside in the road, waiting for their children. Because many students had extra-murals such as sports, library duty, that kind of thing, there weren't as many parents as there would be on, say, a Friday.

One of the moms was sitting quietly in her car, a grey Volkswagen Polo, about forty metres down the road from the school gate, sending a text on her phone. Everyone knew her. She was pretty and friendly and, of course, the mother of the runner.

But this was the wealthy suburb of Bryanston, Johannesburg, and not some quaint English town, where it's safe. Joburg can be like the Wild West, gangsters, drug dealers, hijackers, kidnappers, you name it. All kinds of crooks. So the school employed an outside security company with guards all over the place, especially at the gates when the students came and went. A tall, blonde teenager of about fifteen came through the gate into the road. Her hair was tied back in a ponytail, her school backpack was bulging and she was carrying a big red sports bag.

Unmistakable.

She smiled and waved. Hi, Mom. The woman in the Volkswagen Polo shut off her phone, waved back, opened her door and climbed out.

The teenager was halfway to the car when there was a roaring sound and a black BMW came hurtling down the road on the wrong side. The car's brakes screamed and there was smoke from its tyres as it came to a screeching halt right next to her.

Later, people said that everything happened in slow motion. They could see it all like a horror movie playing over and over, frame by frame.

Two guys dressed in black with hoodies leapt out of the car and grabbed the girl in a kind of bear hug, trying to shove her into their car. But she had this big sports bag and her backpack and they couldn't get hold of her. She screamed like hell and the three of them scuffled onto the ground.

Everyone scattered. The mom ran to her daughter. Three security guards ran towards the struggling group. Everyone else ran away screaming. The mom stood in the road, frozen. One of the kidnappers pulled out a gun and turned towards the people running. He knew it was useless, they'd lost their chance of getting the girl and now they had to escape.

So he just fired off shots randomly, later reports ranging from three to six, or even eight. One security guard was hit in the shoulder. Everyone dived for cover. It was mayhem.

In fact, the thing hadn't been planned very well after all. The backpack, the sports bag, the security guys.

When faced with a life-threatening situation, two basic choices are available to all animals, including humans: *fight* or *flight*. The senior kidnapper, in that unrehearsed, split-second, desperate life-and-death situation, chose *fight*. He stood still, turned towards the mom, screamed, 'Die, white bitch!' and shot her. Twice.

The kidnappers tried to get back into the car but it was useless. The security guards were all over them with their batons and their fists and their yelling and their fear and uncontrolled anger.

Then everything went quiet. People peered out from behind cars and walls.

What they saw was this: a Volkswagen Polo with its driver's door open, a black BMW with three men shoved inside, two security guards, guns drawn, next to it. One security guy on the ground, blood oozing onto the grey tarmac.

A young man stood about ten metres away, his hands held high as if calling to the gods. He had a Head Boy badge on the lapel of his blue school blazer.

THE FINAL LAP

The target, her ponytail in disarray and her bags scattered, sat bewildered on the ground. The mother, already bleeding out from a shot through the aorta, lay sprawled on the white line in the centre of the road.

The boy's name was Deon Coetzee and the mother was Anne Dennison.

The girl's name was Abby Dennison and her life, from that moment, would never be the same.

PART I

Nine Years Later

1

Wednesday, 25 July

LONDON, ENGLAND

It was early afternoon on a warm, sunny day in London. James Selfe stood at the window of his fifteenth-floor office in Regalbank Towers, the bank's international headquarters in the City. He gazed out, deep in thought, considering for the umpteenth time the spectacular view south-east across the Thames, with the Shard and the Tower contrasting the modern and historical faces of the city.

Selfe, teased by his friends as embodying 'the perfect example of a boring London banker', cut an imposing figure. Today he wore, as he usually did, a dark suit with the jacket buttoned, crisp white shirt, blue-striped Old Etonian tie, Regalbank-branded gold and black cufflinks, and highly polished black leather shoes. Just over a metre-ninety tall, with neatly trimmed steel-grey hair and bristly moustache, he was a striking man.

At forty-three years of age, James was at the pinnacle of his career. Not only had he recently been invited to join the bank's board of directors, but the board had, for the past four years, allowed him to combine his portfolio of marketing and public affairs with his other passion, athletics. Back in 2014, prompted by Selfe, the bank had decided to create and become title sponsor of a new track and field event called the Roger Bannister Memorial Athletics Meeting, first staged in the 2012 London Olympic Stadium and designed to revive the waning memory of the world's first sub-four-minute miler. For that first meeting, it was decided that Selfe would act as temporary meeting director. After all, he had successfully overseen several smaller events in his spare time over the years. The temporary assignment had, four years later, become a permanent fixture in his life.

Selfe moved across the room, stuck his head out the door and smiled at his PA. 'Jane, please ask Mary to join me.'

A minute later a tall woman of about thirty, smartly dressed in the bank's uniform of branded grey shirt, black, knee-length pencil skirt and black jacket, entered. This was Mary Southgate, Regalbank's head of communications. She came right to the point. 'I presume you've had those phone calls.'

'Have a seat, Mary, and let's get to it. Indeed, I have good news. This morning I spoke to both Paul Dennison, Abby's father, and Solomon Moyo, Sarah's brother and manager. Odd-sounding character, to be honest. Anyway, the Dennison crew are training in Loughborough and the Moyos are in Eldoret.'

'That's the famous distance-training town in the Kenyan highlands?'

'Yes.'

'And …'

'Both Abby Dennison and Sarah Moyo are confirmed. Contracts being prepared as we speak. It's a real coup, the best field ever for the Roger Bannister Mile for Women.'

'How tough were they in the negotiations?'

'As expected. Paul and I had lengthy discussions over issues such as appearance fees, time incentives and the selection of a pacemaker. We finally agreed on 100 000 euro to line up, and a further 200 000 for the world record, if Abby breaks it. Everything payable, less taxes, to a Regalbank account in the United Kingdom. Plus accommodation, plus Suzy Marshall as pacemaker.'

'No problem, Abby is worth three times that amount.'

Getting Moyo on board had been trickier. 'Solomon demanded four air tickets from Nairobi to London, hotel accommodation "away from the other runners, you know how shy she is", and a 100 000 euro appearance fee. I balked at this and we settled on 50 000. Solomon told me that Sarah would not attend the media conference. That wasn't news to me, I know the score.'

'Well done, James, this is brilliant. Media release time?'

'Of course, what are you waiting for? Time to rock the sporting world.'

Mary left Selfe's office ten minutes later, the agreed text for the announcement rolling around in her head. The media release was posted on two websites simultaneously at 16h00, London time.

Abby Dennison and Sarah Moyo to compete in the Roger Bannister Memorial Mile

Wednesday, 25 July.

Regalbank, proud sponsor of the Roger Bannister Memorial Athletics Meeting, today confirmed the participation of two more top-ranked athletes, South African Abby Dennison and Sarah Moyo of Zimbabwe, in the women's mile race at the Roger Bannister Memorial Athletics Meeting, to be held in the London Olympic Stadium on the evening of Friday, 10 August.

Dennison is currently ranked number one in the world over the 1 500-metre distance. The previously confirmed field, which includes Mary McColgan of Scotland, England's Jane Beardsley, former world number one Olga Fedorova from Russia, and Kenyan superstar Elinah Kiptanui, already boasted the cream of the world's middle-distance athletes. But the presence of Dennison and Moyo in the race is certain to add a new dimension of excitement in what promises to be a genuine attempt to break the old women's world record for the distance.

Ends.

For more information, visit www.regalbank.org.uk/athletics or www.rogbannistermeeting.com

Regalbank was a smart sponsor. The company's media people knew exactly what would happen. Although 'the cream' description seemed reasonable on the surface, everyone knew the race would not be the same without Abby Dennison and Sarah Moyo, arguably the world's best over the distance.

After a few minutes out in cyberspace, the story went viral. Thousands of downloads, hundreds of thousands of tweets and retweets, phones ringing off the hook. Several hundred emails in the first hour. Mary put a dozen volunteers onto phones and computers and retired to her office.

In far-away Eldoret in Kenya's Rift Valley, Solomon Moyo put down his beer bottle, went into a pair of adjoining rooms and woke two men and a woman. 'Get up, I have news.'

In his hotel room in a small mid-range hotel in the English Midlands town of Loughborough, Paul Dennison closed his laptop. Bring it on, he thought. Seventeen days to go, perfect. He powered up his phone and sent a message on 'The Team' WhatsApp group: 'My room, guys, now. Time to rock and roll.'

2

Friday, 27 July

JOHANNESBURG, SOUTH AFRICA

Deon Coetzee exited the Gautrain station in Rosebank and started the short walk through the shopping precinct to APN Towers, where he worked as a senior sports journalist for Africa Paramount News, the biggest and most respected news agency in the country. The southern hemisphere winter was nearing its end and the temperature, close to zero before dawn, had climbed to a more acceptable fifteen degrees for the morning commute. The sun was gently warming the air as it rose over Alexandra in the east and Deon knew that the temperature would peak at more than twenty in the early afternoon.

Typical Joburg, he thought, that's why I love this place. Great weather, great people, great sport to enjoy.

Already the wide shopping precinct was buzzing. Unlike Cape Town, 1 400 kilometres to the south-west, Johannesburg is an early morning town, he thought. Men in tailored suits and women in black skirts and grey jackets sat outside Tashas, sipping steaming cappuccinos *al fresco*. Deon could almost taste the warm chocolate croissants and freshly baked poppy seed muffins beckoning from inside the SuperSpar as he walked past.

His trusty laptop bag in his right hand, he smiled at a pretty shop assistant on her way to work at Woolies. 'Happy morning,' she said, her high heels clicking on the paved walkway.

A homeless man emerged from his sleeping place in a bus shelter, thrust out a hand and said, 'A few bucks for breakfast, sir?' Deon stopped, fished in a pocket and took out a ten rand note. 'Here you go,' he said, 'but buy breakfast, not beer. And my name is Deon, not sir.'

He received a toothless grin in return. 'Thank you, sir.'

Deon looked exactly like a young sports journalist, preferring branded T-shirts, faded jeans, denim jacket and training shoes to the suits and ties of the guys on the finance desk. His three days of beard was the result of consecutive late nights reporting on a T20 game at the Wanderers Stadium and a soccer match at Orlando Stadium.

With a few minutes to spare before his official starting time up on the eighth floor, he sat on a low wall under a jacaranda tree outside Kingsmead College, the local elite girls' school. Closing his eyes, he reminded himself why he loved his job as images floated through his mind: the back staircase at the Wanderers Stadium up to the press box and the vertiginous view from its eagle nest under the roof; the scent of mown grass at Royal Johannesburg golf club just after dawn on the first day of the Joburg Open, the pigeons cooing and the caddies breathing out mini-clouds of fog while holding steaming cups of coffee; standing in awe of a medal-winning asymmetric bars routine in the women's gymnastics final; a bar clearance twenty centimetres above the head of a high jumper; a saved penalty in the cup final; a drop goal in the rain in the Currie Cup final; and the otherworldly ecstasy on the faces of runners who have just beaten the final gun in the Comrades Marathon.

He had also learned to appreciate the genius of a true world-class performer, the fusion of the essential elements of natural talent, a will to succeed as indestructible as tempered steel, the luck of a kitten plucked from the centre of a busy street by an eagle-eyed passer-by and the work ethic of William Shakespeare.

He loved the feeling of breathing in the atmosphere of a packed stadium, the life force of fifty thousand minds in unison, the fervour of their songs, their wide eyes and hopeful hearts. The way sport is able to lift people from a mundane existence in a council flat or squatter shack to a place where dreams are realised, even if vicariously through the successes of others. In packed stadia, people belong, are part of something bigger than themselves.

A taxi hooted angrily and Deon was jolted out of his dreamy reverie. Ten to nine, time to get into it, he realised.

The newsroom was quiet on a Friday morning, most of the reporters busy preparing for the weekend, which was when most of the sports action happened. Deon navigated the route between the workstations to his cubicle, the only sounds being the gentle hissing of the coffee machine in the corner, the click-click of fingers on keyboards and the whirring of printers. White noise came from the endless traffic on Oxford Road far below. The place smelled faintly of air freshener and floor polish.

He arrived at his workspace, a miniscule three-by-three-metre cubicle into which was crammed a desk with a personal computer and printer, a chair and a small side table covered in books, on top of which were two dirty coffee cups. On the floor was a miniature rugby ball autographed by the 2007 World Cup-winning Springbok rugby team, and a pair of ancient Nike running shoes. The partitions separating his workspace from his neighbours were covered with media accreditation cards from events all over the world, numerous images of Deon with a variety of famous sportspeople, including Abby Dennison, and several congratulatory letters from sponsors, sports federations and even the occasional politician.

It was a sports fan's man cave of note.

He collected his thoughts, powered up his laptop and started writing a preview of what would undoubtedly be a pedestrian soccer match between Wits University and Black Aces, scheduled for the next day. *Give me strength.*

He wrote just two paragraphs when it happened. The moment when his world changed forever.

It was a familiar sound, a ping that announced the arrival of an email, the beginning of a cascade of events that would ultimately become one of the biggest stories in the modern history of athletics.

Deon paused his preview to open the mail, hoping it wouldn't be one of those infuriating 'you've won a million dollars, just give us your bank details' spam messages.

It wasn't. It came from a .co.uk address. It said:

Dear Mr Coetzee,

The press office of the Roger Bannister Memorial Athletics Meeting officially invites you to attend our event, to be held in the London Olympic Stadium on 10 August. We routinely invite leading journalists from around the world to be our guests, particularly if there is an important athlete from their country taking part. You will know that Abby Dennison from South Africa has recently agreed to compete in the meeting's Blue Riband event, the women's mile.

You will appreciate the significance of this race, which evokes the history that resides in the mile as a track distance, synonymous with the great Roger Bannister, after whom this meeting is named.

Abby is currently ranked number one in the world in the 1 500 metres, the metric equivalent of the mile.

You are considered to be the pre-eminent athletics writer in South Africa, hence our invitation to you. Regalbank, the event sponsor, will fund your return airfare Johannesburg–London–Johannesburg, as well as six days of accommodation at our media hotel, four days before the meeting and two afterwards.

The meeting is in fourteen days' time (Friday the tenth) and we have arranged with the British High Commission to give you an emergency visa. If possible, we would like you to leave Johannesburg on the overnight British Airways flight the Monday before the meeting.

If you can confirm your availability by Monday afternoon, we will send you the flight and accommodation details.

Yours in athletics,
Simon Hardy
Media and Brand Manager, Roger Bannister Memorial Athletics Meeting

He read the mail again, and again, just to be sure he wasn't hallucinating. Then he stood up, walked through the newsroom past everyone, took the elevator down to the ground floor and stepped out into sunshine on Jellicoe Avenue, Rosebank.

It was busy out there. Minibus taxis crowded down Oxford Road, hooting and jostling for passengers. Pedestrians scuttled across the intersections, doing their best to avoid being demolished by cars, taxis and motorcycles. The faint sound of a mass of cheering girls drifted from inside Kingsmead College across the road. A giant orange crane swept in a gentle arc over a construction site. Hadedas screamed as they flew in convoy overhead, and in between it all he could even pick up the gentle calling of a pair of doves in a jacaranda tree.

He shoved his hands deep into the pockets of his jeans and crossed the mayhem of Oxford Road, walking into the gentle quietness of the shady avenues of Melrose. He thought about Abby Dennison, the reason for this unexpected invitation; first, a young girl in a blue school uniform three years his junior at school; then Abby, the enormously talented runner progressing from school prodigy to international track superstar. Then, with a sudden jolt, he recalled the worst day of his life when he was confronted with the sight of a woman lying in the road, her body covered in blood, breathless.

He turned back. It was time to meet with Charlie Savage.

Charlie, APN's sports editor and the one man who potentially stood between him and the stuff of dreams. Charlie, good old grumpy, unpredictable Charlie, a legend in the world of sports journalism and now top of mind given the email from London. Surely he would understand and give the thumbs-up to go to London?

Charlie Savage was just short of seventy, but looked older, thanks to a pack-a-day Marlboro habit that ultimately ended up in a close encounter with a heart attack.

Everyone respected him because he was wise in the ways of sports journalism and could sniff out a good story like a dog senses a bitch in heat. He seemed to possess a sixth sense that transcended normal communication channels in journalism. Some said he cast bones around his flat at midnight, others that the phenomenon was part of the paranormal universe.

Deon respected Charlie because he was brutally honest. A bad story, poor game prediction or an interview that missed the obvious angle was treated with contempt. 'Get your act together, son. This is garbage. Go home.'

Equally, something good was praised. Sort of. 'This is okay, but don't get too excited, you aren't up for a Pulitzer.'

He was notoriously tight with money, clinging onto his budget like a drowning man hangs onto a floating piece of wood in a storm-tossed sea. Famously skint, lesser mortals than Deon usually gave up the unequal struggle to get a new laptop or even be reimbursed a couple of hundred rand after a meal with the national captain of cricket or soccer.

But Deon took him on as a matter of pride, haggling for long periods over matters financial. 'I like that about you,' Savage once said. 'A good hack will never give up, just keep on going until you get the story, or the money, or the bone, like a dog.'

Five minutes later, Deon stood nervously at his boss's door. 'Come in, Deon. Sit,' growled Charlie. He hadn't even looked up.

Deon sat, hands rubbing nervously together. 'Boss, I have a request. I want to go on a trip.'

'To Durban for the surfing final again?'

'London.'

'What the …?' Charlie didn't normally utter profanities and he managed to retain his composure. Clearly, it was an effort. 'That's not possible.'

'It has to be. This is the story of the year. Really.'

'What could that possibly be?' He sounded doubtful.

'Abby Dennison.'

'Tell me more.' He was listening now, like Deon knew he would. Deon even thought that his ears pricked, like a dog's. Everyone listened when the name Abby Dennison was spoken.

He told him about the Bannister meeting, the Olympic Stadium, the Bannister mile race, the email from Simon Hardy, the flights, the hotel, the emergency visa, the thing about being South Africa's pre-eminent athletics journalist, the lot.

Charlie was quiet for a while and Deon held his breath. Then he said, quietly, 'Get out of here, now. Go!'

'Where to, boss?'

'Where do you think, you moron? The British High Commission. They close at noon on a Friday.'

3

Monday, 30 July

JOHANNESBURG

Mark Whyte was the founder, owner and Chief Executive Officer of MileStar Electronics, a medium-sized, highly successful Johannesburg-based technology company operating in the burgeoning online financial services sector. On this particular Monday morning, he was seated behind a large desk in his wood-panelled, deeply carpeted corner office on the top floor of a new office building on Rivonia Road.

At thirty-two, Mark certainly looked the part of a young, successful, wealthy and eligible executive. A metre-ninety tall, slim, sandy-haired and with boyish good looks, he wore a dark grey Armani suit over a pale blue shirt. His tie sported the navy blue and burgundy colours of St John's College, one of the city's finest boys' schools. A similarly coloured silk handkerchief peeped out of the breast pocket of his jacket which he, very unfashionably, wore virtually all the time at work. Imported brown Florsheim Arcus shoes completed the ensemble. There were no rings on his fingers.

Mark was no fool and for many years had understood the tortured history of his country and how a tiny proportion of the population were vastly privileged compared with the majority of the people. He was one of the privileged ones, thanks to an upbringing in a wealthy family (his father owned a substantial furniture-manufacturing business) and a private-school education. He also understood the strength of his intellect, particularly in mathematics, that underpinned a stellar academic career that culminated with an actuarial qualification, *cum laude*, from Wits University.

That was followed by a stint in the corporate world with increasingly senior posts in one of the country's largest life assurance companies, a period he subsequently termed 'the worst three years of my life'. He soon realised that, for him, the restrictions, rules and politics inherent in working for a large company outweighed the very real advantages of job security and a steady income. But he stayed in the corporate world because he enjoyed being at the cutting edge of the fascinating and rapidly changing world of data science and information technology and their increasing relevance in solving business problems and driving strategy. A comment made by one of his bosses, 'Mark, believe me, data is the new oil of the world', stuck with him.

Towards the end of the three years, it dawned on him that the financial products offered by his employer were aimed at relatively wealthy people with credit ratings and bank accounts, a business model that effectively excluded about eighty per cent of the population. He knew instinctively that the lack of insurance products for millions of low-income people represented a massive business opportunity.

He also had an entrepreneur's unerring nose for business and a hard, unfeeling, self-centred approach to work and life in general. After deciding to venture out on his own at the tender age of twenty-seven, he obtained seed funding from his father and several of Dad's wealthy mates. MileStar Electronics was born.

The company now sold low-cost life and funeral cover entirely online to thousands of low-income families in South Africa and its neighbours. It was a brilliant concept, one that had initially been pooh-poohed by the establishment but was now recognised as a model of how a new, disruptive tech start-up operation could profitably offer the unbanked majority of South Africans a chance to access some sort of financial inclusion and security.

Five years later, he owned a business that employed fifty-one people, made more than five million rand after tax each year and was conservatively worth more than forty million on the open market. How did he know that? Just a few months earlier he had been offered exactly that amount by a large financial services group for direct ownership. But he had turned it down. He was having too much fun to retire. Anyway, what would he do?

Mark also secretly prided himself in a tendency to relieve the boredom of academic and business life by taking calculated and totally unnecessary risks just for the thrill of it. He remembered with satisfaction the first time he'd done this, back when he was eleven. On a family holiday in uMhlanga Rocks he'd dared himself to swim out beyond the line of breakers at the beach, some sixty metres from the shore. His frantic parents scolded him and banned him from swimming for two days after he arrived, safely and smiling widely, back on shore. A photo of the family on that very beach adorned his desk, a reminder of that important day.

He glanced up nervously and made sure that his door was closed. Powering up a laptop that he withdrew from a locked desk drawer, he punched in a series of passwords and opened a file containing page after page of images, 275 in total. Mark scrolled through them for a few minutes, then connected the laptop to the company's central server and googled a name. The search engine responded by rolling out more than a million references. Right at the top was a media release headed 'Abby Dennison and Sarah Moyo to compete in the Roger Bannister Memorial Mile'.

He read it several times, made some notes on a pad and then, deep in thought, walked to the ceiling-to-floor window that occupied most of the north-facing wall of his office, and looked out. There had been an unseasonal overnight thunderstorm and the morning air was crystal clear. The view to the north was spectacular and the Magaliesberg mountains, sixty kilometres away, were silhouetted against a flawless blue sky.

Smiling, he lifted the handset on his desktop phone and buzzed his personal assistant. 'Be a honey, Mandy, and pop in for a second, won't you.' A slim brunette walked into the office.

'I need to go to London next week, preferably on Sunday. Please call Friedrich at Pentravel and book me a business-class ticket and a room at the Thistle, near Hyde Park.'

'Will you be coming home, or do you plan to stay there forever?' she asked cheekily, arching her eyebrows and grinning.

'Oh yes. Mmmm. Book six nights there, then another five at a reasonable place in the Lake District, Windermere if possible. I need a break in a quiet environment. Preferably right on the lake.'

She stared at him. The business was heading into its peak selling season and the company's various agents were scheduled to arrive for the annual sales conference in mid-August. How would Mark prepare for this key meeting while he was running around England?

'Yeah, right. Okay, cool. Next Sunday?' As she left the room she glanced, surprised, at the second laptop open on the desk. Never seen that before, she thought.

Mark closed the laptop, locked it away and left the office. Passing Mandy's desk, he muttered, 'Going out for a while, take messages.'

'What about the meeting with the new group of interns at two o'clock?'

'Change it. Make it at three. I'll be back by then.'

He went to the basement parking and powered up his red Porsche Carrera 911S Cabriolet. The three-litre engine growled as he moved towards the exit. With a wave to the security guard at the gate he accelerated down the narrow road behind the building, the car and its personalised number plate – Mstar GP – drawing envious looks from a group of young men in suits smoking outside.

Travelling through the suburbs, he arrived outside a school, noting that there were few people around, just some kids going home early and guards at the gate. With the engine still running, he stopped, looked over to his left and saw a small marble tombstone. On it were engraved some words and around the base lay a few dried-out yellow flowers.

Crossing the arterial Nicol Drive, he passed house after house hidden behind high walls armed with security cameras. On several corners there were little wooden huts with more cameras, manned by smartly uniformed guards from a private security company. The cameras rolled continuously, capturing the Porsche and its driver and transferring the film to a hard drive twelve kilometres away in a dusty, rundown warehouse in the industrial area of Wynberg.

Clearly knowing where to go, Mark arrived outside a house that, unlike its neighbours, did not have a very high wall. The double-storey dwelling was visible up a long driveway and was fronted by a wide patio, facing a small swimming pool.

A gardener was sweeping up leaves outside. 'Is the lady home?' Mark enquired through his open window. He knew the answer but asked anyway.

'No sir, the boss and the young lady are overseas.'

'When are they coming back?'

'Sir, I think at the end of September.'

Mark drove away, dropped into Hobart Grove Centre for a cappuccino and was back in his building an hour later.

Mandy stopped him outside his office. 'Welcome back at last. The interns have been waiting patiently for you. Today was their first day and they're itching to get to work. The Academy requires them to report back on progress weekly. You know they're with us for seven months. Talented bunch as usual. Two of them are apparently elite runners.'

'I know about the runners and look forward to meeting them. Bring them in.'

Mandy handed Mark four brown files, one for each intern.

As he closed the door, Mandy looked back with a certain level of dismay. It was becoming more common, this erratic behaviour of her unpredictable, impulsive, yet utterly brilliant boss. The hidden laptop, the unexpected trip to London, the sudden departure from the office. She recalled an article she had recently read on one of her favourite websites, one aimed specifically at young professional women. It was titled, 'Warning Signs – don't ignore his secrets'.

She dismissed the disturbing thought. Maybe he's having an early male mid-life crisis? On the other hand, maybe not.

4

Monday, 30 July

ELDORET, KENYA

When the history of Kenya in the early twenty-first century is written, Eldoret will earn a brief mention as a regional industrial and agricultural centre. But the little town will loom large in terms of athletics, for it was here that several of the legendary champions of world middle-distance running were born, grew up, lived, trained and became world beaters. These athletes put Eldoret firmly on the world sporting map.

With parts of the country situated two thousand metres above sea level, Kenya in the 1990s became one of the international epicentres of distance running. The combination of a rich pool of young men and women genetically endowed with the perfect body structure, anatomy and physiology for distance running, plus the fact that the country was high above sea level, meant that hundreds of young Kenyans ran and ran and ran some more, starting, very often, by running many miles to and from school.

And, of those youngsters a tiny, elite group emerged and hit the world of distance running in the 90s like a tsunami, smashing records and winning medals at an unprecedented rate. That pattern continued, producing runners of the calibre of Elinah Kiptanui, the country's current heroine, scheduled to run in the forthcoming Roger Bannister Memorial Mile for Women.

Over the years, the town of Eldoret morphed into an international mecca for runners, ranging from brilliant to ordinary, who arrived at the various custom-built training centres, high up in the African Rift Valley mountains, to train.

Sarah Moyo was one of these. Five days after the news that Sarah would be running the race in London hit the international sports media like a bullet, a man sat in a small room, drinking Tusker beer. Solomon Moyo was thinking about the call he had made a week earlier to James Selfe, the London banker. He smiled. Selfe had held out for a while, but in the end the power of the Moyo name and the stubbornness of the family's oldest sibling had won the day. Fifty thousand euro was more than Sarah had ever won, let alone received as an appearance fee.

In Eldoret, the sun was setting over the mountains and the smell of Nyama Choma, beef roasting on open barbecues on the roadside, drifted in through the open windows. Solomon went outside. Even though the town was close to the equator, it was cool in the Kenyan highlands. He sat on a rock under a wide acacia tree and closed his eyes. His mind drifted back nearly two decades to their modest home outside Harare in Zimbabwe.

For the first time since those days, Solomon Moyo felt confident that finally, his family would reach the glorious pinnacle of success and wealth that the sangoma had predicted. His mother, now part of the family ancestors, had consulted the old man when Solomon was just a boy. She had decided that, at nine, her oldest son was ready to grasp the obligation he had inherited to carry on the family name and, by revering the elders and ancestors, to grow its wealth and status in the community.

On that memorable day the wise old man had thrown the bones and declared that one of the three Moyo children would achieve fame and fortune far beyond their wildest imaginings. The young Solomon was stirred by these words but as the years passed he became ever more sceptical of the prophet's predictions as the three children, with both parents falling victim to a terrifying disease called AIDS, struggled to survive as the policies of their increasingly unpredictable and clearly unhinged president ruined their country.

In the end, running saved them. Little sister Sarah was blessed with an incredible ability to run long distances across the fields that surrounded their modest house, apparently without getting tired. Even as young as twelve or thirteen she would take off, satchel on her back and heavy leather shoes on her feet, to school, six kilometres away. The very evident joy she got from the act of flying along the rough dirt roads caught the attention of one of her teachers, a man with his own history of competitive running.

Wiseman Ngwenya had been a promising junior himself, excelling in the middle-distances and heading for an international career in the sport until his dreams and potential were snuffed out when the national athletics federation collapsed. Undeterred, the young Wiseman studied part-time while working as a waiter in a Harare restaurant, eventually ending up teaching mathematics at the school of the then fourteen-year-old, highly talented Sarah Moyo.

But there had been a problem. From as young as five, Sarah had shunned company, preferring to hide in her room with a book or, in later years, go running alone. Solomon and his younger brother, Samson, had ignored these warning signs until, one day when she was fifteen, Wiseman called them into his office. 'Sarah has what is known as Asperger's Syndrome,' he told the brothers. 'It usually starts early in life and these children have difficulty making eye contact. I have found that Sarah is quite awkward in social situations. The good news is that Sarah can learn to manage her social and communication challenges and has every chance of doing well in school and succeeding as an athlete. She just needs to be managed carefully. We have to be super careful in the way we protect her.'

The brothers sat there, horrified. 'Is she crazy?' asked Samson.

'Not at all. Think of it as being extremely shy. Withdrawn.'

Samson nodded. He knew. 'Long ago I noticed that Sarah never made eye contact and stared past people. She hated social situations and was unhappy when a stranger spoke to her. She also showed few emotions, not even being happy when she won a race.'

Solomon asked, 'Will this affect her running?'

Wiseman replied, 'Not if we recognise her condition, never pressurise her into uncomfortable social situations like press conferences and give her all the love we can. In fact, Asperger's people often excel at what they do. With the correct management, Sarah can become a world champion.'

Wiseman took her under his wing, nurtured her talent with the loving attention of a surrogate father and ultimately secured an athletics scholarship at the prestigious Villanova University in Philadelphia, Pennsylvania, the school where South African runner Sydney Maree had studied and eventually achieved lasting fame when he broke Brit Steve Ovett's world record over 1 500 metres in Cologne.

In America, the eighteen-year-old, painfully shy and profoundly inexperienced Sarah initially floundered under the combined pressures of living on another continent, coping with a completely foreign student environment, and the need to prove herself as an athlete. Her first year was a disaster as she battled academically and failed to achieve anything remotely acceptable as a runner, scoring best times that year of a pedestrian 2:04 for 800 metres and an even worse 4:12 over the 1 500.

Under the watchful eye of her coach and the university student counsellor, the silent, steel-like determination that would eventually make her the world number one emerged the following year as she scored personal bests of 1:59 for the 800 metres, 3:59 for the 1 500 metres, and a fine 8:41 for the 3 000 metres, good enough to guarantee that she stayed at Villanova.

Her final year was a triumph. She won the 1 500- and 3 000-metre races at the prestigious NCAA Outdoor Track and Field Championship, the equivalent of the Olympics for American universities, and ranked sixth in the world over the 1 500 with her 3:55.89 at the Rome Diamond League race.

Along the way, she never attended media briefings, gave interviews or was present at awards ceremonies.

The Moyo family spent the off-season in a small house in Eldoret, and the prize money and appearance fees she earned at races improved the family's finances considerably. Solomon, 'the wise prophet', as he proudly called himself, became her manager and slowly their combined bank balance grew, particularly as she earned in precious hard currency. Both Solomon and Samson, as her support team, were invited to track meetings. The future looked rosy.

At the end of Sarah's final year at Villanova, Solomon and Samson hired Caihong Junren as her coach, much to the dismay of her mentor at Villanova, who called at midnight when he heard the news. 'Do not go near any coach called Junren. Don't you know about the turtle blood episode? Run a mile in the opposite direction, preferably at world-record pace,' he said emphatically.

Solomon ignored the advice. Sarah had no idea that turtles even had blood and, in any case, had no say in the matter of her coach.

A year later she ran 3:53 in Tokyo, the world's fastest time that year. As far as anyone knew, Sarah Moyo had never had an in-depth interview, came from a poor family in Zimbabwe, was shy to the point of possibly being on the autism spectrum and was totally dominated by her two brothers, particularly Solomon.

Sitting under the acacia tree and thinking, Solomon recalled initially being hesitant about employing a coach with the name Junren. He knew about the famous episode back in the 1990s when a group of female Chinese athletes, including sisters Qu and Wang Junxia, broke eleven Asian records and three world records in one memorable track meeting. These and several other improbable, but nevertheless ratified, records survived an incredible twenty years before being broken. Their coach at the time was a man called Ma Junren.

In a letter allegedly written decades later, Wang claimed that she and other runners were forced to take 'large doses of illegal drugs over the years'. Folklore built up around the coach, including the unlikely story that his athletes were forced to drink turtle blood. Eventually, Ma Junren became notorious as the kingpin of Chinese doping.

Solomon dismissed the thought. Even though Caihong Junren was a distant relative of the now-disgraced Ma Junren, no one had raised the issue with him and he presumed it was all water under the bridge.

What was of vital importance now was the acknowledged fact that Sarah was, like Abby Dennison, an athlete with natural abilities seen only once in a generation. She was also the owner of an incredibly strong mind, a quality that had carried her from poor schoolgirl in rural Africa to the very pinnacle of the sport. Another fact was critical: Sarah Moyo and Abby Dennison had never raced head-to-head on the track. In just over ten days, that would change.

Solomon's reflective mood was interrupted by the sound of running shoes on dirt and the hint of rasping breaths. Sarah had arrived back after an hour's run along the dusty roads of Eldoret. She hadn't run hard, just a steady sixteen kilometres.

The pair went inside. While Sarah showered, Solomon woke the two men. 'Time to pack,' he said, 'we leave tomorrow. Let the war begin.'

5

Wednesday, 1 August

LOUGHBOROUGH, ENGLAND

Paul Dennison, Bronwyn Adams and JP van Riet sat in a quiet pub in a small hotel in the English Midlands town of Loughborough. It was just after eight o'clock and darkness had settled in. A football match was playing on a television set on the wall, Chelsea versus some Spanish team, the commentary muted. The only sounds were the occasional clink of glasses, the murmur of conversation across the almost deserted room and soft music from a system somewhere, a series of instrumental versions of The Beatles songs – 'Michelle', 'Yesterday', 'Here Comes the Sun', 'Let it Be'.

Abby Dennison, the other member of what had become known across the athletics world as the Team, was not there.

Paul looked at his companions with a certain fatherly pride. After all, he was their leader, their motivator and their benefactor. And, like any good manager, he had carefully selected them for their skills and dedication to the task and encouraged them to play their respective roles, unhindered and free from interference. They were the experts.

To his left sat Bronwyn Adams, Abby's former high school English teacher, a woman with master's degrees in both English literature and educational psychology. When Abby had been ready to progress from young prodigy to international track star, Paul had persuaded Bronwyn to join the Team permanently as Abby's mentor, counsellor and general shoulder-to-cry-on.

In reality, Bronwyn, or 'Mizadams' as Abby still called her, was a replacement mother figure, filling a yawning gap in her life that had been there ever since that fateful day in the road outside the school.

THE FINAL LAP

JP was an entirely different animal. He was Abby's coach, brought into the group by Paul when he realised that his limited skills and experience as a track coach were never going to be enough to propel his daughter to stardom. Like most world-class athletes, Abby had for several years employed a full-time coach who travelled with her and took care of everything related to her training, rest schedule, gym programme, diet, injury prevention and, equally important, her ability to avoid the very real risks of doping.

Paul smiled as he considered the contrast between the neat schoolmarm presence of Bronwyn and the coach, dressed as always in a shabby tracksuit and grubby track shoes, his unkempt hair flopping over his ears.

Each of them had a drink in front of them – Paul and JP with draft beers that frothed over the sides of the glasses and Bronwyn with a gin and tonic.

After a long silence, JP spoke softly, in a tone that verged on reverence. He could have been in church. 'No woman has ever run that fast, I am certain of that. Not even Moyo or Fedorova.'

'Let me see those numbers,' murmured Paul. He wanted to see them again, to confirm what he already knew. JP handed him a grubby piece of paper. 'That's amazing,' he said a few seconds later.

Another silence, then Paul spoke again, looking at the coach. 'Tell me about it, the training session. From the beginning.'

Three hours earlier, Abby Dennison was bent over, exhausted, hands on knees, head drooping. Her whole body glistened with sweat and little drops tumbled from her nose and chin, splashing onto the rubberised red track below.

JP studied the digital stopwatch in his hand. 'That was 59.3,' he announced in a flat voice. 'Two to go.'

Abby straightened up, turned and jogged back. After twenty metres she stopped, turned and trotted back behind the start line, looking expectantly at her coach. He was standing on the grass next to the white start–finish line, stopwatch in hand.

'Ten seconds,' he said quietly.

She pushed her hair behind her ears and took a deep breath before slowly moving forward, first a walk, then a slow jog, staring ahead along the tartan track.

'Four, three, two, one …'

On the count of zero, Abby exploded away from the line. Immediately she was moving fluidly, her hands reaching above her head, which was angled forward, her eyes fixed on the track three metres ahead of her. Abby's shoulders were hunched as her momentum increased.

After ten metres she was running at high speed, head up and knees rising so that her thighs were parallel with the ground on each stride. To counterbalance the powerful thrust of her legs, her arms drove backwards and forwards like pistons in a steam engine.

It was gloomy now, a typical pre-sunset English evening where, unlike in JP's native Africa, the darkness seemed to take hours to fully form. Apart from Abby and JP, the track was almost deserted, and the coach clicked his watch as his runner sped past a yellow T-shirt which lay crumpled just inside the running surface on the far side of the field. It designated the 200-metre point, halfway through the lap she was running.

'Twenty-nine seconds. Perfect,' breathed JP.

Soon it was over, the fourteenth 400-metre repetition of this key training session. Abby kept good speed right across the line, coming to an exhausted halt ten metres later. Immediately she sank forward, hands on knees again, her breath rasping as she took in great gulps of air in an effort to supply her painful muscles with fresh oxygen.

'Fifty-eight flat. Now the last one. Let's have a good, strong finish.' He made a note in a small wire-bound book, then put it back in his tracksuit pocket.

Once again Abby turned, looked up and started walking forward.

Just over a minute later it was all over. Abby had completed her toughest training session, fifteen 400-metre repetitions, with only a sixty-second recovery in between each one, in an average of 60.2 seconds each.

She had done versions of this session over the years – sometimes ten, other times twelve and occasionally, just before a big race, fifteen laps – as the final test to judge her condition and plan the target time for the competition. But never before had she averaged better than 61.8.

It was a massive achievement.

'Now cool down.'

Abby jogged slowly around the deserted track for fifteen minutes, her pulse rate dropping rapidly, from well over two hundred beats per minute at the end of the final sprint to a more leisurely rate of seventy within three minutes. Later that night, as she lay in a dreamless sleep, it would drop to a snail-like thirty-nine.

By now, the darkness had crept in and lay like a blanket over the track, which was lit by a single beam that spread a flimsy circle of brightness over the finish line. A thin mist had rolled in, making it difficult to see across the field. It was suddenly cold and JP hugged himself and rubbed his hands together. Maybe it wasn't actually cold, but rather the anticipation of it, a post-stress reaction. He was happy that the session was over. Tick the box. As Abby cooled down, JP wandered around the infield, head down, hands thrust deep into his pockets.

As per her normal post-training ritual, Abby chose not to engage in endless post-mortems with her coach about the session. They both knew how good it had been.

She flopped down onto the grassy infield, now wet from the misty air. Sitting alone in the darkness, she took off her spikes and put on a loose-fitting tracksuit and heavy jogging shoes. From her tog bag she withdrew a small bottle and rubbed fragrant lotion onto her legs. Arnica. Then she lay back, alone with her thoughts, her mind a jumble of metres, seconds, average speeds and comparisons with similar sessions in the past.

The voice of the groundsman, patient as always, broke the rhythm of her thoughts.

'You all finished, guv? I gotta close up now,' he called in a heavy cockney accent from somewhere in the darkened grandstand off to their right.

'Sure, thanks,' replied JP, already moving towards the exit.

With a click the single light went out, leaving just a pale moon struggling to make its presence felt in the foggy air. A dog barked somewhere and a car coughed as it passed the track. The air smelled of mown grass and fragrant Arnica.

As Abby and JP drove away in a rented Toyota, the groundsman locked the gate and stood motionless in the dark, staring as the tail-lights disappeared into the mist.

'My Gawd,' he muttered. 'I ain't never seen anyfing like that.'

By now, the beers were drained and only flecks of foam remained in the glasses. 'So, that's how it all happened.' JP's voice was even quieter than before. 'She's in pretty good shape. With her session of two-hundreds on Monday, where she averaged 24.2 for all ten, she has the speed as well. I think we're looking at a sub-4:12. If it all goes to plan.'

'If it all goes to plan,' repeated Paul, standing and stretching. 'I'm off to bed, coach, Bron. See you in the morning.'

While her father, mentor and coach were gathered in the pub, Abby spent an hour in the High Performance Centre of Loughborough University, a ten-minute walk from the Team's hotel. First she had an expert massage, where the muscles of her back, shoulders, buttocks and legs were worked, the masseuse gently easing the toxins out of the muscle cells and into the bloodstream where the liver reduced them to harmless waste products.

Then it was Abby's private heaven, the aromatherapy chamber. She lay on the wooden benches while heavily scented steam swirled around her and the humidity opened the pores of her skin and for the second time that day the sweat flowed freely.

Dripping perspiration, she plunged into the unheated pool, the cool water shocking her system and revitalising her brain as she swam several leisurely lengths, her powerful legs rippling the water, sending a flurry of wavelets across the surface.

Then she walked back to the hotel through the gloom and went straight to bed. It was close to midnight. After just a few seconds, she passed from consciousness into the deep sleep of those who have taken their bodies to new levels of effort and exhaustion, for no woman had ever run so fast for so long in a single training session.

As she moved from the dreamless phase of early rest into the wild-eyed, brain-jangling one of REM sleep, Abby dreamed of a big noisy crowd that pressed around her, of men shouting questions, of runners in a kaleidoscope of multi-coloured running clothing; reds, greens, luminous yellow, ominous purple, monstrous pink.

She tossed and turned, her face furrowed and troubled. Then she dreamed of a track with white lines on a brick-red surface. Slowly the crowds receded, the noise in her brain subsided and there were no other runners. Everything went silent and she was running, flying almost, her feet not touching the ground, floating over it. The white lines became a channel and she raced between them, running until all she could hear was the sound of the wind in her hair. The Final Lap.

She dreamed of the week ahead and, somewhere deep down in her subconscious mind, she knew she was ready.

6

Thursday, 2 August

LOUGHBOROUGH

Abby stood on the small balcony of suite 204 of The Link Hotel in Loughborough. The sound of the traffic was muted as few cars passed in the street that separated the modest two-star hotel from a row of houses on the far side.

It was warm and she was dressed casually in a pink short-sleeved blouse, a pair of skinny Levi's, and sandals. Around her neck was a thin gold chain with a small cross hanging down the front. Her thick blonde hair was a mass of curls that framed her face and tumbled down onto her shoulders. Subtle blue and pink highlights cut through the blonde, adding a touch of mystery without overpowering the startling effect of the mass of unruly hair. A pair of high-fashion sunglasses perched on the top of her head.

Abby stubbornly refused to spend her free time wearing what she called 'boring athletics kit' of tights, branded T-shirts, tracksuits and colourful running shoes. 'When I'm not running or on duty for some sponsor, I'm a real girl,' she would tell anyone who was interested.

Her clothing may not have hinted that her chosen career was that of a professional athlete, but in her head there was little else to think about but running, particularly after her ground-breaking training session the afternoon before.

JP may have written down all the various details, but Abby had them safely tucked away in her head, the result of an apparent photographic memory that never ceased to amaze people. 'How can you remember fifteen numbers when your body is stretched to the absolute limit?' Paul had asked earlier that morning.

'I don't remember them, they're saved in my mental hard drive,' she replied obliquely, munching cornflakes.

Bronwyn Adams entered the room through an open door and sat quietly on the bed, looking at the girl who had, over the nine years since Anne Dennison's death, become like a daughter.

The English teacher in Bronwyn could never convert a person's height into those complicated metres and centimetres, so all she saw was a tall figure, just short of six feet tall. So striking was Abby Dennison the athlete that her presence often drew the attention of passers-by in the street or people sitting in coffee shops. Many stopped and frankly stared at her, a phenomenon that Bronwyn was not sure she enjoyed. She had become aware of numerous accounts of celebrity women being harassed, stalked and even molested by strange men in raincoats and she had to admit that all this attention on Abby made her a little nervous.

Abby, in contrast, seemed not to notice such things and, to be honest, hardly registered the effect she had on strangers.

At sixty-one kilograms, she carried no excess weight and was well proportioned for her height. Her shoulders were broad, her breasts small and her waist tiny. Her hips were narrow and her upper legs radiated power, even through her jeans. When she wore tights, her quads and hamstrings rippled like moulded bronze and her calf muscles bulged and pulsed with a life of their own as she walked. Today, her shoulders and arms presented well-defined deltoid, biceps and triceps muscle groups that caused the narrow cuff of her blouse to bite tightly into her upper arm, seemingly strangling it.

Although her body appeared god-like and perfect, her face had certain imperfections. Her teeth, although ivory-white, were slightly skew in front, the central incisors overlapping slightly, and the left canine in the upper jaw was slightly on the long side. She also considered her nose to be too large, but this impression was not shared by others, who, on the whole, considered it rather cute, like some sort of olfactory trademark.

'For my next birthday, I want a nose job,' she once asked Paul.

'But you'll end up looking like Michael Jackson, all nips and tucks and with a permanent manic grin. Anyway, you're an athlete, not a ramp model.'

Truth be told, Abby's Team had received more than one offer for their star runner to do classic modelling, usually involving skimpy swimsuits and white beaches. They all had a good laugh over this.

'Not a chance,' Abby had said, although the idea of white beaches had a certain appeal.

There was certainly nothing wrong with her eyes, which were the centrepiece of her face. Set far apart, they were large and blue, flecked with faint traces of gold if you looked closely enough. They were crowned with long lashes that, if anything, accentuated their beauty, and there were faint but definite laughter lines around their edges.

Her pale skin was flawless and clear, even though she had spent 'too many hours in the sun as a teenager', according to Bronwyn. It had to be said that, in deference to her mentor's wishes, Abby never ventured too long in the bright African sun without a cap or bonnet to protect her precious complexion.

As Abby gazed out over the tranquil morning scene in the provincial English town, Bronwyn remained still, quietly watching her. Bronwyn was in her mid-forties, but looked several years younger. Tall and thin, her light brown hair cut short, she had a face that could be described as handsome rather than pretty. She wore steel-framed glasses that sat too far forward on her nose, giving her a myopic, bookish look. This was not surprising, considering that she had been a high school English teacher before transforming herself into what she now called a 'glorified nanny to the rich and fast'.

She had never married ('I never wanted to be tied down to a man who always wanted to climb on top of me at the wrong time, would ultimately get fat, boring and probably demented, before eventually dying and leaving me alone'), was a confirmed bibliophile, amateur poet, movie buff and now full-time surrogate mother to arguably the world's most famous female runner.

She wore an elegant dark green sponsored Maxx tracksuit, trimmed with a mass of tiny yellow diamantés down the sleeves and across the shoulders, over a matching yellow T-shirt, with its ever-present triangular logo in green on the left side. Although it was covered, Abby knew that on the back of the T-shirt 'Team Abby' appeared, together with the South African flag, its shining yellow, green, black and blue hues reflecting the colours so popular in the flags of Africa. Completing her outfit was a pair of Maxx trainers, white with the iconic four stripes in red and blue of the world's newest running shoe brand. There were no rings on her fingers and she wore a slender pearl necklace, a matching pearl bracelet around her left wrist and small white pearl earrings.

'Abby,' she called from inside the room.

Abby turned suddenly, taken by surprise. 'Didn't see you there, Mizadams. I was just thinking …' She stopped mid-sentence and gave Bronwyn an affectionate hug. She was five centimetres taller and had to bend down to embrace her.

'And what were you *thinking* about, may I ask? Your training session last night?'

'Actually, no. I was thinking how few birds there are in England. Not like at home. I hardly saw any when I was out there on the balcony, probably fewer than five birds in ten minutes. I miss home, if you really want to know. The jacarandas, the thunderstorms, even those noisy guinea fowl. I don't think I could live here. I'm too African.'

'Well, we're coming to the end of the northern hemisphere summer. In six weeks your track season will be over and you can go home to the jacarandas and hoopoes and woodpeckers and loeries.' A pause, then, 'How are you feeling about next week, the Bannister meeting?'

'Mizadams, they're no longer called loeries. Now they're turacos. And the grey loerie is the grey go-away bird, which I think is pretty dumb.'

'The Bannister meeting, Abby. Don't change the subject.'

Abby sat down on one of the chairs scattered around the room and stretched out with her feet on a low coffee table. Her eyes lost focus and it was as if she was talking to herself. 'I'm processing that. You know, it was quite a training session. Although it was my fastest ever over fifteen four-hundreds, I have to say that I wasn't completely destroyed afterwards. Sure, it was hard work and at the end of each circuit my pulse was up well over two hundred, and I was in pure oxygen debt. But as I ran I had this amazing feeling of peace. I could hear nothing, just the wind in my ears. I felt so *powerful*. It's not something I've felt many times before, especially not in training. In races, I often get that out-of-body experience where the whole world is blocked out. That's when I've run most of my best times. But not in training. Training is usually hard work, unpleasant. You want to puke, to be honest. But not last night. Last night was *radical*.'

Two cellphones chirped simultaneously. 'It'll be Dad,' said Abby. 'You reply. He probably wants a meeting or something. Just when I wanted to sleep.'

The message had come from Paul on the Team's WhatsApp group. 'Guys, we must meet. Sorry to interrupt your busy schedules. Two o'clock, the Ovett Room. Abby, go sleep.'

Bronwyn looked at Abby. 'How did you know?'

'Telepathy, another of my many talents.'

Bronwyn said nothing and the silence lasted for several minutes. Abby continued to stare at the wall as if in a trance. Eventually, Bronwyn stood up and left the room. She hesitated at the door. 'Rest a bit, my baby. You deserve it. Lots of time to chat later.'

Abby was still lying there, her feet on the table, her backside deep into the cushions. She'd heard nothing of what her mentor had said. Her eyes slowly closed, the gold-flecked blue no longer visible. She slept peacefully for two hours.

Body rested and showered, hair washed and blow-dried and tummy filled, Abby wandered into the Ovett Room, one of the small meeting places in the business section of the hotel. Each was named after famous British middle-distance athletes. Apart from Ovett, rooms were labelled Coe, Cram and Holmes. Right away she felt at home.

She was the last to arrive. 'Well, hello,' said Paul, 'we were about to start without you.'

'You wouldn't dare. Without me, none of you would be here anyway.' The comment was offered with a smile, but not without a suggestion of quiet authority. She took her seat and placed a bottle of chilled sparkling water on the table. Each person had their favourite drink: Bronwyn had iced tea, JP a half-litre of Coke Zero and Paul had ordered a giant cappuccino, which stood under a layer of foam in front of him.

Clutching several coloured marker pens, Paul walked to a whiteboard. 'Okay, here we go. Abby runs the mile in eight days' time in the Olympic Stadium. That's Friday of next week, at 8pm, prime television time across Europe. Against the strongest field in the world.'

He sipped his cappuccino. 'So, we need to agree on the following: training so far, training and peaking up to the race, strategic resting, the move into London, and the media conference on the Thursday.' Looking at Bronwyn, he said, 'Bron, obviously your role over the next week is crucial. You and Abby need to find time to sit and plan the race mentally. JP will go through the actual tactics just before the race as usual, but your job starts now, right after this meeting, effectively. Neither JP nor I will interfere.'

Bronwyn relaxed and spent the rest of the meeting listening, her usual role in meetings such as these. Part of the information came from the spoken word and part from nuances, body language and the general tone of what was said, especially by Abby. Mizadams was an English teacher and she could read her student like a grade twelve setwork book.

JP stood. Abby grinned, he was such a nerd! Unlike the rest of the Team, JP van Riet did not cut an impressive figure. He was half a head shorter than Abby, rather thin and scrawny and wore a faded green Nike tracksuit above ancient, dirty running shoes. There was a large digital watch on his left wrist and his fingers were devoid of rings. His hair was brown and longish, drooping over his ears and covering his forehead. He looked almost hippy-like, but what he knew about sex, drugs and rock 'n roll could be written on the back of a small postage stamp.

Abby smiled, appreciating for the hundredth time that JP's appearance was completely at odds with what the man was really like and what he had achieved. Christened Johannes Pretorius Albertus van Riet by his staunchly Afrikaans parents (he was named Johannes and Albertus after his paternal and maternal grandfathers respectively, and Pretorius after one of the fabled leaders of the Boer pioneers who fled from the British, trekking their way from the Cape Colony into the hinterland of nineteenth-century South Africa). To be honest, JP did not even want to know the true identity of the Pretorius that gave him his second Christian name. When he turned five, his family got tired of using Johannes and he had been known as JP ever since.

Abby was in awe of him. To her, he represented everything that was pure in sport. He loved athletics and, effectively, had devoted his life to it. He was scrupulously honest and, even with Paul, spoke his mind, often in the face of opposition. He was Abby's greatest fan and they shared a strange, platonic relationship based on a combination of skills, experience, talent and pure hard work that resulted in extraordinary achievements. Symbiosis was the biological word for it – two plus two equals five or, in this case, fifteen hundred. There was absolutely no doubt that Abby would not have achieved as much as she had without JP.

He had been a good athlete in his own right. At Stellenbosch University near Cape Town, he'd studied Physical Education while building his career as a runner to its natural limits, which happened to be a 3:42 effort in the 1 500 metres. Although he attempted to do so on several occasions, JP never actually broke four minutes for the mile, a fact that had left him feeling strangely empty.

All that effort with relatively scant reward ultimately caused the man's metamorphosis – from average athlete to world-class coach. In nature, a caterpillar miraculously becomes a butterfly, a tadpole breathing through gills becomes a frog with lungs. JP, through years of conscious, dedicated effort, similarly moved from one species of human to another; not physically, but intellectually and emotionally. It was a brilliant example of the power of the human spirit to achieve an extraordinary outcome.

Part of JP's success was also grounded on his superior academic ability. He was a brilliant student. After scoring seven distinctions in the matriculation examination at Paarl Boys' High in the Cape, he was flooded with scholarship offers from most of the country's top universities.

But once he had realised that he would never really make the big time as an athlete, JP set his goals on that other facet of the sport that could garner him the success that had evaded him as an athlete – coaching.

And so, from his third year onwards at Stellenbosch University, until he graduated *cum laude* with a doctorate in education, JP attended every coaching course available, read every book, personally corresponded with most of the world's top coaches and interviewed as many top distance runners as possible. He also exhausted the financial coffers of his scholarship backers, his family and as many sponsors as he could persuade to fund his quest to become the middle-distance coach that would change the face of athletics.

The Team meeting rolled on. Reports, questions, answers, suggestions, debates, discussions, a couple of arguments, some disagreements, many decisions made and concrete plans laid down.

They agreed on training sessions, gym work, peaking strategies, train rides into London, the media briefing. It was hectic, but necessary, all part of the Abby pre-race strategy build-up.

After nearly two hours, Paul looked across the table. 'That's it. Done. I believe we've covered everything. We all know what we have to do. Now, go and chill out. Abby, Bron, JP, the rest of the day is yours. Bronwyn, they have a great collection of Shakespeare and Milton in the Loughborough library. JP, check out the weight-training guy in the gym. The trainer told me he has some suggestions to get Abby stronger, if that's even possible. Now, scram.'

They were dismissed.

7

Friday, 3 August

LOUGHBOROUGH

It was exactly a week to go before the Roger Bannister Memorial Athletics Meeting in the London Olympic Stadium.

Thousands of kilometres south of Loughborough, a typical scene in the deep bush of the Kruger National Park is playing out: a zebra kill, on it a pride of lions growling, ripping flesh and chewing contentedly, but keeping a wary eye on a group of hyenas circling and eyeing the meal hungrily. Three black-backed jackals are sitting quietly under a bush nearby, too small to enter the fray yet, but knowing that their time will come. In the sky, more than fifty Cape, white-backed and even a few lappet-faced vultures circle patiently. Vultures – the ultimate guardians of cleanliness in the bush. After they are finished with a carcass, only white bones remain.

The Roger Bannister Mile was something like that. It was the big prize and the various players were circling, hovering, watching, like hyenas, jackals and vultures. Waiting, planning, preparing for their roles. Runners, coaches, sponsors, the event management team, the media, spectators and a worldwide audience.

For most people, it would be a spectacle to be savoured, anticipated and enjoyed. For others, not so much. Money, reputations, careers, investments, records and titles were on the line. And, like the predators, they were waiting for their chance to fight for their particular piece of the pie. Two of the players in the game that morning were at opposite ends of the world and both had the race on their minds.

The first person was Abby.

It was early morning in Loughborough. The eastern sky was showing the first glimmers of dawn as Abby left the hotel. There was an eagerness inside her, a desire, a *need* to run that manifested itself as a rising pulse rate and goose-bumps on her arms. She had realised a long time ago that she was born to run fast and she couldn't wait to get out there.

Some would call it an addiction. It probably was.

The early morning air had a distinctive fresh, clean smell and texture that always seemed to evaporate once the day got going, a purity unspoiled by noise and traffic pollution. For non-runners unable to grasp this, imagine the smell and feel of misty, soapy air swirling around inside a shower cubicle; pretend you can touch the crackling atmosphere after the lightning, thunderclaps and torrential rain of a Highveld thunderstorm have moved off; sit inside a concert hall with an orchestra and choir rendering Handel's 'Hallelujah' chorus. The air seems *alive*.

Abby clicked her digital watch, pulled her sunglasses over her eyes and set off slowly. The hotel was close to the outer boundaries of the town and after a few minutes she was running down a narrow lane that wound between neatly fenced farmlands. Soon she was into her full stride, moving ever faster and relishing the sensation of cool air across her face, air that delivered a rich stream of oxygen, absorbed by her lungs and transported swiftly into the working muscles of her legs, arms and upper body. After fifteen minutes she was completely warmed up and feeling like the proverbial million dollars. Now it was fully light and the view of the lush English countryside was exceptional.

The farmlands were interspersed with stands of densely packed trees that became a forest that ran for several kilometres down one side of the road. On the other side was a golf course with a pretty clubhouse and wide expanses of manicured fairways.

She went off-road onto a sandy track through what was described in the hotel's brochure as a park but in reality was a forest. The trail wound between tall leafy trees that cut out the sun and cast broad shadows, making it gloomy in parts. The air was pleasantly cool and she could hear a quiet symphony of bird sounds, their calls cutting through the otherwise-silent air. But the birds were invisible, hidden deep in the foliage.

The place reminded her of the Knysna Forest back home, large tracts of hillside covered by dense foliage no more than ten kays from a busy town. A wilderness bordering on chaotic civilization. Beauty and the beast.

She stopped midway through the session and found a grassy patch between the trees. It was time for JP's morning stretching routine to which she adhered every day without fail. This was essential to ensure that her muscles – what JP called 'your secret weapon' – remained flexible and stretched to their maximum extent.

Twenty minutes later she ran back to the road, turned and headed back to town.

After eighty minutes away, she arrived at the hotel. The town had woken up and cars passed by in numbers, students walked and cycled towards the entrance of Loughborough University, one of England's pre-eminent sports-related teaching institutions, and hotel guests hurried in and out of the building. The lobby was crowded and she felt the eyes of a dozen people on her as she passed through. Feeling distinctly uncomfortable, she ran up the stairs. Must have been my sweaty body they were staring at, she thought.

The second person contemplating the Bannister Mile race was in distant Johannesburg. It was mid-morning.

Mark Whyte was feeling relaxed. Mandy had booked his business-class London flight and secured his favourite London hideaway, Suite 504 in the Thistle Hotel.

Now he had a single task to complete, but the outcome was by no means certain. He felt a familiar dryness in his mouth and his pulse rate went up a notch or two. The occasional high-risk move, his secret addiction.

He picked up the phone, dialled a number and waited. After six rings a voice answered. 'This is Simon, how may I help you?'

'Good day, Simon, my name is Mark Whyte and I hope you have a minute for me. Just to confirm I have the correct number, you are Simon Hardy, media manager of the Bannister meeting?'

'Indeed I am.'

'Then let me explain. I know it's mighty late in the day, but I'm hoping that you can help me. I am from Johannesburg, South Africa, and will be coming to London next week on a sudden, unplanned business trip. I own a small technology company. But, more important, I am also an athletics fan and, I suppose, play a small role in the athletics media in South Africa. I'm not a journalist in the true sense of the word – working for a big media house or anything – but I own a website, a blog I suppose, specifically focusing on track athletics. It's a niche site that has expanded its reach over the past few years and is linked to my Facebook and Twitter platforms. I've got more than twenty thousand dedicated followers, mostly in South Africa but also around the region. I also focus on regional athletes, particularly in Botswana, Zimbabwe and Namibia. My number of followers is growing fast, doubling every few months.'

'Okay, Mark, how can I help you?'

'Let me be frank. I was hoping to score a media accreditation for the Roger Bannister meeting. Abby Dennison will be running and she is massive in South Africa. My blog and social media coverage will definitely add value back home if I can set up in the stadium. Am I too late?'

'Technically, yes. I have already accredited nearly two hundred media people and that excludes the BBC, our host broadcaster. But, seeing as we would like to expand our international coverage, and Africa is a particular target for our sponsors, I may be able to make a plan. Give me an hour. Oh, and what is the web address of your blog?'

'My site is called MileStar Athletics with a .co.za address and I suggest you have a quick look at it to decide whether I'm worthy of an invitation. Then you can call me on my private number. If so, I'll be happy to squeeze into a tiny corner of your media area. Just me and my laptop.'

He gave Hardy his private number, hung up and settled down for what would be a nervous wait. There was plenty riding on this and the normally unflappable Mark was distinctly anxious. He would be at the Bannister meeting anyway but didn't relish the thought of buying tickets like an ordinary fan and sitting high up in the cavernous stands of the Olympic Stadium. No, thank you. He wanted the precious media pass that would give him access to the inner sanctum of the event. In the world of high-end sport, the media centre is where you want to be. And, crucially, where Abby would be found.

The MileStar Athletics blog had been difficult to set up, particularly as it was done in a hurry, two days to be exact. Getting the template and populating it with appropriate information was easy enough, but it definitely had to pass the scrutiny of an expert such as Hardy, who was probably studying it at that very moment. It had to be one hundred per cent authentic-looking and, to achieve this, Mark had worked through most of two nights. He downloaded video clips from track meetings, created 'unique' interviews with several leading athletes, including Wayde van Niekerk, and wrote an 'exclusive, in-depth profile' on Abby Dennison, which included details of the fateful day nine years earlier that changed her life.

He had even created false pop-up advertisements to give the impression of financial viability and, for the fun of it, included a section that dealt with injuries and nutrition. It was indeed a masterpiece of creative online fraud. But would it pass muster under the scrutiny of one of Britain's foremost athletics media managers?

It did. An hour later, Mark's iPhone buzzed. 'Simon, so good to hear from you. Thanks for getting back to me so quickly.'

'Pleasure, Mark. Look, your website seems excellent at first glance. Because we only have one dedicated South African journalist coming to the meeting, I am happy to accept you. Better than just relying on the news services. Can you come and be accredited at the media centre two days before the event, at the stadium? That's next Wednesday. Just ask a volunteer the way. We'll be open all day from nine o'clock till late. Give yourself time, it's a big place. Oh, and please bring some identification, just for the record, you know. Your passport will suffice. Is that all good?'

'Wow, thanks Simon. That's fantastic. I'll be there next Wednesday. By the way, who is the South African journo coming?'

'Deon Coetzee.'

'Oh.'

In London, Simon hung up and called his boss, James Selfe. 'Hi James, I just had an interesting call. Can we chat? Won't take long. Cheers, I'll be up in a minute.' Simon always enjoyed the view of the Thames from the office of the meeting director and this Mark Whyte thing was a good excuse to go high up in Regalbank Towers.

After a brief lunch, Mark had another look at the Regalbank media release about the Bannister Women's Mile and spent a few minutes deep in thought. Then he left his office, walked down the passage and knocked on the door of a corner office on which a sign said, 'Prabesh Venkathan, Head of Technology. Enter at your own risk'.

'Come in,' said a voice.

Mark entered the secret world of the complete computer nerd. The head of tech was a tall, gangly man about the same age as Mark. His black hair was long and tied back in an untidy ponytail. He wore jeans with holes in both knees, sandals and a T-shirt that read 'When all else fails, Ctrl/Alt/Del'.

The room was a mess of books, files, piles of paper, cables, various bits of random computer hardware and dirty coffee cups lying everywhere. A battered acoustic guitar leaned up against the far wall.

Prabesh's desk had two computer screens, a single keyboard, a laser printer and a kettle spread across its vast surface. The man himself was working on both computer screens, the keyboard plus a cellphone and an iPad at the same time. He wore wraparound dark glasses.

There was no visitor's chair and Mark had to stand. He smiled. Ever since the two of them had been undergraduates all those years ago, they had been pretty much inseparable. They were both addicted to the strange and rapidly changing world of programming, coding and the internet, and theirs was a deep and abiding friendship. When Mark had moved into the world of business, Prabesh had remained in the academic environment, earning several more degrees, attending international conferences and publishing papers that not even Mark could understand. When Mark started MileStar, he persuaded his friend to leave academia and join him in the exciting world of a tech start-up. It was a partnership made in heaven.

The most significant difference between them was the fact that Prabesh, at the age of twenty-five, had married his girlfriend from school, the delightful Farida Pather, and the couple had since then added three children, a girl and twin boys, to the family.

Venkathan continued tapping away as if there was no one there. In the near silence, Mark gazed for the umpteenth time at the framed items on the walls. Along one side were his Wits University degrees, BSc (Honours) and MSc in computer science, both *cum laude*. A framed certificate announced that he was a member of the Actuarial Society of South Africa and next to that hung another one indicating that Prabesh Venkathan was the winner of the Society's Academic Prize in 2012 for Risk Modelling and Survival Analysis. Various photographs adorned the walls showing a smiling Venkathan with a variety of well-known people including Mark Shuttleworth, Adam Habib, Jonty Rhodes and Johnny Clegg.

Mark coughed. 'Hey bru,' came a voice from behind the array of equipment, 'what brings you into this particular hole?'

'I need your help.'

'So what's new, brother, you always need my help.'

'True, but this time it's somewhat, how shall I say, under the radar.'

'My game. Bring it on. But first we shake.'

Prabesh stuck out a hand and the two men engaged in a complex series of handshakes and fist bumps that lasted at least five seconds. An old ritual from their student days.

'What do you need me to uncover? Hopefully not from the dark web, you know I don't go there.'

'Hell no. It's about a runner.'

'Of course, the delightful Abby. Why not just phone her? How can she possibly resist your charms?' He grinned knowingly. 'I've told you a million times, get married like me. It's the best thing ever. Have kids, grow up.'

'It's not Abby. She's in London. It's another runner.'

Prabesh dug into a drawer and pulled out a black beanie with 'Hacker Supreme' embroidered on the front.

Mark laughed out loud. 'We're not going into the secret files of the CIA, my friend. Just some information about a particular runner. But stuff not readily available about a person who is totally, profoundly, missing from regular media and even social media. Some sort of extremely talented ghost.'

'My territory. Everyone has a presence somewhere on the web. Everyone has a phone, a computer, a hard drive, an email address, emails, photos. Who is this mystery person?'

'Write this down. I need you to dig up everything possible on Sarah, Solomon and Samson Moyo, Caihong Junren, Wiseman Ngwenya, the athletics department of Villanova University starting five years ago until now, especially regarding this particular Sarah. I want to know everything that's hidden. I want to know their secrets, their plans and what toothpaste they use.'

'No problem, consider it done. My pleasure.' He pointed at his beanie and grinned.

Two hours later, Prabesh entered Mark's office, closed the door and sat. 'Hey bru, what can I say. This is one mighty interesting family. And have I got some juicy stuff for you.'

'Bring it on,' said Mark.

'May I ask why all this digging into a Zimbabwean runner? I thought Dennison was your passion?'

'I need to get in touch with the Sarah circus.'

'But she's off the radar. No interviews. Did you know she has mild Asperger's Syndrome? Amazing that it didn't stop her from becoming this brilliant runner. Wasn't there a tennis player like that?'

'Not sure, but the Asperger's business explains a few things.'

'So how are you going to get into the inner-Moyo-sanctum?'

'Money, my friend, money. Opens every door.'

8

Tuesday, 7 August

LONDON

Deon arrived at Heathrow Airport after an uneventful and largely pleasant flight. For some reason the aeroplane had been half empty, which allowed him to stretch across three seats and get a decent six hours' sleep.

A subsequent email from Simon Hardy instructed him to take a taxi from Heathrow to the designated media hotel, adding that the organisers would give him a per diem of one hundred pounds to cover incidental costs. Oh, and could he pay the cab fare until he could receive the cash? He could, but only just. Paying in pounds with South African rand was always depressing.

He eventually arrived at the Premier Inn, Stratford, the official media hotel for the Bannister Meeting. It was an unassuming, generic business-traveller hotel. Eight floors, plastic chairs and tables in the reception area, purple walls and plastic vases. At least the flowers were real.

Check-in was quick and efficient. When he gave the reception clerk, whose purple and green name tag read 'Emily Williams', his name and passport, she fished around under the desk and hauled out a Regalbank-branded backpack labelled 'Deon Coetzee, APN, South Africa'.

'This is from Mister Hardy,' she explained. 'Each invited media person gets one. You're from South Africa? I'd love to visit Africa one day. Can you tell me about it when I get off shift at six o'clock?'

'Sure, but now I need to get cleaned up.'

Deon's room was comfortable and functional but the view from the window, of an empty back street and the rear walls of an office block, was less than inspiring. He immediately tested the shower and fifteen minutes of bliss under a cascade of warm water cleansed both body and mind. A thorough rub-down with a massive fluffy towel and he was ready to take on the world.

Next step was an investigation of the bounty inside the large media backpack. It was chock-full of goodies. There was a branded golf shirt (a quick check showed it was the correct size – brilliant planning), an excellent lightweight waterproof hooded windbreaker with numerous zip-up pockets, and the obligatory branded cap.

There was also a treasure trove of edible goodies – chocolates, biscuits, a large bottle of some local sports drink and several packs of snack-type foods. Good, now there was no need to spend the precious per diem on dinner.

Most important for Deon was a sealed envelope, inside of which was a personal letter from Hardy and twelve fifty-pound notes. Cash flow revived, he thought.

Clad in a fresh T-shirt, clean jeans, the Bannister meeting baseball cap and windbreaker and his best Adidas trainers, Deon left the room, took the elevator and, with a friendly smile, went past reception.

'Mister Coetzee, just a minute please!' Emily was almost breathless with excitement. 'I didn't tell you. I'm volunteering at the Roger Bannister meeting. When Mister Hardy arranged for the media to stay here, I asked him if I could help out. I love athletics, in fact I run for a local club, Victoria Park Harriers, we race on the track in summer. I'm studying at university and Mister Hardy arranged for me to work in the media centre, so I'll see you a few times.'

'You don't look like a sprinter or field-event person. Maybe the longer distances, I guess five or ten thousand?'

'Too long. Fifteen hundred mainly, although I dabble in the eight.'

'Best time for the fifteen? Under 4:50, maybe under 4:40?' Be gentle, if the girl hasn't broken five minutes, don't make her feel bad.

'4:17.'

Deon stopped. 'Wow, that's impressive! That must put you up there in the rankings.'

'Nationally it's nowhere. At least twenty girls are faster. Debbie Feltman has broken 4:10. She's from my club. And of course, Jane Beardsley and

Mary McColgan are internationally ranked, although Mary is Scottish. Does that count?' He said he didn't know and she continued, 'But in the London leagues I'm ranked in the top five. My hero is Abby Dennison, she's the best. Close to 3:53 this year. Amazing.'

'And what are you studying?'

'I'm finishing my master's in media studies at London University. Being a receptionist helps with my uni fees. Oh, please don't forget to tell me about South Africa.'

'I won't. Promise. Later maybe.'

Deon went to the nearest tube station, bought a five-day pass on the London Underground and hopped onto a train that took him to Marble Arch station. When he was a student, he'd spent six weeks in London with a varsity mate whose distant uncle let them stay in a tiny flat in his basement at no cost. Even though it had been freezing in London – mid-winter – they had a ball, doing the usual sightseeing stuff and even attending a couple of West End shows, sponsored by the uncle who seemed to have plenty of money and a burning desire to force-feed culture into a pair of long-haired, culturally ignorant students from Rhodes University, Grahamstown, South Africa.

That's when he learned, through desperate and sometimes hilarious trials-and-errors, how to master the Underground.

Going from the claustrophobic intensity of a tube train up the rattling, crowded escalators, through the echoing halls of the station and out into the maelstrom of the noisy organised chaos of a London high street had always been thrilling. The moving sea of people and vehicles, the high buildings, many of them world-renowned, and the wall of noise stood in sharp contrast to the muted, stuffy atmosphere of the Underground. He stared at the famous arch and, across the road, London's iconic Hyde Park.

It was a typical warm, hazy British summer's day, when time seems to drift along without any noticeable change. It could be nine in the morning, midday or even supper time, but everything, somehow, looks and feels the same.

Crossing the road, he entered the park close to Speakers' Corner. The traffic noise and general mayhem subsided as he entered the gentleness of the beautiful environment – vast stretches of green grass on which people lay and sat, soaking up the sun as if it were something rare and wonderful. Wide paths crisscrossed the park and he wandered between the trees and stretches of water on which ducks flapped, squabbled, squawked and swam around busily.

This trip was, of course, all about Abby Dennison. Abby ...

He recalled watching her race in Joburg, Pretoria, Stellenbosch and Potchefstroom, from when she was a gangly fifteen-year-old 800-metre runner, all long legs and blonde hair. Even then she was wonderful to watch as she edged ever closer to the two-minute barrier that separated a good national runner from someone of international stature.

The fact that she broke two minutes just a month after her sixteenth birthday marked her as someone special. It was a story that every true-blue sports fan would love. A once-in-a-generation thing.

In all his days as an athletics writer, he had never encountered an athlete with such supreme natural talent. She was a cut above, possessing that intangible something that all great natural sportspeople have. Ernie Els, George Best, Naas Botha, Messi, Pelé, Ronaldo, Federer, Nadal, Woods, Graf – they were all cut from the same cloth.

Natural talent is not the only essential thing in the mix, he thought. Add good old-fashioned hard work: the grind of gut-wrenching, muscle-destroying, mind-numbing speed, strength and endurance training, two to three hours a day, six days a week. Could she do it? Everyone had asked that question in those early days when she was at school, when the boys called and her girlfriends texted her about sleepovers and trips to the mall in tight jeans and tank tops.

Would this talent ultimately reach its full potential?

Abby had worked really hard, even in those early days. She trained with a kind of pioneer spirit, like someone conquering new, unchartered territories. She did interval training on the track, an hour of 200-metre repetitions – as many as thirty – or 600-metre intervals in under ninety seconds, and kilometre reps in under three minutes; Deon remembered seeing her out in the park in the afternoons doing fartlek until she almost collapsed from fatigue;

she ran for an hour some mornings on the road in winter and the golf course in summer to build crucial stamina; she spent six hours a week in the gym, slowly building her upper body strength until she could bench press her own body weight.

She reached full physical maturity, nearly six feet of lean beauty and athleticism. She won junior races and broke junior records, both national and international; started winning senior races before she turned seventeen; and won her first national title, the 800, in 1:58 by forty metres. Through all of this she still scored excellent grades at school, matriculated and became a full-time athlete.

In those days Paul coached her. When asked whether she would not be better served by employing a professional, Paul simply said that he understood her mind and her moods, he could motivate her and hold her back when she neared breaking point. He talked to her and hugged her when she was down, celebrated with her when she was happy and tucked her into bed at night. He loved her, she was his daughter, his own flesh and blood.

No coach could do that, not for a young girl with all the pressures, fears and insecurities that come with the teenage years without a mother. Maybe they would get a coach at some point, he said. When the time was right, he would hand over the coaching reins, bring in a pro.

Everyone agreed that Abby had the athletics world at her feet.

But there was one element still to be nailed down, the big unknown. This was the fabled issue of Big Match Temperament, or BMT, as it has been called by generations of sportswriters and psychologists.

There are, in the final showdown, two or three individuals possessing, in equal measure, talent and work ethic. Then the question arises: who will win the race and who will lose? It is then that BMT becomes the final judge, the arbiter, the cruel master who decides who is truly great and who should have been truly great but wasn't.

As Deon made a final turn through the park and saw Marble Arch tube station across the road, he realised that the question of BMT had hung over Abby Dennison all those years. Did she, or did she not, have it? The Bannister Mile race would finally put that debate to bed, one way or another.

Twenty minutes later Deon was back in the hotel. Emily was just finishing her shift for the day. 'You alright after the flight?'

'Sure, just a bit tired. Need some sleep.' He rubbed his eyes for effect.

'Can you sleep after a shot of caffeine? Why not join me for a cappuccino, on the house.' Deon made a swift mental calculation: cappuccino at four pounds is about eighty rand. Three times the price back home. Great deal.

They went up to a neat little coffee shop on the first floor. It doubled as the breakfast room but there was only a smartly dressed woman tapping on a laptop, cellphone at the ready, earphones in ears. Modern-day mobile office, work anywhere, any time.

Two cappuccinos arrived, Deon's accompanied by a hot croissant oozing butter and melted cheese. On the plate were several slices of ham and a small salad.

'Hope you're not vegetarian?'

'Hell, no. I eat pretty much anything, dairy, carbs, meat. Especially if it's free. It is free? I don't want to blow Simon's hundred pounds in one hit.'

She grinned. 'Complimentary. One thing I have learned to do in this job is suss out clients. I took you for a bachelor journo who is very successful but underpaid, who works too hard at weird hours but doesn't care because he loves the job. No wedding ring unless you've taken it off. Maybe a girlfriend, but I doubt it – too young and busy travelling around to settle down. You probably live in a small flat with a fridge, microwave, a double bed and a bookshelf with a hundred books. A big flat-screen TV, a couple of mismatched chairs and a coffee table covered with dirty mugs. Different-coloured curtains. Maybe a cat. Oh, and being South African, from what I've heard, a decent wine collection. Right?'

'Wrong. I live with my mother on a sheep farm in the Karoo desert.' He grinned.

They both laughed. Deon ate and drank hungrily.

Then, 'Why this super hospitality?'

'Good question. I'm fascinated by this whole Bannister thing. Being a volunteer, working with journos from around the world. Japan, America, Germany, South Africa. I don't have a very exciting life. In fact, the furthest away I've ever been is Scotland and that was in the rain.'

It suddenly dawned on him that he had an obligation, a duty, to make Emily's fleeting encounter with the outside world a special one. 'You asked about my life and I could tell you. But I'm not going to, it's not important right now. I'm going to tell you a story, a terrible story, that will keep you awake tonight. It will open your mind to both the beauty and tragedy of South Africa and the wonder, the incredibleness, of Abby Dennison.'

He spoke for a long time. The hiss of the coffee machine, the traffic noise, the smell of cooking coming from the kitchen and the rumble of vacuum cleaners in the passageway disappeared as Deon entered a zone of sadness and anger. His mind rewound nine years to that fateful day at the school gate, recalling the numbness that only profound shock can generate. Until then, he had never known what evil meant or imagined the depths to which a human being could descend.

He told her how he had seen Anne Dennison die.

'Oh God,' said Emily at the end. She went pale and a small tear stole down her cheek.

There was silence for a time, then she asked, 'What happened after that? How did you all recover?'

'It took a long time. The police discovered that this was a known kidnapping ring that had previously stolen five children for money. Abby was their target because she was well known and they figured her parents would cough up a big ransom. They ended up being found guilty of murder after a hell of a trial. Abby had to testify and look all of them in the eyes. I've never understood how she did that. I was in court that day and also had to testify. I was a wreck, especially during the cross-examination. She was calm all the way through. Incredible.'

'Who were the kidnappers?'

'There were three of them. The leader and the second guy were career criminals with all sorts of convictions and jail time behind them. They got life sentences. The third guy, the driver of the car, was different, younger with no previous convictions. He claimed not to know what they were planning, said he was just the driver. He cut a deal with the prosecutor, was seriously remorseful, broke down in tears on the witness stand, the whole big drama thing. Then he threw the other guys under the bus. It worked for him and he only got ten years. I think he was paroled last year.'

'What happened then?'

'For the Dennisons it was a long and hard road. They were broken, as you can imagine. Lots of post-traumatic stress counselling, and the whole community pitched in. Bronwyn Adams took over as a sort-of surrogate mom for Abby. The support was amazing. Paul spent less time at work and more time coaching Abby, who soon got back into training, determined to reach the very top for her mom. Later, Paul hired JP van Riet to coach her, and she became a full-time athlete and continued to shoot up the rankings.'

'And how did you cope? You were pretty young yourself.'

'Badly. For months I had flashbacks and nightmares. Then I started to come right. Amazingly, it was Abby who helped me the most. She showed me how to be strong by focusing on the future. By forgiving.'

'Forgiving? What the hell is forgiving?'

'You'll have to ask her that. I don't understand how it works. She says she forgave her attackers, her mom's killers. Beats me, but it certainly helped Abby recover.'

'Did that crazy time bring the two of you together?'

'Yes. For the rest of the year we saw each other often. I visited her house and we did the coffee-in-the-mall thing. But we were just kids. Then I went off to university, she became a superstar, and we only connected a few times a year.'

'Did you ever feel there may be some sort of relationship developing?'

'Yes, to be honest, but maybe it was wishful thinking. One gets a different sort of vibe, some sort of mutual attraction. But there was not much opportunity. We were never together long enough.'

'The price of fame, I guess.'

'I guess.'

There was a long silence as they absorbed the tale of the previous hour. The lady with the laptop left, the dishes were cleared and a few people came into the room and ordered drinks and supper. Deon realised he'd finally reached the end of his strength. 'I'm so sorry, I'm done in,' he said, genuinely exhausted.

'I'm sure you are,' she replied. 'Let me take you to your room.' At the door he fished out his key card. Emily gave him a brief hug and a quick kiss on the cheek. She left, looking sad and thoughtful. Fifteen minutes later Deon was asleep, still wearing his previously clean T-shirt and partially clean jeans. At least he'd removed his shoes and brushed his teeth.

9

Wednesday, 8 August

LONDON

Deon was excited. It was accreditation day.
Many sports journos, especially the old guys, go through life saying, 'What's the big deal? It's just another golf tournament or soccer match or Wimbledon final. Boring. Where are the beers?' But not Deon. Sport had been his passion for as long as he could remember. Tennis, cricket, golf, athletics. Especially athletics.

He carefully packed the essential tools of his trade into a sturdy backpack – his APN card, laptop, wire-bound notebook, high-school pencil case with five different coloured pens, a calculator, the latest World Athletics yearbook replete with about a million statistics, a litre of Coke, two slabs of Lindt chocolate, his cellphone, credit card, London Underground map and passport.

Was this going to be the biggest gig of his life? He'd covered every major sporting event back home – from the Currie Cup final and the Million Dollar golf, to the Comrades Marathon and the Dusi Canoe Marathon – plus a few major international athletics events, the biggest of which had been the world junior track champs four years earlier. The highlight of that event had been Abby Dennison's win in the Girls' 800 metres in 1:57.32, at that stage the third-fastest ever by a junior.

But today was something special. It wasn't a major championship or a Diamond League meeting, but the aura of the event had been carefully built up around the history and magic of the mile distance – immortalised all those years ago on a dusty gravel track in Oxford by Roger Bannister – and the iconic London Olympic Stadium. This had captured the hearts and minds of sports fans across the world. Outside of the World Athletics Championships, the Bannister meeting had the highest television audience of any track meeting in the world, apparently in excess of two hundred million viewers in a hundred countries, and that was last year. This year, who knew?

And he was one of only two hundred accredited journalists. And he had been invited! Very cool.

As he passed the reception desk on his way out, he noticed that Emily wasn't at her post. 'Where's Emily?' he asked the man behind the desk, whose name tag read 'Archie Grimsby'.

'Oh, she's taken the day off,' Archie replied casually without looking up from his cellphone. 'She's volunteering at the athletics meeting. Crazy. If I had the day off, I'd go to the Alien Kids concert at Wembley. You know the A-Kids?' he enquired, looking up.

'Not really,' Deon replied. 'But I'm also going to the athletics meeting.'

'Oh dear, sir, I meant no offence. I hope you do well in your race.'

'I expect to win,' Deon told him with a grin.

It was an easy ten-minute walk to the giant stadium and the designers had built little walkways and bridges and overpasses and underpasses, all well signposted. He had no trouble finding the way.

For the average fan, a sports stadium means just that – a place where sports events take place. Not so. Pioneered by the Olympics (mainly) and the FIFA World Cup, modern stadia are more than a track or pitch with some seats around them. They are effectively mini-cities. This stadium was huge, seating about eighty thousand people. But that was only the start. Inside were hospitality areas, media areas, VIP areas, athlete changing rooms, a substantial and sophisticated security infrastructure, numerous ablution facilities, a fully equipped medical centre, indoor warm-up areas for competitors, numerous meeting rooms, costly corporate suites with excellent views of the action, several restaurants, food vending areas and sophisticated access and evacuation systems, designed so that all those people could get out of the stadium in less than twenty minutes if necessary.

Outside, the entire precinct was open to the public, with food outlets and grassed areas where people could walk with their kids and dogs. There was also a dedicated bus terminal, and during big competitions there was a fan park where people unable to score tickets could watch the action on a giant screen. A tube station was a few hundred metres away.

Close by was a warm-up track comprising a full 400-metre synthetic track with grass infield. It was the only facility outside the stadium that was access-controlled, allowing competitors and their coaches to prepare unhindered by fans.

Deon followed the 'Media Accreditation' signboards that were complete with the Bannister meeting logo in red, white and blue, evoking the Union Jack, unashamedly British.

The entrance was under the main grandstand and the same 'Media Accreditation' sign was over the door, only much larger. Deon couldn't miss it, nor could he miss the small figure of Emily Williams. She looked pretty in a Roger Bannister Memorial Meeting golf shirt – red, blue and white, with the meeting logo sitting on the left side. She trotted out to meet him.

'Deon!' she said excitedly. 'Welcome to Bannister accreditation.'

'You don't need to get so excited. I'm just another media person.'

'No, you're not. You're my South African friend and you told me about Abby's mother and you …' Deon held up his hand like a traffic cop on Jan Smuts Avenue.

He grinned at her. 'Stop! Please show me the way, or I'll never get accredited and you'll never see me again.'

She called another volunteer to stand at the entrance, turned and led the way along a passage and into an elevator which went up four levels. The doors hissed open and they exited into another passage.

'I never would have found this by myself,' he said.

'My pleasure. Never forget that in sport, the media are kings. They ultimately pay your salary. That's what Mister Hardy taught us. Except I'm a volunteer and don't get a salary.' She led the way to the media centre and left with a small wave.

Putting Emily out of his mind, he walked into a room that buzzed with excitement and activity. Along one side was a long table, behind which sat six volunteers typing busily on their laptops. On the far side a guy sat next to a contraption that took a photo, printed it onto a special card, labelled and laminated it, and hooked it onto a coloured lanyard. Further along this conveyor belt of activity stood the information area, where media packs were distributed and questions answered.

Deon had arrived at a busy time and there were another eight media people being processed. Everyone seemed to be speaking at once and, to add to the general noise level, music played over a hidden sound system. A Beethoven concerto, if his memory was correct. Of course, Beethoven was Bannister's favourite composer.

First up on the accreditation conveyor belt was the approval table, where each media person had to be identified and approved. Deon had his passport and APN card ready and the volunteer stared silently at him then took the card and passed it through some sort of scanner that lit up bright red and clicked as it captured images. He typed something rapidly on his computer before handing the card back.

'Do you need my passport?'

'No sir, just your South African media card. Thank you, Mister Coetzee.' He pronounced it 'Coat-Sea'.

'Please proceed to the data desk.' Deon was dismissed, with a vague thought that the guy probably worked for MI5, the CIA or Mossad.

It took ten minutes to work his way through the system. First, he was logged into the database, then had his photo taken and personal accreditation card issued, complete with an image of himself that, for a change, did not look like a prison mugshot. 'Deon Coetzee. APN South Africa. Media Level A1', it read. He was good to go.

Then came the information station. The bulging media pack contained everything from a stadium map (complete with directions to gender-neutral toilets) to bios of every athlete taking part, details of the media conference – to be held the following day – and details of the food and beverages available to the media, including a section for the vegan and gluten-free folks.

He was just about to wander off to take in the view into the stadium when he heard his name being called. 'Mister Coat-Sea! Deon! Please, this way.' Deon looked around to see the Mossad/CIA/MI5 guy waving at him.

'What is it?'

'Someone needs you, sir.'

Just then, a tall figure emerged from a side room. He looked about forty-five and wore a dark grey suit with a black waistcoat, white shirt and blue and white striped tie. A matching silk handkerchief sat in his left breast pocket and his polished black leather shoes reflected the overhead lights of the room. He had thick, wavy steel-grey hair cut neatly and he sported a handsome silver-grey moustache. Steel-rimmed reading glasses perched on the end of his longish nose, and a bulky gold watch was visible next to the cuff on his left wrist. Rolex?

All in all, he cut a handsome, prosperous-looking figure. Possibly a successful City of London stockbroker, a captain of local industry or a medium-level politician.

In fact, he was none of those. This was James Selfe, meeting director of the Roger Bannister Memorial Meeting and one of the most respected – and feared – meet directors in all of world athletics. Formidable.

'Mister Coetzee!' His voice boomed across the room and everyone looked up. Conversation stopped. 'Welcome to London. I'm happy that at least one South African athletics writer has been able to attend our humble event. Especially as your wonderful Abby Dennison is competing.'

Deon felt all the eyes in the room swivel across to him. In sharp contrast to Selfe's sartorial elegance he wore a Nike T-shirt that had survived a hundred washes, a pair of jeans and New Balance running shoes. He felt like a refugee from a Hillbrow jumble sale. Not my finest moment, he thought, but it's only accreditation. 'Thank you,' he squeaked, feeling his ears turning red. 'It's an honour to be here. And not only for Abby, but for everyone else as well …' His voice trailed off.

'Come, come,' boomed Selfe, 'we're honoured by the presence of our South African colleagues. Now, I have something to tell you, but in private only,' he said, waving a hand in the direction of the mass of people in the room. Deon noticed that the volunteers quickly turned their attention back to crossing names off lists, furiously typing on computers and shuffling papers around. There was little doubt as to who was in charge.

Turning abruptly, Selfe walked down a passage, unlocked a door and held it open.

They entered a large room with glass sliding doors that opened onto an outside seating area. The floor was thickly carpeted and there was a bar counter along one side. Hand-painted portraits of members of the West Ham United club, the stadium's resident Premier League football team, covered one of the walls. In the centre of the room was a rectangular boardroom table with twenty chairs. The place smelled of furniture polish. The same classical music played softly in the background.

Selfe moved behind the bar. 'Drink?' Deon asked for a Coke, which James poured from a can into a tall glass, adding ice from a fridge. The ice clinked and the drink fizzed.

Deon moved to the glass doors and stared out into the deep recesses of the stadium. It was his first sighting of the legendary arena, the holy ground where, back in 2012, Mo Farah and Jessica Ennis-Hill had thrilled British crowds with Olympic home victories and David Rudisha had run the greatest 800-metre race in history. Deon stared in wonder at the track and the grandstands, all under wide roofing, the tiered seats disappearing into the shadows.

There was silence for a full minute as James allowed him to take it in. 'Your first visit here? I thought so. She is rather special, isn't she? Now, come.' Deon reluctantly joined him at the massive table, its dark wood surface reflecting the soft lights recessed into the ceiling. Each seat had a small microphone and a set of headphones in front of it and Deon presumed these were for simultaneous translation purposes. And, no doubt, to facilitate the recording of meetings. He wondered if it was turned off now.

They sat at one end, with eighteen empty chairs neatly placed around the table for company. For a moment there was silence, then Deon asked, 'Okay. What's this about? What do you want to tell me?'

'Deon. May I call you Deon? We Brits are a little formal sometimes, but it goes with the territory. Like warm beer and Brexit. Part of the package, I'm afraid.'

'Just Deon, of course.'

'I'm James, then. It's settled.'

He was quiet again, seemingly gathering his thoughts. Then he leaned forward, all business. Deon sipped his Coke, the water droplets on the chilled glass wetting his fingers. He felt vaguely nervous, like being called unexpectedly into the principal's office at school.

'You obviously know that we at Bannister sponsored your trip here to London. What you don't know is how delighted we are to have you here. South Africa has produced many wonderful athletes over the years. Spence, Van Reenen, Thugwane, Budd, Ramaala, Meyer, De Reuck, Van Niekerk. And now Dennison, one of your best ever. But World Athletics has never been able to influence, if you want to use that word, the sporting media from your country. You have a large population, close to that of the UK, and we need to reach it. We know that athletics as a sport in South Africa has declined over the past twenty years. Apart from Abby and Wayde, that is. No doubt much of that was political, but the mismanagement for years after your democratic elections, plus a few other things, has added up to a steady decline in the standard of your athletes.'

Once again, he stopped to gather his thoughts. Deon realised that Selfe was being careful, making his point without wanting to get his guest's back up. But he was on safe ground as Deon agreed that the sport of athletics was in decline back home.

'What I'm about to tell you is off the record. It's for your ears only. We are fortunate here in British athletics to have access to extensive databases on the world's sporting media. We have to know who is coming to our meetings. Hundreds of so-called journalists seek accreditation each year for various events, including this one. It's like an avalanche, a tsunami. If we allowed them all in there would be no room for anyone else, no athletes, hardly any spectators. We have to be selective. Some are from newspapers, others from reputable media agencies like yours. Many are from television networks, radio stations. Most of these we know. And if we don't know them personally, at least we know their principals and how genuine these are. But we still have to be selective as we can only accommodate about two hundred people. More than that and it would be chaos.'

Abruptly, Selfe stood and went to the bar where he poured himself a glass of orange juice from a large bottle. Deon said nothing, waiting for him to continue, settling deeper into his seat. This was going to take a while.

'We do thorough research on new people coming in. We are flooded with new-age digital media. Websites of every possible description. Sports, fashion, celebrities, you name it. Dozens of them, all claiming millions of followers. It's impossible to sort out who's who. These people change every year. We've never heard of most of these websites, let alone the so-called journalists.'

Deon could see Selfe's point about the dramatic increase in sports media, particularly since the digital age and the internet allowed basically anyone with a laptop and connectivity to be a reporter, irrespective of their skills or motives. Track athletes were celebrities, role models. The fastest, strongest and, sometimes, the most beautiful people in the world. The rock stars of sport. Everyone wanted to get a piece of that.

Deon waited for Selfe to reach his conclusion. What he said was ridiculously far from what he expected.

'In fact, we've done some research on you, Deon. Now don't be alarmed, we routinely look for genuinely talented new journalists from countries World Athletics is targeting. It's one of the key objectives of the World Athletics president. There are databases, media-tracking agencies, even diplomatic channels we use. And we are certain that you are a successful, committed athletics journalist. Your record speaks for itself. Although most of your work has been done in South Africa, it is of high quality, original and possessing some really good investigative angles, which is not common in the average sportswriter. I confirmed all this with your editor.'

That floored him. Charlie Savage? Giving me a good report? Come off it. He would probably say that I was a third-rate beginner. He smiled, realising suddenly that the old dog must have known about Deon's invitation to London. Selfe confirmed this. 'He gave you a strong commendation and, coming from him, that's high praise indeed. You see, we researched him as well. How's his health, by the way?'

'He'll probably live to be ninety.'

James continued, 'We would like to see South Africa become one of the big players in world athletics. You already are in rugby and cricket. You used to be in athletics, so why not again? Africa is such a massive potential market for the sport and right now Kenya and Ethiopia are grabbing the headlines. South Africa is perfectly positioned to be a launching pad for athletics coverage across the continent. You have your excellent SuperSport digital platform that reaches across Africa, not to mention a number of influential radio stations. We want to partner with these platforms to build athletics across Africa.'

Once again Deon was impressed with Selfe's detailed analysis, and it dawned on him why Abby was being positioned as the star of the show on Friday.

He asked, 'With all the world-class athletes on display here, is this why you're focusing so strongly on Abby? She's just one of many stars.'

'Excellent observation. People have asked why I positioned Abby as the prime attraction this year, when I have Keino, Washington, Kiptanui, Safarova, Moyo and many more top performers. Apart from the desire to reach both South Africa and the whole continent, there are several other reasons. Firstly: she's big news. Really big news. This mystery woman, still only twenty-four years old, who seems to beat everyone all the time. In two years, virtually unbeatable over eight and fifteen. And no one really knows who she is! Then, face facts, she's the poster girl of the sport. Tall, attractive, with a nice smile. In an event dominated by East Africans, brilliant as they are, Abby is something different. She's simply a one-in-a-million athlete. No one knows how fast she can go. People are talking about world records.'

Deon knew the answer to his next question but asked it anyway. 'The women's mile is hardly ever contested these days. It's all about the 1 500 metres. How do you compare the two in terms of records and statistics?'

'A critical issue. You will know that in the first few Bannister meetings both the men and the women ran the 1 500. It was the gold standard distance. Everyone understood it. And we had great results, sub-3:30 every year for the men and even a 3:55 one year by a woman. But we wanted to honour Bannister so it was a no-brainer to change to the mile.'

He glanced at his watch – the Rolex – before continuing. 'I'll be brief. The women hardly ever run the mile, in fact the world record of 4:12 was set up twenty-two years ago by Svetlana Masterkova of Russia. Ancient history. The current world best over 1 500 is just over 3:50. Now consider that the mile is exactly 1 609 metres, or 7.26 per cent, longer. Add that percentage to 3:50 and you get 4:07, more or less. That means the mile record is about five seconds slower than the equivalent 1 500 time. That's because it's so old. Standards are not what they were in the 1990s.'

'Even though that was allegedly the era of widespread doping.'

'Even so. In today's environment, a world-class mile time would ideally be under 4:10 or even faster. That would equate to about 3:51, 3:53 over 1 500.'

'Wow! That's only ten seconds, about sixty metres, slower than Bannister.'

'To be honest, and this is off the record, we are hoping to get a time under 4:10. It would be history-making. So I have arranged a pace-setting regimen that will see to that. Just wait and see, Abby will be the big star on Friday. Her coach JP and I chatted privately last week, but Abby doesn't know about that. He thinks she can go close to 4:10, even 4:09. Sixty-two, sixty-three seconds per lap.'

Deon took a deep breath. A potential world record!

James again glanced at his bulky wristwatch. Time was marching on and he was all business again. His voice dropped a fraction. 'Changing the subject somewhat, I know we can trust you and that's why I am taking you into my confidence.'

Now what?

'Two weeks ago, Abby Dennison's father, Paul, called me. You know him, of course?'

'We've met many times but he's kind of distant. For some journos, he's rather intimidating.'

Selfe smiled knowingly. 'Indeed. I've been on the receiving end of Mister Dennison's not-insignificant negotiating skills. But that's not what his phone call was about.'

'Oh.'

'No. He asked me to speak to you off the record. Paul and Bronwyn feel that Abby is too, how shall I say, closeted. Tied up with her coach and father. Her public persona is that of an absent runner, a recluse almost. She doesn't even tweet or have an Instagram profile. People perceive her as not willing to engage. They need to know more about her as a person, rather than just a runner.'

James leaned back in his chair and thoughtfully rubbed his chin. They both took sips of their drinks. Deon said nothing.

'Here's the point. Paul asked me to suggest that you use a couple of days after the meeting here to spend one-on-one time with Abby. Get to know her a bit better. Take her around the city, get her to relax. I can arrange a nice trip to a London art gallery or out in the country. Whatever place both of you will enjoy visiting.'

'And what must I do? Surely you don't want me to be a nice distraction for a day?'

'No. You're an excellent writer and Paul knows it. That's why he wants to do this, to get some more, how shall I say, personal stories out there. About Abby the person, the woman behind the athlete. Rather the real, live individual than the ice maiden many people perceive her to be. Also get some images of her doing fun things, non-running things, in non-running clothing. She needs to become a person, not a robot or a machine.'

'Does Abby know about this, or is she just a puppet and everyone else pulls the strings?'

'Definitely not a puppet, not that one! In fact, I believe that she actually initiated this exercise, although Paul never said so to me. To check, I called Bronwyn Adams confidentially and she admitted that Abby feels a bit "too controlled" by Paul. Not in a bad way, of course, but Bronwyn realises that Abby needs to assert her independence, as it were.'

'She was an excellent student as well, got a bunch of distinctions in matric.'

'Exactly. Abby wants to be seen as more than just a runner. Bronwyn believes that this is part of Abby kind-of reinventing herself.'

'Who actually asked for me to work on this?'

'It seems to be a group decision. They know and apparently trust you and, of course, you went to the same school. Reading between the lines, I believe that Abby insisted she work with you.'

'How will it work?'

'They don't want this to be some sort of big, once-off scoop. Rather a series of little profile pieces, small interviews that will roll out over a couple of months, while the excitement of this meeting is still on everyone's minds.'

'What's the drill?' Deon asked, feeling part of some larger-than-life sporting soap opera.

'Chat with them after the media conference tomorrow. The trip can spread over two, three days if necessary. She is resting after Friday, taking time off from training. Paul will discuss the details with you.'

Deon felt like a pawn in a chess game. Still, it was a great opportunity to get exclusive interview time with a world sporting icon. So what if Paul, Bronwyn, Selfe, Abby and whoever else had set the whole thing up? By-lines all over the place. A proper career move.

'It's time to go,' James announced. 'Can you be at tomorrow's conference fifteen minutes before it starts? I've arranged a seat in the front row for you. Paul will chat to you afterwards to sort out the Abby pieces. Stay here for a while if you like. Enjoy the view.'

Deon stayed, deep in thought. On the surface, Selfe's story was plausible. Abby, the athletics icon, but to most people a mystery woman. What does she do for fun? Does she prefer pasta to steak? Does she have a secret boyfriend? What impact had her mother's death had on her?

The fact that Abby needed to assert herself from within the confines of the Team, take a bit of control, determine her own destiny, was news to him, but not surprising. He knew that, under the elite-athlete façade, she was tough and determined. He wondered what her ultimate destiny would be. He had no idea.

His thoughts were interrupted when Selfe popped his head back into the room. 'One more thing, Deon. Have you ever heard of a website called MileStar Athletics?'

'No, sorry.'

'And an athletics writer called Mark Whyte?'

'No.'

'I thought so.'

Then he was gone.

It took Deon ten minutes to make his way out of the stadium into the bright sunshine. Emily was still at her post welcoming people. She was busy with someone, so Deon gave her a cheery wave as he passed. Halfway across the open area he stopped and looked back, but they had gone inside.

He was sure that he recognised the man with Emily from somewhere. He stopped and tried to recall the name James had mentioned. What was it? Malcolm Watson? Martin West?

Then it came back to him. It was Mark Whyte, the MileStar guy.

Interesting.

10

Wednesday, 7 August

LONDON

At 10h33 Mark Whyte arrived at the stadium to register and was greeted by a smiling Emily Williams. He looked her up and down, liked what he saw and gave her his widest smile.

'I'm Mark Whyte, I'm here to register for media. South Africa, MileStar Athletics.'

She consulted a multipage printout covered with names and designations. 'Whyte, MileStar, Whyte, MileStar. Oh, here it is. I see you only applied a week ago. That's unusual, most people apply months in advance.'

'I was coming to London suddenly.'

Emily beckoned to her partner just inside the door. 'Rosie, please take Mister Whyte up to the media centre.'

Mark gave her another broad smile and left with Rosie. As they disappeared into the cavernous stadium, Emily speed-dialled a number on her cellphone. Seconds later it was answered. 'James, this is Em. He's here. Whyte. I sent him up with Rosie. He'll be with you in a minute.'

She hung up and turned to a pair of Japanese men. 'Welcome to the Roger Bannister media centre. You must be Mister Takahashi and Mister Nakamura from the *Tokyo Sports Illustrated*. Welcome to our humble meeting.'

Four floors up, Mark arrived at the media centre and began the accreditation process. As he was finishing up at the first table, James Selfe arrived with a flourish and greeted the newcomer warmly. 'Mark, greetings, I'm James Selfe, meet director. Welcome to London.' The two men shook hands.

'The pleasure is mine. I was sure that my late application would be rejected.

And yet, here I am. An honour.' The same broad smile and Selfe could have sworn he saw a flash as the overhead lights reflected off Whyte's teeth. No, it must have been his imagination.

'Come, come, let's make this quick.' He clicked his fingers at a volunteer. 'Richie, please make sure Mister Whyte is processed quickly. Oh, and Mark – you don't mind if I call you Mark, we're all simple sports fans here – won't you just give your passport to Richie? We need to check the passports of all our international media people. Bureaucracy and all that. Government nonsense. Hope you don't mind.'

Mark pulled out a green South African passport. 'Sure.'

'Richie will hustle your accreditation through and give you everything before you leave. Meanwhile, have you seen inside the stadium?' Mark shook his head. 'Well then, come and see.' Taking Mark by the arm, he led the way to the large window that overlooked the giant stadium. 'Isn't she wonderful? Just wait until there are eighty thousand fans in there. Then you will truly see why sport is so important to people.'

While the two men stood side by side, staring into the vastness of the arena, Richie took the passport into a side room and carefully scanned some of the pages on a large machine that clicked and whirred and flashed red and then green. After withdrawing the document, he entered a number on a keyboard and clicked on the 'send' button. He came back and joined Selfe and Mark at the window. 'All in order, sir. Sorry for the delay.'

Selfe escorted Mark through the remaining steps in the accreditation process. It took less than five minutes. At the end, Selfe made a big show of hanging the media accreditation lanyard around his guest's neck. A couple of the volunteers even clapped.

'Come, come, Mark. Let me show you the holy-of-holies, the VVVIP centre. Honestly, not even I go there very often. It's mainly for royalty. And big sponsors, and lords and ladies. You know the drill, all very British.' He chuckled.

They went into the same room where Deon had sat less than an hour earlier, had the same Coke with ice, the same glass of orange juice and sat at the same table in the same chairs.

On the south wall of the media centre, recessed into the surface, a tiny surveillance camera had followed Mark from the moment he entered the room. More than a hundred metres away, a security official wearing a black bomber jacket, camouflage trousers punctuated with several zip-up pockets, a black baseball cap with a red eagle logo in the front, dark glasses and calf-high black boots sat deep underground in one of the bomb-proof security rooms of the Olympic Stadium.

In front of him was a large console linked to dozens of cameras scattered around the stadium. The man ignored all of these except one that looked, unblinking and undetected, into the media accreditation room. As Mark moved around, the operator changed the direction and aperture of the camera, moving it up and down on Mark, first a wide shot, then a series of close-ups of his face.

After three minutes, the operator decided that there were sufficient quality images stored on the security computer's hard drive and he remotely locked off the camera, which now became static and non-operational, its tiny eye closed. Then, like Richie in the media room, he typed a message on a computer, instructed the machine to activate a secure line to a building across London, and clicked 'send'.

At that very moment, Selfe and Whyte were sitting in the VVVIP centre six levels above the security room. James asked, 'Do you know a South African athletics writer called Deon Coetzee?'

There was a long pause. 'Yes, I know of him. Well-respected guy locally. Covers lots of sports other than track and field. Kind of a jack-of-all-trades.'

'And master of none?' Selfe's stare was intense.

Whyte's reply was smooth. 'Not at all. On the contrary, he does a great job on golf, cricket and hockey as well as athletics.'

'But athletics is his main sport.'

'Yes it is.'

'Have you met him?'

'Not officially. I have my own business in Johannesburg and it keeps me mighty busy. Life insurance cover for lower-income folks. Big market. So my athletics work is a side-line and I try to cover the whole of Africa with lots of interviews with Kenyans, Ethiopians, that sort of thing. Profiles, background pieces. The website is just a hobby really, software is my main activity as you can imagine. But my website does have a niche following and that's quite important in Africa where athletics doesn't have the same quality coverage as it does in Europe, for example.'

Selfe lied smoothly. 'Indeed. That's why I was keen to squeeze you into our media contingent.' He moved across the room to the bar area. 'Another Coke? A beer? It's nearly noon and you know what they say about the sun going over the yardarm?'

Mark stared at him blankly and shook his head. 'No thanks.'

'No matter. How well do you know Abby Dennison?'

The sudden change in direction caught Mark by surprise. He hesitated, gathering his thoughts. This sounded like an interrogation and he was starting to feel uncomfortable. 'Not personally, not on a friend basis, shall I say. Obviously I know about her times and medals. Everyone does. But I've never been able to get an interview with her. Her father is quite the gatekeeper. But JP is much easier and I've spoken to him a few times on the phone.'

'Well, you'll get up close tomorrow. Maybe even get that precious one-on-one at the media conference. You will be there, won't you?'

Mark found himself sweating. 'Of course.' He stood. 'James, I must thank you for accommodating me, especially at the last minute. Now I have to go. I have a meeting with a supplier across the city. If you'll excuse me.'

The men shook hands and Mark made his way out of the media centre, down the elevator and out into the bright London sunshine. He noticed several office workers sitting on the grass nearby. A few of the men had their shirts off, celebrating a warm, sunny London day. There was a chorus of bird calls as a group of pigeons flew overhead and disappeared behind the giant stadium.

Emily greeted him as he passed. 'Mister Whyte, don't you say goodbye? I hope you got accredited.'

'Oh, thanks,' he replied vaguely. 'See you tomorrow at the conference. Ten o'clock?'

'Yes. Ten.'

As he crossed the Olympic precinct and went along the walkways, over and under bridges and into the tube station, Mark felt vaguely troubled. All that attention. The tour of the VVVIP centre. The questions. In all likelihood it's nothing, he thought.

It wasn't. After bidding a cheery farewell to Mark, James went back into the main media centre, where Simon Hardy stopped him. 'Got a minute, boss? In private?'

The men went into the VVVIP area. Hardy spoke quickly. 'I know you've got plenty on your plate right now, but here's the info you wanted on Whyte. His ID is genuine. QSH's people went into the South African national database, which the two countries share. No criminal record, a squeaky-clean guy. His company, MileStar Electronics, is genuine. In fact, it looks like a very successful operation.'

'What's the problem then?'

'Well, the MileStar Athletics website isn't genuine. There is an actual website of that name and Whyte is the registered owner, but nothing on it is original. Interviews are lifted from other sites, photos downloaded from Google, my friend Danie at Athletics South Africa has never heard of it. I think Mister Whyte, for whatever reason, badly wanted to get accredited here.'

'Weird. Why go to all that trouble? He could just have bought tickets.'

'I think I know why. Yesterday I asked Zack, Regalbank's chief computer nerd, to do some serious digging and he hacked the MileStar Electronics mainframe. Naughty but necessary. He said its firewalls were, quote, "piss-easy to get around", unquote.'

'You never told me that.'

'Of course not. But what I can tell you is that Whyte's own computer, which is networked to the mainframe, has more than two hundred photos of Abby Dennison on it. Mostly of her running and mostly lifted from other sources, but some clearly taken personally, paparazzi style. Personal stuff like shopping, driving her car. A few even looked like drone shots of her in her garden by the swimming pool. My guess is that he has a rather unhealthy obsession with our precious Abby.'

'Set up a meeting with QSH and Mary Southgate at Brooks's this afternoon. I want to have Whyte watched. Just in case. He must be kept well away from, as you call her, our precious Abby.'

11

Wednesday, 8 August

LONDON

Brooks's is one of the oldest and most exclusive gentlemen's clubs in London. Situated in St James Street, it has a proud history dating back to 1762 when a pair of seriously miffed and extremely embarrassed gentlemen, having been blackballed entry to White's club, decided to go into competition. So there.

Late in the afternoon, three people sat in a quiet corner of a private room in Brooks's on deep leather chairs. Two of them were men, both wearing dark suits with waistcoats and blue-striped Old Etonian ties. The other person was a woman in her thirties, dressed in a long black cashmere coat over a grey tailored business suit and white shirt. A pearl necklace gleamed in the soft light.

On the walls hung several landscape paintings, including a Turner and two Samuel Palmers. Along the other walls were glass-fronted bookcases filled with leather-bound volumes. On a low table in the centre stood a bottle of South African Kanonkop Black Label Pinotage, costing more than a hundred pounds on the club's seriously expensive wine list, and three glasses.

James Selfe was one of the men. On his left sat Quentin Smythe-Harrison, known by an entire generation of felons as QSH, senior compliance manager at the British Serious Fraud Office (SFO). On Selfe's right was Mary Southgate, executive vice-president, communications, of Regalbank.

Mary spoke first. 'I hope you gentlemen realise the concession I am making to be here. After all, Brooks's is notorious for being one of the last bastions of male domination in the city. It's only in the last fifty years that women are even allowed through the doors as guests, and even now we cannot become members.' She sniffed, but there was a smile in the corner of her mouth.

'My dear Mary,' replied Selfe. 'You must know that we men are an endangered species. Until recently we had a woman prime minister and even our bank chairperson, the venerable Baroness Quilter, is most definitely female.'

As he raised his glass, Mary said, 'To the survival of the male species in the modern world!'

The trio clinked glasses and got down to business.

'What's going on, James?' asked QSH. 'Why the sudden meeting? And why the clandestine scanning of some journalist's passport?' He dug into a pocket and pulled out a copy of Mark Whyte's passport photo.

'QSH and Mary, thank you for coming. A week ago we received a late application for media accreditation at the Bannister meeting from a Johannesburg-based athletics writer called Mark Whyte. He claimed to have a website called MileStar Athletics, was coming to London on business and wanted accreditation. Normally it would have been an immediate "no" – the closing date had long passed – but Simon Hardy, our media manager, was intrigued. He studied this MileStar website and on the surface it looked legit. Good content, well-informed stuff, excellent interviews and educated comments from Whyte. He gave the man his accreditation, but remained curious and asked Zack to dig a bit more.'

'Who is Zack?' asked QSH.

'Zack Abromowitz, Regalbank's head of data science,' answered James.

'And an amateur hacker,' added Mary.

'And what did this Zack person find?'

James selected his words carefully. 'Of course, all of this is off the record. I don't want us to take this info out of the room. Whyte is the owner of a successful tech company in Johannesburg called MileStar Electronics, which sells cut-rate life insurance to lower-income clients. Quite legitimate and very successful, I might add. But Zack found more. On the hard drive of Whyte's personal computer, hidden deep in a series of encrypted folders, were more than two hundred photos of Abby Dennison, some clearly taken paparazzi style. And, believe it or not, MileStar has a couple of subsidiary shelf companies called Abbyden Holdings 1, Abbyden Holdings 2 and Abbyden Holdings 3.'

'This is almost comical,' said QSH. 'Why did this Whyte chap come here, now? All this way, creating a false website, just to get into the media centre?'

Mary spoke. 'James told me about this earlier, hence our meeting now. The whole story worries me. It sounds innocuous on the surface, and it may be. But I have a niece who is a fashion model with Storm Models, one of the city's biggest agencies. She does mainly photographic work, some of it a bit risqué, swimsuit and lingerie stuff. Her bosses warned their models to be on the lookout for stalkers and she became aware of a man who seemed to be trailing her on a regular basis. She told her bosses. Long story short, this guy had started off by collecting photos of her, stored on his computer. Turns out most were taken by him and were definitely invasive, through her bedroom window, for example. Then it became nasty and, before they could nab him, he confronted her one night on her way home from work, begged her to marry him, said he loved her. She freaked out, smacked him right there in the street. Then he threatened her with violence. The next day the sex-crimes squad tracked him down and now he's locked up pending trial. My point is this: stalkers often escalate. This must not happen to Abby, certainly not in London. We need to watch him like a hawk.'

She continued. 'This Whyte character seems to be besotted with Abby Dennison. I spoke to a psychiatrist friend recently who said that some people, usually men, become fixated on a famous person, usually an attractive, successful, high-profile woman. Movie stars, singers, models, sportswomen. Stalking can become pathological and dangerous when things get out of hand, like with my niece. So far, this sounds pretty benign but you never know.'

James said, 'While he is on British soil I want him watched. I don't want anything to disturb Abby. The race is in two days' time. QSH, can I ask you to get one of your spooks to keep an eye on the lad?'

'Consider it done.' He paused before adding, 'To be sure, I'll dig up the relevant authority in South Africa and alert them.'

They all agreed that the meeting, not to mention the wine, had been worthwhile and went their separate ways at 19h00.

THE FINAL LAP

At that exact moment, Mark Whyte was in his hotel room, reading the latest Daniel Silva novel about an Israeli spy. He paused, reflected on the day and decided that it had been a good one. He was accredited, officially in the system, and tomorrow was media conference day, when he would probably get his first shot at meeting AD. What a win. I really am a smart boy, he thought. And who knows where this may lead … after all, she's young and impressionable, probably longing for decent male company outside the athletics world. I'm good looking, wealthy, an athletics lover and well equipped to take her around London after the meeting. See the sights. Show her my hotel room. A man can fantasise, can't he?

The phone next to his bed tinkled, destroying the mood. Annoyed, Mark picked it up. A voice said, 'Mister Whyte, sorry to trouble you but you have a call from a Prabesh Venkathan. He says he's your business partner. Can you take it?'

What the heck? Prabesh? His body went cold and his pulse raced. 'Put him on.'

There was no small talk. 'Mark, this is Prabesh. We've been hacked. The mainframe, the server, all the computers, the lot.'

12

Thursday, 9 August

LONDON OLYMPIC STADIUM

By 09h00 Deon had been for a forty-minute jog through the Olympic precinct, showered, grabbed a quick hotel breakfast, packed the essentials into his backpack and was strolling towards the stadium.

He wore his smartest jeans, Nike trainers, socks (for a change) and a black windbreaker. He was, by his own low standards, smartly dressed, meaning a real shirt with a collar and sleeves. The only slightly embarrassing feature was the branding on the back of the windbreaker that should have read, 'Soweto Marathon 2014'. But part of 'Soweto' had fallen off and it read 'S wet Marathon 2014'. Evidently the glue on the 'o's was sub-standard. He hoped no one would notice.

His mind was in overdrive – it was another huge day. Media conference day.

Deon arrived at the media centre twenty minutes later. The elevator door opened with a hiss and he was greeted by a wall of noise and plenty of activity with people rushing all over the place.

The media centre inside the Olympic Stadium – and most other world-class sports venues – was a series of rooms designed to do several things, the main one being to offer journalists access to the arena where two hundred work stations in prime positions opposite the finish line on the track were reserved. These were long benches onto which the journalists could place computers and writing materials. While regular spectators sat in conventional seats, media people needed a workbench.

The main room in the centre – the one that adjoined the outside seating area – was the conference venue. It was large and configured in such a way that more than two hundred members of the media could be accommodated comfortably in rows of chairs – fifteen rows of fifteen chairs each. There was space at the back for the television cameras and their operators.

In the front was a table, about eight metres long, behind which were four chairs, each with a microphone on a low stand. The table was covered with a linen tablecloth that reached the floor and was branded with dozens of small Regalbank logos. On the table were four bowls of predominantly yellow flowers and there was plenty of bottled water, the offering of a supplier-sponsor. A podium with a microphone stood next to the table.

Behind the table stood a wide backdrop covered with a chequerboard of small logos: the Bannister event itself, the title sponsor – Regalbank – and four supplier-sponsors.

Recalling what James Selfe had said the previous day, Deon scanned the front row of seats. Sure enough, one of the chairs had a 'Reserved – Deon Coetzee' sign on it. Very cool.

He checked out the media area. Linked to the main room was a series of work areas, designed to give journalists the chance to file their stories away from the chaos outside. There was access to the mainframe computer, on which was stored vast amounts of data about the event, its history, the participants and, of course, the legendary Roger Bannister himself. There was Wi-Fi throughout the area and the access code was in the media pack.

One of the satellite rooms was set aside for catering which, during the event, would serve everything from Red Bull to roast beef for hungry and thirsty journalists.

Deon now grasped what Charlie Savage had drilled into his head for years. 'The single best way to attend any world-class sporting event is to be a media person. Work your butt off, sweat and toil, take risks, kick plenty of backsides and maybe, maybe, one day you will get there.'

As he gazed out at the empty stadium, it dawned on him – he was 'there'. And, he realised, without the sanction of the old man he would never have reached this career pinnacle. The thought gave him a deep sense of satisfaction.

His quiet contemplation was broken by a tap on the shoulder. 'Deon, what are you thinking about?' He spun around, slightly embarrassed. It was Emily Williams.

'Oh, hi. You on duty today?'

'Yes. My job is to run around keeping all you media guys happy. Fetching drinks, answering questions. Vitally important stuff like that. Oh, I have to know: did you run the Swet Marathon? It's on your jacket. Sounds difficult. And hot.'

'Well, no, not really, but I was there. And it's not the Swet Marathon, the "o" letters fell off. Actually … never mind. I'll explain later.'

She giggled, then regained her serious face. 'To be honest, I need to show you something … someone, to be precise. Come with me.'

She moved back into the big room with all the seats. 'There he is,' she said quietly, tilting her head to the right. 'Mister Whyte, spelled with a "y", the MileStar man.' For a moment, Deon was confused.

'Who?'

'Yesterday, just after you left, he came to accreditation. His name is Mark Whyte and he has a website called MileStar Athletics and comes from South Africa. And Mister Selfe gave me strict instructions to call him from downstairs when he arrived. So I did, straight away. Selfe never asked me to flag anyone else and that's why I remember Whyte and his website so clearly. Don't you know him? He's one of your neighbours.'

Deon stared across the room at the man in question who was standing by himself close to the back row near the door, scanning the room. He was an imposing figure. Tall, slim and athletic looking, maybe just over thirty, but his thinning blonde hair made him look older. He sported a trendy half-beard of about ten days' growth and wore a light blue double-breasted jacket over an open-necked white shirt with a dark blue collar and cuffs. His navy-blue trousers fitted neatly and accentuated his slim frame. His shoes were polished black leather. He carried a thin leather briefcase and his accreditation hung around his neck.

Distinctive about his appearance were his spectacles, black, thick-rimmed and tinted so that they looked like dark glasses in the brightly lit room. They dominated his face. Deon thought that he looked nothing like a typical sports journalist.

'Do you want an introduction?' enquired Emily.

'Later, maybe.'

The names Whyte and MileStar were unknown to Deon, which was a problem. How did someone from his country get accredited when so many other journalists had no chance? He must have somehow suckered Hardy into giving him one and that was a potential issue. Deon's scam-antennae went onto full alert. Whyte, MileStar, designer beard, ostentatious wealth, big thick tinted glasses. Filed away for future reference.

The place was really busy now and the noise from dozens of excited voices was almost deafening. Looking around, he saw Paul, Bronwyn and JP seated at the end of the front row near a closed door. Paul looked around and waved, signalling for Deon to come over.

Deon went across and stuck out his hand. The handshake was not exactly bone-crushing, but it came close. 'Deon,' boomed Paul, 'good to see you. It's been a while.'

Five months. 'How are you, Mister Dennison, and how is that fine daughter of yours, the reason I'm here as you no doubt know?'

'Fine, fine, thank you. All of us, the whole team, Abby, Bronwyn, JP. Very excited about tomorrow, of course. Wonderful event.'

'I can't wait to see how she flattens the lesser mortals in the mile.'

'Don't count your chickens.' He paused, then lowered his voice to a conspiratorial semi-whisper. 'I gather James spoke to you about our little project this weekend?' Deon nodded. 'We need to plan this carefully, lots to discuss to get it right. But not until after the meeting. I don't want to distract Abby at all.'

'Does she know? Is she happy with the idea?'

'Yes and yes. It was her idea, truth be known. I think she hatched it with Bronwyn, but that's fine.'

'Why don't we meet on Saturday sometime, when the dust has settled?'

'Maybe lunch, at the athletes' hotel?'

'Fine. Honestly, Mister Dennison, jokes aside, I am really looking forward to this assignment. I'll do a good job, I promise.'

'I'm sure you will. That's why we selected you. Oh, and it's Paul, by the way. None of this mister stuff. Makes me feel old. Look, the boss is here.'

Deon looked up. Simon Hardy was at the podium.

Deon went back to his assigned seat and Hardy called the room to order. Everyone sat down, silence descended and the distinctive clicking and whirring of television cameras could be heard. The room was jam-packed and several writers had to stand along the side walls.

Simon welcomed everyone and gave the usual spiel about important things like where the toilets were, and escape routes in the event of a fire or earthquake. He also announced that the conference was being live-streamed on rogerbannistermeeting.com, which they all knew anyway. It was in the media pack.

Then, with something of a flourish, he announced the arrival of the athletes. There was a hush of expectancy as a side door opened and James Selfe entered, followed by four athletes. They were easy to recognise, although Deon had only ever seen two of them in action. They were world famous, all either Olympic or World Championship gold medallists. One even held a world record.

Cameras rolled and flashbulbs popped. They took their seats and Deon realised that Abby Dennison was not among them. He wondered why, then it dawned on him. Of course, the golden girl would have the table all to herself. The centrepiece in a glittering array of talent, the *pièce de résistance*.

Jackie Washington was the flamboyant American who had famously broken the decade-long stranglehold that Jamaicans held in women's sprinting when she won the World Championship 100-metre gold medal ahead of a brace of Caribbean runners. Today she sported a USA tracksuit, dark blue with crimson and gold trim down the arms and legs and on the collar. Her wraparound sunglasses were parked on her head, nearly disappearing into a mass of curls.

Kenyan Benjamin Kiplimo Keino was the shy, almost reclusive middle-distance runner who had broken the world record for the mile just six weeks earlier. He looked distinctly uncomfortable in the glare of the media centre's lights and the frank stares of the audience. The fact that he was also the reigning world 1 500-metre champion only added to his aura and mystique. No one knew much about him, apart from his exploits on the track. Today was possibly a plan from his management to open him up a bit.

Tatyana Safarova was instantly recognisable. The Olympic women's 100-metre hurdles champion from Ukraine was one of the glamour-girls of the sport. Unlike the other athletes, all of whom wore their sponsored outfits, Safarova sported completely non-athletic clothing. She wore tight-fitting black Levi's that must have been shrink-wrapped around her lithe figure and white, calf-high boots covered with little glow-in-the-dark stars. Above the jeans was a loose-fitting blouse of alternating yellow and blue vertical stripes – the national colours of Ukraine – unbuttoned to the waist. Under that was a black figure-hugging cotton T-shirt. Like Washington, Safarova sported sunglasses, but in her case they were over her eyes. She looked like she had a hangover.

Scott Huffner was the reigning world pole vault champion, a man who had cleared over 6 metres outdoors and 6.14 indoors. Tall and lean, with the look of a gymnast that most world-class pole vaulters have, he was instantly recognisable by the tattoos that adorned his arms from shoulder to wrist. This decoration involved a bizarre range of iconography, among which Deon could identify the Olympic rings, the American flag, a bird flying (bald eagle?), the Taj Mahal, an insect that looked like a dung beetle, a snarling wolf face and the words 'Love' and 'Mother'. Deon knew that he was an outgoing, friendly man and a practising Quaker.

Selfe had rolled out the rock stars of track and field. If nothing else, this would guarantee his sponsors acres of space in the tabloids.

The genius of the man, though, was that each of these athletes was the best in the world at their particular event. The crème de la crème. This was no freak show.

But no Abby. Yet.

Hardy got the ball rolling and for the next thirty minutes the questions and answers flew. It was fascinating to watch as the athletes, like most world-class sporting heroes, had been drilled in the art of the interview – open faces, plenty of smiles, thanks for 'great questions', thoughtful pauses before answering, avoidance of anything remotely controversial, absolutely no denigrating of competitors, fulsome praise for the event, its sponsors and the 'wonderful, loyal fans'. Etcetera, etcetera. All by the book.

Mostly, Deon learned little new. Athletes are notorious for not opening up about their private lives, their training, predictions about likely success in the meeting, and their beliefs.

However, there were a few gems. When asked how the Kenyan nation seemed to have some sort of production line of middle-distance champions, Kiplimo Keino offered, 'We are all one big clan, just a few big families of runners. We come from the same region in Kenya, which is at very high altitude. Most of us started off poor and I had to run to school, eight kilometres each way, from when I was seven. When I was fifteen my father got his first car and we could drive to races. My second cousin's great-uncle's father was Kip Keino,' he added proudly.

Kip Keino was, of course, the legendary miler who had changed the face of world middle-distance athletics when he won the gold medal in the 1500 at the 1968 Olympics in Mexico City. Since then, African domination of these distances has been all but total.

Deon felt a slight chill as he remembered that Elinah Kiptanui, another Kenyan, would line up against Abby the following evening. And Sarah Moyo was rumoured to have grandparents that originally came from Kenya.

In reply to a question about whether her victory over the Jamaicans signalled a resurgence of American sprinting, Jackie Washington offered this gem, 'Let me tell you, the days of Usain Bolt and the Jamaicans are over. I had lunch with Donald Trump and he told me it was time to make America great again.' No one really believed that story but it made a good soundbite.

When asked whether he would put the image of his current girlfriend – long jumper Kerry Stevenson – on his arm, Huffner replied, 'No. What happens if she dumps me?'

Safarova waxed lyrical about 'my plans to become a world-class fashion designer after I stop with athletics. I designed these clothes myself'. To emphasise her talent, she moved her chair back and plonked a sparkly boot on the table.

But it was far more than fun and games. These were real champions and the world's sporting media lapped up the opportunity to interact with them. It was clear that they all took this meeting very seriously and had peaked for it. Everyone was in for a glittering feast of athletics.

At exactly 10h40 Hardy called an end to that segment of the conference and the quartet left the room. James Selfe went up to the podium and the room was silent, almost breathless with anticipation. Unasked questions hung in the air: where is Abby Dennison? Surely she will be attending the briefing? Hadn't that been mentioned in the media pack?

Selfe purposely built the tension by hesitating, then he smiled at everyone. 'You all know that Abby Dennison will be running the Bannister Mile for Women tomorrow evening. We as organisers also realise that she, like the athletes that have left the stage, is one of the best in the world in her event. However, because she is so seldom available to the media, we thought it appropriate that she has the stage to herself. But first let me remind you of some statistics. Dennison, in four years, has become one of the biggest names in world athletics, even though she has never competed at a senior World Championship or Olympic Games. Her single Junior World Championship four years ago saw her take the gold medal in the 800 metres.'

He paused for effect as the scribes scribbled.

'She has run 1:55.39 for the 800, which was the fastest time in the world two years ago and she has another six times run under 1:57. Over the 1 500 metres, which she only started running three years ago, she has broken four minutes on six occasions, her best time of 3:53.80 being one of the fastest in the world this year. Oh, and she ran 4:01 in a warm-up race three weeks ago, winning by sixty metres. Of course, she has broken 50 seconds for 400 metres as well. That was at high altitude in Johannesburg.'

He hesitated, turned to his left and said, 'Please welcome South Africa's Abby Dennison.'

Abby entered and took the centre seat at the front table. She was the centrepiece in this display of athletic brilliance, the diamond in the crown that everyone wanted to meet, greet, talk to and touch.

Deon thought that she looked brilliant, fabulous, happy, radiant. Am I going over the top? he asked himself. Probably. But who cared, this was his girl, the one he'd watched in awe when she was fifteen and running barefoot around the more-or-less 400-metre-long high school grass track in under fifty-eight seconds. She was a once-in-a-generation athlete then and remained one to this day.

She wore the standard Team kit of dark green tracksuit with gold trim on the collar, cuffs and down the side of the legs, the standard South African national sporting team colours. Her apparel and shoe sponsor, Maxx, appeared in logo form on the upper left front of her tracksuit top. Deon knew from experience that on the back of her jacket would be the 'Team Abby' name and a small South African flag.

Abby's hair was shorter than he'd seen it for a while, styled to reach just above her shoulders. As usual, it was a mass of blonde curls that bobbed and swayed as she walked and was decorated with pink and blue highlights. Deon had a sudden thought that, after the media conference and the avalanche of coverage on social media that would inevitably follow, several million young girls across the world would make a beeline to their local hairdressers to copy the signature AD hairstyle.

She carried nothing except a half-litre bright yellow plastic bottle with a screw-on top and retractable drinking port. Down the side was written, vertically and in large letters, 'Xtend'. This was another Abby sponsor, the supplier of her specially designed pre-competition drinks. Paul must have obtained permission from Selfe for Abby to bring a product onto the podium that was a different brand to the event's water supplier. Deon could imagine Paul's grin of satisfaction as the Xtend logo entered cyberspace.

He knew all of this would be there but what surprised him was her left ring finger. On it was a silver ring holding several small blue gemstones.

The room burst into spontaneous applause as she sat, and Deon wondered what Huffner, Washington, Safarova and the other athletes thought about that. Abby had to briefly put a hand in front of her eyes as the flashbulbs popped.

The room settled and Hardy fielded questions. Modern media conferences have a certain standard modus operandi in which the chairperson – in this case Hardy – invites a journalist with a question to identify themself and their publication before asking their question.

The session lasted for almost thirty minutes before Hardy called it a day. It had been the longest single media conference that Abby had ever handled and Deon thought she did well, but at the end she looked tired.

Mostly the questions were reasonable and the answers clear, well crafted, apparently honest and definitely helpful. By the end, the media contingent had a far better feel for Abby the person and Abby the athlete.

Some of the questions were too personal or just plain silly and these Abby deflected with a smile and considerable charm, so when she replied, 'I cannot comment on that at this time, if you don't mind,' no one seemed annoyed.

Many were technical, about her training methods and diet and to these she answered vaguely, the norm for elite athletes. Similarly, she would not be drawn into any predictions about the race the next day. She was effusive in her thanks to the organisers for inviting her and generous in her praise of the stature of the meeting.

To Deon's single question, she replied, 'Thanks, Deon, good to see you here. My family, the Team, is everything. We're a tight group. I owe everything to them and I wouldn't be here if it weren't for their contribution. To be honest, they've dedicated their lives to me. For sure.'

Further questions about the Team elicited a number of interesting replies. 'Each one plays a key role. JP is my coach. I don't argue with him or question him. Mizadams is my rock, my conscience, my mentor. And Paul, well, he's my dad.'

'I am proud to be South African. If I'd grown up in America or Canada or Australia I wouldn't be the same person. There are no wild elephants, cheetahs or wild dogs in Canada. There is no Kruger Park or Karoo or Soweto in Australia.'

'My main athletic hero? I don't know. Roger Bannister, perhaps. He broke the ultimate barrier. Since then you don't know who did, or did not, take drugs to break records. At least I know Roger didn't. So I have no modern heroes on the track.'

'I definitely don't want to be a professional athlete forever, hanging around till I'm forty trying to win races. I also don't know when my career will end, but it will be sooner rather than later. Maybe when I'm not enjoying it anymore. It's not about winning as much as the thrill of the competition, of doing my best, of reaching my potential. Is winning enough?' she asked rhetorically, shaking her head in a clear 'not for me' gesture. Most people jotted that down. It was a significant moment.

'Drug use in athletics is a massive issue. It's huge, like a monster lurking in the room. I don't take drugs, I simply could not live with myself if I did. The problem is that you don't know who does and who doesn't.'

'What do I enjoy the most about running? Hmmm, I know the answer to that. Try to understand this: it's the final lap of a race, after the bell. I love it. The speed, the adrenalin, the power, the competition, the desperation of everyone around me, the strength of the ones who can last till the final fifty metres, then the sky-high rush of winning, if I can. I race for the final lap.'

Eventually, Selfe stood up and made a 'T' with his fingers and wrist. 'Timeout folks. That's it. Let's get out of here and file stories. Oh, I see a hand going up. One final question. Mark Whyte, I believe?'

A couple hundred pairs of eyes swivelled around, looking for the questioner. A tall man wearing a smart jacket, tailored trousers and thick-rimmed glasses stood up. 'Mark Whyte, MileStar Athletics, South Africa. Miz Dennison, I see you have a ring on your left hand. Does that mean you somehow got married without anyone noticing?'

He sat down and the room was strangely silent for many seconds. Deon held his breath. What the hell question was that?

Eventually Abby smiled. It was the widest smile she had given all day. 'Mark Whyte, is that correct? Sorry, I didn't recognise you. The answer is yes, I am married. To my Team and to running. But, mostly, to the final lap.'

The room erupted. Laughter and applause competed for prominence as cameras caught close-ups of Abby's left ring finger as she raised it, alone, pointing towards the ceiling, the sapphires reflecting the flashes of the cameras. Deon was not the only person in the room that appreciated the subtle double meaning of the gesture. On the surface she was, like any girl, showing off a beautiful ring, but underneath lay a message. The single raised finger sent a clear signal, as it would countless times on social media: 'Stuff you, Mister Whyte.'

It was the perfect middle-finger salute. Brilliant.

As the crowd slowly dispersed, Paul said, 'Join us for a minute, Deon.'

They went into a side room, where Selfe, Hardy, Bronwyn, JP and Abby stood waiting. She gave him an unexpected hug, which lasted at least five seconds. He pulled away, embarrassed.

Paul said, 'It's been a while, Deon.'

'*Ja*. Only a few times in the last year unfortunately. But now I hear that's going to change …'

'Indeed. Abby is delighted that you guys are spending time together this weekend. So it's confirmed then. Deon will join us at the hotel for lunch tomorrow and we can plan the weekend's interview session.'

That was it. They were dismissed. As they left the room, Abby put her hand on his shoulder. 'Don't mind Dad,' she said. 'He's just being the boss, as usual. I can't wait to chill out and do some fun stuff. See you tomorrow.'

Deon noticed the small figure of Emily Williams down the passage that led to the elevator. 'Paul,' he asked, 'can Abby sign an autograph for my friend Emily, a volunteer?'

Without answering, Abby went up to Emily and the pair had a brief chat before Abby wrote a message in a small notebook. They shook hands and hugged.

JP, Bronwyn, Abby, Paul and Deon walked across the broad paved area outside the stadium towards their respective hotels, then Deon turned in the direction of the Premier Inn. Some morning it had been. He stood still for a while, neither hearing the traffic noise nor feeling the bright sunshine on his face. For a humble sportswriter, this was some kind of heaven.

He felt a light tap on his shoulder. Deon hadn't seen Emily following the group and was jolted out of his thoughts. 'Look over there,' she said, pointing. As the Team disappeared down a side street, a tall figure emerged from behind a pillar and followed at a discreet distance. He wore a light blue jacket over tailored trousers, and thick-rimmed dark glasses hid his face.

'It's Whyte,' she said, 'and he's following them.'

13

Thursday, 9 August

LONDON

Mark Whyte trailed the Team as they made their way back to the elite athletes' hotel. They went inside and he moved off and caught a tube to the Hyde Park area, close to his hotel. Before leaving the stadium precinct, he had removed a Nikon Coolpix camera from his briefcase and, taking full advantage of the instrument's substantial 125x optical zoom, snapped a dozen images of Abby and her group from as far away as fifty metres. No one noticed him in the crowds around the stadium.

It was a beautiful warm day, the temperature up into the high twenties. Londoners, relishing a short spell of real summer weather, a welcome break from the cool and rainy June and July they had endured, were out in their hundreds in the central London park, soaking up the sun during their lunchtime break.

Feeling peckish – the food at the media conference had been cold and tasteless – he found a restaurant right on the Serpentine. Accepting a table outside, he enjoyed a splendid view of the large expanse of water and ordered a chicken salad and noted that the price – fourteen pounds – would have bought him at least three such meals at a decent restaurant back home.

Even so, the ambience of the place was worth the cost. The calm water glittered in the bright sunlight and dozens of people wandered around on the many footpaths that criss-crossed one of the world's most famous parks. Several sat at the edge of the lake, cooling their feet in the water.

The grass was thick, a rich green colour, thanks to plentiful summer rainfall. Even the water birds seemed excited. Pure-white swans paddled gracefully around as if they were the regal kings of the waterway, while mallards, brightly coloured mandarin ducks and Canada geese flew around, landing with great splashes and squabbling noisily over scraps of food tossed into the water by eager children.

Mark was in no hurry. He dug into his briefcase and extracted a slim laptop computer. After booting up, he connected it to his Nikon and downloaded a few of the best images taken of Abby outside the stadium. He saved these in a password-protected folder in the cloud and deleted all the images on the camera itself. Making sure that the screen of the computer was not visible to other diners, he logged into one of his image folders and scrolled through. There were more than a hundred of them, all of Abby, either on her own or with other people.

They were taken in a wide variety of situations: some were competition shots downloaded from the internet while others were images he himself had surreptitiously taken – Abby training with JP at the Wanderers in Johannesburg, Abby shopping in Sandton City with Bronwyn, Abby walking in Bryanston and now, Abby in the streets of London. A few special ones had even been taken over her house last summer as she sat by the pool. The drone had been a good purchase but using it had been risky. Not a good idea.

Feeling relaxed and filled with anticipation about the days ahead, he spent two hours taking in the sights of South Kensington. Just before he reached his hotel, his cellphone buzzed. He didn't recognise the number and hesitated before answering. What now? Later, he realised just how important the call had been. If he hadn't answered …

A voice said, 'Mark, it's Prabesh. Remember I told you that we'd been hacked? Well, the hack came from someone or something called Regal, it was well disguised. I think it's a bank.'

'Bloody hell.'

They spoke for a few minutes and when Mark returned to his room he used the hotel phone to call a cellphone in Johannesburg. 'I know it's nearly dinner time,' he said, 'but you know me, Mandy. I own you twenty-four seven.'

'Mark, be quick for God's sake. I'm having drinks with Justin.'

'Which Justin?'

'Grow up, will you!'

'Okay, Mandy. I'll be serious. Remember I asked you to book me a trip to the Lake District? Well, things have changed and I need to come home earlier. Get me a flight from Paris to Joburg on Saturday night. Emirates.'

'Paris? What changed?'

'I miss you too much and decided that I couldn't wait to see you again.'

'Of course. So I'll dump Justin. And just when the relationship was looking so promising.'

'Seriously, Saturday the eleventh. And confirm when it's done. Bye, darling.' He hung up. Why did Mandy focus on men called Justin? As far as he knew, there had been at least three in the past two years. If this was a new one, it would be four. Crazy.

Mark paced around the room for several minutes, deep in thought. Although he always worked hard at appearing relaxed and in control, especially in front of women, inwardly he was worried. He knew the only thing that was remotely suspect was the false website. And the fact that the MileStar mainframe, and possibly his own PC, had been hacked that very day was too much of a coincidence. He had no desire to be under the Regalbank microscope.

He decided what he would do. First, he would change hotels and go seriously downmarket, where passports would not be checked. It would suck, but it was worth it. Then he would keep a seriously low profile. Stay out of the limelight at the meeting and just watch Abby. He was certain that she would win and get close to the world record for the mile – he knew the numbers in detail. Maybe she would break it and show those arrogant Kenyans and Eastern Europeans a thing or two.

How could he not be there when his girl became the fastest in the history of the sport? No way.

Three floors below, out on quiet Bayswater Road, a man dressed in scruffy jeans, a battered, nondescript leather jacket, sneakers and a cloth cap, stood under a lamppost and spoke on a cellphone.

'Got it all, guv. He's in his room, saw him standing by the window. Been a long day, but productive. He didn't have a clue. To be honest, I would have preferred a smarter mark, but it is what it is. He trailed the Dennison group back to their hotel, but they had no idea. Funny thing, though – the Coetzee guy, the other journo, he spotted Whyte following Dennison. He's a smart one, way sharper than Whyte, who looks like an arrogant jerk to me.

'Anyway, Whyte had a decent camera – maybe a Pentax or Nikon – and he snapped away at Dennison all the way back to her hotel. He may be some sort of stalker. I've seen his type before.'

'What happened then?'

'He took a tube to Hyde Park. Then it got interesting and challenging for the first time. He went into the restaurant next to the Serpentine so I found a seat right behind him. He got out his laptop and downloaded the pics he'd taken. Then came the best part – he tried to cover the screen but did a bad job of it. He had hundreds, and I mean *hundreds*, of Dennison pics. After that he wandered around for a long time, looking at the sights. Then he got a call on his mobile and went straight to his hotel. He rushed and looked anxious.'

'And now?'

'He went to his room and made a single call on the hotel phone. Later I'll get the number from the hotel operator.'

'Tomorrow? The same routine for you?'

'Sure thing guv, I'm on it. Same fee?'

'Add twenty per cent. It could be a long day.'

'Thanks, guv. Chat tomorrow.' The man walked off, with a final glance at the now-darkened window.

Knightsbridge is no more than a kilometre from Bayswater Road and is one of the city's most fashionable districts. A dim light could be seen shining from the window of a fifth-floor apartment. QSH, wearing a deep crimson smoking jacket, switched off his cellphone, drained the last of his favourite port from a small glass and patted the beagle lying sleeping next to the chair.

He addressed the dog. 'We'll see what our friend Mister Whyte gets up to tomorrow, won't we, Winston? Should be interesting. Come along now, time for bed.'

The light in his window went out.

14

Thursday, 9 August
LONDON

After the media conference, Deon took a ninety-minute walk back to the Premier Inn, sorting out the jumble of facts, impressions and general information that crowded his brain. Being honest with himself, it felt like he inhabited an unpredictable, vaguely scary world. Mind racing, he stopped suddenly outside the hotel entrance. A lady pushing a pram had to swerve around him. 'Idiot,' she muttered, and the baby started crying.

'Sorry, ma'am,' he mumbled, but she had already disappeared around a corner.

Get a grip, he told himself sternly, this is serious stuff, career-altering if you play your cards right. Emily, who had in the meantime returned to her post at the hotel, came through the entrance doors. 'What are you doing? That lady nearly crashed into you.'

'I'm jet-lagged?' he offered hopefully.

'Nonsense. You were miles away. Come in, it's time for lunch.'

His phone rang. '*Nkosi Sikelel' iAfrika*'. He peered at the screen – 'The Savage', it read, the words placed between a set of jaws sprouting sharpened teeth.

'Got to take this. My boss.' Then, 'Charlie, I was just going to call you.'

'Good boy. How's it going? James tells me you are totally on top of things.'

James? 'Well, yes, I suppose so, boss. Yes, of course. I mean, I hope so … How's the cough?' Trying to appear in control but failing badly. Why did Charlie always have that effect on people?

'Get a grip, man. Of course you're on top of things. Otherwise I would never have agreed to this whole nutty plan. Listen, no need to give me all the details, I spoke at length to Selfe. He filled me in on everything, the race, the runners, the whole Abby deep profile thing.'

'Thanks, boss.' Savage and Selfe had obviously been talking.

'Anyway, I'm glad that our plan, James's and mine and the guys from Regalbank, is coming together. Now listen, Deon, you have work to do. I need a story by, let's see, it's just after two o'clock here and I need to get it out by five at the latest. I need twelve hundred words max, a preview of the mile race, the runners, the stats, Abby's chances, you know the drill. Just email it to me. Two hours should do it; no, make that ninety minutes. I'll probably have to edit a lot of it. You junior guys have so much to learn.' His words tailed off into some sort of unidentifiable noise.

'Got it, boss. Glad to hear your cough is better.'

But Charlie had already hung up.

He turned to Emily. 'You'll never believe this … oh, forget it.'

'I guess you have work to do,' she said, sounding disappointed. 'I was hoping we could have lunch.'

'Sorry, my boss needs a preview. And he actually pays me. And there is a huge race tomorrow. And if I don't meet his deadline he will probably fire me and I'll have to stay here in your terrible weather and get a job washing dishes in your hotel and you will be my boss.'

'Sounds wonderful.' She grinned. 'What time will you be finished?'

'I need an hour and a half.'

'Happy writing.'

It was 13h15 in London, British Summer Time, an hour later in South Africa. Charlie needed to get his story onto the wires by five in order to catch the evening news broadcasts on radio and television, as well as to comfortably make the deadlines of the hugely influential morning online newspapers like *Daily Maverick*, which had almost totally taken over the early news slots from old-fashioned newspapers. Deon had less than ninety minutes to prepare one of the biggest stories of his life. Twelve hundred words? No pressure.

In his room it was all business. He took his time, thinking about the main points of the story, the statistics and the various scenarios that could play out. And in the centre would be Abby, given that the audience would be entirely South African. Previews can be tricky – too specific and readers will rip you to shreds when you get it wrong; if it's too bland, the editor will say it's boring. But previews are often the chance for a good journalist to make a name for himself, to rise above the mediocre. Deon generally enjoyed writing previews, thanks to his relentless research, in-depth interviews, impeccable record-keeping and a deep understanding of the sport and the participants.

Sixty-three minutes later it was done, the Bannister Mile for Women preview. He read it over, much of the content centred on the magnitude of the event in the global sports scene, the immense amount of attention being focused on Abby, the 'mystery woman' and 'golden girl' of world athletics (horrible, horrible clichés).

He picked up the phone and dialled nine for reception. 'Mister Coat-Sea, what can I do for you?' It was the Alien Kids guy.

'Hi. May the force be with you. Is Emily around?'

'She's in the bar doing the Guinness shuffle. A new dance involving lots of bottles.'

'That's fantastic. Please ask her to come to my room. I need her to scrutinise an article.'

Peals of laughter. 'Hey bro, that's a good one! Never heard that before. Scrutinise? As far as I know, she's not a policewoman. At least I hope not. Oh no, is she a cop?'

'Part-time drug squad. Undercover.'

'Really?'

A few minutes later there was a gentle knock at the door. 'Room service,' a female voice said.

Deon let her in. Emily was pushing one of those shiny hotel carts on wheels. This one had several dinner plates on the top level, and he smelled grilled prawns and spotted a small chocolate cake topped with cream. On the lower level sat a few bottles of Guinness.

She smiled. 'What did you say to Archie? He went white and made a few rapid calls on his cell. Strictly not allowed on duty.'

'I told him you were an undercover drug-squad cop.'

She stopped giggling when he turned his laptop toward her and gave her the preview to read. Normally, a writer will only give an article to an outsider if that person has a decent level of interest in, and knowledge of, the subject. Emily had both.

'There's some background about the meeting in the first paragraphs,' he explained, 'so whip through that. There is also a bit of background about Abby, which you know. The real stuff I want you to crit comes after that. Imagine you are an athletics fan eager to understand what all the fuss is about. How come the whole world is going crazy about a track race?'

He scrolled down on the screen to the meat of the article.

Who are the competitors?

In a world-class race even the lowest-ranked runners, Jane Beardsley and Ashley Donaldson, are highly rated, being respectively twelfth and thirteenth in the world. Both are British – Donaldson is Irish and Beardsley English – which is one of the reasons they have been invited. Both are relatively young, under twenty-five, and will be happy to tag along in a very fast race, with a huge international audience to boost their profiles and improve their chances of lucrative sponsorship opportunities down the line. Any time quicker than 4:15 for the mile, equivalent to 3:57 for the 1 500, would be a fine outcome for either of them.

The Europeans, Birgit Lennartz of Germany and Brigita Karlovic of Croatia, have outside chances of making the podium. In a quick, even-paced race, both will try to stay in touch for as long as possible, the chance of running close to 4:12 being a huge motivator.

Elinah Kiptanui and Mary McColgan are definite wild cards. Both are enormously talented and capable of springing a surprise, which would be to beat either Dennison, Moyo or the Russian, Olga Fedorova. Kiptanui and McColgan will be targeting a podium finish and will play a cat-and-mouse game with the favourites. McColgan has the advantage of being the crowd's favourite.

Olga Fedorova, of all the athletes, has the biggest point to prove and the most to lose. Undisputed queen of the middle-distances on the track for five years, she has seen Abby Dennison climb through the rankings and grab her number-one position, based on the fastest times last year. This is only the second time they have met – Fedorova beat Dennison by a massive six seconds in the Weltklasse Zürich 1 500-metre race last year – but she has ducked a head-to-head with Abby this whole season. Friday night is literally make-or-break for the thirty-year-old runner from St Petersburg.

Then we have Sarah Moyo, the so-called mystery woman from Zimbabwe, ranked number two in the world and definitely the biggest threat to Abby. Although she lacks the pure sprinting speed of Dennison, she can hold a fast pace over 600 or even 800 metres at the end. She's never raced Dennison before and this is what the world will be watching.

Finally, there is the American Suzy Marshall, who has been invited to act as race pacemaker. Marshall is a specialist 800-metre runner and has proven to be adept at holding an accurate, fast pace at the front of the race for the first two laps. Given the organisers' intent to stage a race that attacks the world record, it is essential that an expert pacemaker be used to keep the field on track until the halfway mark. Expect Marshall to run two laps of around sixty-three seconds each, the perfect platform for the first women's world record for the mile in more than twenty years.

Emily looked at Deon. 'What else is important?'

'Here's the key paragraph. The numbers. To me, this is the key to the whole thing.'

Why are the numbers so important?

Athletics is all about statistics and this race offers athletics fans the real possibility of a world record.

The mile distance is not often included in athletics meetings, having been supplanted by the 1 500 metres, its metric equivalent. In fact, the mile distance is more famous for its glorious history – the Bannister sub-four-minute race back in May, 1954 – than anything else.

The mile is exactly 1 609.34 metres long, in other words, about 110 metres longer than the standard metric distance. The inside lane of an athletics track is exactly 400 metres long, which means that the mile starting point is 9.3 metres before the finish line. The athletes run those nine metres, then four laps.

The current women's world record for the mile has stood for more than twenty years. It was set by Russian athlete, Svetlana Masterkova: 4:12.56. To beat this time, Dennison and the others have to run four laps of 63 seconds each, but also set aside another second or two for the extra nine metres. In reality, an even-paced race of 62.3 seconds per lap will guarantee a world record. And this is exactly what the meeting organisers are planning for and that is why they have assembled the strongest possible field plus the best pacemaker in the business, Suzy Marshall.

Putting this into perspective, the women's world record for the 1 500 metres is a fraction of a second over 3:50. This equates to exactly 61.33 seconds per lap. Extrapolating that to the mile would result in a time of 4:06, a little over six seconds faster than the current record.

No wonder there is so much excitement. Dennison (especially) and Moyo, Fedorova or Kiptanui could break the record and create another Bannister moment. Except that world records aren't spat out like tins of Coke from a production line. There are reasons why they are as rare as the proverbial hen's teeth. Tactics, pace-making, weather conditions, collisions, poor form and a host of other complications can cancel any thoughts of a record. That is why tomorrow night's race has such a tantalising, mysterious feel to it.

And that is why the Bannister meeting organisers have – brilliantly – created the possibility, no, the likelihood even, that one of these runners will somehow emulate the historic feat of the great Roger all those years ago.

Except this time there will be an audience of hundreds of millions, not three thousand spectators around a lumpy field in Oxford.

Personally, I cannot wait.

Emily sat back, quietly absorbing what she had read. 'I love it,' she said, 'genuinely love it. It's got key facts, something about the runners that makes it alive and a real sense of tension, the unknown, who knows what will happen? I am even more excited now and I've been part of this thing for ages. Well done.'

Deon was happy. He read it over a few more times, tweaked a couple of metaphors and beamed it up to Charlie in Joburg, fingers crossed behind his back. What seemed like ages, but was probably just a couple of minutes later, his computer pinged.

'Great preview. But don't let it go to your head. You've set the bar – to use high jump parlance – now you have to stay there.'

Deon heaved a sigh of relief and went to the mini-bar and cracked open a Diet Coke. It would cost him two pounds but he didn't care.

Emily asked, 'What do you do tomorrow?'

'My normal big workday routine. Go for a long slow run, then enjoy a leisurely breakfast. I take care to check everything, my laptop, accreditation and so on. I go to the stadium at one o'clock, get the best position in the media work area. Then I sit and relax, read, watch the place fill up. Chat to other media guys. Chat to the volunteers.' He smiled.

Emily went to the trolley and wheeled it across the room. 'Time to guzzle and imbibe,' she said.

Two hours, three bottles of Guinness, a dozen fried prawns and a quarter of a chocolate cake later, she asked, 'Oh, I nearly forgot. Tell me more about this mysterious Sarah Moyo person, the one with the syndrome. What was it again?'

'Asperger's.'

15

Friday, 10 August
Race day afternoon

LONDON

The Hotel Olympia in Earl's Court wasn't far from Mark Whyte's original hotel and QSH's Knightsbridge flat, but it could have been on another planet in terms of neighbourhood, appearance and quality. But no questions were asked, no passport requested and the two hundred pounds for four nights' accommodation had been paid in cash.

'Thank you, Mister Lincoln, enjoy your stay,' the clerk had said, happily pocketing the cash when Mark had arrived, unannounced, that morning. He wondered how much of it would actually reach the owner. With no register, he suspected only some of it would. Not my problem, he thought.

It was time to go to the athletics meeting. Friday afternoon traffic meant that the taxi ride would take as long as an hour. Mark dressed casually in a long-sleeved shirt, slacks, heavy jacket and track shoes, with his trademark thick-rimmed glasses in place. He carried a backpack containing his laptop – not that he would need it, but he wasn't sure that it would be in his room when he returned – camera, accreditation, passport, wallet with several hundred pounds in cash and the media pack. There were also two baseball caps, one black, the other white.

Ten minutes later, he was on his way in a taxi. 'London Olympic Stadium please,' he instructed the driver.

'Going to the Bannister meeting? It's all over town, that thing. Even bigger than the football match, but maybe that's because Man U will probably beat Chelsea and half of London will be in mourning.'

'I'm media. Very privileged.'

'I'll say. Will you get to meet that Dennison girl? She looks like Miss World in spikes.'

'Maybe. If I do, I'll give her your love.'

In a coffee bar across the road from the Olympia, PI Coopersmith, dressed in scruffy jeans, a battered, nondescript windbreaker, trainers and cloth cap, stirred his coffee and spoke on his cellphone. 'Hi Boss. Whyte changed hotels this morning, checked into the Olympia on Warwick Road. Seems like he's trying to cover his tracks after that call from his office. The desk clerk was reluctant, but fifty quid changed his mind. He paid up front for four nights in cash, no questions asked. Our Mister Whyte is now Mister Lincoln. Four days should give us time to find out what he's really up to and if he's a threat to Abby. He took a taxi, no doubt he's off to the track meeting.'

Knightsbridge

Quentin Smythe-Harrison was enjoying himself. This Whyte-Lincoln character was becoming more interesting by the minute. And if Coopersmith's undoubtedly accurate analysis was to be believed, he could even be some sort of stalker as well.

'Well, well,' he turned to Winston the beagle. 'Stalking isn't something I know much about, old boy, but you know me well enough by now. Always eager to learn something new, especially about criminal behaviour. So we'll keep eyes on him for a while. You never know what hanky-panky he'll get up to. Then we can nab him. Possibly when he leaves Heathrow on Tuesday.'

The dog looked up, wagged his tail a few times and scratched his ear vigorously.

Snapping out of his thoughtful state, QSH pulled his overcoat off a peg near the door, took his phone out of a deep pocket of his jacket and punched some numbers. 'Hello Ricky. Coopersmith says that our Mister Whyte is on his way. Pick up the trail when he goes into the media centre at the stadium and don't let him out of your sight until he gets back to his hotel. By the way, he's changed to a fleapit hotel in Earl's Court, so stay with him. Then follow him again tomorrow. Thank you, my good man.'

The next number was on his speed-dial. 'Jerome, old boy, please bring the car around. I need to get to the athletics meeting. And be a sport and check where the VIP entrance is. We don't want to be caught up in the thousands of people crowding in to see the Dennison woman, now do we?'

Athletes' hotel
At exactly 15h55, Abby emerged from her room, wearing full track gear and carrying a bulky kit bag. Thirty minutes before, she could have been mistaken for a relaxed, even sloppy kid going out on the town to a pub or club with her friends on a Friday night. Bronwyn and Paul stared at her, as did everyone when she transformed herself from an overgrown teenager into one of the most complete female athletes in the world. The change was remarkable and Paul had never become accustomed to seeing his daughter like this. On some level he resented it, as if his little girl had suddenly been lost to him.

Her racing outfit consisted of two layers, the actual competition gear and the protective tracksuit outer garment. Not visible now was the competition clothing, a short-sleeved bodysuit top, mainly green but with gold panels on the shoulders and down the sides, traditional South African sporting colours. Her racing shorts were tights that reached to just above her knees, opposite in colour to her running vest, mainly gold with green trim down the sides and along the bottom. Given the clear rules regarding branding, she had a five-by-ten-centimetre Maxx logo on the left side of her chest. On the back was a single word, 'ABBY', and a small South African flag.

Her tracksuit top fitted snugly and was made of light, weatherproof material. Long-sleeved and with a hood, it was similar in colour and design to her racing top – green with gold trim. The pants went to her ankles and continued the colour theme.

A slim gold digital running watch on her left wrist, tiny pearl earrings and an almost-invisible gold chain around her left ankle were her only accessories. A pair of Oakleys perched on the top of her head, while bright pink and white Maxx training shoes and thin pink running socks completed the ensemble.

Bronwyn and Paul stared. Even though they had seen her in all sorts of clothing, running and otherwise, the sight of Abby in full racing gear never ceased to amaze them. She had such a presence.

She smiled. 'Okay, you two, it's time to get going. Let's get out of here and find the terrible people of the world of track. Runners, managers, coaches, hangers-on, journos, officials, drivers, perverts, the full catastrophe.' She hesitated. 'Where's JP?' she asked, looking around.

'Here I am,' said a man in a shabby green T-shirt and faded green cap, carrying a tatty old kit bag, coming out of the bathroom.

16

Friday, 10 August
18h00

LONDON OLYMPIC STADIUM

Bronwyn Adams, her precious VIP accreditation around her neck, stood inside the VIP suite of the Olympic Stadium behind a floor-to-ceiling panel of inch-thick glass. The suite was positioned in line with the middle of the finishing straight on the upper tier of seating. On the far side, the seats were already filled with excited spectators as, before the meeting had started, more than seventy thousand people were already inside. It was the first sold-out crowd for a track meeting since the 2012 London Olympics.

From this vantage point her gaze swept across the vast arena, taking in the massive double-tiered grandstands under the structure's all-around roof, on top of which were the stadium's signature triangular steel structures that anchored bank upon bank of blazing floodlights. Outside, London was gloomy under grey, cloudy skies, but the huge floodlights turned the competition arena into a pool of crisp brightness that could probably be seen from satellites passing overhead as they busily transmitted live television to several hundred million viewers across the world.

Inside the glass capsule that was the VIP area, sounds from the stadium were muted. To experience first-hand the raw emotion of the place, Bronwyn stepped outside into the VIP seating area and immediately the noise hit her like a hammer blow. The chattering, shouting and singing of thousands of excited voices coalesced into a wall of sound that echoed around the stadium and produced a constant roar, not unlike that of a couple of jumbo jets taking off at once.

Bronwyn almost recoiled from it, to seek relief from the assault to her auditory system in the relative quiet of inside. Instead, she paused, for there was more than just noise out there. Then she understood: the excitement in the stadium was like a living thing, a massive creature with a life of its own. It could not be seen but it was there, rising and falling with the action on the track, holding its collective breath as a pole vaulter started his run, then exulting with a roar as he cleared the bar, nearly six metres above the ground.

In crowds, she thought, especially big ones, people lose their identity as individuals and become just a unit, a cell in the body, a brick in the wall, part of something far bigger than themselves. Individuals melt together and metamorphose into a single unit – the crowd, the mob, the army – driven by any number of normal human motivators: celebration, patriotism, worship, fear, hatred, religious zeal, greed or a range of other emotions; some noble, others not.

Bronwyn stood there, mesmerised. It was like nothing she had experienced in her life. Then she started to analyse what was happening and from her youth studying history she extracted images of massive crowds of human beings.

The armies of Caesar or Hannibal or Alexander or Napoleon or Patton or Montgomery plunging head-first into battle, the cries of their generals ringing in their ears; a huge crowd at a political rally, listening with eager hearts and minds to a leader waving his arms, punching the podium and promising utopia to all who follow; an angry mob plunging through a neighbourhood of Hong Kong or Harare or Paris or Caracas or Pietermaritzburg, united in their hatred of something – foreigners, immigrants, a different religion, poverty, the government, rampant inflation, no food; a hundred thousand people at a football match in Spain: Real Madrid versus Barcelona, *El Clásico*; pilgrims pouring in their thousands into the Great Mosque in Mecca, or into Saint Peter's Square in Rome as the Pope gives his blessing.

These are the images Bronwyn pulled into focus. Essentially, they were all the same, a generic crowd of people in a dozen different settings with a dozen different objectives on their minds, yet essentially all the same: the individual lost in the mass of people. The giant organism moves and breathes with a life of its own. Cells in a body, bricks in a wall.

It was the same here. People from all over the world who simply love the sport of athletics, gathering to experience the drama, the skill, the hundredth of a second that means the difference between winning and losing, the sleek baton changes in the relays, the joyous twist at the apex of the pole-vaulter's leap, the animal-like scream of the discus thrower on release, the frantic pedalling of the long-jumper's legs in the air, the desperate body-thrust of the sprinter on the line, the wild arms of the middle-distance runner in the final charge for victory.

Citius, Altius, Fortius. Faster, Higher, Stronger.

The people also came to see the beautiful bodies, sculpted in the gym and on the track, with sharply defined pecs, glutes, deltoids, quads, biceps, triceps and gastrocnemius muscles. There were multi-coloured headbands, some with flashing lights; women with long blonde manes or frizzy afros or sleekly gelled hairstyles; competition clothes carefully designed to accentuate lithe bodies and couple them with valuable sponsor logos.

Eye candy, all of it.

Bronwyn stepped back into the quiet of the VIP area, where she could hear the hiss of the coffee machine, the gentle notes of a Mozart concerto and the hum of several dozen voices, sounding like a swarm of bees gathering in a tree. The contrast between inside and outside was a shock to the senses, like going from a freezing, rain-lashed pavement into the blissful warmth of a coffee shop, the windows misty with condensation, the air saturated with the aroma of cappuccinos and hot croissants.

She slowly readjusted her senses, then she heard, 'It's more than just the sport they come for, you know.'

Bronwyn spun around. James Selfe stood at her shoulder. 'Goodness, you startled me,' she said.

'Sorry, but it's always like that with people who experience a huge sports crowd for the first time. My guess is that you have never been in the middle of seventy thousand people before?'

Her composure was back and she smiled. 'No, but last year I went to the Weltklasse meeting in Zürich and they only get half of that number. And, of course, they're Swiss, and very orderly. What do you mean, it's more than just the sport?'

'Ah, my dear Bronwyn, let me explain. Come and sit, please.' Taking her by the arm, Selfe led her to several leather chairs in the corner of the room. He waved at a young woman nearby. 'Emily, come and meet Miss Bronwyn Adams. She's part of Abby Dennison's team. Bronwyn, this is Emily Williams, my most valued volunteer.'

Emily's excitement showed and she said, 'My pleasure, ma'am. I am a huge fan of Abby's. In fact, a South African journalist, Deon Coetzee, is staying in the hotel where I work. It's the media hotel.' Her voice trailed off as she shook Bronwyn's hand.

'Ah yes, Mister Coetzee. An excellent writer, highly regarded.' Bronwyn hesitated for several seconds, then continued, 'All the girls seem to like him for some reason. Must be the smile. Definitely not the elegant attire.'

Emily blushed. 'I noticed that.'

Selfe stepped in. 'Tea, Bronwyn, maybe a cappuccino, or something stronger? Do South African women drink beer?'

'Some do, but I prefer something a little more refined. G and T?'

Without a word, Emily hurried off in the direction of the bar.

Selfe was all business again and Bronwyn suspected that there was some sort of agenda behind this apparently random chat. He turned and she felt the full power of his personality, the half-smile, straight teeth, bright blue eyes, the steel-grey moustache and beard-shadow. He made her feel as if she was the only person in the room. No wonder he was on the board of one of the world's biggest banks and at the same time the director of the Bannister meeting, no small job itself.

As if to confirm her vague thoughts, he started by saying, 'Please excuse my forthrightness, but this is an important discussion, one that I have been wanting to have the whole week. Let me explain. You are at the epicentre of the Abby Team and they all respect you. I respect you. Paul is a bit too much of an alpha male to pay much attention to me, and JP is only concerned about Abby's times and victories. You, on the other hand, are a level-headed person and fully committed to Abby's welfare, and therefore likely to take to heart what I am about to tell you.'

Bronwyn accepted the tall glass of colourless liquid presented to her by

Emily. Ice cubes and two slices of lemon swirled around as she mixed the drink with a paper straw. Condensation ran down the outside of the glass. The swarm of bees was quiet. All that mattered was James's voice, soft and compelling.

'Thank you, my dear,' she said to a grinning Emily.

Selfe continued without pause. He had Bronwyn's full attention now. 'I saw you looking at the crowd just now. And you were amazed by the atmosphere, the passion of all those people. Now you need to understand why they are here. It's pretty much all about worship, almost in a religious sense. Of course, they come to see the excitement of the sprints, the skill of the pole vaulters, the power of the throwers, the guts and endurance of the distance runners. Most of them understand the technicalities of the sport. But that's not the main thing. What they have really come to see are the athletes themselves, the people behind the headlines, the faces and bodies on TV and in adverts. They come to see their heroes.'

He took a long draught from the beer Emily had brought him. Bronwyn said nothing.

'Everyone needs something to revere, to worship, to emulate. With modern media being what it is, especially since the advent of the explosive power of social media, this vast array of heroes and heroines is everywhere. Movie stars, rock singers, sports men and women, even television evangelists and reality TV stars. These people have become the gods of the new social media generation. Millions of people follow their every move on Facebook, Twitter, Instagram, dedicated TV channels, online platforms, YouTube, and in newspapers and magazines. You name it, they are there. And with four billion people now having access to online media, the audience is beyond vast. Fascinating.'

Bronwyn said, 'Scary, is what I say. All those millions of people, in a way worshipping other human beings, all of whom have frailties and weaknesses and secrets. I find it profoundly sad.'

'At one level it is sad, I suppose. But it's reality, you cannot make it go away. Some people are the genuine modern gods of our world. If Tom Hanks or Meryl Streep are in a movie, most people will go to watch it without even knowing what the film is about. If Roger Federer makes the final of Wimbledon, the television audience is double what it would have been had he been knocked out earlier. Footballers Messi and Ronaldo collectively earn about two hundred million dollars a year. The Kardashians and Paris Hilton are famous simply because they are famous. It's a mystery. There is genuinely no end to the desire of humanity to worship someone as their own personal god, if I can put it that way.'

'James, I hear you and I have my own view on this topic, which I would love to share with you. But why are you telling me this now?'

'Because you and your team have an opportunity, but it's tempered with several risks. Very soon, you will have to decide whether you want to grab the opportunity, knowing the risks. If you look around the world of sport over the past twenty years, the superstars jump out at you. Famous names like Beckham, Federer, Williams, Nadal, Sharapova, Tiger Woods, Lewis Hamilton and Michael Schumacher. People will pay hundreds of dollars to see Roger and Rafa in an exhibition match. It's all about hero worship and not their forehands. You get the picture.'

The silence was broken by a burst of laughter from a group of men walking into the room. Emily arrived at the table and asked if they needed more drinks. 'Just a Diet Coke for me,' said Bronwyn quickly, 'I need to stay sharp tonight.'

Emily left.

'What has all of this to do with me, the rest of my team?'

'Here it is. You will note that the list I gave you excludes any track athletes. I did that on purpose. Now go back thirty years in track and field and list the superstars. Go on, do it.'

Bronwyn hesitated, then started slowly. 'Usain Bolt, Michael Johnson, Sergey Bubka, Carl Lewis, Sebastian Coe and Steve Ovett, but that goes back a long time. Haile Gebrselassie and Kenenisa Bekele, but that's stretching it a bit. Mo Farah. A number of Kenyan and Ethiopian women, but I forget their names.'

'Excluding the East Africans, virtually no women,' added Selfe.

He paused, collecting his thoughts. 'Here's the point I want to make,

Bronwyn. It's actually none of my business, but I thought you might like my opinion, a heads-up from an expert if you like. I'll keep it short. Abby Dennison could be the next athletics super-heroine, in fact, the first woman to get that status for a long time. She's not there yet, but her trajectory is spot on. She has the ability, no doubt, probably one of the most naturally gifted female middle-distance runners in a generation. She has the looks, the youth and the quiet gentle personality. She's polite, smiling and has a brilliant public profile. Part of her appeal is the mystery around her, partly because she's relatively new on the scene and partly because she's been well shielded by yourself and Paul. Now here's the thing: tonight is a huge stage for her. A decent proportion of this crowd has come just to watch Abby Dennison in action. And she's up against the best, including Fedorova and Moyo. If Abby wins and is close to the world record, she will be ratcheted up quite a few notches in the most-famous-and-loved-sporting-woman-in-the-world stakes.'

Selfe sat back and sipped his beer. Bronwyn stood up, walked around, absorbing what she had heard. She sat and said, 'What does that mean? In reality?'

'First of all, it means big money. Appearance fees and prize money in athletics are nowhere near those of tennis, for example, but the cash would come from sponsorships. The media and the giant brands across the world love beautiful, successful sportswomen. That's not a chauvinistic comment, it's fact. Then, of course, there is the lifestyle, if that appeals to you. Invitations to speak, be guest of honour, endorsing charity foundations, that sort of thing. And of course,' here Selfe patted Bronwyn on the shoulder, 'it's not just for Abby, but for her entire supporting team as well. You could all be set up for life in a couple of years, provided she keeps winning, keeps healthy and never gets caught doping.'

'Ouch. That's harsh.'

'But true, my dear Bronwyn.'

'I know about risk and reward, Mister Meeting Director. You've very eloquently outlined the rewards, now what about the risks?'

'Ah yes, the risks. Not to make too fine a point here, there are several. But forewarned is forearmed, as they say. If Paul, JP and yourself want to build her career, you need to do it with your eyes wide open. The first challenge is the time involved. Athletics will have to remain your sole focus for about eight months of the year. Training, hotels, airports, gyms, physios, doctors, competitions and so on. That means a reduction in normal social life for all of you, especially Abby. Can all of you accept that is how you will live?'

He paused to let that sink in.

'Then there is the second risk. Failure, a spectacular fall from grace. This could come from poor training methods, injury, demotivation, over-racing, fatigue and other factors. Middle-distance running is hugely demanding in terms of physical and mental strength. The next big risk is doping. Now I am certain that Abby never has, and never will, knowingly take a banned substance. But with modern out-of-competition tests, you have to be certain that absolutely everything she puts into her mouth is vetted. No drinks, no medicines, no special foods, no supplements can be taken without expert advice as to their dope-free status. I'm being serious. A percentage of positive dope tests come when the athlete has unknowingly eaten, drunk or injected a banned substance. Many athletes claim it wasn't their fault, but you never know. Then, of course, there are the trappings of fame – life in a fishbowl, paparazzi everywhere, in the supermarket, through the bedroom windows, on the beach. Famous people hardly ever have real privacy. They are public property, thanks to the very social media that made them rich and famous in the first place.'

'Please tell me there are no more risks. I'm beginning to feel sick.'

'Finally, and I mean *finally*, there are very real physical risks in being a famous woman. Stalkers, psychopaths, sexual predators, muggers, thieves and even kidnappers are out there. Famous people need to have very tight security and that weighs on everyone's mind. For many people, it's simply not worth it.'

One of the VIP guests opened the sliding doors to the stadium and the roar of the crowd blew into the room in a fresh gale. Selfe said, 'I hope I haven't been too intrusive, metaphorically rushed in where angels fear to tread. But I genuinely like Abby, she's a lovely, down-to-earth talented woman. She has a brilliant career ahead of her and the right people to guide and protect her. But you all need to understand what happens out there in the big, bad world. And if I can help, so much the better. If not, I'll shut up. Now, I need to tend to my guests, not the least of whom is the chairperson of our bank, my boss.' Selfe waved to a woman wearing a black suit and standing next to the bar. She smiled and beckoned him. He stood and said, 'Bronwyn, I hope this hasn't been too much, but I trust you and Paul will factor these suggestions into your plans and the way you manage Abby. It is completely possible, hundreds of successful sportswomen have done it over the years. It just needs planning. I have a feeling that tonight may just be the four-odd minutes that will change your lives.'

He left and joined the bank chairperson, guiding her outside to the padded seats of the VIP area. By now, there were four pole vaulters left in the competition and the bar was at 5.90 metres. One high jumper had cleared 2.35 metres and the men's 110-metre hurdles had been won by the French athlete Jean-Jacques Rousseau in just under thirteen seconds, the fastest time in the world for the year.

The time in London was 18h20, a hundred minutes before the start of the Bannister Memorial Mile for Women.

17

Friday, 10 August

THE ROGER BANNISTER MEMORIAL ATHLETICS MEETING

JP and Abby sat on the bottom row of concrete steps next to the warm-up track outside the stadium. They sat close together, their knees touching. It was exactly one hundred minutes before the start of her race. The coming discussion was a key step in the racing and winning process.

JP's planning was thorough. He'd analysed the competition, their strengths and weaknesses, their fitness levels, recent performances and their likely tactical approach to the race; there was the issue of the pacemaker, Suzy Marshall, and her key role in the record attempt. Abby and JP needed to agree on several issues about her own approach to the race – her early positioning in the field, whom to follow, when to take the lead, what to do if the early pace was too slow, and who was likely to be there at the death.

JP also used this discussion to motivate his athlete, to make her believe in herself. Abby looked expectantly at him, waiting for his briefing and committing every detail to memory. 'Apart from Suzy, there are three people in the race that matter, Sarah Moyo, Mary McColgan and Elinah Kiptanui. Of these, Moyo will probably be the strongest. McColgan will be the crowd's favourite and a dangerous floater. Marshall will start out well, she's got excellent pace judgement and I think we can trust her to take you through seven, maybe eight hundred metres. Then she'll step off the track.'

'I don't understand,' said Abby. 'Olga Fedorova has been number one for ages. She ran 3:56 the other day and looked like she was jogging. And she will literally kill to beat me. I know you are a genius, JP, but sometimes I think you are just *dof*.'

THE FINAL LAP

The coach smiled, a rare occurrence. 'Okay, Abs, listen to me carefully. I know who will be a threat and I'm pretty certain who won't be. Moyo and Kiptanui, so focus on them. Olga probably won't be a candidate for the podium but you definitely need to stay away from her if possible. Remember that. Now, far more important, let's talk about the pace and why Marshall is the key.'

Abby leaned back onto the concrete step, the rough edge digging into her shoulders. 'Ouch, that hurts!' Then, 'Okay, let's forget Olga and talk about Suzy.'

'Here's what James Selfe and I have agreed. Marshall will run through four hundred metres at a sixty-one second pace, which means she will go through the finish line after a lap and a bit between sixty-two and sixty-three. The second lap will also be sixty-two, which means 2:05 with two laps to go. There will be digital clocks mounted on the finish line and around the first bend to show you the lap times.'

Abby thought about that. 'I've never gone through two laps that fast in a 1 500-metre race before. In Koblenz last year it was 2:06 and I ended up with 3:58. At the end I faded badly and Elinah nearly beat me. This will be three seconds quicker at halfway, which translates into about five seconds at the end. That will be 3:53 for the fifteen hundred and 4:10 for the mile. No one in the world has run that fast for about three years!'

JP agreed. 'It's hugely ambitious and entirely dependent on Marshall keeping a perfect pace. If it's too slow, you'll have to make up time on the third and fourth laps, a difficult thing to do. If she starts out too fast, the runners will have to either go with her, a risky option, or hang back and make their own pace. I know it's easy for me to say, "Go and run 4:10." Then I sit in the stands while you bust your lungs and put your reputation on the line in front of all those people.'

He lowered his voice. 'Abby, you are the best woman mile runner in the world, have been for two years. Only a few people have run as fast as you since the London Olympics. You've run sub-four for the fifteen hundred on ten occasions. Your training times are the best ever. You've rested up and the conditions are perfect. The best pacemaker in the world will be out there, running specifically to our requirements. I think you can go under 4:10, which means going through fifteen hundred metres in 3:53.'

Abby stared at him. Could she run that fast? If JP said so, it had to be possible. Theoretically. He had never overestimated her potential and she had complete faith in his judgement. He was waiting for her to accept the challenge. She knew if she declined, he would accept her decision. She looked him straight in the eye, a little smile playing around the corner of her mouth. 'I can get to the bell in 3:08 or 3:09, but my mind will have to take me through the final lap. And I think my mind can tag on another sixty-two at that stage.'

It was done. Abby had committed to running a time of under 4:12. JP was elated, but he didn't show it. Game on.

She started her elaborate warm-up routine on the track with her mind a jumble of numbers. How did she feel? Scared? Terrified? Overwhelmed?

None of these. 'Bring it on,' she said, loud enough for a nearby javelin thrower to smile and wave.

Paul was outside the VIP seating area when his cellphone chimed. He quickly moved inside, away from the stadium noise. Briefly JP confirmed that Marshall should go as planned. Paul listened intently, said, 'Got it,' and hung up.

He gave a thumbs-up signal to Selfe, who was across the room chatting to a group of men in business suits, one of whom was QSH. 'Excuse me for a moment, gentlemen,' he said and joined Paul.

Dennison was brief. 'Tell Marshall to hit two laps to go in 2:05. They're going for 4:10.'

Selfe said nothing and made a brief call. Joining his friends, he was all smiles. 'Gentlemen, it looks like we are in for something special tonight.' It had taken less than ninety seconds.

After warming up, Abby sat down next to the coach. He put his hand on her shoulder. 'The race will start at exactly eight o'clock, in forty-five minutes' time.'

Abby picked up her tog bag. Every runner, from the casual jogger in a short road race to the elite athlete aiming for a world record, needs such a bag

THE FINAL LAP

at a race, its contents as precious as gold.

Abby's bag contained a small, dog-eared photograph of herself and her mother taken two days before the fateful kidnapping attempt; her matric poetry book; twenty British pounds in a sealed plastic bag for 'just in case'; and a small copy of the Gospel of John. There were also two pairs of custom-made running spikes, a warm tracksuit top to put on after the race, a towel, lip balm and her dark glasses.

The final item was a bright yellow one-litre plastic bottle with a retractable drinking port. The bottle was from Xtend, a sports drink company licenced to use her name and image in its marketing. Part of the lucrative deal was that Abby would carry this bottle with her to all her competitions. On one side of the bottle was the green Xtend logo with the company's payoff line, 'Expand your physical limits'.

The bottle contained exactly half a litre of fluid, the very last drink she would have before the race. It was a recipe that Abby and JP had designed specifically to meet her need for hydration and carbohydrates, her source of energy during the race. It was half-filled with bottled water, to which fifty grams of white sugar and a teaspoon of salt were added. For flavouring, two teaspoons of concentrated orange cordial had also been mixed in.

She took it out and downed the first half. She would have the rest after exiting the call room, out on the track just before the race.

She picked up her bag, turned without a word and set off at a brisk pace for the athletes' private entrance to the stadium and the Roger Bannister Memorial Mile for Women.

Neither her nor JP noticed a man, dressed in nondescript dark clothes and wearing a wide-brimmed hat, filming the action on the warm-up track with a video camera. His accreditation said 'Coach' and he could have been with any one of the several dozen athletes warming up at the time. He left the warm-up area at the same time as Abby and headed for a side entrance to the stadium, where the regular spectators would enter. He was quite happy to sit with them, anonymous.

It was forty minutes before the start of the Roger Bannister Memorial Mile for Women.

18

Friday, 10 August
19h15

THE ROGER BANNISTER MEMORIAL ATHLETICS MEETING

Abby Dennison walked away from JP, her anchor, into the unknown.

The stadium sound hit her like the roar of the ocean, but the noise wasn't the ocean at all, it was eighty thousand people shouting and screaming and whistling while ABBA's 'Dancing Queen' reverberated through the deep canyon of the stadium.

She realised with a shock that all those people were there to watch her race. Would she be their dancing queen, the running queen, the winning queen? The losing queen? She was on her own now.

When she reached the athletes' entrance, a young female volunteer inspected her accreditation. Above them, the stadium seemed like a giant fortress in a horror movie, all jagged edges, grey concrete and grotesque, grinning faces behind windows. The volunteer smiled. 'Good luck, Abby,' she said. Abby smiled grimly and walked through an open, black door into a narrow passageway painted an ugly, dull yellow with bright lights set into the ceiling and fire extinguishers in glass cases on the walls.

Abby walked and walked. The passageway seemed never-ending and she began to wonder if she was in the wrong place. It was completely quiet, the yellow paint yielding to white tiles on the walls, the air smelling faintly of antiseptic.

Just as she was considering turning back, she heard noise, a gentle rumble of voices that got progressively louder, like an approaching train. The passage turned a corner and opened up, quite suddenly, into a bright space, wide and long. The underground warm-up zone.

THE FINAL LAP

There were people everywhere, some jogging, some doing short sprints, others stretching and limbering up. No one was standing still, everyone deep into their last-minute mental and physical pre-event routines. Conversation bounced around the walls and filled the space with sound.

For elite athletes, this is time to enter the mental zone before the race actually starts. A private place carved out in your mind after thousands of hours of training, where the rubber that is the vast unknown of the competition meets the road of reality.

Athletes will say that the best part of a race is not the finish line, but rather the crack of the starter's gun. That's when the waiting is over and the thrill of competition erupts as adrenalin rushes into the bloodstream, arrives at the brain in seconds and sets off a series of specific physiological reactions.

Adrenalin. Abby always imagined a crack appearing suddenly in the wall of a giant dam, unleashing a million litres of water a minute downstream; or the sudden stampede of a three-hundred-strong herd of buffalo across the wide plains of Kruger. That's how adrenalin works at a molecular level when it kick starts the primeval human survival instinct, from back when people lived in caves and a hungry lion arrived unexpectedly. People had to choose between fleeing the sudden danger or facing it head-on. Fight or flight.

Adrenalin is super cool. It causes the liver to break down glycogen into glucose, providing an instant energy boost; it enhances lung capacity, boosts muscle contraction in the heart and speeds up the pulse rate. It also contracts the arteries in the skin to divert blood flow to the working muscles. The adrenalin rush is the reason why the starter's gun is so important to runners.

But in the minutes before the start of the race there lurks the middle-distance athlete's silent but very real fear: the possibility of failure, the humiliation of defeat. A step wrong here, a brief hesitation there. A surge too early, a sprint that runs out of steam ten metres before the finish line. The agony of another person slowly moving past, first their breathing, then the hint of movement in the peripheral vision, then the athlete passing, arms raised in victory, and the awful realisation that the race is lost, plucked from your hand in those final metres.

Fear of failure is like a stalking predator, silent and deadly. Abby had seen predators in the bush: the crocodile, just a grisly face visible above thick, foul-smelling green water; the leopard, eyes gleaming yellow in the dark, silently stalking a warthog.

She remembered with a shudder the human predators, the muggers, kidnappers and gun-toting hijackers waiting silently like the crocodile for their innocent prey: the hiker on Table Mountain; the sleeping family in their home; the lone driver stopped at a traffic light at midnight.

The mom fetching her kid from school.

But, for Abby, the predator was not a live thing. It was failure.

What, exactly, was failure? Abby briefly considered this. For four of the nine runners, there really wasn't any sort of failure – for them success was just making the cut and being there; for the pacemaker Marshall, failure would be an incorrect pace by a second or two a lap; for Sarah Moyo, Mary McColgan and Elinah Kiptanui, not making the podium – the top three – would constitute failure; for Olga Fedorova, not beating her nemesis Dennison would be failure. If Abby was last and she was second last, that would be success.

But how would Abby define her own success and failure? Would failure be not winning, or not setting a world record? Would failure be winning in a slow time, or coming second but still beating Fedorova? The permutations were endless.

Just then, an Afro-coiffed man charged past, missing her by inches. 'Look out,' he yelled. A warm breeze followed him. The air was thick with sweat, the humidity dribbling down the walls in little droplets.

Abby sat on her tog bag. Failure, she knew, was none of those things, measurable things, numbers, times, positions. It was simple. Failure would be not to do her best.

She knew that she had the strength, the speed, the coach, the research, the all-time best training times, the Team, the number-one world ranking. She also realised that everyone else in the field knew all that as well and it would make them fearful. They would probably be running for second place, even Fedorova. She knew it deep down in her soul. The race was hers to lose.

This realisation shot from her brain to her body and her pulse quickened. She smiled, stretched and did twelve run-throughs, back to back, with a decent break in between, all of them fifty metres long. The first few were slow – nine seconds – then she sped up to eight, then seven seconds. Her final pair of sprints took six seconds each.

She was exhausted and it took a while to get her breath back. Then she realised that the place had gone strangely quiet. Looking around, she saw that there was now little movement or conversation. More than thirty world-class athletes, across a number of disciplines, had stopped what they were doing and were watching her, among them Olga Fedorova. Abby smiled and gave a little wave. Hi Olga!

Just then, a voice called out on a loudhailer. 'Women's Mile. Will the competitors please move to the call room. We have twenty-four minutes to the start.' Abby picked up her Team-branded tog bag and walked into a small room at the end of the warm-up zone. They had checked it out earlier in the week and she knew that on the far side of the room was a door that led directly out into the arena, near the start of the hundred-metre sprint.

Seven runners were already in the room, none of them sitting. As she entered she felt the tension ratchet up. Virtually the entire field was in one place now – only Olga Fedorova was missing – and most of them knew one another well. Everyone was pacing around anxiously, stopping to stretch every few seconds or to lean against the wall to target calf muscles or quads.

Keep moving, keep warm, keep your mind off the race, keep avoiding eye contact with everyone.

It was hot in the call room. The outside temperature was nudging thirty degrees, it was humid and people had been warming up. They were all sweating freely.

In a crowded room like this, invasion of a person's private space can be excruciating. Abby just wanted to get out of there and onto the track. She tried to distract her mind by welcoming the manic roar of the crowd that leaked through the door. She studied the room and noticed that the benches around the walls needed varnishing and the place smelled of stale sweat and menthol heat rub; there were a few unisex toilets behind a door and a dozen bottles of water sat untouched in a cooler filled with ice. From time to time, someone would go into a toilet, and Abby timed her visit there as late as possible.

Suzy Marshall stood by herself. As the pacemaker, she was in a unique position. Not quite up to the standard of the others, she was still considered a world-class performer, excelling over the shorter 400- and 800-metre distances.

Her hair was black, long and teased into a thick mass of curls kept in place by a shiny gold headband. She wore a gold crop-top with black trim. Her warm-up tights were black and Abby knew that her racing shorts underneath were miniscule and black with gold trim. She was lean, with a body-fat ratio of about ten per cent. Her arm and shoulder muscles showed fine tone and the clean curves of their peaks and valleys produced little patches of shadow in the glow of the call-room lights. Her stomach muscles were hard and flat, the result of hours of regular gym work, where many repetitions with the light weights produced tone and strength, but without the bulk that resulted from brutal work with the heavy weights.

She moved with the easy grace of the teenage ramp model she once was. It had become something of a minor piece of athletics folklore that she had, at the age of nineteen, elected to focus on developing her precocious athletic talent, deciding that running was more lucrative and much more fun than strolling up and down a catwalk being gawked at by a bunch of fashion journalists.

Abby glanced at her left hand and immediately spotted it, the famed wedding band, broad and heavy, fashioned from gold and platinum and topped with a massive two carat diamond. The ring had been given to her by Björn Lundberg, the Swedish tennis player currently ranked fourth in the world and for the previous two years, her husband. The pair were considered the elite couple of the international sporting world and were fêted like royalty. Abby wondered how two people so highly ranked in different sports could make a marriage work. She also wondered what it must be like to be married, period.

Elinah Kiptanui was a typical East African distance runner, tiny – probably weighing less than forty-five kilograms – with negligible body fat and long, skinny legs. Her hair was long and braided and clipped at the back with a silver bangle. She smiled shyly at everyone.

Brigita Karlovic and Birgit Lennartz were typical European distance runners, lean, short and powerfully muscled. Both had short-cropped brown hair and they wore identical sponsored outfits. Fortunately, Karlovic was short-sighted and wore glasses when running, otherwise it would have been difficult to tell them apart.

Mary McColgan, the young Scot, had long, thick, flame-red hair that trailed untamed like a mane when she ran. She had a boisterous, confident personality that belied her age, which was twenty-one. Her running outfit featured the blue and white of her native Scotland.

Sarah Moyo was a silent ghost-like figure, huddled in a corner, staring at the floor. She was short, thin and clutched a tog bag as if someone was about to steal it. Everyone respected her issues and no one made any attempt at contact.

The call-room official walked in from the underground warm-up area and Abby recognised him from several previous meetings. He was Kurt Hunsler, one of the super-rich Hunsler brothers who owned the giant German software company PAS. Unlike his brothers, who worked full-time in the business, Kurt, a fanatical athletics enthusiast, had managed to work his way into most of the big European meetings as call-room official. He was renowned for being both dour and extremely good at his job. The fact that he apparently paid organisers several thousand euro per meeting for the privilege of working with the athletes only added to his appeal.

'Ladies, can I have your attention?' Hunsler's precise English was heavily accented. 'Your race is due to start in exactly twenty minutes and I see that you are all here except for Miss Fedorova, who is apparently on her way.'

Just then, the Russian came into the room. Her shoulders were hunched and she looked nervous.

She gave a weak smile and sat down in the far corner. Hunsler glanced at his watch, synchronised with the official meeting running time, and again checked the field. He announced briskly, 'Ladies, I trust that you can all understand English?' There were assorted nods. 'In six minutes you will go out onto the track. Then there will be exactly twelve minutes until your race starts. At the start line you will each meet your personal helper who will have a basket for your clothing and your bag, which will be taken to the finish. Of course you know this is a mile race, not fifteen hundred, so you will start exactly 9.34 metres before the finish line. You can do some warm-up sprints down the front straight but please not to go into the corners. Four minutes before the start you will be called to the line for stadium and television introductions.'

He peered through black-framed spectacles. They knew the drill and no one said anything.

'Now, two very important things. First, please let me check your bib numbers.' Each athlete lifted her tracksuit top to reveal her individual race numbers, pinned to the front and back of her running vest. He ticked a few boxes on a clipboard. '*Danke*, you are all very well organised.' The idea of a well-organised group of runners clearly sat well with him.

'Second, and very important. Miss Marshall here,' he waved in the general direction of Suzy, 'is your pacemaker. Because the first lap of the mile race is 409 metres, in *uzzer* words, about one and a half seconds slower than the normal first lap, the first checkpoint for the pace will be on the finish line, in *uzzer* words, with three laps to go. The meeting organisers, as is their right, have decided to set a pace of sixty-three seconds for the first lap, of 409 metres, and sixty-two seconds for the second lap.'

There was silence in the room as everyone digested the fact that they were going out on world-record pace.

'That is very fast,' exclaimed McColgan, '3:53 for fifteen hundred.'

'Your *massematics* is correct, Miss McColgan. Very good. *Zat is ze* whole point. The organisers believe that *zis* field can attack the record. Of course, it is your right not to go with the pace.'

Then Hunsler was all business. He lined them up in lane order and handed out the sticky lane numbers they had to attach to their legs just below or on their running shorts. He called the names one last time, Donaldson, Beardsley, McColgan, Fedorova, Kiptanui, Karlovic, Moyo, Lennartz, Dennison, Marshall. 'Shall we proceed? Your race starts exactly twelve minutes from now. Please follow me in a line. I will leave you in the start area and come back here for the next group of competitors.'

He turned and walked out of the door leading into the mayhem of the London Olympic Stadium. As they walked onto the red tartan track, Abby waved to the crowd.

Time to rock and roll.

19

Friday, 10 August
19h50

THE ROGER BANNISTER MEMORIAL ATHLETICS MEETING

Abby had never experienced a scene like this. The floodlights bathed the arena in bright white light that turned the dull evening into dazzling day. There was colour and movement everywhere. The first thing she saw was a television camera mounted on a Steadicam harness that enabled the cameraman to move around freely, his pictures transmitted to the outside broadcast van via a microwave link. The lens was thrust into her face but Hunsler waved the cameraman away.

As they filed along the perimeter of the track on the grandstand side of the arena, the men's 400 metres was in progress and the eight athletes thundered past on their final hundred metres, their arms and legs glistening, their feet thumping heavily on the track and their breath coming in harsh, animal-like bursts.

The infield was a mass of colour and action. The grass was impossibly green, marked with a network of white lines demarcating the various field event sectors and distance-marker lines. Field athletes jogged around, stretching and talking nervously. The huge male shot-putters, some weighing over 120 kilograms, rubbed white chalk dust into the area between their chins and shoulders. For some, their necks brawny and distended from years of gym work with the heavy weights, there was hardly any space for the chalk. Their hands were a dusty white colour, smeared with sweat and dirt, and their biceps, triceps and trapezius muscles rippled large and hairy, stretching their grubby T-shirts to the limit. Most had a few days' growth of beard and several were prematurely balding. Abby knew the likely reason.

The female javelin throwers, tall, powerful and clad in tight bodysuits that stretched down to their ankles, paced nervously as they waited for their turn to throw. Some stared at the ground while others watched anxiously as their competitors sprinted up the runway, heaved the spear into the dark sky with a shout that could be heard in every corner of the stadium, before coming to a sudden, agonising stop just centimetres shy of the barrier line at the end of the runway.

The stadium was awash with a cacophony of sound. The public address system blared forth a combination of event information and exhortations to the crowd to give one or other competitor extra support.

Behind the straggly line of mile athletes, at the start of the main straight, loomed a giant television screen, showing live pictures from the competition interspersed with sponsor messages.

But it was the crowd that made Abby's throat constrict as she sensed the sheer emotion of eighty thousand people. She felt warm tears begin to well as she gazed upwards at the vast mass of humanity. The stadium was at capacity and the tiered rows of seats stretched high into the dark caverns of the grandstands until the people vanished into purple blackness under the roofs where the floodlights could not reach.

Flags and banners were everywhere. The national flags of at least a dozen countries were visible, waved by groups of eager fans who had gathered for arguably the biggest night of athletics in the year. The Union Jack flashed red, white and blue, while the brazen black, red and gold of Germany was particularly prominent. The black, red and green of Kenya signalled support for the elegant and silent distance runners from the African Rift Valley, and Abby immediately felt a twinge of fear as she thought of the pure speed of the young Kiptanui, who had been smiling in the call room but who would be a deadly opponent in a few minutes' time.

Abby spotted a large South African flag, waved by a group of people about twenty rows up and in line with the home straight and who were jumping up and down in excitement. She waved and they waved back. She had no idea who they were.

The crowd soon realised that the runners in the women's mile were on the track and a fresh buzz of excitement rippled through the fans nearest Abby. For most of them, this was THE event of the night, where the South African icon Dennison was to compete head-to-head against the Russian champion Fedorova and the local record-holder, McColgan.

The rest of the action on the field was temporarily forgotten as thousands of necks craned for a better view. Binoculars were hoisted to eager eyes and cellphone cameras flashed in a starburst of blinding light. For them, this was a moment to be captured for posterity.

Abby stared upwards and the blinding flash of a camera right alongside the track temporarily dazzled her, leaving only a swirling, greenish wash of colour in her vision. She shaded her eyes to prevent herself from walking into somebody.

After a minute they arrived at the start of the mile race, a line across the track just before the finish point of all the track races. A girl of about fifteen came up to her. 'Miss Dennison,' she said, staring into Abby's face, 'I am your carrier. Please leave your clothing and tog bag with me when you are ready. As you know, you are in lane number nine. I will follow you after the race until you need your stuff.' She pointed to a large red basket. There was a large '9' on the side.

Abby stared at the girl then smiled warmly. 'Thank you.'

She peeled off her tracksuit top and the loose-fitting blue T-shirt under it, removed her tights and placed the items into the bag she had carried into the stadium. Out of the same bag she removed her running spikes. Although it sounds like a mundane, routine activity, putting on a pair of spikes is anything but. Abby's racing footwear was by far her most important piece of clothing and she made sure that the shoes were perfectly laced up. A loose, flapping shoelace in a race inevitably spells disaster.

In the bag were several other items, including one which she now withdrew. It was the Xtend bottle. She took a long drink, exactly two hundred millilitres, then placed it back in her bag.

She stepped onto the track to perform a series of strides. Although her full warm-up and stretching routine had taken place much earlier with JP, she had consciously been moving since then, first in the underground warm-up area, even in the call room, and now on the track itself. The ambient temperature was close to thirty degrees, which meant that her muscles were loose and warm. Her pulse rate was a comfortable fifty beats per minute.

Abby deliberately stood still in the middle of the track, staring down at her feet for a long time. The red rubber tartan filled her vision and slowly the sound of the stadium faded until she could hear nothing. She focused her eyes on the beginning of the finish straight eighty metres away and started her first run-through. There would be three, run back to back, and covering seventy metres each. The first was done at half speed as she coaxed her body back into full racing mode.

The second was quicker, as she concentrated on rhythm, style and cadence. Now, the energy mobilised in the lengthy warm-up flowed back into her body like a river. Her pulse increased to seventy and her blood pressure crept up, dilating the aorta that took blood from the heart to the great working muscles and forcing wide the pulmonary artery that carried the surge of oxygen-poor blood back to the lungs for re-oxygenation.

The final run-through was done at full speed, shocking her body and mind with the realisation of what was to come. Her pulse shot up to 130 and she covered the final fifty metres in six seconds. From close up, she was a blur of arms and legs, tanned by the African sun to a polished gold, her athletic top and running shorts an amalgam of green and gold. Her mass of blonde curls, untethered and streaked with highlights, rose and fell with the rhythm of her legs, while on her feet, the spikes – the left bright green, the right golden yellow – traced a path along the tartan reminiscent of the northern lights seen in a Scandinavian winter.

She heard nothing and saw nothing of the crowd and the rich variety of action taking place in the stadium. She was fourteen years old and back on the grass running track at high school on a chilly Thursday afternoon in winter when, suddenly, she discovered that she could run fast, really fast. Until that day, running had been fun, the occasional interhouse competition when she had easily won the girls' hundred-metre race and even, on one occasion, had challenged and beaten all the boys, even the older ones.

But that Thursday had been different. Mizadams had said, 'Abby, see how fast you can run all the way around the field.' The track was exactly four hundred metres long, but was rough, with thick grass in parts and the occasional small hole. She ran as fast as she could for as long as she could. Mizadams was silent for a while as she stared at her ancient analogue stopwatch. 'You did that in fifty-eight seconds. Abby, I think you have a future as a runner.'

Within two years, she had discovered that she could run simply for the joy of it, for the feeling of speed and freedom that running brought. And, strangely, the faster she ran, the less tired she seemed to become, until she entered the strange, trance-like state athletes call the runner's high. Hearing nothing, her entire being was centred on the physical act of running as fast as she could, the only sensation the wind whipping across her face.

Now, years later, she was in the Roger Bannister Memorial Meeting, running the mile against the best women in the world. Reality.

She jogged back, stopping metres before the white line that crossed the track and that marked the start of the race. She looked up and immediately her senses sharpened, and she was once again aware of her surroundings. The other athletes were milling around, waiting for the starter's call and the introductions. Her world now consisted of nine runners and a red surface with lines on it. She blotted out the commotion in the stadium as the announcer started the build-up towards the high point of the meeting. She never looked at the crowd or at the faces of the other runners, did not respond when her name was announced to the crowd and a television cameraman moved right in front of her. In fact, she heard nothing, not the announcer, not the roar of the crowd.

Less than two minutes to go.

20

Friday, 10 August

THE ROGER BANNISTER MEMORIAL MILE FOR WOMEN

An unexpected hush, like the sudden silence as the eye of a cyclone passes over, settled over the crowd as eighty thousand pairs of eyes focused on a curved, fifteen-metre-long white line on a red rubberised surface where ten women stood waiting in full racing kit. Three of them were hopping up and down, one was touching her toes and five were jogging nervously on the spot. Only one stood perfectly still, a silent statue in a city square buzzing with traffic. Her arms were down at her sides, eyes staring forward, seemingly oblivious of the excitement around her.

The thrill of the unknown settled like a blanket over everyone. For weeks, since the announcement that Abby Dennison, Olga Fedorova, Sarah Moyo, Elinah Kiptanui and Mary McColgan would be taking part in arguably the most competitive women's mile race in thirty years, the excitement had cranked up as the media, prompted by successive releases from the organisers, predictions from experts, and the occasional comment from the participants themselves, had built the race up into something extraordinary, like a moon landing or Krakatoa erupting.

Such was the power of social media and fake news, where so-called experts were even predicting a sub-four-minute outcome. 'That's ridiculous,' McColgan had said in one interview, 'none of us is Superwoman.'

Bronwyn Adams, her hands twisting and untwisting in front of her, stood just inside the glass window of the VIP suite. A few metres away, Paul Dennison, his knuckles white, gripped a glass of beer as if it was a life raft in a stormy sea. He took a sip and foam settled on his upper lip.

Each was in a tiny universe of their own. No words, no eye contact, just a shared gnawing ache in the gut.

Mark Whyte was also there. He had arrived four minutes earlier after timing his entry into the media centre carefully. He had no desire to engage with anyone, least of all Bronwyn, Paul, James Selfe or Deon Coetzee. Especially Deon Coetzee.

Whyte stood in a deep corner of the media centre, yet with an excellent view of the arena through the glass. His powerful Nikon binoculars were raised, converting the distant figure of Abby Dennison – tall, elegant, her arms and legs shining erotically with a sheen of sweat in the bright lights – into a full-frame reality, close enough to touch. He reached his free hand out to stroke her soft skin, but all he felt was the disappointing coldness of glass. In the close-up of the Nikon's lenses, she stood motionless in lane nine, the group of runners around her in constant movement. She was half a head taller than the rest. He could see the ripple of flat abdominal muscles under her running vest, the tantalising hint of cleavage above her running top. Her quad muscles were like polished steel and her green and gold running shorts reached to just above her knees. Her spikes sparkled in the powerful floodlights.

At that moment she looked directly at him, smiled and gave a brief wave. Then the moment passed and the motionless statue returned, eyes hooded as they stared straight ahead. Mark almost jumped with excitement until he realised that the brief smile was for Paul or Bronwyn or Deon or whoever. Just not for him.

Still, he felt his pulse racing and a familiar warmness invaded his stomach. His hands started to sweat and his shirt moistened, even though the air conditioning cooled the media centre.

Although he was less than thirty metres away, Deon Coetzee could have been in a different world. Strangely dissociated from what was going on around him, he sat behind a bench in the outside media section, directly opposite the finish line. Perhaps it was the years of training as a journalist – impassive, uninvolved, an observer whose job it was to report, analyse and present the facts – that caused his apparent dissociation from the rampant emotion of the occasion. Reaching below his desk, he grabbed a tin of Coke, ripping at the tab that sealed it. It spluttered and foamed as the contents spurted out, wetting his trousers.

'Damn it,' he shouted and several nearby journalists grinned.

Deon looked around at the dozens of media people in the immediate vicinity – journalists tapping feverishly on laptops, earphones in; radio commentators chatting away in a dozen different languages, lip-microphones clamped just below their noses; television commentators, headphones in place, staring at monitors parked on their desktops, and speaking excitedly in staccato bursts. The total live audience following the race on radio, television and the internet was later estimated to be about two hundred million, roughly three per cent of the world's population.

It had been the most anticipated sporting moment in the world for weeks. Now the waiting was down to a few seconds. In less than five minutes the outcome would be known and dreams would have been realised for some, hopes dashed for others. For only a tiny percentage of the massive, heaving crowd, the outcome would be immaterial. Everyone had a stake in this race. It was like waiting outside the delivery room to hear about the successful birth of a baby, or peering at a list of names on a notice board to see if you had passed a crucial exam at university. The tension was an unbearable, living thing.

Although the official media-accreditation number had been capped at two hundred, there were many more unofficial, amateur reporters out there. Deon knew that the modern information machine, powered by the engine of social media and riding on the giant superhighway that is the internet, meant that stories could reach every corner of the planet, from the Arctic tundra of Alaska, Canada, Greenland and Russia to the jungles of the Congo and Amazon rivers, within milliseconds.

But not even Deon could imagine what was really going on at the receiving end of the information deluge.

Shack dwellers in Orange Farm, south of Johannesburg, gathered around a communal television, its blurry images received through a mud-stained, once-upon-a-time-white dish perched precariously on a corrugated-iron roof that was leaking badly; several dozen people crowded into the Bar Lacubaco in Rio de Janeiro's famed Vidigal favela in the mid-afternoon, on this occasion not enjoying a view of the brightly lit Ipanema Beach far below, but instead peering expectantly at a wall-mounted screen that showed the bright circle of light that was the Olympic Stadium; a group of several thousand athletics fans in the country that had made modern middle-distance athletics a world-famous sport — Kenya — gathered in Nairobi's Central Park as a local radio commentator regaled the crowd with his own live commentary as he listened on a pair of headphones to the BBC World Service broadcast of the meeting; in bustling New York City, the afternoon traffic was slightly less busy as bars and restaurants filled with people briefly pushing the pause button on their lives and looking to see why the world had become so interested in a white female track runner from Africa.

In the holy-of-holies, the VIP boardroom adjacent to the main media centre, James Selfe stood with a gaggle of important guests: Simon Hardy, Quentin Smythe-Harrison, and Mary Southgate of Regalbank. Other guests included the president of World Athletics and, for the first time at a track meeting, the Lord Mayor.

Hurrying around them in a frenzy of drinks-carrying was Emily Williams, Selfe's carefully chosen personal assistant. Her neat athletic frame, tight-fitting jeans, figure-hugging Bannister-branded shirt and ready smile were not lost on the likes of Hardy and QSH. And, if truth be known, on the ferociously single Mary Southgate as well.

Kurt Hunsler had joined the group of shot-putters, who had by now completed their competition. They stood outside the track at the start of the final straight, waiting for the action.

Of everyone, JP was the least tense. He had elected to sit opposite the start line, six rows up from ground level, where he could watch the race and get Abby's splits as she passed. It was the perfect place to judge how her race was progressing.

His lack of tension could be explained thus: he was the best judge of Abby's form, based on her training times and recent racing results. He understood the pace-making regimen and how it would play into Abby's race plan. He also knew that she was in the best shape of her life and that it all depended on how the others would tackle the race, tactically. Barring a calamity, he was confident that she would win. Only the finishing time remained an unknown component of the puzzle. That would depend on numerous factors outside of Abby's control.

JP also realised that the winning time would determine whether this race would become one of track history's greatest, or just a big anti-climax. It was an all-or-nothing situation for everyone concerned.

Virtually all the spectators had some form of electronic equipment with them. Mostly they were cellphones, held high to capture the images and atmosphere inside the stadium. WhatsApp messages and pictures by the thousand poured into cyberspace. There were hundreds of hand-held cameras, their owners snapping away happily, capturing images that could be viewed at length later, only the very best downloaded onto computers and emailed to friends around the world. 'I was there … look.' Flashbulbs exploded to create a mass of blinding light as fans stretched to the limit the technical capabilities of their equipment in the vastness of the stadium.

Only a few people had video cameras. Mostly they were of the happy-home-movie variety, but one was a state-of-the-art Sony 4K Camcorder, capable of producing a broadcast-quality product. It had the latest telephoto lens that could focus on a person fifty metres away and bring them close enough so that the target's face would fill the viewfinder. The operator sat in the middle of the stand close to the start line and, from the moment Abby had entered the stadium until she was called to the start, her every action had been captured. This was not the first time that particular camera had been busy. It was the same one that had been filming the interaction between Abby and JP, up to the moment she had walked off the warm-up track.

As the starter raised his pistol, the camera was switched off. It had done its job.

21

20h00

THE RACE

'Women's mile,' called the starter, 'please go to your starting positions.' He read out their names and they stepped into position five metres before the line. 'Donaldson, Beardsley, McColgan, Fedorova, Kiptanui, Karlovic, Moyo, Lennartz, Dennison, Marshall.'

The runners' helpers had long since departed onto the infield with their baskets, where they stood in a row, silent and watching.

Scientists and psychologists have shown that some of a person's senses can, in situations of extreme stress, be partially shut down so that the one or two remaining faculties are enhanced. In darkness, hearing becomes more acute; when danger lurks, vision, especially peripheral vision, improves.

That's what happened to Abby on the start line. She closed her eyes for two seconds and when she opened them the sound of the crowd dimmed to a faint roar, like the sea at night in the distance. She couldn't feel the track beneath her feet. Her vision sharpened, every movement of the runners around her was amplified and the colours of the stadium – the blood-red of the starter's jacket, the crisp white lines on the burgundy track – brightened.

'On your marks,' barked the starter. The athletes trotted up to the curved start line and settled into their starting positions, motionless and poised for action, heads down, arms in the running position, toes centimetres behind the white line. The assistant starter walked quickly along the row of runners, making sure that no one was over-stepping.

There was a brief pause as the starter checked for movement in the field. There was none. For the smallest fraction of a second there was no sound in the stadium.

Eighty thousand pairs of eyes were riveted on the starter who was standing on a small platform, his right arm thrust into the air, the pistol gripped firmly, a blue cord connecting it to the electronic timing system and the computers that drove the algorithms that recorded, millisecond by millisecond, the progress of the race.

Millions of television viewers in over a hundred countries worldwide halted conversations, called family members from outside and settled down for four minutes of drama.

Selfe, Hardy and their team had done their work well. The athletics world held its collective breath.

This is what happened.

The pistol cracked and the sound rushed around the stadium, igniting a roar from the crowd as the runners burst forward, heads down and arms flying as they sought to gain early momentum and rhythm.

Marshall, running in the outside lane, started hard and ran around the athletes on her inside. Before they had reached the first bend at forty metres, the American had claimed the lead as planned. She was running fast and fluidly and the race was off to a perfect start. Abby, in lane nine, just inside Marshall, kept going straight and made no attempt to chase the inside lane, electing to expend a little extra energy running wide, meaning that she would avoid anyone charging up on her inside.

It was Fedorova's race plan, evident after the first few seconds, to track Abby all the way through. She sat on her heels, a risky tactic for both women as only a few centimetres separated their spikes. With their cadence being four strides per second, it meant that, between Abby and Fedorova, there was a blur of around eight individual footfalls every second, each one pregnant with the possibility of one foot touching another, potentially spelling disaster.

As she approached the first bend, Abby glanced to her left and made a beeline for the spot just behind Marshall. To her surprise, it was a relatively simple task. Then the penny dropped: the rest of the field knew that the first four hundred would be a scorching sixty-two seconds and they had collectively decided to let Marshall, Dennison and Fedorova go. For now.

THE FINAL LAP

Abby, with Fedorova in her wake, tucked in behind Marshall going round the first bend. By now, Kiptanui, McColgan and the rest were five metres back, far enough for them to collectively start losing contact with the leading trio.

Abby, who seldom had words with the other runners in a race, felt comfortable at this speed – sixty-two seconds per lap – and spoke to Marshall, 'Perfect, keep this pace.' The American responded with an almost imperceptible thumbs up.

In slower, more tactical distance races where there is no designated pacemaker, the runners often bunch up with no one wanting to take the lead. This happens regularly in championship races such as the Olympics. Often the first part of the race is slow and the eventual outcome is a tremendous sprint over the final lap – or shorter – where the runner with the greatest sprinting speed wins the race. Usually the end result is a relatively slow time.

This was completely different. Coming out of the first bend after a hundred metres of running, Marshall was leading with Dennison on her shoulder, almost touching and running half into the second lane. Fedorova was inside Abby, and McColgan, Kiptanui and Moyo were together four metres back and slowly catching the leading trio. The rest of the field was three metres further back.

The athletes had settled into the rhythm of the first lap. The pushing, barging and general stress of the first fifty metres was behind them and it was time for the initial tactical decisions to be made: how fast to run, who to follow, which position to aim for at the end of the first lap. All ten women were now deep into private worlds of excitement, tension, fear and, eventually, pain.

In fast-moving sports, where circumstances can change rapidly – motor racing, tennis, boxing, rugby and middle-distance athletics – decisions are often not made after a definite thought process. The thoughts in the runners' brains were not fully formed but instead expressed in some sort of fleeting images, nanoseconds long. There was no time to think things through logically and they reacted instinctively. Years of conditioning – the classic theory of ten thousand hours of training – caused their brains to react automatically. While a spectator sees a runner making a move that looks carefully planned, often this is more a conditioned response to a given situation than a conscious thought process.

Suzy
I've done this dozens of times before. Sixty-two feels exactly like this, but I mustn't get carried away and run under sixty. Keep my rhythm and relax my arms. Don't get tense. Forget about the others. Wait for the clock at the first checkpoint.
Mary
Damn, only a hundred metres and I've lost contact! And the pace is not even that quick. Slowly, close the gap on Olga. Not too fast.
Elinah
Stay with Mary.
Sarah
Coach said I must stay with Elinah in the first lap.

The 1 500-metre finish point was on the bend, 109 metres before the finish line of the mile. Marshall, Dennison and Fedorova swept towards the digital clock standing at this point, which was 300 metres into the race and the first key checkpoint. McColgan, with Kiptanui, Moyo, Lennartz, Karlovic and Beardsley in a line behind her, was now a metre behind Fedorova. They had closed the gap.

Around the bend, Marshall relaxed a little, just enough to slow down a fraction. She had a series of key targets stored in her brain and she recalled the first one. To reach sixty-two seconds through 409 metres, she should pass the first checkpoint in under forty-six seconds. She glanced up as she passed. Forty-seven, forty-eight! Too slow, she realised, ten metres too slow!

'Pick it up, Suzy!' Abby's words carried, clear, urgent.

JP
Too slow! Get your arse moving, Suzy, don't blow the record.
Deon
They've caught up. The pace must have dropped and they're definitely off record pace. McColgan wants to pass Fedorova, and Abby is crowding Marshall as well.

They all know what's going on.
Suzy
I must get them back onto the agreed pace. Hit the finish line in sixty-three. No need to start sprinting, but I have to go sub-sixty per lap for a while. That's fast, but necessary.

Marshall increased her pace, and it was anything but gentle, rather like a sudden changing of gears down the finish straight. Abby knew this would happen and reacted immediately but Fedorova was slow to respond, allowing McColgan to slip past into third. Kiptanui and Moyo were now on the Russian's shoulder as well. It was pell-mell sprinting towards the end of the first lap. Karlovic and Beardsley were out wide in the second lane, trying to get a decent position. They were all surging, and not even a quarter of the race was done.

Dangerous territory.

Suzy Marshall, with Abby on her shoulder, charged over the finish line. Three laps to go, 1 200 metres.

The digital clock displayed two numbers, one above the other. The bottom number kept on rolling, the hundredths of a second kicking over in a blur. But the top level had stopped as the leader passed. This was the key indicator, the end of the first 409 metres. The target was sixty-three seconds.

The top level showed 62.74.

The crowd, knowledgeable in such matters, roared even louder. They had all seen the split and this was exactly what they had come to witness – a world record. Could it actually happen, a kind of Bannister Moment? The whispers of those more experienced said, 'Hang on. Three laps to go. Anything can happen.'

Marshall, aware that she had pushed the envelope down the straight, dropped her pace slightly. She swept into the bend with Dennison right behind. McColgan, Fedorova, Kiptanui, Moyo, Karlovic, and Beardsley were in a line behind the leaders.

Lennartz and Donaldson were ten metres back and effectively out of contention, just hoping for a decent time in a world-class race.

Marshall settled back into a reasonable pace and went through the next hundred-metre sections in sixteen seconds each. Dennison, McColgan, Kiptanui, Moyo, Fedorova and Beardsley were behind the pacemaker in a row, all very business-like now that the mayhem of the first lap had abated. They went around the bend towards the same intermediate checkpoint, which showed sixty-one seconds for the previous four hundred metres, a product of the crazy sprint down the straight.

Abby's brain kicked in and, coming out of the bend into the finish straight for the second time, she spoke to Marshall. 'I'm going past.'

Suzy
That's crazy early. I thought she would wait until into the third lap. She must be feeling good. Fantastic, now let's see how the others respond. Wow, what a race! I love that girl.

Entering the home straight, Marshall moved into the second and then the third lane and slowed down to a jog. She hadn't even run eight hundred metres and had been pressured off the track by the world number one.

Abby picked up the pace and roared into the lead for the first time. The crowd went ballistic, standing, waving, jumping up and down and screaming their heads off. The amazing Abby was going for the world record! Flags and banners fluttered across the stadium. Cellphone cameras flashed, commentators had to shout above the noise, and the stadium announcer was almost apoplectic. It was pandemonium.

Abby approached the finish line and the clock ticked over, relentlessly, waiting for no one. The bottom line was the accumulated time, the top line the time for that lap.

Abby glanced to her left as she approached the line: 57, 58, 59, 60, 61.

She had passed the clock by the time it stopped but she saw the time on the second clock on the bend. 62.11 seconds. Perfect. That meant the accumulated time was 2:03.85 with eight hundred metres to go. Two more laps of sixty-three seconds each would give a final time of under 4:10.

Easy? 'Not so fast, everyone,' warned the stadium announcer, but few people heard.

Deon
The announcer's correct. This is a risky move by Abby. She is obviously feeling good, but taking the lead with more than two laps to go – eish!
JP
Abby was spot on. Suzy was slowing. If she'd stayed behind for another half a lap she would have lost two or three seconds and the whole field would have been on top of her. No one else would have taken the lead. It would have been a mad sprint for six hundred metres and I'm not sure if she could beat Kiptanui or Moyo in that situation. She had to go early.
Abby
I know what I'm doing here, Suzy was slowing. If I'd stayed behind for another half a lap we would have lost two or three seconds and the whole field would have been on top of me. No one else would have taken the lead. It would have been a mad sprint for six hundred metres and I'm not sure if I could beat Olga, Elinah or even Sarah in that situation. I had to go early.
JP
I'm worried about Olga.

The third lap of a mile race is usually the trickiest. The runners are tired and it's too early to sprint. Once they get to the bell it's different – just four hundred metres to go, the final lap, hang in there, sprint, it's nearly done.

But the third lap …

Going into the first bend of the track for the third and penultimate time, Abby dropped the pace slightly, knowing that no one would dare pass her at that stage. They didn't and were in a straight line behind her. Kiptanui, Moyo and McColgan had slipped past Fedorova but the Russian was still there, six metres behind Dennison. Beardsley was next and even Karlovic and Lennartz had made up ground. Only Donaldson had lost contact completely.

You could have thrown a large blanket over the top eight. Suzy Marshall stood, hands on hips, on the finish line, watching the race develop.

Elinah
Stay with Abby.
Sarah
Perfect, I'm still with Elinah.
Mary
I have to stay with Moyo. Don't lose contact.
Olga
Watch, everyone, here I come!

As Abby hit the back straight, she increased the pace, imperceptibly at first, then noticeably. The runners, the spectators and those who understood athletics watching around the world on television, knew it. Her stride lengthened, her arms lifted and her cadence rose by about eight per cent. It was enough to increase her pace by about three seconds per lap. Again, the sudden acceleration caught the others by surprise, opening a small gap on McColgan and the other three.

At the same time, Fedorova made her move. She went into the second lane and increased her pace, but more markedly than Dennison had done. She passed Kiptanui and Moyo midway down the back straight and then McColgan fell prey to the surge of the Russian woman and she surrendered her second place before the bend.

There was a collective gasp from the crowd as the entire character of the race changed. 'It's no wonder that Olga Fedorova was world number one for three years,' yelled the stadium announcer.

But there was an even bigger collective shout as Fedorova moved wide in the bend, first running right next to Abby, then, amazingly in such a strong race and with more than a lap to go, passing her.

With five hundred metres to go in the Roger Bannister Memorial Mile for Women, Olga Fedorova, world number three, was two metres ahead of Abby Dennison, world number one.

Suzy, Deon, Elinah
What the hell is she doing?

Mary

Fantastic. She's blown the whole race open. Now we all have a chance.

JP

As expected. I thought maybe she would wait for the bell. This is perfect for Abby but she needs to be very careful now. Hope she remembers my advice.

Abby

Don't panic, don't panic. Focus. This is a huge gamble, to go so hard, so early. She has a great sprint, so why this tactic? Something's going on. Catch her then stay with her.

Dennison, with McColgan, Moyo and Kiptanui in tow, reacted to Fedorova's surge by speeding up. Within thirty metres they were back in touch, the five women charging down the home straight towards the bell, the crowd roaring. Flags waved, hooters hooted, flashbulbs flashed and cameras clicked, capturing historic images.

In the media centre, people stood like statues, some of them with hands over their mouths, others with drinks unknowingly spilling out of tilted glasses. Bronwyn was silently crying, small tears leaking out of her eyes. Paul's pulse rate had hit 180. James Selfe was smiling. Only Emily Williams was shouting, her voice filling the normally sedate, ultra-British VIP suite. No one took any notice, there were other things on their minds.

The numbers ticked over on the finish line clock and a blue-jacketed official stood impassively next to it on the grass, a large brass bell in his right hand poised in readiness. One lap, four hundred metres, to go.

The final lap.

It was anyone's race, anyone's record, anyone's little place in the crowded pantheon of historic athletic achievements. But there was room for only one name – the winner's. No matter the time, it was turning out to be one of the classic mile races in the recent history of women's track athletics.

Olga Fedorova passed the finish line, the bell ringing loudly in her ears. Dennison was centimetres behind, running slightly wide to avoid the Russian's flying feet. McColgan was third and Kiptanui fourth. Less than five metres separated them. Nothing, in the context of a race. But one thing had changed – Sarah Moyo had lost contact with Kiptanui and was a crucial three metres behind the Kenyan.

Sarah
It's okay. I feel fine. I was just worried about being crowded on the bend. You never know what might happen.
JP
This is a problem.

None of the runners glanced at the clock – they were far too engaged in the tactical savagery of the previous few hundred metres. Now it was all about positioning themselves in the final lap. But everyone else – people inside the stadium and those outside watching on television, did look at the clock. It said, in simple arithmetic that a five-year-old could understand: Accumulated time: 3:06.95. Previous lap: 62.10 seconds.

The world record was on.

Sub-sixty-six for the final lap would do it. Sixty-four or better would give someone a sub-4:10. And sixty-two would result in the unimaginable – 4:08.

JP, Deon
The final lap.
Abby
The final lap. Risk time. I'm going to stay on her shoulder. Contact, contact, contact, breathe into her neck, make her know I'm here and not falling back.
Olga
Сейчас! Now!

For months, years probably, the next sixty seconds would be played over and over and over and over on television screens, iPads, computers and cellphones. In slow motion, ultra-slow motion and real time. From close-up, medium distance and drone shots from up in the night sky. With comments from experts in a dozen languages: English, Russian, French, Afrikaans, German, Croatian, Spanish, Swahili. Especially Swahili.

Research conducted months later showed that it had become the most watched, downloaded, tweeted and retweeted sporting clip of the year, in the top fifty news clips of any genre.

YouTube was flooded, news broadcasts were interrupted with breaking announcements. CNN pronounced it 'one of the top fifty most viewed stories of the year' in its year-end summary. ESPN said it was 'a classic moment of twenty-first century sport'.

Steven Spielberg was rumoured to be planning a movie based on it but that turned out to be an urban legend.

Sixty seconds of a track race. Not a nuclear war or the assassination of a president or a tsunami in Thailand.

No, it was just the final lap of a track race.

Such is the power of sport – occasionally, amazingly, the ultimate human drama.

An in-depth documentary broadcast on Netflix three months later looked back at what had happened. It explained that there were twenty television cameras in the stadium covering the various events, each feeding pictures into a massive outside broadcast van owned by the BBC, parked beneath the giant grandstand. Inside the OB van, a group of forty-six people managed the various feeds, sifting and sorting them, recording and selecting the best one to be sent out at any given time to viewers across the world.

Twelve of these cameras were placed around the track, giving simultaneous views of the action. Each camera's feed, even though it was not necessarily being broadcast, was recorded on disc inside the replay section of the OB van.

Other cameras were placed in the VIP area, high up on two of the floodlight towers and on the infield focusing on the crowds. One was in a drone circling high above the stadium.

The most important camera, from the point of view of the documentary producers, was held by an operator sitting on the back of a slim, quiet motorcycle, purpose-designed and purpose-fitted, that rode alongside the leaders in the outside lane of the track. This camera filmed the race leaders from a distance of about fifteen metres.

All twenty cameras, and the technology that supported them, enabled the officials and producers to examine every sound, every frame, every nuance, every movement, every facial expression and every crowd reaction from numerous angles. Pictures ranged from ultra-close-up to distant drone shots and track-side cameras.

The producers, video editors and sound engineers slowed the footage down, sped it up and zoomed in until the images of a single shoelace or knee-cap filled the screen. They amplified the sound and enhanced certain colours to get better and more useful images.

In the end, not surprisingly, it was mainly from the motorcycle camera that officials and producers eventually figured out what had happened, long after the recriminations and accusations had died down. The bike driver and camera operator, BBC Sport's most experienced mobile motorcycle crew, had done a brilliant job. They hadn't flinched or lost control or missed a beat in the midst of the drama.

The evidence was, to be honest, irrefutable. This is what all the cameras saw.

Going into the bend after the bell, with Dennison on her right shoulder, Olga Fedorova led the race. They were close and virtually touching. Two metres behind them, Kiptanui was on the rail directly behind Fedorova and McColgan was another two metres back, running wide in the second lane. Moyo was also in the second lane a further two metres behind McColgan. She had a perfect view of the quartet ahead.

Beardsley, Lennartz, Karlovic and Donaldson were together, passing the finish line, twenty metres behind Moyo.

Midway round the bend, Fedorova's right arm swung outwards half a metre, but because the runners were so close together, the movement was enough to clip Abby's left arm. At the same time the Russian shifted slightly to her right, forcing Abby to take evasive action by reflexively swerving into the third lane. Fedorova's moves were slight but, given the proximity of Abby, potentially lethal. In a tightly-bunched situation, runners never make sideways moves.

THE FINAL LAP

It was later agreed by experts that Abby's swift evasive action, entirely justified, triggered another situation that rapidly developed behind Fedorova. Kiptanui, who was directly behind Olga, saw a sudden change in the body positions of the runners in front of her and had neither the time nor the space to react. She was boxed into a nightmare of rapidly shifting bodies moving laterally across her path.

It was inevitable. Her right foot connected with Fedorova's left heel and within a split second both women became airborne, arms swinging wildly, legs pedalling in the air as they desperately tried to get purchase on the track below.

But the physical laws of momentum and G-forces and circular motion and gravity and biomechanics were always going to win.

It had to happen, the unthinkable. Kiptanui lost her balance and fell forward onto Fedorova, who was now virtually airborne in a desperate effort to involve Abby in the collision. Moving at twenty-four kilometres an hour, they had no chance. Both women lurched forward, their arms thrust out in front of them in the human being's instinctive reaction to a forward fall. All thoughts of continuing to run evaporated as the awful realisation dawned that they were about to crash onto the track.

In the chaos, Fedorova's flying body side-swiped Dennison, who again swerved away to her right. She lost her rhythm, and her arms swung wildly as she desperately tried not to fall. She eventually landed on one foot out in lane seven, slowing down and nearly colliding with the television motorcycle. When she eventually regained her balance she had to run back from nearly the outside lane into lane one. In the process, she lost about four precious seconds but, amazingly, had remained on her feet.

Kiptanui was the first to crash onto the track and, a few milliseconds later, Fedorova hit the tartan right in front of her. At that sort of speed it took several metres and a full three seconds for the pair to eventually come to a stop in a tangle of legs and arms. As the other runners disappeared, Fedorova crawled off the track and lay with her face buried in the soft grass of the infield, while the Kenyan remained where she was, a small, pitiful, crumpled heap in the centre of lane number one of the London Olympic Stadium.

The entire complexion of the race had changed completely. As Kiptanui and Fedorova were doing their death-dive, McColgan, Moyo, Beardsley and Karlovic were able to weave their way between the flying bodies without losing speed. In one way, the chaos had worked for them.

Dennison, not so much. She had somehow not fallen and had regained her rhythm, but now found herself in fifth place. It was a disaster.

Going into the back straight, McColgan led Moyo, Beardsley and Karlovic. Dennison was fifteen metres back, just ahead of Lennartz and Donaldson.

Although the race had entered its final, crucial stage, it was as if time had stopped as the crowd tried to process what they had seen. One moment, their focus had been on the race, nine women chasing a world record; a few seconds later there were two entirely different situations to absorb: the continuing race, and the collision that ended with two bodies on the ground.

Humans react instinctively and characteristically to situations that are sudden, unexpected and profoundly negative. First, people go silent and totally still, then they collectively thrust their hands over their mouths. A couple of seconds later, they react: they scream or cover their eyes or cling to the person next to them or jump up, wave their arms and shout.

The images from the four cameras focused on the crowd showed these standard responses in the later documentary.

The stadium was weirdly silent for a few moments, then it erupted into sound at a level not experienced before. It was the primeval roar of the crowd – instinctive and unreasoning, drawn from the millennia of human evolution. It was like thunder.

Sarah Moyo also reacted instinctively. Years of training and racing had taught her mind to process information in less time than the other runners. Suddenly she found herself jointly in the lead, running alongside McColgan, with just three hundred metres of open track in front of her.

She surged strongly and the brilliance of her natural talent, coupled with years of grinding speed-endurance training on the tracks of Zimbabwe, Kenya and America kicked in from somewhere in her subconscious mind. She charged into the lead, swiftly opening a five-metre gap on an amazed McColgan.

THE FINAL LAP

Sarah
I can win today.
Mary
What the …?
JP
Go Abby, you can still do it. What the hell was Olga thinking?
Abby
What the hell was Olga thinking?

By the time Moyo had taken the lead, the crowd realised that it was pointless to stare at two prone bodies on the ground when the race was entering its climax. Everyone swung their gaze back to the competition, where someone would win and break the world record and eight other people wouldn't.

Moyo, running in the green, gold, red and black national colours of Zimbabwe, raced towards the final bend, where a line across the track designated the start of the final two hundred metres. McColgan was eight metres back with Beardsley and Karlovic following. A yawning gap of another ten metres lay between Karlovic and Dennison, now twenty-six metres behind the leader.

Unlike the instinctive Moyo surge, Abby's sprint was a calculated affair, motivated by a combination of anger, frustration, bloody-minded determination and pure fear. It was likely that she would lose this race – and the world record.

A race and record that were rightfully hers.

She was back in Loughborough and JP was on the sidelines. He said in his quiet way, 'One more circuit, give it everything!' The sun had set, the field was deserted apart from the groundsman, and she opened the throttle. One more lap, one more lap!

The final lap.

By the end of the back straight, she had caught and passed Beardsley and Karlovic in a blaze of green and gold. But both McColgan and Moyo were running as if their lives depended on it and both had formidable finishing kicks, worthy of their high rankings.

Abby was closing the gap on the Scot, but Sarah was still far ahead. Even though Mary had started out as the crowd's darling, by the time the Fedorova-instigated mayhem had settled, it was clear that it was now Abby who had become their favourite. The power of eighty thousand voices screaming, 'Abby, Abby' helped her to pass Mary as they came out of the final bend. Less than one hundred metres to go.

McColgan could only stare in wonder at her retreating back. 'My God,' she breathed, exhausted, broken.

But Moyo was still twenty metres ahead.

Everyone realised that it was all over. No female runner in the world could have caught Sarah Moyo that night, not with a twenty-metre gap and less than one hundred metres to go.

Sarah Moyo won the Roger Bannister Memorial Mile for Women in a new world record of 4:07.25, nearly five seconds faster than the old mark. She had run the final lap – including avoiding the Kiptanui/Fedorova chaos – in 61.3 seconds, her fastest of the race. Her final two hundred metres had taken 28.9 seconds.

Abby Dennison finished second, eight metres behind the winner. Her time was 4:08.17, an agonising 0.92 seconds slower than Moyo and also well within the existing record. But it was not good enough. Only winning was good enough.

Later, an analysis of the last lap showed that Abby had run the final two hundred metres in 26 seconds flat, the fastest ever last half-lap in women's middle-distance history. Faster, even, than the final half-lap run by the winner of the men's mile race earlier in the evening.

Mary McColgan finished third in 4:10.31, the third-fastest mile by a woman in history and 2.14 seconds behind Dennison. Jane Beardsley held onto fourth place, finishing in 4:11.83, also under the record. Brigita Karlovic finished in 4:14.85, Birgit Lennartz in 4:14.92 and Ashley Donaldson, after a valiant last lap effort, couldn't quite catch the two Europeans and ended up with 4:15.33. All eight finishers broke four minutes for the 1 500 metres, a first in world athletics.

It was the greatest women's mile/1 500-metre race in the history of the sport.

But the cost, for two women, had been immense. One had lost her chance of being part of history by breaking a world record and possibly winning the race.

The other had entered the sparsely populated universe of world-class sportswomen who had sacrificed career, reputation, potential earnings and self-respect on the sad altar of all-consuming jealousy.

It hadn't been a moment of madness. It had been a carefully constructed and – almost – perfectly executed plan.

22

Friday, 10 August
20h06

THE ROGER BANNISTER MEMORIAL MILE
FOR WOMEN

The digital display on the finish line froze when Sarah Moyo flashed past. The top line read, '4:07.25'. The bottom line exclaimed, 'New World Record!'

The big screen at the far end of the arena flashed the same message and the stadium announcer yelled, '4:07.25, a new world record for Sarah Moyo of Zimbabwe!' Pretty much everyone knew what had happened.

On the ground, broadly speaking, several things were happening.

A lone little girl, about ten years of age, stood on the track. In her hand she held a small bunch of blue, white and red flowers wrapped neatly in coloured paper and secured with a strong elastic band. She had only one task, something she had been dreaming about ever since her Uncle James had sat down next to her and said, 'How would you like to do me a big favour? It might even get you onto TV.' The big favour that would get her onto TV was to give the winner of the women's mile race a bunch of flowers directly after the finish, a tradition in elite track races.

But the race winner had left the scene. As had been arranged by Solomon beforehand with the organisers, Sarah Moyo collected her tog bag from her assistant, walked into the athletes' tunnel close to the finish line where she was met by a specially designated doping-control official who escorted her to a private room under the grandstand where she took off her spikes, put on her tracksuit and urinated into a plastic bottle. She left the room, exited the stadium at the door where Abby had earlier entered, and met her brothers and coach outside. The four of them climbed into a waiting car and went directly to their hotel.

THE FINAL LAP

As the winner left the scene, only the little girl's parents noticed that, after about a minute, she quietly walked away in tears, still clutching her precious flowers. She would not get on TV this time but maybe next year she would have another chance.

Exactly sixteen minutes after breaking the world record, Sarah Moyo was enjoying a soothing hot shower. She had spoken to no one, nor would she until breakfast, taken in her room the next morning, shortly after an easy ten kilometre post-race, cool-down run.

As Moyo was taking her leave of the Olympic Stadium, on the first bend of the track officials and medical staff were gathered around Fedorova and Kiptanui, talking soothingly to them and checking for injuries. Stretchers were being rolled out and people were giving orders and speaking on phones. It looked like a minor war zone.

Abby had slowed down after the finish line, coming to a stop about thirty metres further on, head slumped forward, hands on knees. Most people think that an athlete, after a massive physical effort that drains any sort of energy reserves, would take many minutes to recover. That may be true for someone finishing a marathon, but for superbly conditioned track athletes it is different. Recovery is normally just about pulse rates: in the intense effort of finishing a race, Abby's pulse rate would have shot up to over two hundred but, such was her conditioning, it would have come down quickly, to under a hundred in less than three minutes. She could have walked off five minutes later almost as if she had been for a brisk stroll in the park.

But she didn't. For her, it was all about getting her mind, rather than her body, back to normal.

Slowly, she mentally returned to planet Earth. As her pulse rate dropped and her breathing normalised, her brain started to register her surroundings. Her world expanded from twenty square metres on the ground to the stadium, the crowd and the sounds. She could feel the track under her feet, hear the crowd, sense the media horde approaching. Her world expanded and she became a normal person again.

She had no idea at that stage what her time was. She never even saw the digital display. All she had picked up from the wall of sound in the minute or so since the race had ended were the words 'world record' that boomed over the public address system.

The only thing she knew was that she was second. She hadn't won. It was a crushing blow, a realisation that she had failed people – her father, Bronwyn, JP and, most important of all, herself. People, in the immediate aftermath of some sort of disaster, a motor accident for example, think to themselves, 'If only I could rewind the clock, go back to before this happened. If only I had known, I could have avoided it. If only I had been a metre wider on the track, I would have won and the world record would be mine.'

If only …

As she approached the railing separating the spectators from the track, someone stuck out a South African flag. Without a word she grabbed the colourful cloth, with its pair of green lines merging into a single one, symbolising the unification of the nation after 1994, and draped it around her shoulders.

Then the media circus arrived. In sharp contrast to Elinah Kiptanui, still sitting dejectedly on the grassy infield fifty metres away, Abby had no medics or officials to keep them away.

She just saw cameras. There seemed to be dozens of them but in fact there were only twenty. On the night, sixteen stills photographers and four television camera operators were accredited to go onto the track itself, but only after the race was over. They descended on Abby as she walked around the first bend of the track. The cameras flashed continuously, almost blinding her. Television camera operators jostled with stills photographers to get close and, possibly, even claim a precious soundbite. Hand-held microphones were thrust into her face and questions flew like arrows.

Abby stood trapped against the perimeter railing, where the media had basically forced her, draped in her flag. She raised her hands, signalling quiet. Amazingly, the media realised that she had something to say and quietened down. Flashbulbs still popped and cameras rolled, but at least she could be heard.

'Guys, thanks for being here,' she shouted. 'This has been an amazing night. Right now, I don't even know what my time was.'

'Four-oh-eight!' someone yelled. She had broken the world record after all. But it wasn't much of a consolation.

There was a flurry of questions. Again, she signalled for quiet and again they fell silent. 'I'll answer all your questions later. There is so much I have to say, people to thank. But now I have a much more important task. Please excuse me.'

In another sequence that entered the YouTube most-watched list for August, she strode purposefully to her right, putting her hands up to ward off the encroaching photographers. 'Give me some space, please,' she was heard to say above the din, 'I'll be with you guys in a while.'

Five minutes after crossing the finish line, she was bending down next to Elinah Kiptanui, her hand on the now-seated Kenyan's shoulder. 'I'm so sorry, Elinah. I couldn't do anything. You shouldn't have fallen. It wasn't your fault.'

'I did nothing wrong,' came a small voice that Abby struggled to hear. 'She tripped me.'

'I know. It wasn't about you. She was after me and got it wrong.' This was whispered into the Kenyan's ear so that not even the most sensitive microphone close by could catch the words. 'But say nothing now. Wait for the official investigation.'

Kiptanui stared at Abby, who was now kneeling beside her. 'You mean …' Her voice trailed off.

'I think so. But I'm not certain. Say nothing.'

'I won't, I promise. Sorry you couldn't catch Sarah, no one could, not even me.' She smiled for the first time.

With a final pat on Elinah's shoulder, Abby set off on her lap of honour. With the brightly coloured flag flapping around her, she jogged around the track, going wide and reluctantly high-fiving spectators close to the barriers. The show must go on. The media contingent chased after her, cameras swinging wildly. But, like McColgan and the other runners earlier, they had no chance of keeping up and, by the time she reached the finish straight, just two obviously fit young reporters were still in touch.

She gave both reporters a hug. 'Well done, guys. You must be pretty fit!' Then she made a beeline for a spot opposite the finish line. Stopping at the barrier, she reached over to JP. In another classic media moment, athlete and coach hugged over the barrier for a long time. And, for the first time, Abby's emotions boiled over and the tears flowed.

Pulling away eventually, she raised her eyes to the VIP box and saluted, military-style, her precious Team, Paul and Bronwyn, who stood outside waving and blowing kisses.

It was only then that her patient helper could hand over her tog bag.

Suddenly it was all over and a green-jacketed female official tapped her gently on the shoulder. 'I'm Rachel Vanderhoven, part of the doping-control team. Please come with me now to doping control. You know, of course, that international regulations dictate that you need to pass a dope test for your time to be ratified. The other runners who also broke the record are already there. Have you taken in any drinks since you finished the race?'

Abby shook her head. She knew the drill. 'Let's do this,' she said.

The two women went down a tunnel into the depths of the stadium, took the elevator up to the fourth floor, entered through a black door guarded by another official into a white-tiled room that looked, to the uninformed person, like a standard changing room with toilet cubicles but no showers.

Five other women were there, including Mary and Jane, and Abby recognised the American sprinter Jackie Washington in a far corner. The three mile runners exchanged quick hugs and muted congratulations. Washington ignored them.

'I hate this place. Peeing into a plastic cup.' McColgan grimaced, showing little of her earlier exuberance. 'It always takes me ages. My frigging bladder freezes,' she explained somewhat crudely, pointing downwards.

'I'm good to go,' said Abby with a grin. 'I always am. My bladder is super well behaved. Come on,' waving to Vanderhoven, 'where do I pee?'

Apart from the shouting, the apologies, the accusations, the denials, the recriminations, the investigations, the reviews and interviews, the endless analyses, the relentless replays on television, the more-than-seventy-five-million YouTube views, the disciplinary hearings and the media announcements, it was all over.

The Roger Bannister Memorial Mile for Women passed into history.

23

Friday, 10 August
21h47

THE ROGER BANNISTER MEMORIAL
ATHLETICS MEETING

Simon Hardy certainly had his hands full.

The media centre was crowded to overflowing. In a venue designed to comfortably seat two hundred people, at least forty more were crammed in. Two extra rows of seats were added in front, chairs were placed down the centre aisle, and the front table was moved back a couple of metres, allowing a few photographers to sit on the floor right in front. A few more people stood at the back or peered in from crowded doorways. Others stood in the passageway outside, hoping to hear something, even if they couldn't watch the action.

The problem was not the media at all. With just two hundred accredited journalists, the post-event media conference should have been a doddle. It was an army of VIPs – later estimated by disgruntled reporters, who eagerly took pictures and videos of smartly dressed bankers, lawyers and sponsors fighting for precious seats, to be more than sixty – who had invaded the press conference area long before the conference started. Many were clutching colourful cocktails and happily munching smoked-salmon sandwiches and assorted sushi delicacies. iPhones were everywhere.

Technically, the VIPs were not allowed into the media conference, but when you are chairman of a City bank, managing partner of a major law firm or – amazingly – even the Lord Mayor, such minor technicalities are just silly restrictions placed by lesser mortals. One simply HAD to see and hear Abby Dennison, *dahling*, close up and in the flesh. Maybe even get a selfie or autograph. At the very least, it would make for excellent one-upmanship at the next dinner party with the Trafford-Wilkes.

The excitement from the stadium spilled over into the media centre. Normal British social barriers vanished in the melee. Smartly dressed women clutching Gucci handbags squeezed into chairs alongside journalists wearing faded jeans and ancient Asics trainers. Their knees touched but no one cared. A couple of muted squeaks and giggles from one elderly lady elicited a hug and a cheek-kiss from her much younger, bearded and heavily tattooed neighbour.

Bankers in pin-striped suits leaned against walls. Someone had managed to get into the sound-control room and George Harrison's 'Here Comes the Sun' blasted from the overhead speakers. Most people were confused until someone announced loudly that the song came from The Beatles' *Abbey Road* album. That got everyone laughing and Hardy had to shout into the microphone and several volunteers clapped their hands for silence. When that eventually happened, the sense of anticipation was a palpable thing.

'Ladies and gentlemen, in light of the new world record in the women's mile race, we have decided to change our advertised media protocol tonight. Originally we planned to have a single media conference at the close of the meeting with a selection of winning athletes and that will happen directly after this special briefing, so please remain for that. But, as was agreed with her management team before the meeting, Sarah Moyo, the winner and new world record holder, is unavailable right now.'

This announcement was greeted with confused stares from most reporters. Hands shot up and questions flew. 'Why not?' 'We want to see the winner!'

Hardy was firmly in charge and silenced them with a wave. 'Sorry, everyone. Let's move on.' Some of the more experienced journos in the room knew the reason: Asperger's, borderline autistic. Whispers could be heard explaining this.

Hardy continued. 'But I am delighted to welcome Abby Dennison – who less than two hours ago finished second and also smashed the decades-old world mile record – together with her coach, JP van Riet. But I must warn you that neither of these two individuals, nor anyone else in the meeting organising team, will comment on the unfortunate collision between Olga

THE FINAL LAP

Fedorova and Elinah Kiptanui. We need to wait for the official investigation to proceed and the relevant announcements will be made by the national and international athletics federations. That process may take several days or longer. It is out of the hands of this organising committee.'

There was an audible buzz in the room and several hands shot into the air. Three reporters jumped up at the same time and questions filled the room. 'Who was at fault?' 'Have they been disqualified?' 'Was it deliberate?'

Hardy raised his hand again. 'I urge you to be patient. The situation is complex and we as the Roger Bannister Meeting organisers cannot offer opinions. I also urge you to treat with caution comments made by any of the athletes in the race, particularly Olga and Elinah, although we have no control over the runners. They may not have the full picture.'

The hubbub died down as the eastern access door opened and James Selfe came into the room, followed by JP and Abby, both wearing the full Team tracksuits. JP looked solemn and decidedly nervous, while Abby was unsmiling. Eventually, she smiled thinly and waved to the assembled crowd, which broke out into spontaneous applause. This lasted two minutes and twenty seconds. The show must go on.

Hardy controlled the conference well. He was an experienced media man and allowed questions and answers to flow smoothly. Reporters waited their turn patiently and, by the end, there were not many different questions. Most people wanted to know the same things: How do you feel now that you have a world record? Are you disappointed about not winning?

'That's a pretty dumb question,' Abby replied rather rudely. The media men grinned; well done, Abby, it certainly was ridiculous.

Did the race go as planned or did you have to alter your tactics? Why did you take the lead so early? Did you expect to run so fast? What's next on your racing schedule? Tell us about the roles played by your support team. Do you have a message for the people back in South Africa?

A couple of reporters tried to sneak in questions about the collision but Abby deflected them. 'Honestly, I don't know what happened. It was too fast. Like everyone, I'll wait for the official review.'

JP sat beside Abby and happily let her field the majority of the questions.

But inevitably he was on the receiving end of a few, mainly about Abby's training and race plan. He answered smoothly, but without divulging any real detail. He acknowledged that she had a definite race plan that involved the important role of the pacemaker. 'Suzy agreed to set a pace so that the runners could go for the world record and she did that, superbly.' Until she hadn't, of course, but the ever-diplomatic JP failed to mention that.

On the subject of mental conditioning, he was even more circumspect. 'One of our team, Miss Bronwyn Adams, is Abby's mental coach. Maybe you should ask her that.'

After twenty minutes, Hardy knew that not much more of value was going to emerge. 'Ladies and gentlemen, all the track and field events were concluded before the final race. We timed it in such a way that you wouldn't miss any of the action. Now, once Abby and JP have left, I ask you to remain here, as we have invited four more athletes to join us for the next media briefing. This should be in about ten minutes' time.'

In fact, it only started twenty minutes later, such was the clamour for quick one-on-one interviews with Abby – requests quickly denied by Hardy as it would probably have lasted all night – and a seemingly endless stream of photographs to be taken, mainly by the illegally present VIPs. Hardy, try as he might, had little influence over the bankers, lawyers, captains of industry, lords, ladies, earls and yes, the Lord Mayor, and they hung around like groupies at a rock concert.

Human nature, be it in a screaming teenage girl or an ageing lord, never changes: people have an irresistible need to create heroes out of other people, irrespective of their failings and frailties. As the Abby circus was winding down, Emily Williams tapped Deon on the shoulder. 'What a night we've had,' she whispered in his ear. 'Later I want to hear your analysis. But now, James asked me to direct you out of the room with Abby and JP. Apparently, there are some arrangements that need to be made. Something about a private meeting tomorrow. So, bye … for now.'

He gave her a quick hug, said 'Thanks' and wriggled his way through the throng and, finally, out into the passage with Abby and JP. The trio was whisked away.

The conference room quickly quietened down and the VIPs departed, leaving a trail of empty glasses and small pieces of sausage roll and lettuce in their wake.

Few of the regular media remained behind, such was the scramble to get Dennison, Moyo, Kiptanui and Fedorova stories, images and videos out into an information-hungry world. The proverbial early bird may catch the worm, but in the media world it's the early reporter that gets the accolades.

When Jackie Washington, Scott Huffner and two other notable winners came in for their conference, the room was three-quarters empty, with the forty or so extra chairs making the place look even more deserted and bleak.

'Where the hell is everyone?' enquired the American sprinter, who had earlier set the fastest time in the world for the year for 200 metres at 21.71 seconds.

'Where do you think?' chuckled Huffner, ever the smooth operator. 'Give the mile girls their due. You and I definitely played second fiddle tonight.'

'Second fiddle, my ass,' responded Washington. 'It's just because she's a gorgeous blonde bimbo.'

Huffner said nothing.

They sat, with just twenty-two dispirited reporters in the room. Downstairs, the Lord Mayor was climbing into his bullet-proof Rolls-Royce.

24

Friday, 10 August–Saturday, 11 August

LONDON AND PARIS

Throughout the media conference, Mark Whyte remained seated quietly on a chair near the front of the room, close to the exit. He was one of the media people who realised what was going to happen and had claimed an early seat. He wore the white Bannister baseball cap which kept his face largely in shadow. Gone were the black-rimmed glasses and expensive leather jacket. In their place he wore a bulky black denim jacket over a black polo-necked sweater with Levi's jeans and heavy Asics trainers. He wanted to be easily missed in the crowd.

He carried a briefcase that on closer inspection would have revealed contents entirely unsuited to a sports media conference. Such an inspection would have confirmed that Mark Whyte had no intention of remaining in Great Britain for long. No one gave him a second look, apart from one particular volunteer, the only person in the room wearing an earpiece.

As Hardy called 'time', Mark stood, quickly moved to the front, snapped a couple of close-up shots of Abby on his iPhone and exited the room through a side door. Moving quickly, he was the first person to reach the special media-only elevator and the first to go through the restricted entrance into the drop-off area outside the stadium. Following a route he had planned earlier, he walked towards the Stratford tube station.

Upstairs, the volunteer with the earpiece spoke into a walkie-talkie. 'Gary, subject has exited and I expect he'll leave the building soon. Go to the media exit door and continue to follow. We have to see where he goes. Get on a train or bus with him if necessary. QSH wants to know what he's up to. We think he'll go to his hotel in Earl's Court but just make sure. Whatever you do, for

THE FINAL LAP

God's sake don't lose him. Technically he's not committed any crime and the boss's only concern is that he somehow interferes with Dennison. Honestly, in my mind this is just a sad guy and the sooner he leaves England the better. We have to watch him until Tuesday apparently.'

As Mark expected, there were throngs of people moving in the same direction, and he joined them, slowing down noticeably. As they approached the tube station, the crowds thickened and slowed even more. The second tailing man moved closer to Mark but the crowds kept getting in the way. Fortunately, a white baseball cap on a tall man was a useful beacon as it bobbed up and down in the crowd.

Just before they reached the entrance to the station, Mark removed the white cap and gave it to a tall young man next to him. 'This is a limited edition souvenir cap from the meeting, I don't need it, I have two,' he said, smiling. The man looked at him for a moment then said, 'Gee thanks, mate' and put it on.

As he did that, Mark reached into a pocket, withdrew a black baseball cap, put it on his head and swerved quickly out of the crowded station entrance. Joining a crowd outside a pub in the street, he went inside. Following another planned route, he walked down a narrow, dark passage away from the bar area towards the men's toilet, and exited through a service door into a deserted alley.

About thirty metres away, the tailing man was becoming frantic. Then he spotted it, the key white cap. He approached, only to find to his horror that the cap now belonged to another man. 'Where did you get that cap?' he asked anxiously.

'Dunno, some bloke gave it to me as a souvenir. Nice chap, he was. First a world record by that Zimbabwean lady, now a special edition cap. What a night!'

What a night indeed. The second man got onto his walkie-talkie. 'Bloody hell, Johnny, he gave me the slip. Definitely planned. He was really good in the crowd, I had no chance. Better call QSH.' Johnny did that and the words uttered by his boss upstairs in the VIP centre caused three smartly dressed women close by to look up startled, then blush, then giggle into their hands.

A kilometre away, Mark walked westwards in the direction of the Holiday Inn. Just before he arrived, he pulled his phone out of his jacket pocket. Less than a minute later, an Uber driver pulled up in a hybrid Toyota. Whyte climbed in and instructed the driver to take him to St Pancras station.

Arriving there, he checked into an inexpensive hotel across the road, where he enjoyed a good night's sleep and was reunited with the rest of his luggage, which he had arranged with a local courier service to deliver earlier in the day from the Earl's Court hotel.

He rose early the next morning, caught the 07h55 Eurostar train, travelled across the English countryside for a while, read *The Guardian* during the uneventful underground crossing to France and exited the Gare du Nord station in the French capital two hours and twenty-two minutes later.

During the crossing, a bored-looking British immigration official casually glanced at his South African passport with its valid multiple-entry Schengen and United Kingdom visas. Just before the train arrived in Paris, his French counterpart, smelling of garlic and Gitanes, didn't even bother to look at it.

It was mid-morning on a beautiful late summer's day in the French capital. The Emirates flight out of Charles de Gaulle was only due to leave at ten that night, so Mark enjoyed a relaxed breakfast of hot croissants and coffee at a sidewalk café close to the Eiffel Tower before taking a Métro train to the Musée d'Orsay, where they were holding a special exhibition of Impressionist paintings. Crossing the Pont Royal bridge over the Seine towards the Tuileries Garden afterwards, Mark reviewed the events of the previous week. All in all, he decided, it had been a worthwhile exercise, the world record, the media conferences, everything.

The website thing had been a bit stressful, but in the end the exercise of changing hotels, catching the Eurostar and spending a day in Paris had been an unexpected pleasure.

But perhaps the most fun had been fooling the guys following him. They really didn't have much of a clue. He'd spotted the man following him in Hyde Park and then the same guy lingering under a lamppost outside his hotel. What did they think he was, some sort of idiot?

Less than twenty-four hours later, Mark came through immigration and customs at Johannesburg's OR Tambo International Airport into the middle of an unseasonal late winter thunderstorm.

25

Saturday, 11 August

ATHLETES' HOTEL, LONDON

A deep low-pressure front had moved in from the northern polar regions overnight, bringing a sudden chill to the air and causing the temperature to fall by about eight degrees. Grey clouds blotted out the sun and a steady rain was falling, the monotonous drip-drip adding to the gloom of a wet London day.

The Team plus Deon had moved into a new central London base, the Parkwood at Marble Arch, that morning. It was a relief for everyone to get away from the Stratford area, a bit run-down and boring by London standards. To be honest, they all wanted to get away from the looming edifice of the stadium, now more of a reminder of the disastrous mile race than a symbol of sporting brilliance.

Deon had joined the Team for lunch and Abby had been pleased to see him. Avoiding any discussion about the race, the five of them had concentrated on deciding where Abby and Deon would be going for their 'escape from the city and everything to do with athletics', which is how Paul had described it. Abby brightened noticeably at this and, after evaluating a variety of possible destinations, they agreed that Oxford would be ideal.

Abby said, 'I love the idea of the place's history, architecture and general beauty. Nothing at all like what we've been living in for the past months. A total change.'

Paul called James, who promised to set it up with a rental car and a night's accommodation. They would leave the following morning, Sunday.

Now it was mid-afternoon, Deon had gone for a long walk and Abby was sitting at a table in the Team's suite, idly scrolling on her iPhone. Bronwyn sat close by on a couch, watching her. 'The forecast says it will clear tomorrow. That means our trip to Oxford will at least be dry,' Abby said, without taking her eyes off the phone. Her mood had deteriorated noticeably since lunch.

'Good.'

'I'm not sure it will help. I mean, what's the point?'

'You know what the point is. It's about getting stories out there, like we all agreed. That's the point.'

'Stories of a loser. Who will be interested now?'

'Come here.'

Abby crossed the room and sat next to her mentor. She burst into tears and flung her arms around the older woman's neck. 'It's not fair, it wasn't my fault. All that work for nothing.'

'I know, you know, we all know, everyone knows. It wasn't your fault. And it wasn't for nothing, you broke the world record, for heaven's sake.'

'That's also not the point.' Between sobs.

'What is the point then?'

Abby wiped her eyes on the sleeve of her tracksuit top. 'This is the point. When Mom was killed, I suddenly learned that there are bad people in the world. People with bad motives; no love, just pure selfishness. Then I kind of got over it and running filled the gap. Mom is still here in my head and I run for her, you know that. Now that thing called evil, or whatever it is, has hit me again. Olga, a runner, a sportswoman, supposed to obey the unwritten laws of sport, fair competition, the best person wins and all of that. She goes out there, in front of all those people and tries to destroy my life, while ruining hers at the same time. I don't get it. It's a bit like a suicide bomber. Diabolical.'

Bronwyn said nothing for a while, then, 'You are completely correct. We can never escape bad people for ever. It's a life lesson. Somehow, we need to cope with that and make sure we never do the same to others. Always remember, like your mom, it was not your fault. You were the victim.'

'But in a way it was my fault. I was warned.'

Bronwyn looked at her, startled. 'What?'

'JP.'

'JP what?'

'He warned me, said he had followed Olga's life story, analysed interviews and online posts and found early photos available on obscure Russian websites. She grew up in a sad family with physical and substance abuse. She developed an unhealthy streak, allegedly even some sort of criminality in her past. But she was a brilliant natural athlete and the Russian athletics system took over. That effectively saved her and eventually she became number one in the world. Amazing story. But once I took her ranking away, which was basically everything she had, she developed some sort of hatred for me, according to JP's analysis. He said that she would do anything to destroy my career. Take it away like I had taken hers away. He told me to stay well away from her in the race and I didn't. It was the only thing he told me that I ignored. And look what happened.'

Bronwyn was shocked. 'When did he say that?'

'In the warm-up area, just before the race.'

'Where is JP now?'

'I don't know. Haven't seen him since lunch. He's probably out walking in the rain. We've hardly spoken since the race. He looked broken last night, poor guy.'

Just then they heard a voice raised in anger in the next room. It was Paul. 'James, I don't care what you say. That was a deliberate attempt to sabotage the whole race. You can't just let that chaos be handled by a bunch of athletics officials. It was economic sabotage or something. This is England, not some banana republic where criminals walk free. That woman must be arrested, charged with something. Millions of pounds were invested in that race. Get the police involved, for God's sake, do something!'

There was silence for a while, then Paul said, 'I know it was completely out of your control, unprecedented, but people like Fedorova need to be taught a lesson.'

More silence. Bronwyn looked at Abby, whose face was now a stricken mask, tear-stained.

She said quietly into Bronwyn's shoulder, 'Stop it, Dad. Please.'

Paul's voice quietened, 'Okay, James, let me know. Thanks, I know you and your bank have also suffered damage. And please know this: my outburst is not because my daughter lost a race she should have won. Moyo was in the right place at the right time. I just want some sort of justice.'

Paul came into the room. 'Hello baby, how are you feeling? Sorry you had to hear that.' He put his hand on Abby's shoulder and she held it tightly with both of hers.

'Oh Dad, I don't know what to say. I've never felt so disappointed in my life. It seems like it's all a waste of time, this running stuff. I just got a text from Marie-Louise, remember her, she was in my matric class. She messaged me to say she saw the race and was sorry that I didn't win, but well done anyway for nearly breaking the record. I mean … Anyway, she's in her final year at med school and is going to be an intern at Victoria Hospital in Cape Town next year. And Jennifer Adams has just given birth to twins. Can you believe that, two kids and she's only twenty-four. She's now Jennifer van der Walt, the gorgeous one, married Craig, the rugby captain. Deon's big mate.'

'Good for them. Anyway, you're now the second-fastest mile runner ever. Not too shabby. Soon you will be the fastest, if some lunatic doesn't try to stop you.'

'How do I know that there aren't more lunatics out there?'

'There probably are. But it's up to us to identify them, protect you and stay well away from them. Give them no chance.'

'I don't know, Dad. That's easy to say. Right now, I'm honestly considering taking a break from running, maybe a month, maybe a year, maybe forever.'

Bronwyn raised her hand. 'Abby, we all love you. Go to Oxford with Deon tomorrow, take your mind off the race.'

'Okay. Deon is just what I need right now. No disrespect, but someone my own age, outside the Team, smart, funny, adorable in a way.'

Paul raised his eyebrows. 'Adorable?'

'*Ja*. My type of guy. Cuddly, if you ignore his old clothes and smelly shoes.' She smiled for the first time in a while.

'Have fun, baby. With your smart, funny, adorable friend. And, honestly, our family has suffered under two separate criminal attacks, the first when

Mom was killed, now the Olga thing. The chances of that happening again are close to zero.'

He was completely wrong.

Fifteen minutes later, Abby left the hotel. The rain had reduced to a misty drizzle but she walked under a wide umbrella anyway. No one noticed that one of the most recognisable sportswomen in Britain was walking through London on a Saturday afternoon in the miserable weather.

She dawdled aimlessly, head down, shivering in the cold, hidden under her umbrella. She opted to move away from the busy roads around Hyde Park and soon found herself in Oxford Square. She smiled. Oxford? Maybe some sort of foretaste of what was to come with Deon.

Rounding a corner, she found St John's Church, a beautiful early Victorian Anglican building. A sign outside read 'Welcome' and, hoping just to find somewhere dry, she pushed open the high wooden door and went inside. Immediately the warmth, calm and beauty of the interior took her breath away. She stood and stared at the high, beamed ceiling, wooden pews, stained glass windows and shining altar. There were a few people seated silently on the pews and Abby sat down in the back row. She didn't know what to do, so she just closed her eyes.

After a few minutes she heard movement as people came and went and then there was a whispered voice nearby. 'You look a little lost. Can I help you?' She looked up into the smiling face of an old man with white hair and round, rimless glasses.

'I'm Father Clive, and you look cold.'

'Oh, goodness, I just came in and sat down. Is that okay?' She stared up at him.

'Of course. You look familiar. Have you been here before?'

'Well, no. I'm from South Africa.' She waited for the inevitable.

There was silence for a few seconds, then, 'It wasn't fair,' he said quietly.

'What!'

'That Russian woman crashing into the two of you. And poor Elinah.'

Abby was speechless. 'I was there,' he continued, 'a big athletics fan. Up in row WW, couldn't afford anything closer.'

'You mean …'

'Yes. But now, why are you here? How are you feeling? You must be devastated.'

Abby was breathless. This was totally weird. 'I am. Honestly, I don't know if it's all worth it, this running stuff. Nine years ago, my mom was shot by kidnappers, and now this. Why is the world such a bad place? I am genuinely considering stopping this running business, getting a normal life.'

Father Clive sat down next to her. 'My dear Abby, you are completely correct. I read about your mother, I've followed your career for years. Indeed, the world sometimes seems to be a bad place. But we as Christians have a view on this. Why not come into my humble office, have a hot cup of tea and we can discuss things. I'm pretty sure it will help you decide whether or not to continue running. Everyone has a gift, including you, and we are taught to use our gifts, whatever they are.'

'Is running fast for a few minutes a gift?'

'Of course, a very special gift from God. The Apostle Peter wrote, "As each has received a gift, use it to serve one another, as good stewards of God's grace."'

'What does that mean? Use my ability to run fast to serve others?'

'In a way, it's a duty we all have, to use whatever gifts we have, be it running fast like you, or preaching in a church like me. I can explain if you like. Come with me.'

They went through the church, across a courtyard and into a small office. 'Tea?'

They sat. 'Thanks, this is such a beautiful, peaceful place,' said Abby in wonder.

An hour later, she went back to the hotel. The drizzle had stopped.

26

Sunday, 12 August

LONDON AND OXFORD

The M40 goes from London to the university city of Oxford through Buckinghamshire, an easy two-hour drive. Abby and Deon left after a late breakfast. The weather had cleared and she'd gone for an hour's run in Hyde Park, early enough for the place to be deserted, apart from a few joggers and dog-walkers.

Deon recalled the discussion he'd had with James at accreditation about this trip with Abby. It seemed like a lifetime ago.

He was delighted with the Oxford idea. The cherry on the top had been a call from Charlie Savage that went something like this, 'You and your precious Abby have interrupted my weekend poker game, so I'll make this quick. Your reports on the Bannister meeting got us the highest readership ratings we've had so far this year, but don't get too cocky, the story was too big to spoil. Now you're going off gallivanting for a dirty weekend with the lady in question, but all I ask is that you produce the goods. I want in-depth stuff about her, profile pieces, well-balanced, informative content that includes more than just running. But leave out the parts where …'

Deon cut him off. 'Charlie, this is no sort of dirty …'

'*Ja, ja.* Heard that before. But hormones will always be hormones. Now I have to get back to my game. See you in a week, champ. Oh, and your reports were superb. Top drawer. Keep it up.' With a chuckle he was gone.

Selfe had rented a mid-sized Toyota and they carefully navigated traffic out of the city, threading their way from Marble Arch onto the A5, then onto the A40 at Edgware Road tube station.

The first few minutes, with only the two of them in the car, were awkward. Being together for a couple of days was new territory for them so Deon decided to lighten things up. 'You know my boss, Charlie Savage? Well, he likes to stir things up and believes he can say anything and get away with it. He told me we're just going off on a dirty weekend.'

'Sounds exciting. I've never done that. I wouldn't know what to do.' She giggled. 'Have you ever done it? A dirty weekend, I mean.'

'A couple of times.'

'Were they fun?'

'Hell no. I was worried about someone finding out. Every time there was a knock at the door from room service I dived under the bed.'

She laughed, genuinely amused. That broke the ice.

Deon asked her, 'Honestly, Abs, how are you? That chaos on Friday night was the worst thing I've ever seen at a sports event.'

She hesitated. 'Initially, I was completely confused, had no idea what was going on. It all happened so fast. Then it sank in – I had lost the race and the world record through no fault of my own. After all that work. I went into a kind of depression yesterday, even told Dad and Mizadams that all this running stuff wasn't worth it. I wanted to be like my schoolmates with university degrees and starting families. Then I met an old guy called Pastor Clive, who told me about using gifts to help people. Don't ask – I'll tell you about it when the time is right. But that was yesterday and this is today. Right now, I don't know, honestly, my mind is a jumble. So here's the plan – let's do this Oxford thing, but with one rule. You don't try to counsel me, make me feel better. Let's have fun, pretend we're on holiday. I've put the whole running thing on hold, at some point something will just click and I'll move forward. The direction of that move? I don't know. Do we have a deal?'

'Deal,' he said, and that was that.

She switched on the radio. 'Eighties music, my dad's favourite stuff. Queen, Whitney Houston, ABBA, Bruce Springsteen. Dad found a station called Absolute 80s Radio.' She punched in some numbers and the music started.

'That's pretty cool,' he said, and meant it.

London was much like any other English city. Low-rise houses packed together, rows and rows of them, their front doors leading directly onto the street, chimneys peeping out of roofs. Small shops – mom-and-pop grocers, tobacconists, hair salons, pharmacies, pubs, gift stores and dress boutiques – lined the streets in a never-ending stream of commerce.

The road was busy. There were cars, bicycles, red London buses, black London cabs, ladies pushing prams, a few joggers, hawkers and newspaper sellers. There seemed to be endless signs telling people what to do: stop, go, slow down, park here, don't park here, taxis only, pedestrians only, walk, don't walk, pick up your dog's poo, no dogs allowed.

Abby looked relaxed and her eyes closed for a while. Then she sat up straight, clicked her knuckles one by one, yawned and said, 'How is this going to work? I mean, what's the plan? Are you going to question me about everything a hundred journalists have already covered?'

He thought about that, then responded carefully, 'Here's how: you make the rules, you decide what to do, what to say, when to say it. I'm not a reporter, I'm your friend.'

'Sounds like a therapist. But what about wearing your reporter's hat? You have to tell people stuff about me that they don't already know. Build the profile.' She made it sound like a criminal's rap sheet.

The question was one he'd been pondering. 'The idea *is* to build a profile, but I'm not going to question or interview you in a formal kind of sense. Basically, I want you to have a good time, relax, get away from the stress of competing and just talk. You choose the subjects. Whatever's on your mind. Whatever you want to share.'

'Talk. Mmmm. I can do that. But what are you going to do with all this talk?'

'Paint word-pictures.'

She thought about that for a while. 'Can I talk about anything? Will your so-called word-pictures include everything I say?'

'Absolutely not. There are broadly two types of things we can talk about. The first is stuff you are willing to share with the world. The second is private stuff. Just you and me and no one else. But be sure to alert me so that I know when to stop making word-pictures.'

'That works for me. Actually, this is really funny. And sad. All those people wanting to know what I like, don't like, hope for, am scared of, dream about, plan for. Haven't they got better things to do? I mean, like, I'm just a person who can run fast.'

He said, 'Psychologists understand that people have a deep need to create heroes and role models for themselves. As children our first role models are usually our parents and, as we grow older, we form relationships with admired mentors at school or work. Later, some people obsessively study the lives of athletes, movie stars, television or music personalities, sports teams. Sometimes the adulation borders on some sort of worship or even fantasised romantic love.'

'Sounds unhealthy.'

'It's seldom pathological, although in extreme cases it can be. Many people have boring, humdrum lives and escape by having imagined relationships with their heroes. Another common reason is that these figureheads give them stability during challenging or dangerous times. When people have role models to look up to, they feel comforted, at least for a while. Often, if a person is passionate about a particular area of life, like music or sport, they find a hero in that same space to look up to.'

Abby thought about that. 'And mass communication is king.'

'Absolutely. That's my game and that's why I'm so careful to put information out there that is factual, without bias. Relevant, uplifting and interesting. Never, ever, salacious.'

'No fake news.'

'Sadly, there is more fake news than real news. Every Tom, Dick and Mary with a phone and a Facebook page is now a reporter and journalist. Sad, and dangerous.'

'Dangerous?'

'Yes. Incorrect information about someone can be dangerous, especially if it's salacious or inflammatory. Images and videos are taken without consent. Pictures are doctored, innocent women are turned into centrefolds.'

She groaned. 'Imagine that. A million men ogling me. Hilarious.'

The conversation went on for the next two hours. She talked, he listened;

he talked, she listened. They were serious, they laughed, they covered reddening faces in embarrassment, she cried (twice), they told jokes (badly), shared secrets, expressed hopes, fears and ambitions, opened up about what they liked and disliked and whom they unreservedly loved.

The conversation wasn't wall-to-wall, though. It stopped and started, punctuated by long silences, especially when they were passing through interesting or pretty countryside. By early afternoon, they had reached the outskirts of Oxford and pulled into the parking lot of The Head of the River, near the centre of town, overlooking the Thames.

By now, they were relaxed in each other's company and navigated the check-in procedure – two separate double rooms – without any embarrassment. 'This is a business trip,' Deon told the proprietor, a stern-looking lady in her fifties who seemed doubtful. Halfway through the registration process, the inevitable happened. The son of the owner, a guy in his twenties with a shaven head and beard, stuck his head around a door and exclaimed, 'My God, it's Abby Dennison! 'Struth! Look, Ma, the runner! I'm Liam. Welcome to our humble hostelry.' Grabbing Abby's hand, he pumped it vigorously. 'You're the most famous person to come here since Ringo Starr back in the nineties. This is one for the gallery in the pub.' He fished a phone out of the pocket of his jeans.

Abby grinned sheepishly. 'Never been compared to Ringo,' she muttered as images were captured.

Liam ignored Deon totally. He could have been invisible.

They emerged from their rooms forty minutes later. Abby had transformed into a person he scarcely recognised. Gone were the jeans, T-shirt and running shoes from the morning. In their place she wore a long-sleeved pale blue linen shirt that buttoned up to her throat under a figure-hugging brown leather jacket with several pockets guarded by shiny silver zips. For one of the first times since school he saw her in something other than athletic gear, jeans or tracksuit pants. She had on a black and white checked mini-skirt that ended a few centimetres above her knees. She wore brown calf-length boots, dangly hooped earrings and around her neck a thick gold chain with a crucifix at the end.

'We good to go?' she asked, grinning, hooking her arm through his. 'Show me the sights of Oxford, kind sir.' Liam looked up, dropped his phone.

Neither of them had been in Oxford before, but Deon had taken a virtual tour on Google and had a rough idea of where to go. It was a brilliant Sunday afternoon, temperatures in the high twenties with clear skies. They stepped out.

It was like walking into some sort of fascinating freak show.

The local folk were out in their droves in what was clearly a university town. The average age was under thirty and there was every sort of fashion statement out there: cut-off jeans full of ragged holes, numerous T-shirts with a variety of slogans ranging from a fat guy with 'I beat anorexia', a girl with 'I'm not as think as you drunk I am' to Abby's favourite, 'FBI. Female Body Inspector'. Footwear ranged from unshod filthy feet, through sandals and ancient running shoes to knee-high boots and fluffy slippers.

They weren't all shaggy students, however. Earnest looking older men in tweed jackets and clutching briefcases walked along, eyes on the ground. One old lady had a ginger cat on a lead. A barefoot homeless man wearing black garbage bags tied up with pieces of string held out an empty tin, hoping for a coin. Two policemen in smart navy-blue uniforms and pointy helmets spoke into walkie-talkies.

There were numerous tattoos, beards, shaven heads, Afros and piercings all over the place, many hidden and undoubtedly in unmentionable places.

A foursome of rowers powered down the river, the cox screaming instructions through a bullhorn. Preparing for the Oxford and Cambridge boat race?

Shirtless men with ponytails piloted skateboards, a girl rode a bicycle with a ginger cat in a basket in the front, a yellow Rolls-Royce cruised past, rap music blaring.

Abby looked like a fashion icon at a jumble sale. Even so, in that environment, no one gave her a second glance.

They wandered around the city, its ancient buildings and narrow cobbled side-streets contrasting, ancient versus modern, with posh boutiques and

Michelin-graded restaurants.

There were the colleges – Merton, Balliol, St Peter's, Magdalen – big cathedrals and small churches, libraries, art galleries and renowned institutes. It was like walking through history.

There was also the natural beauty of the place: rambling parks, grassy and welcoming, narrow little walkways alongside the river, bridges, moorings with small barges, clusters of brightly coloured flowers in window pots, doors painted red, green, purple and yellow.

Part of the plan was for Deon to take a series of images to go with the written profile pieces and reinforce the story of Abby, 'the person behind the athlete'. He had taken a photographic course as part of his training and over the years had developed an excellent eye for composition, light and mood.

After two hours he had captured several dozen images of the kind never before seen of one of the world's most recognisable sportswomen.

In the parks, the streets, the shops and alongside the river, he photographed her smiling happily, then frowning, then sad and wistful. He captured her face staring up at the sky, eyes wide in wonder; in other images she raised her arms to the sky, wrapped them around herself as if cold, and made fists as if ready for a fight.

She thoughtfully contemplated Magdalen College, its ancient buildings hinting at half a millennium of scholars, statesmen, poets, scientists and philosophers passing through its doors, changing the world and building its history.

He captured her image in a smart boutique, the saleswoman showing her a slinky evening dress; another was of Abby grinning as she posed wearing a broad sunhat with faux sunflowers around its rim.

They sat outside a coffee shop, drinking cappuccinos as a bearded musician serenaded her while playing a battered guitar. Deon captured an image of him bowing deeply as she put a ten-pound note into his hand.

As they approached their inn, Deon photographed her in the late-afternoon sunlight gazing at the gentle Thames and the elegant, snow-white swans that made their way under Folly Bridge.

These would become images that would travel the world on the internet, be downloaded, studied, photoshopped, printed and stuck to walls, licensed for advertising campaigns, enlarged, framed and hung in galleries, turned into fuzzy black and white renditions in photographic magazines, used in a new Oxford tourism marketing campaign – look who was here!

Images that would forever change the world's perception of Abby Dennison, athlete.

Then she said, 'Deon, please stop. Stand over there, under those trees.' They were in a small park and few people were around. 'I want another picture, just for me, on my phone. I want to remember today, the peacefulness of it, the lack of pressure to perform, the chance to be just me.' A woman walking past offered to take a photo of the two of them. Snap. Smiling, she walked off without a word. Clearly not an athletics fan.

Abby put her arm around his waist, leaned in and kissed him on the cheek. A long kiss, maybe five seconds. 'Thank you,' she said simply as he just stood there.

Eventually they arrived back at their hotel. Liam, predictably, was there to greet them. Before Deon could say anything, he began to speak. It was like a machine gun firing. 'Time for a drink, we have four different local ales, what about a G and T for the lady, you look pretty hot, all the drinks are on the house, are your rooms okay, no, I'm sure alcohol is not what you want, we have local fruit juices and I make an excellent Steelworks and …' Gasping for air, he seemed to run out of things to say.

Abby smiled at him. He was funny in a strange, loveable sort of way. 'Here's where you can really help,' Deon said, and Liam almost sat up and panted like a dog, so excited was he to help the great Abby D. 'There's this athletics track on the other side of the park. Can you perhaps find out if we can go and run there tomorrow morning early, about seven o'clock?'

Liam scurried off and they walked to their rooms. 'Fifteen minutes from now in the pub?' Abby looked tired, relaxed and happy all at the same time.

'Done.'

Liam was waiting, clearly excited, back in the bar. 'Spoke to the guv'nor at the track. He'll be there early to open up. Special concession. Just wants a selfie and an autograph.' Abby sighed.

The evening rolled on, drinks, a decent dinner in the hotel restaurant presided over, not surprisingly, by Liam, who mercifully left them alone most of the time. They talked some more. It was like a floodgate opening. Deon didn't do much more than ask a few questions and make the occasional comment. For Abby, this was like a release, the chance to express herself as a person, not a runner. The more she spoke, the more liberated she felt.

It was after ten when they finished their coffees and, a first for Abby, a small glass of Jägermeister. After spluttering as the potent liquid hit her throat, she leaned across the table and whispered in his ear, 'Thank you, Deon. I feel free, like a weight has been lifted off my mind. I'm not sure exactly what you're going to do with all this stuff, but I trust you with it.'

'I will use it carefully. I need to think about today and how I'm going to frame Abby Dennison as more, far more, than just an athlete. But you can trust me, I promise.' And he meant it.

They were about to stand up to leave when her hand arrived on his wrist. 'Hang on a sec, Deon,' she said. 'There's one more thing, but this is between you and me, no media, no Paul or Bronwyn, just us.'

'What?' The air seemed to have cooled.

'It's probably just my imagination, but every now and then, back in Joburg, I feel watched. Like someone is out there, tracking me. It's not something I can pin down like an actual face, but rather a presence, if you know what I mean.'

'Sort of, tell me more.'

'It's always a car, driving slowly along, kind of on the same route as me. Twice I've changed my route and it's still there. Also outside my house. A fancy sports car. But this has only happened a few times, maybe four or five.'

Deon was horrified. 'Let me chat to Paul, maybe you need security.'

'Absolutely not. Paul will freak and then I'll have security guys all over the place. No, when I'm home I'll be extra careful and call you if this happens again. Thanks, Deon, I just need to know someone has my back. End of discussion.'

It was, and they mounted the creaky flight of stairs to the first floor, where her room was. Deon went up another flight to his room which looked out over the river.

For a while he stared out at the now eerily quiet city and reflected on the stuff that Abby had said about the kerb crawler, filing it away mentally. Then he went to the desk in the corner of his room and made notes, lots and lots of notes. It took an hour of careful remembering. The notes weren't in any way verbatim, but designed, in a short-hand sort of way, to capture the essence of what she had said. He teased out the highlights, knowing that they would become the foundation of the series of articles to come.

He wrote:

Why do you run?
Because I love it/the freedom/the feeling of going faster and faster/the initial pain in my body that goes away/the beauty of my surroundings/it's my gift from God, like the pastor said.

Why do you compete?
Because I have been blessed with remarkable ability/it's in my genes/to be honest, I love winning/improving my times/setting records/being the best I can be.

The best part of a race?
The final lap.

Why is the Team so important?
Like lions, we are family-oriented, communal creatures/they are my family/each has a different role/Dad loves, guides and protects me/Mizadams listens to me, motivates me, gives me strength, in a way my replacement mother/JP is my coach/he helps me do my best and win.

How much do you enjoy the lifestyle of being a full-time athlete?
It used to be exciting but I resent it now/it's become tedious/I feel like I have no real home.

Is running enough for you now and if not, what do you miss?
Many things/a regular, predictable day-week-month-year routine/a permanent home/girlfriends/a break from running without feeling guilty/driving and walking in the bush with the animals and birds/a Highveld thunderstorm/sleepover parties/a puppy of my own/being free from constant intrusive attention/not being 'on show' the whole time/most of all, intellectual stuff, brain stuff.

Brain stuff?
My brain is not used, only my body/my brain feels like my appendix, it's there but has no apparent use/I want to learn, study, become something besides a runner/I want to debate, converse, argue, research, teach, influence people, write exams, graduate, be a thought leader.

Other passions?
The African bush, the animals and birds/Kruger, Sabi Sands, Kgalagadi, Sossusvlei/classical music, especially Liszt, Tchaikovsky and Mozart/science-fiction movies/Scrabble/concerts at the Linder in Johannesburg/singing and maybe being in a choir/Greek mythology/the Bible.

What effect did your mother's death have on you?
Profound/life-altering/but motivating/I run for her as well as myself and the Team/I believe that she knows about my success but I'm not sure.

What are you afraid of in running?
Afraid of injuries/afraid of being caught for doping even though I would never use a banned substance/afraid of not doing my best.

What are you afraid of outside of running?
I am afraid of illness or death in Team members/flying in a thunderstorm/spiders and snakes/being poisoned (isn't that ridiculous?)/waking up naked in a busy street/being raped, hijacked or attacked in the dark/I'm still affected by the attack on my mother/being thought of as a symbol rather than a person/being old and lonely and alone/never having children.

Do you feel conflicted because your running stops you from all those other things, and yet it is your destiny, your calling?
I never used to feel conflicted but now that thought is becoming more prominent.

Finally, what thought would you like to leave with me?
Is winning enough?

Deon switched off the light at midnight, crawled into bed and slept the sleep of the truly exhausted. He had no idea that, just before 01h00 Abby, unable to sleep, put on a tracksuit, quietly left the hotel, walked to the river in the moonlight and sat on a bench watching the slow, gentle passing of the water. Only the murmuring of night-time frogs broke the silence. Then, cheeks moist from silent tears, she went back to her room, closed her eyes, said a quiet prayer and finally fell asleep.

They met outside the next morning just before seven. Abby was back in runner mode and he was half asleep but they did a few loops of the park in gorgeous early morning sunshine before heading off to the Iffley Road Sports Centre, where Joseph Henderson, the chief groundsman, stood with local runners Davis, Meryl, Tom, Harold, another Tom, and Beatrice, who wasn't a runner but wanted to meet Abby.

After a shower and a quick bag pack, they were downstairs for breakfast, which included Liam's 'house special: a self-styled omelette with local 'erbs and spices, local farm-fresh eggs and full-fat milk'.

Abby enjoyed that while Deon stuck with muesli and coffee.

The trip back to London was strangely subdued. Conversation was sporadic and brief, rather like the end of a holiday or the first freezing wind and frost of a Highveld winter.

About twenty minutes before they arrived at the Parkwood at Marble Arch, something happened that would be etched in Deon's memory for ever. It was such a bizarre, unexpected surprise. They were in the traffic when his phone rang. It was James Selfe. On an impulse, Deon stopped the car and said, 'Let me take this outside. It may be important.' Abby looked at him, confused and a little apprehensive. It was an unwelcome intrusion.

'Deon, can you speak privately?'

'Yes. What's up?'

'Plenty. Listen carefully. For now, this is for your ears only. It concerns Abby and the Team, and Paul has been briefed. I suggest you tell Abby now, before you get back to the hotel. We trust your judgement on this. Don't worry, it's nothing sinister or bad, just very different. You need to pitch it to Abby as a wonderful opportunity.'

Deon was surprised that James hadn't asked about the Oxford trip, like it was some sort of past-tense issue, done, gone. A truck passed by, belching black smoke and Deon hoped it wasn't some sort of omen.

'Shoot.'

'After the Moyo win on Friday, the crash on the track, Abby's second place and several runners breaking the record, the board of Regalbank had an emergency meeting this morning. Paul Dennison was there. Looking at the vast exposure it generated all over the world, especially in America, which is now an emerging and key market for us, we as a bank have a brilliant commercial opportunity. Today the board decided to create a once-off incentive in the women's mile. Next year there will be a mile race specially set up to achieve a particular time. The eight best runners in the world will be invited. There was a lot of discussion about the venue and Paul suggested that this special, once-off race takes place in Durban, South Africa, in April next year. We debated this for ages and eventually the board agreed. Paul and I then called the president of the South African athletics federation and he immediately agreed to it. We chose Durban because of its perfect southern hemisphere autumn weather and, obviously, because it's in Abby's home country. Tomorrow we will announce this incentive to the world through the bank's media machine. Now …'

Deon stopped him in mid-flow. 'Wait a minute, James, just hang on there! You are going to make the biggest track race of the year *in Durban*?'

'Think about it, Deon. Abby is the biggest name in women's athletics but Sarah Moyo beat her. Abby is South African, Moyo is Zimbabwean. We can't wait a year for this thing to happen, it has to be in less than eight months' time. Later than that and the momentum will be lost. We can't risk doing it in the northern hemisphere winter or even spring, too risky weather-wise. Durban is perfect, April is perfect. What a way to kick off the world track and field season.'

Deon thought about that, standing in the street with his phone pressed to his ear, with cars, buses and pedestrians passing by. Abby peered through the window, opening her hands and raising her shoulders in a 'what's going on?' gesture.

Deon said, 'I presume there's more.'

'Yes, but that will come later, after the board has spent more time doing the budgets. We'll announce the details as soon as we can.'

'Thanks for the heads-up, James, I'll tell Abby now.'

Sitting in the car, he told her about the new race, the date and the Durban venue. It was quiet for a while and they heard nothing but passing traffic. Then she said, 'I don't know what to say. I have no idea whether I'll run this race. I'm tired of all the pressure. First the Fedorova thing in the Bannister race, now this big race in Durban. It's all a bit much right now.' She looked at Deon with beautiful, wide, wet blue eyes and said, 'Please, Deon, I just want to go home.'

27

Two weeks later

LONDON

The announcement was put on Twitter and Facebook, and posted on two websites simultaneously at 09h00, London time. It said:

**Regalbank announces the biggest-ever
financial incentive in athletics**

Monday, 27 August.

Regalbank, proud sponsor of the Roger Bannister Memorial Athletics Meeting, today announced that, as a result of the worldwide interest generated by the women's world mile record established by Sarah Moyo two weeks ago in London, a follow-up race, to be known as the Regalbank Women's Mile Challenge, will offer the biggest-ever financial incentive in the sport.

Should the winner of the Regalbank Women's Mile Challenge break Sarah Moyo's world record time set at the recent Roger Bannister Memorial Athletics Meeting, that athlete will receive an incentive payment of one million American dollars.

Sports fans are reminded that Moyo ran a time of 4:07.25 in London.

The venue for this race has also been decided. After consultations with the relevant athletics authorities in South Africa, it was decided that the race will be held in Durban on 12 April next year.

Further announcements about who will be competing will be made in due course.

In order to simplify the name of this historic race for the media and athletics fans, the Regalbank Women's Mile Challenge will in future be known as R1609, given that the mile distance is exactly 1 609 metres long.

Ends.
For more information, visit www.regalbank.org/athletics or www.r1609.com

PART II

Nearly Five Months Later

28

Monday, 7 January

JOHANNESBURG

It was back-to-work day for Deon and he was in a chirpy mood as he drove up Corlett Drive to the office in light traffic. He loved Johannesburg in the summer holidays as the long, hot days, tempered by the city's high altitude, meant that he could enjoy the warmth without the winds of Cape Town or the stifling humidity of Durban.

In one respect, he didn't enjoy the year-end period. Unlike most folks, he had no close family to share the holidays with, to give presents to and celebrate the new year with. His mother was living in a single room in a government-supported old-age home in Somerset West and his father was into his third marriage and living on the KwaZulu-Natal South Coast.

Just before the sports office at APN had been reduced to a skeleton staff for Christmas, Charlie Savage had called Deon into his office. 'I have to commend you on the Oxford–Dennison series. It was excellent, not only for us as a media house and for you as a journalist, but I'm certain it was good for Abby as well. She's clearly an outstanding young woman, with many interests and talents other than running. You captured the conflict going on in her life – the breadth of her talent, her drive to succeed on one hand, and her intellect and desire to be more than just a runner on the other. It's a difficult situation.'

Deon said, 'I knew intuitively that the series would be good. It's difficult to write something substantial when you have nothing to work with. Silk purses and sows' ears and all that. But Abby is the opposite, she's multi-dimensional and it's difficult to know what to leave out. She is a rich vein of human-interest material, I think I nailed that aspect.'

'I have a question: surely she must have been gutted by the Fedorova incident? Where is she mentally?'

'The Oxford weekend helped a lot. For the first time we connected on a different level. I was no longer the reporter and she the runner, we're close friends now. Remember we have this unique bond – I was there when her mother was killed, I testified at the trial. On the surface she seemed okay, but this is the second time something really bad has happened in her life. She hinted that she may take a break from competitive running. Paul told me she's gone quiet and spends lots of time on her computer.'

'Let's move on.'

The old Charlie returned, the tough boss, looking for more hard-hitting material. 'In January I want two sets of stories from you, to roll out over three weeks. Punchy, informative, a quick read, ending with a teaser to the next one. The first six will look back at what happened after the Bannister meeting in women's middle-distance running.'

'And the second series, a sequel to the first?'

'Yes. In essence, "where to" for that section of athletics this year, including the R1609 plan. Focus mainly on Abby; how do you see her year playing out? What about Moyo? Not a prediction, but an informed outlook. Maybe this, maybe that.'

'Got it, boss.'

Deon always worked better at home, and two days later he went into Charlie's office holding a thin file.

'Here's my plan for the first series. When these are done, I'll bring you the plan for the next six. I'm pretty happy so far, and now you also need to be.'

They worked through the summaries for an hour, changing here, de-emphasising there, adding more emphasis somewhere else. It was intense as they debated, argued and eventually agreed on everything.

Article 1: The Fedorova/Kiptanui incident
Extensive studies of race videos showed that Fedorova intentionally tripped Kiptanui, but she had intended to trip Dennison and mistimed it.

Three months later Fedorova broke down and admitted that she 'kind-of-hated' Abby because she had 'stolen' her ranking. She expressed remorse and said she hoped people would forgive her. Although she formally retired from athletics, she was banned for life by World Athletics and faced charges in the UK if she ever set foot there again.

Article 2: Elinah Kiptanui after London
Kiptanui recovered in a week and was soon back to full training in the Kenyan highlands. She said that she harboured no ill-feelings towards Fedorova, but 'felt sorry for her'.

She ran two more 1 500-metre races before the season's end: a brilliant 3:55.11 in Monaco and 3:59.99 in Barcelona.

Experts were divided as to whether, had the Bannister race proceeded normally, she would have been able to outsprint Moyo and Abby and win the race. The consensus was that she would have achieved a top-three place at best.

She was named Kenyan sportswoman of the year.

Article 3: Sarah Moyo after London
Given the hype around the Bannister race, there was enormous interest around Moyo, her family and coach. The media labelled them 'The Triple-S Brigade'.

After London, Sarah went back to Eldoret in Kenya and did not compete again. It was agreed that she suffered from a type of Asperger's Syndrome, the reason why she avoided media interviews. Note to self: research several other high-profile sportswomen with the same problem, including a ranked tennis player.

Article 4: The world's response to the Regalbank R1609 incentive
Very positive, so much so that the value to Regalbank in marketing terms was calculated to be more than one hundred million dollars before the project had started. It was considered by experts to potentially herald one of the biggest athletics stories in recent years.

The top contenders backed the incentive and promised to be there if possible. The exception was Moyo, who could not be contacted, and Abby, who initially said that she 'would see'.

Regalbank's corporate launch in the United States was a success and the bank was named among the ten most successful sports sponsors of the year in a representative poll across the world in all sports. The bank also announced it would be opening a South African office to 'capitalise on the emerging African market'.

Article 5: The Team's response to the Regalbank incentive
Initially, the Team would not comment on R1609 but in November a South African TV channel persuaded Abby to go on the record. Both Paul and JP were in the interview. She said that she had not decided whether or not to enter the R1609. 'It's a long way off and a lot can happen.'

When questioned about whether the record could be broken again, JP said, 'I suppose everything is possible, like a sub-two-hour marathon. But it will take a super-human effort, and the conditions, both around and in the race, will have to be perfect. No tripping, for example. Perfect pace-setting. A twenty-to-one chance, I'd say. The bank's money is pretty safe. They were very smart with this thing.'

Article 6: The rest of the season
Because of contractual issues, Dennison ran two more races and won both, 3:57.23 in Rome against Beardsley and McColgan and an 800-metre race in Newcastle, England, where she ran 1:56.09, her fastest time for a year and the third fastest of her career.

'I'm tired,' she said after the Newcastle race. 'It's like coming to the end of the lollipop.'

'What are you talking about?' asked the interviewer.

'All you've got left is the stick,' she said, which made no sense to him. It emerged later that she was referring to a 1960s pop song by Max Bygraves.

In the World Championships, the 1 500-metre race was a typical championship competition where no one took the lead. It was won by Jane Beardsley, who found a 58-second last lap to win in 4:08, equivalent to about a 4:30 mile.

Suzy Marshall won a medal in the 800 metres, the bronze; her first-ever championship podium place.

Everyone agreed that, after London, racing became a 'drag' (McColgan's words) but McColgan was aiming to 'become a multi-mega-zillionaire next year'. This comment was voted 'one of the top-five sports quotes of the year' by *Mad* magazine.

Deon and Charlie had a few laughs about all of that and, after a couple of changes, agreed to the format. Deon was about to leave the room when Charlie said quietly, 'Deon, one more thing.'

'Sure, boss.'

'I often like to look behind the sports-star image of successful people and ask what is really going on in their heads, in their lives. Abby is one of these. My gut feel tells me here is a person with huge potential as a runner, but also with fears resulting from her mother's death, and now this Fedorova thing. She's had her support system for years but now I believe that she needs someone new, smart, young and caring to jump in. You are this person. You can help Abby achieve her full potential. Think about it.'

29

Sunday, 27 January

DENNISON FAMILY HOME

JOHANNESBURG

Abby was settled in a chair next to the pool, coffee steaming, waiting for the rest of the Team to arrive for the first planning meeting of the year. Mizadams had spent a month in Australia with her sister, and JP, as usual, went to Stellenbosch, where he kept a small apartment a stone's throw from the Coetzenburg track, centrepiece of the university town's historic sporting precinct.

JP had accepted the temporary post of visiting coach for the Maties Track Club, the athletics section of Stellenbosch University's vast sporting infrastructure. He also spent many nights and weekends completing a coaching manual for middle-distance athletes he'd written a year earlier. The manuscript had been snapped up by an international publisher of sporting books. So widely had his fame as a coach spread that the initial print run of ten thousand copies was sold in less than a month. 'It's going well,' JP said, as if he was talking about the weather.

As she waited for everyone to arrive, Abby thought about the amazing three years since her first international breakthrough race, before JP and Mizadams were on the scene.

It was a Saturday morning and she and Paul were in Brussels. The night before, she had competed in the famous Ivo van Damme Memorial meeting and had been overawed by the sheer scale of the event. It was a 1 500-metre race and six of the top-eight-ranked women were there. She was ranked eleventh and was fortunate to be in the race at all.

The start was slowish and she stayed in the group, not knowing what to do. When Olga Fedorova kicked hard at the bell Abby tucked in behind her as the other runners fell back. She stayed there round the final lap and into the straight. Suddenly she realised the power of her sprint as she ran past Olga and beat her by ten metres. It was the first time she had broken four minutes and she had entered a new world of opportunity.

The next day she was walking in central Brussels past the famous Atomium. On a whim, she stopped next to a traffic officer and told him, 'I can do this. I can be the best runner in the world.' He looked totally confused when she said, 'I'm Abby Dennison, and one day I will break a world record.' They shook hands solemnly.

She charged back to the hotel and breathlessly told Paul, 'This is my life now. I want to be the best and am prepared to sacrifice everything to do that. But I can't do it alone and I need you to work with me.'

'Deal,' he said.

Three months later, Paul hired JP and Mizadams, and the Team developed a professional, full-time plan. They accepted the risks and the sacrifices that would have to be made, especially by Paul and Bron, whose careers would take a ninety-degree turn. Everything was centred on Abby's running. It was all-or-nothing, and they accepted that the normal things people did would no longer be possible for them.

For Abby, it was fun and exciting, new experiences every day: racing, training, travelling to exotic places, meeting people, being interviewed. She was young, talented, earning lots of money, famous and having a great time. But she soon discovered that it was also a fragile, stressful, unstructured existence. At times, she longed for a normal life and became tired of the relentless pressure to perform, to improve, to win more races, set personal bests.

A big challenge was the dope testing. These were both at competitions plus the random tests, where the World Anti-Doping Agency official would arrive after a day's warning wherever she was in the world. Abby had never failed a dope test nor missed an out-of-competition test. In total, she had been subjected to forty-three and the most recent had been two weeks before Christmas.

Now, at the start of another year, the Team had almost reached the pinnacle of the sport with another shot at securing the world record and the chance of an incredible payday.

All these thoughts were put aside when Paul arrived with JP and Bronwyn from the airport. Abby leapt up with a shriek and ran first to Bronwyn and then JP, hugging them in a joyful embrace. The warmth of family, friends, safety, protection and guidance spread through her like a wildfire. Now she knew why she did all of this – it was because of these people, her family, her reason for living.

It was warm but Paul wore a thick pullover, khaki shirt, dark brown trousers and hiking boots. It looked like he was heading off to the bush. Mizadams was in a conservative cream pant suit, a wide-brimmed hat and wore her trademark pearl necklace. She looked like Meryl Streep in *Out of Africa*. JP had on his normal shabby tracksuit over a Bannister T-shirt, running shoes and, bizarrely, a New York Yankees cap. He didn't look like any sort of film star.

Abby had splashed out on a new wardrobe and sported a short, strappy polka-dot sun dress. Her sunglasses were perched on her head. She wanted to look like a modern twenty-four-year-old and JP's frown confirmed that she'd succeeded.

They sat down and Paul said, 'Firstly, our thanks to Bronwyn and JP for coming back to our little Team. For a while I thought that all the ups and downs at the end of last year might have frightened you both off.' He chuckled. 'I know Bron's sister claims she has a boyfriend waiting in the wings for her in Australia and, apparently, Suzy Marshall is looking for a new coach.' He winked and Bronwyn stared daggers at him.

'Marshall doesn't know if she's a runner or a model,' said JP, looking serious. 'I'd never coach her.'

They were quiet for a while, then JP said gently, 'Guys, we all know what this is about. It's the Regalbank Challenge in Durban ten weeks away. James Selfe called Paul yesterday and we need to decide. Either Abby is in, or she's out. By the way, everyone is calling this race R1609, short-hand for Regalbank Mile, quite catchy.'

Abby didn't know about James's call, but she realised what was going on: the R1609 race, with all that money at stake, had actually been built around her participation. The venue, the timing, everything. It could take place with the other athletes, especially if Sarah Moyo was in the field but, from James's point of view, Abby Dennison was the hook, the centrepiece. They all knew it.

Paul spoke in his best CEO voice. 'Let's get this straight. This is Abby's decision, she's the one on the line. She will have to do the work, take the risks, run the race, win or lose. It's her financial incentive, her career, her life. I will abide by her decision and I know that the rest of us will play our roles if she decides to run.' The other two nodded.

Abby walked to the pool, took off her shoes and sat on the side, dipping her feet in the cool water. A crested barbet trilled its long call from a nearby tree. She waited for it to finish before speaking. 'Thanks, guys, you know I love all of you and appreciate everything you do. We really are a family. Ever since Deon and I were told about this race by James, I've been evaluating the risks and rewards of taking part. I know that I don't need to run, but obviously everyone wants me to. I've been monitoring my physical and mental condition through this off-season period and I've worked hard, sticking to the programme. After all these years, I am the best judge of my fitness and general conditioning, especially my mental preparedness.'

There was silence. She walked to Paul and put her hands on his shoulders. 'Over Christmas, Dad you know this, I spent quite a bit of time with Deon. Ever since our Oxford weekend, he's become a useful sounding board. Not once has he advised me on what to do, he just listens and comments. After the Fedorova thing he's been a quiet source of strength, a new person to give support. Is this okay?'

'Of course,' said Paul. 'Anything to build your confidence.'

Abby sat down beside Bronwyn. They waited for her decision.

'Forgive me if this comes as a surprise, but I've told Deon what I'm going to tell you now. It was crucial as he is now unofficially part of my support team. I've studied my training times and they're pretty good compared to other off-seasons.' She rolled out a few numbers. 'This is normally where I am in June, but this year is different because of the April race.'

Paul said, 'What's your decision?'

She waited a beat. 'I'm in. I'm running the R1609 in Durban. I'm going for the world record. And the million dollars.'

In the ensuing silence the only thing to be heard was a collective sigh around the table. Paul grinned, Bronwyn hugged Abby, and JP pulled out a grubby notebook. Eventually he said, 'Brilliant, this is a good decision, one I knew you'd make. It's ten weeks to R1609, you've done the base training and we need to start the full build-up. I've started on the programme and Paul must sort out all the manager stuff with James Selfe, sponsors, accountants and the rest. One thing though – normally you have at least three warm-up races in Europe. You absolutely cannot just go into R1609 as your first race. I'll look into that.'

They high-fived, group-hugged and soon were sipping tea and munching choc-chip cookies. The atmosphere was relaxed after the weight of uncertainty had been lifted. They knew what lay ahead, and were ready.

Then Paul spoke, 'Abs, I almost forgot with everything going on. I had a call yesterday from a guy called Mark Whyte, who owns some sort of computer company. Apparently he was in London at the Bannister meeting. He told me that his company employs young interns, students at an academy that trains them in technology. Apparently they are super bright, motivated and two are locally ranked distance runners. He wants you to come for a few hours to his offices for a workshop with them. Motivation, goal setting, hard work, that sort of stuff. It's close and no preparation is required. Just a chat and Q and A session. On Wednesday. What do you think?'

She hesitated. The name vaguely rang a bell, but she couldn't place it. 'Sure, Dad. Should be fun. Set it up.' She definitely needed a change of scenery and Mark Whyte and his interns would fit the bill perfectly.

30

Monday, 28 January

LONDON

The Regalbank executive boardroom was a wonder to behold. Situated on the twentieth and top floor of the bank's headquarters, it had a spectacular view of the city.

James Selfe, Mary Southgate, Simon Hardy and six others sat at a long table. Three were media people: Gretchen Steinhold and Hilary Green, bank employees, and Rupert Anderson, Hardy's head of media management for the Bannister meeting. Another two, Evan Herold and Wallace de Lange, were employed part-time by the Bannister meeting and managed technology and infrastructure. Emily Williams was also there, having been employed full-time by Regalbank since November.

Selfe spoke, 'Ladies and gentlemen, welcome. It's just over ten weeks to go to R1609. Paul Dennison called me yesterday and I am delighted to tell you that Abby will be competing. Now, it's time to get down to business.' There was an audible sigh of relief, and smiles across the room.

Over the next three hours, the group discussed key aspects of the event. No one underestimated the challenge of organising a world-class event in an old stadium in a country none of them had ever visited. They discussed the partnerships with the South African athletics authorities and the city of Durban, the structural upgrades to the stadium to increase seating capacity, security arrangements for VIPs, ground transport for athletes, coaches and VIPs. The media plan, the layout and equipping of the media and VIP centres and, critically, technical upgrades to bring the facility in line with world standards, were also discussed.

Selfe said, 'I would like each team – media, logistics, technology and infrastructure – to prepare a detailed action plan and budget, to be presented to this group, along with our chairman and other board members, on Friday.'

Simon Hardy asked, 'I know that a team will soon be travelling to Durban. What are the plans for that?'

'There will be an advance party of seven going to Durban in a week's time to do the work locally. Simon, Gretchen, Hilary and Rupert will be looking after media issues plus the VIP and hospitality facilities in the stadium. Evan and Wallace will manage the buildings, infrastructure, security and technology upgrades. Emily will manage accommodation and transport, including for athletes and VIPs.'

He spoke quietly, as if to himself. 'This is a huge deal, people, the biggest sponsorship ever in athletics. Regalbank is going big here and we can't allow anything to slip. Our reputations and even our careers could be made or broken here. But I trust all of you. This is a single track meeting with twenty items on the programme. Please keep everything simple, just the essentials. The only event that matters is the women's mile, the rest are just fillers with local athletes. All the media activity is focused on one thing, the mile, the record and the incentive. Does everyone understand?'

Heads nodded.

Emily Williams asked the question on everyone's mind, 'Who is running the R1609?'

'Now that Abby Dennison has confirmed, the media team must prepare a story for release today. I have sent word to McColgan, Beardsley, Kiptanui and Karlovic through their agents and I have also invited Ekaterina Vinitskaya of Russia and the American, Molly Fields, who has yet to go under four minutes but we need her to get the American audience on board. I've asked Suzy Marshall to be pacemaker again. So far, everyone is available.'

'Not surprising, considering the money on offer,' quipped Hardy.

'And the sunshine,' added Steinhold.

Hilary Green nervously put her hand up. 'James, do we know if Sarah Moyo will be running?'

Selfe hesitated. 'No one has heard from Moyo or her handlers since Bannister. I have no idea if she will be in Durban or not.'

31

Tuesday, 29 January

ELDORET, KENYA

Sarah Moyo and her group were in Eldoret when the news broke that Abby Dennison would be running the R1609. Three men sat around a table in a small room, drinking Tusker beer from the bottle. The fourth member of their group, the small, powerfully built athlete, was asleep in another room. The men were Solomon and Samson Moyo and Sarah's coach, Caihong Junren. They were deep in discussion about R1609 and the vast opportunities it opened.

Junren spoke, 'The million dollars is possible for Sarah, we all know it.'

'Is she as fit as she was for the Bannister meeting?' asked Solomon.

'She is even fitter. Her times in training are a little faster than back in June. We have been focusing totally on Durban, and the record and the million.'

'Caihong, do you think Sarah can beat Dennison?' Samson asked.

'Impossible to say. She has the talent, but it will depend on the way the race plays out.'

'But she's good enough?'

'Oh yes, definitely.'

Solomon said, 'We have two decisions now. The first is, does she run in Durban, and the second, can we do anything about Dennison?'

Caihong drained his beer and banged the bottle down on the table. 'You guys are pathetic. We must go for it, call Selfe now and tell him Sarah is in, and tell her tonight. She needs to know. Then, how to beat Dennison, we need to plan carefully and we tell Sarah nothing. You boys need to understand how things work. This is not athletics, it's war.'

Solomon made the call outside. Twelve minutes later he was back.

'Done. He's as happy as anything. Now he has the two best runners in the world in his precious race.'

'What about Dennison? We can't expect someone to trip her,' said Samson, which got a laugh from the others.

Solomon stood and with a broad smile and a low bow said, 'Let's have another look at that video footage my clever brother took in London that night.'

32

Wednesday, 30 January

JOHANNESBURG

Paul set up the meeting with Mark Whyte. 'The company is called MileStar Electronics and it's in the Eastview building on Rivonia Road,' he said. 'Get there just before ten and Whyte will introduce you to the interns.'

The name Mark Whyte rolled around in Abby's mind. Mark Whyte, Mark Whyte? Then it struck her – this was the guy at the Bannister media conference, the reporter who asked the stupid question about her ring. The same reporter she had subtly shown the middle finger. Now he was running a tech company in Joburg with interns that needed motivating? Sounded crazy.

She called Deon. He was anything but subtle. 'Whyte is a chancer. I checked with Simon Hardy and his so-called website is a sham. It was a ruse to get him into the media centre instead of sitting out in the stands. Also, I suspect he has a crush on you.'

'What!'

'Why else would he go to all that trouble? I mean, it was just a track meeting. I don't trust him.'

She absorbed that and asked, 'Should I still go?'

'For sure. The guy is a very successful and wealthy business-owner. Squeaky clean, apparently; I did some digging. If anything, it'll be an interesting encounter. He's pretty pushy, calling Paul and everything, and probably has some fantasy about dating you. Go to the meeting, get those interns fired up and check out the famous Mister Whyte. Apparently he has a Porsche, so he could even have long-term boyfriend potential!'

'Fat chance. Maybe you should come along as my bodyguard.'

He laughed. 'And ruin the poor guy's day? No way. But seriously, Abby, be careful out there. You honestly don't know who you can trust.'

She drove into the underground parking garage of the Eastview building just before ten. The security guy's nametag said 'Denzel' and as she was pulling away from the boom gate she saw him wave excitedly to someone. She stopped and called him over. He was ecstatic when she scribbled 'Best wishes Denzel' on a scrap of paper and signed it. 'Thanks a lot,' he said, grinning and staring at the paper.

She scanned the vehicles parked in the 'MileStar/Reserved Parking' bays, looking for a Porsche. There wasn't one, there was just a shiny red Toyota Yaris.

Abby was met at reception by Mandy, a twenty-something woman smartly dressed in a grey business suit, black blouse with sparkly buttons and platform shoes with extremely high heels. Abby was no expert on makeup, but hers was too thick and made her face look like that of a wax model. Her smile was bright, but her eyes told another story: this is my life – smile for the important clients.

'Miss Dennison, I am so happy to meet you. Thanks for coming to our humble company. I know that Mark, Mister Whyte, admires you greatly.'

A voice boomed down the passage. 'Abby, welcome! Thank you for coming. My interns are excited, especially Angie and Mathews, who are serious runners.'

She stared at him. He certainly was imposing close up. Tall, with sandy, unkempt hair and five days of beard. Trendy. A lightweight tan suit, jacket buttoned, pale pink shirt, St John's old boys tie. Wide smile.

She stuck out a hand and they shook. 'My pleasure. I remember you from London, the media conference. How did you manage that?'

'If you don't ask, you don't get. So I asked, told them I was an amateur media person from South Africa,' he said smoothly. 'Anyway, I wanted to watch the biggest meeting of the year and better in the media centre than in the stands.'

'Why did you do it?' she asked, genuinely interested.

'I'm a big fan of the pole vault,' he answered, which stopped the discussion.

Then it was all business. They went into his office with its splendid view of the Magaliesberg. She noticed that there was a model Porsche on the desk. 'You a fan?' she asked, pointing to the small car.

'I love cars,' he said, rather sheepishly. 'Boys with toys and all that. I have three.'

They sat. 'Let's get to it. In the tech business, there is a proper shortage of data management skills, huge demand, low supply. The universities misunderstand the technical skills needed out there and actuarial science courses are full of academic stuff and few real practical skills. There are now private academies that offer one- or two-year courses, mainly sponsored by big corporates, banks and the like. A core part of these courses is an internship of between six and nine months. We get four students at a time, bright kids, motivated and super talented. They get snapped up after graduating, big starting salaries.'

'What do you want me to do?' she asked, suddenly a bit nervous. These were mathematical geniuses, after all.

'Talk about your career, the hard work you have to put in, the sacrifices, the single-mindedness. Especially the crucial role of goal setting.'

'Who are these people?'

'Here are their files. Take a few minutes to get some background.' Abby read four thin files as he went to get coffee.

Boitumelo Molefe, Angie de Villiers, Mathews Sithole and Angus McDonald. Clearly a mix of gender, race and background, and two with serious athletic talent.

'Let's go and meet the boffins,' she said.

They went to the boardroom where the four interns were seated. 'This is Abby Dennison, the runner,' said Mark. 'Ask her anything.'

They did. It turned out to be a wonderful morning that stretched far beyond the allotted two hours. They asked, she answered; she asked, they answered. They told her about their backgrounds (ranging from a Soweto shack to a private school in the KwaZulu-Natal Midlands), the shortage of data science skills in the economy and the challenges of being accepted by the Academy ('Unbelievably difficult, a bunch of crazy-hard online tests, then a hectic interview and a tough bootcamp. Only one in three hundred applicants gets in,' explained Mathews, the young man from Soweto.)

By the time they finished, Abby was as motivated as they were. These were amazing youngsters, so full of drive, raw intelligence and ambition. A new world had opened up, something she had no idea existed.

Just before the session ended, Mark stuck his head around the door. 'Gotta go. I'll call when you have time, Abby, catch a coffee maybe? Thanks again.' Then he was gone.

On the way home, Abby revised her opinion of Mark Whyte. Opinionated, definitely. Arrogant, for sure. But hidden somewhere under the bluster, smart suits and fancy cars was a spark of caring, a genuine desire to build a business that served people at the bottom of the income chain. And as for good old-fashioned grit and determination? Plenty.

A coffee maybe? Not out of the question.

Afternoon

The Team gathered on the patio. It was a beautiful Johannesburg summer's day. Paul hadn't said what it was about but, intuitively, they knew – crunch time for the R1609 had arrived.

He said, 'Team, I've been thinking about our plans now that Abby has committed to R1609. We need to up our game and get completely professional. This is the biggest race of her career and could be life-altering for all of us. This place, Joburg, is not ideal for training; too many distractions, phone calls, journos asking for interviews.'

They listened. 'JP and I met this morning when you were at that intern motivation thing and we looked at a few alternative training venues. Then I called my friend Oscar Rogers, I went to school with him. He's got a compound in White River near Mbombela, you know, the new name for Nelspruit. Big grounds, a few houses, very private. We chatted and he offered us two of the small houses, each with a couple of bedrooms, a kitchen and bathroom, for eight weeks starting this weekend. There are some lovely roads out there for long runs, there's a small gym and an excellent four-hundred-metre grass track and fifty-metre pool at the local high school. He'll organise for us to have access to these facilities whenever we like, and the security team there will ensure no disturbances when Abby trains. The gym will give you two hours each day, privately. JP has also organised for a physio and massage therapist to be on standby.'

JP said, 'I called Magnus Marais from the Mbombela Athletics Club this morning. They have three young male middle-distance runners who are showing lots of promise. All of them have run under four minutes for the 1 500 and 1:55 for the 800 metres. There also is a female runner who has run 53 seconds for 400 metres. I want Abby to have a few warm-up races but that would be difficult in Joburg with too many people in the know and too much attention. Magnus will organise three races for Abby. They won't be official races but he will make sure they are close to being genuine. Timekeepers, officials, a few spectators, the works. Even a call room and bib numbers. You will run one 800 and two 1 500-metre races in Mbombela.'

There was a general chat and Paul wrapped up the discussion with, 'Pack your bags, ladies, we are off to Mpumalanga province, the place of the rising sun!'

The whole White River plan was a bit sudden – in her mind Abby thought that she would be training locally as usual, but she immediately realised that White River would be perfect for the work that lay ahead. The three races also sounded interesting. It was a good plan.

Even better, White River was less than an hour's drive from the Numbi Gate entrance to the Kruger Park.

Early evening

It took a while but eventually the call got through. In far-off Eldoret, Solomon Moyo's cellphone rang. He didn't recognise the number and said, 'This is Solomon, who are you?'

'Solomon, you don't know me and I apologise for disturbing you. My name is Mark Whyte and I own a technology company in Johannesburg. I was in London at the Bannister meeting and watched your sister Sarah break the world record. It was breathtaking.'

'It was, Mark. But I have to ask, how did you get this number? And what do you want?'

'Of course, getting your number was a challenge, to be honest. All sorts of calls around the world, but, as you know from Sarah's success, you have to keep working and eventually you get what you want. Know what I mean?'

'Yeah. Please get to the point. You know Sarah doesn't do interviews.'

'This is not about an interview. Let me be honest. I am a big athletics fan and understand the amazing work your family has done to get Sarah to world-record standard. Putting it simply, my international corporate technology partners and I would like to talk to you about sponsoring Sarah. She is a valuable property and we as African sportsmen need to support our athletes. Potentially, I'm talking big numbers here.'

There was silence for a while. 'But Dennison is South African, why don't you sponsor her?'

'Exactly, that's the point. Dennison has had a golden path to success, being a privileged white South African and everything. She doesn't need any more sponsors, but Sarah can be the next superstar. I know she is quiet and reserved, but that's no problem. We have an international sponsorship agency in mind to deal with that.'

'Sounds interesting, but I need much more information. When can we meet? I will be in Joburg a week before R1609.'

'Perfect, let me know when you're here. My company is called MileStar Electronics, we have a website, check it out. Solomon, this is a big deal, don't blow it. All I ask is an hour of your time.'

A Highveld thunderstorm was building up as Mark drove his Porsche out of the underground garage an hour later and into Rivonia Road. Going down William Nicol Drive he turned into a road in Bryanston where an image of a red car was captured by a security camera mounted on a pole.

33

Saturday, 2 February

WHITE RIVER, MPUMALANGA

The Team left three days later in Paul's Hyundai SUV, loaded with bags, running gear, essential medicines, clothing, computers, binoculars and cameras ('for birds', explained Bronwyn), food for the road, and all sorts of things considered essential by Bronwyn and Abby. There was so much luggage that Paul had to attach the trailer.

They arrived mid-afternoon, a little hot and travel-weary, at the Rogers compound. It was set in a five-hectare plot a few kilometres outside White River, a medium-sized town some twenty kilometres north of the regional capital, Mbombela. Significantly for the local tourism industry, White River was only fifty kilometres from the Kruger National Park's Numbi Gate, one of the portals to Africa's most famous game reserves, visited by nearly two million wildlife enthusiasts each year.

The setting for the training retreat was ideal. The compound consisted of five houses built in a quiet, secluded grove of macadamia trees where the relaxed atmosphere and the lack of distractions were crucial. The surrounding countryside was hilly, and commercial timber forests stretched like a dark green carpet over the rolling hills into the distance. Narrow winding tracks meandered through the forests and, while some were on private land, many were accessible. Perfect for long runs.

It was now all systems go and the Team would hunker down, isolate themselves, eliminate any sort of interference or temptation, just four people ready to battle fatigue, injuries, boredom and, ultimately, the stopwatch and the relentless march of the calendar.

That evening Oscar Rogers hosted a braai under the stars and they sat outside to hear JP's training proposal for the next six weeks. It took more than an hour and the fire eventually became a small pile of red and gold embers glowing under rows of fairy lights twinkling in the macadamia trees. The chirping of a thousand crickets, the occasional hoot of an owl, the *kwaak-kwaak* of a bullfrog in the pond and the rest of the Lowveld night-time sounds came alive as JP rolled out the plan: stamina and strength training in the forests, track work at the school, gym sessions, swimming, cross-training, aromatherapy, physiotherapy, massages. Everything was present in perfect harmony. It was a superbly constructed plan.

JP drained his glass and filled it again with a deep red cabernet. He sighed with pleasure, a true Stellenbosch man. He continued, 'Then we have the races. Time-trials if you like, but we will do our best to turn them into proper races. These are essential because Abby won't have the usual European season to sharpen her racing skills. The races will be at the Mbombela Athletics Club grounds up in the Steiltes area where they have a decent gravel track. The running club will bring the best track athletes from the whole area and these guys are not shabby. Also other athletes to make up a proper field of about ten. They'll race hard and won't give an inch.'

'Will there be spectators?' asked Bronwyn.

'Controlled. About two hundred specially invited people. The first 1 500-metre race will be at the end of week three to see how Abby is doing speed-wise. The 800 and second 1 500 race are at the end, exactly eight days before R1609. There will be a day's rest before these races, which will happen on consecutive days.'

Bronwyn said, 'My role is crucial, as you know. Abby and I will have a session at least every second day for two hours to check on motivation levels, tiredness, discuss any problems you may have and simply relax. We can do these here or we can go for walks, maybe a drive down to Sabie or the Botanical Gardens in town. I also plan to take the two of us into Kruger on three of the rest days.'

Paul had been silent through the discussion, letting the experts play their roles. He said, 'Looks like your days will be pretty full. When do you sleep?'

JP looked serious. 'Very, very important. Abby will sleep the rest of the time. Apart from the sessions with Bronwyn and the physio, you will just eat, sleep and train the whole time, at least ten hours a day, even more. At night, obviously, but at other times as well. Afternoons, late mornings. Whenever.'

As if on cue, Paul stood and stretched. 'Talking of sleep, folks, off to your rooms now.'

Everyone went to bed, exhausted but excited, committed and eager, apprehension balanced by anticipation. There were many 'What if this? What if that?' questions in Abby's head, but she was sure that, between the four of them, they could handle all the routine challenges faced by elite athletes.

She knew, as she lay in bed staring at the ceiling, the full moon shining through the window and the night-time noises reaching a crescendo outside, that it was all down to her. She had to do the work, strain every muscle, test every reserve of determination and mental fortitude, produce the goods.

Could she do it?

She closed her eyes but her mind was in a strange place, floating around like a leaf in a storm. She shook her head to clear it and realised that she was super tired after a long day that had ended with the realisation of what lay ahead. Unusually, she'd also enjoyed three glasses of the cabernet, not something she did on any sort of regular basis, but this evening had been different as the familiar embrace of all the people she loved flowed like a benevolent river around her under a comforting canopy of macadamia branches.

She sat up, climbed out of bed, wrapped herself in a fluffy dressing gown and went to the window. Moon-glow lit the trees; Oscar's fox terrier Bonnie walked across the lawn, yellow eyes gleaming. Four chairs circled a table; faintly glowing fire embers and several empty wine glasses were the only reminders of the dinner; a few lights still shone in the main house but none were visible in the satellite houses. Everyone was asleep. Except her.

She went outside and walked to the entrance gate of the estate, about fifty metres away. A snuffling noise caught her attention: it was Bonnie. She scratched the dog's head and asked, 'Bonnie, old girl, am I ready for this?'

Bonnie wagged her tail and her eyes said yes, of course you are. Abby took her word for it, went to bed and slept the sleep of the truly exhausted.

The following morning, JP's R1609 programme started.

34

Monday, 4 February

APN OFFICES, JOHANNESBURG

Deon was in the middle of writing a report on an excellent T20 cricket match between the local Lions provincial side and the Gazelles, their counterparts from Mpumalanga, when his cellphone chirped. He didn't recognise the number.

'Deon, this is Bronwyn Adams.'

What? Bronwyn? On a Monday morning?

He mumbled, 'Hi, Miss Adams. Where are you? What's up? Is Abby okay?'

'She's fine. I know that Abby told you we're in White River on a training camp. Hush-hush, secret, off the record and all that.'

'Yes, I know that.'

They swopped updates for a while. Then she said, 'The reason I'm calling is to ask a favour, or get your advice, or something. Honestly, I'm not even sure if this is a problem or not and if it is, you are the only person I can share it with. Over the past few months, Abby has mentioned that she's occasionally had a weird feeling that someone has been watching her. In particular, a car apparently following her around.'

He was wary. 'Yes … she mentioned that back on our Oxford trip. Don't say it's happened again?'

'I think so. A couple of times, mainly when she does road work around home. But she's not sure, says she could be imagining it. Being paranoid.'

'What do you want me to do?'

'That's the crazy part. I don't know. I just want to tell someone, share my concern. Maybe you know someone who could do some checking, if that's even possible.'

He thought for a moment, then said, 'When was the most recent sighting?'

'That's the problem. Abby told me confidentially that it happened again last Thursday, close to her house. A fancy sports car driving slowly, then leaving, then coming back. She wasn't sure but thought it may be a Porsche. They have security cameras on the corners and guards in huts …'

Her voice trailed off but the message was clear. Bronwyn wanted him to do some investigating, maybe get the police involved. She said, 'Please keep this between us. We haven't told Paul, he'd go ballistic. And when she went to MileStar to speak to the interns, she found out that Mark Whyte is a Porsche fan and has a model of one on his desk. Maybe now it's my turn to be paranoid, but this Mark Whyte fellow could be worth investigating.'

'Bronwyn, one thing that my boss Charlie taught me is this: there are no such things as coincidences.'

'I agree,' she said, 'see what you can do.'

He spent the next hour calling people, asking questions and making notes. Then he waited.

After about an hour, his phone chirped again. For the second time that day he was caught unawares. 'Howzit Deon. Can I call you Deon? Thanks, man. I'm blessed with the label of Warrant Officer Ignatius Willem Petrus Swanepoel, but you can call me Natie. I work for the Family Violence, Child Protection and Sexual Offences, or FCS unit, of the South African Police Service. Basically catching people doing sex crimes. Okay? Cool.'

'Cool, Natie,' he said. What else could he say?

'Look man, my mate from M and R down the passage here in Rivonia Central told me you'd called about some possible Abby Dennison problem. Now if this was anyone else, I wouldn't have jumped so quickly, but Abby is special, you know what I mean?'

He said that he did. 'What's M and R? Sounds like a construction company.'

'Murder and robbery.' Then Deon realised what was going on. One of his former schoolmates was the head of Fraud at SAPS Rivonia. He'd called him earlier and word had spread. Everyone jumped when Abby's name was mentioned, especially in the context of a possible stalking scenario.

'Natie, listen man. I need to chat to you about a potential stalking issue around Abby. Nothing concrete, just vague suspicions. Can you help?'

'Sure, but I need details. Right now I'm busy, but can I come to your offices at four today? I just hope this isn't some sort of a wild duck chase, but let's see where it takes us. Okay?'

'Sure, Natie. Anything I can do to protect Abby. See you at four. Do you know where it is?'

'Deon, *ou maat*, I'm a detective. I know stuff.'

Deon ended the call and immediately dialled Geoff in Fraud at SAPS Rivonia, and asked about this Natie fellow.

'That guy,' said Geoff, 'is one of the most feared and respected detectives in the force. For twenty years he's tracked down, pursued, arrested and prosecuted numerous, probably hundreds, of sexual predators, rapists and child molesters. He is brilliant at his job. Although he has been targeted many times by the criminals operating in his area of the underworld jungle, he's never been nailed by them. Don't be fooled by his appearance, he looks like a relic from the bush wars, all camouflage clothes and, oh *ja*, a big ugly army surplus belt. Some sort of lucky charm, that belt, according to him. He always wears it, probably sleeps with it on.'

Two hours later, a wide-eyed and clearly nervous Nothando Mtolo, APN's receptionist, arrived at Deon's desk. 'Warrant Officer Swanepoel is here to see you.' Then she fled.

Warrant Officer Ignatius Willem Petrus Swanepoel ('just call me Natie') of the FCS unit looked exactly like a policeman and could have just walked off the set of an American TV crime series. Khaki and green camouflage pants, held in place by a dangerous-looking broad leather belt with metal studs, were tucked into shiny black combat boots. He wore a simple white T-shirt under a navy-blue bomber jacket that had the spiky gold SAPS logo embroidered on one side of the chest, and an elaborate FCS unit emblem on the other. He also managed to find space for a metal nametag ('Swanepoel') on the jacket. His face sported a thick, droopy moustache that came straight out of the 1970s, untidy brown hair that needed a cut, and at least four days of stubble.

He only removed his dark glasses after flopping down into Deon's visitor's chair. 'Howzit Deon,' he said cheerily, 'how goes things? Where's the coffee, I need a caffeine shot badly.'

They collected coffee in polystyrene cups from the corner drinks station and swopped background information for a while. Deon's job, Natie's job ('gender-based violence in South Africa is, how do you say, a pandemic, like the Portuguese flu a hundred years ago'), the risks famous women run daily.

After fifteen minutes of chatting, Natie said, 'Give me everything you know about Abby.'

Deon did, although it wasn't much. The Dennison home address, the feeling that she was being followed in different places that went back even before the Bannister meeting. Also the definite sighting just a week earlier, the sports car, the security cameras, the neighbourhood street guards.

'I suppose, if you're looking for a possible suspect, you could start with a guy called Mark Whyte,' he said eventually. He told Natie about MileStar Electronics and the bizarre story about Whyte inveigling his way into the Bannister meeting using a bogus website. He mentioned that the London guys – 'a big deal banker called Selfe and the head of some government agency, a guy called QSH' – had been alerted to Whyte's scam and had checked him out. 'I'll give you Selfe's number and you can call him for more details.'

He then told Natie about Bronwyn's call, Abby's visit to the MileStar interns, and the little piece of information about the garage and Whyte's Porsche.

'It's not much, but I trust Abby's intuition.'

'As I said, man, this woman is pure gold, a national treasure, like Table Mountain, *braaivleis* and Charles Barnard the heart surgeon. If there's someone stalking her we need to find him. You say this isn't much info? Actually, it's plenty. I've put okes behind bars with less. Leave it to me, I won't let the grass grow under my fingernails.'

He left after consuming two more cups of APN's highly suspect coffee.

Wild duck chases, Portuguese flu, grass under the fingernails, Charles Barnard?

35

Monday, 11 February

SAPS, RIVONIA CENTRAL

Natie Swanepoel was sitting in his small, windowless box of an office behind a deeply scarred and ancient desk, on top of which were an open laptop computer, an old-fashioned landline telephone and a yellow legal pad. A steel filing cabinet with five drawers stood in one corner and a quick glance inside would have revealed ninety brown government case files, seventeen of which were marked 'open', sixteen 'cold' and fifty-seven 'solved'. The 'solved' ratio was the envy of his colleagues.

It had been a week since the meeting with Coetzee and not much else had occupied his mind. This was unusual for Natie, who was renowned for being able to juggle several cases simultaneously.

A small fan on top of the cabinet circulated hot, stale air. The legal pad was covered with scribbled notes, words circled, sentences crossed out and little arrows connecting random phrases. It was Natie's personal and very successful way of approaching complex crimes. He called it 'my brain map', much to the amusement of his colleagues. No matter, it worked.

With a smile, he recalled the phone conversation with James Selfe. The Regalbank people had been smart about getting into Whyte's and MileStar's computers and flagging him as a potential risk to Abby, but the part about how the undercover guys had lost him after the meeting and how he had managed to get back home undetected had been a bit embarrassing. 'At least that was the fault of QSH's guys, not mine,' Selfe had quickly concluded.

Natie ripped off the top page of the pad and, under the heading 'Today', wrote three tasks. Then he made four phone calls, each time making brief notes on the legal pad. He put his cellphone into the pocket of his SAPS jacket, strode purposefully out of the office and down two flights of stairs, said a cheery 'I'm off on a duck chase, hope it's not a wild one' to the bemused sergeant at reception, climbed into his SAPS-branded Opel Corsa and drove up Rivonia Road, direction Rosebank.

He parked outside a certain office building, strode into the basement parking, and flashed his police badge at the guard at the boom, who scrambled to attention, mumbling, 'Good day, Officer, can I assist?'

'Where is the MileStar parking?' he asked, and was led to the far corner where, twelve days earlier, Abby had parked. He looked at the vehicles, in particular a Porsche. He wrote down the licence plate number, gave the guard a smile and a quick 'thank you', and left the building.

Then he drove seven kilometres to the industrial precinct of Wynberg, took a few lefts and rights and ended up outside the offices of SecuriSure, one of the larger security companies operating in Johannesburg's northern suburbs. He gave his name to the young lady at reception and was ushered into the office of Hank van Heerden, the overweight, heavily bearded general manager.

'Good to see you, Natie,' said Van Heerden. 'Coffee?'

'*Ja*, thanks. Black, strong, no sugar.' Van Heerden made a call and coffee arrived.

'What brings you here? Another *blerrie* sex offence?'

'Don't know yet. Hope not. But listen, Hank, this is hypo-confidential. Okay?'

'You know me. Confidentiality is my middle name.' He chuckled.

'It's about Abby Dennison.'

'Oh hell, don't tell me. Not her. Please not.'

Less than thirty minutes and more coffee – strong, black, no sugar – later, Natie left the building. Nothing was in writing, but in his head he had a clear undertaking from Van Heerden. 'I will have my best guys go through every second of the camera footage on the two corners at the end of the Dennison road. A Porsche, its licence plate, times, number of sightings. The last two months. Hell of a job, Natie, it will take my guys at least a week.'

'Thanks, Hank, I'll be back for the report the day after tomorrow.'

He returned to his office building and, posing as a journalist from the eminent British business journal, *World Entrepreneur*, made two calls. One was to Mark Whyte's personal assistant, Mandy, the other to the Willows Retirement Home where, Mandy had told him, Mark's father lived.

After lunch he changed into a set of clothes that he kept in a cupboard.

At exactly two o'clock, Natie Swanepoel, earlier that morning a policeman but now a journalist, sat uncomfortably in a far-too-deep chair in the guest lounge of the Willows Retirement Home. He wore a regulation white shirt, narrow striped tie, neatly pressed grey trousers, black lace-up shoes, shabby grey blazer and a pair of black-rimmed glasses. On the table in front of him were a cup of lukewarm tea, a scone covered with cream and strawberry jam, and a small digital recorder.

The room was oppressively warm, thanks to a large fan heater that blasted hot air into the confined space. At a neighbouring table, four ladies were silently engaged in a serious game of bridge, while the strains of 'The White Cliffs of Dover' could be heard coming from an ancient piano down the passage. The room smelled of boiled cabbage and furniture polish.

Natie felt slightly ill. Over the years, though, he had learned how to push an unpleasant environment out of his mind and get on with the job. As far as environments go, this is hardly the worst ever, so get on with it, he told himself. He drank his tea and looked across the table.

Opposite him sat an impressive man. Although in his mid-sixties, he sat ramrod straight and his piercing brown eyes had no need for spectacles. He stared at Natie with frank curiosity and clear mistrust. James Earl Ambrose Whyte had learned many years earlier not to trust strangers, especially those that suddenly arrived out of the blue.

Natie came straight to the point. 'Mister Whyte, I'm a freelance journalist contributing to an influential British journal that covers economic development in emerging markets, particularly focusing on successful start-up businesses in the technology field. My brief is to analyse case studies so that there can be more of these disruptive businesses starting up. As you know,' he smiled broadly, 'countries like South Africa urgently need job creation and small business development is the best way to go.'

THE FINAL LAP

Whyte nodded. This fellow certainly had all the jargon. He said, 'Why talk to me? Go directly to Mark.'

'I will, but he is apparently a bit on the shy side about personal stuff, so all I really want from you is some background to Mark as a boy, then a teenager, then a student, then a successful entrepreneur. It will give me a proper background to the man himself. I will talk to other people about the company and how it grew. Then Mark himself. He really is a remarkable young man.'

Whyte considered this and decided this fellow was legitimate, even though his jacket was probably purchased at the Oriental Plaza in a season-end sale.

'Okay, Mister Swanepoel, fire away.'

Natie made a great show of switching on the small recorder that had no batteries. No matter, it was the impression that counted. They spoke for nearly an hour, in that time consuming several more cups of lukewarm, weak tea. Natie even finished two more scones, delivered by a beaming caregiver in a blue uniform.

As the lengthy conversation progressed, Whyte became more relaxed and clearly enjoyed telling somewhat long-winded stories about his son's prowess both academically and on the rugby field. Natie discovered that, in the early 2000s, the family always spent the Christmas holidays in Durban. 'But not Durban itself of course, too crowded. Also the wrong type of person. Bargain hunters. Legions of noisy kids.' His nose wrinkled at the memory.

'So where did you go?'

'uMhlanga Rocks of course. Much more genteel, classy. And they had a Blue Flag beach. Those were the good days, before my wife Muriel died. Pancreatic cancer, terrible disease. She was just fifty-three. And now, of course, the beach no longer has Blue Flag status, thanks to incompetent management.'

Natie thought that, for the old man, the loss of Blue Flag status probably equalled the loss of his wife, but he put on his saddest face and patted the old man on the shoulder. 'At least you have the memories,' he said. Pause. 'And where in uMhlanga did you stay?'

'Every year it was the same. The uMhlanga Sands, the best hotel – other than the Oyster Cavern – in the region, but that was completely overpriced of course, even then.'

'They must have loved you at the Sands, regular customers and all that?'

'Of course. We got royal treatment. In later years, the manager gave us the Emperor Suite at normal rates, right in front, second floor, with a balcony overlooking the ocean.'

'Splendid. And Mark, did he enjoy the beach?'

'It was his best place.' Chuckle. 'Between you and me, even when he was fourteen, fifteen, I realised that he would be a ladies' man, like his dad.' Wink, sly smile. 'He would sidle up to the prettiest girl on the beach and start a conversation. And they always responded to him. He had the gift, you know.'

'And he never married?'

'Yes, well, I wondered about that.'

Ten minutes later Natie was in his car. 'Gotcha,' he mumbled to himself. 'The R1609 is in Durban and I bet Mister Mark Whyte will be there. With a bit of luck we might catch the Emperor in his Suite.'

Natie stopped outside a Mugg & Bean bistro, inserted two batteries into the same recorder not used in the interview and switched it on. For ten minutes he dictated a series of instructions to himself, pausing the machine between each one to think. At the end, he had five points of investigation into the mysterious Mark Whyte, who was quite happy to approach girls on the beach but never had a serious girlfriend.

He also needed to confirm that Whyte would be booked into the Sands over the R1609 period. Then he went into the bistro and sat down. The waitress noticed the broad smile on his face. 'Having a good day, sir? My boyfriend's a fisherman and that's how he looks when he hooks a big one,' she said.

'Oh yes,' said the policeman. 'This is a really big one. Probably a shark. Speaking of which, can I have the hake and chips?'

It was only later that afternoon when it occurred to Natie that the Willows Retirement Home was less than a kilometre from the Dennison house. Just down the road, in fact.

36

Thursday, 14 February

APN OFFICES, JOHANNESBURG

It was report-back time and Natie was in Deon's visitor's chair. This was a different Natie, smartly dressed, hair combed, no stubble. Deon realised that the man was the human equivalent of a chameleon – blending into the environment. The transformation was remarkable.

He spoke for about fifteen minutes from clear, meticulous and detailed notes. Dates, exact times, specific places, direct quotes. Deon imagined him in court, a witness for the prosecution, the accused shrinking down into his seat, head down as the evidence rolled on, relentless details of the crime. Testimony perfectly planned and professionally delivered. The defence counsel scribbling notes furiously then standing and facing a smiling Natie. Bring it on.

He was all business now. 'I took note of your comments about Mark Whyte. After the London episode, I realised that he has a particular personality type.'

He stopped. 'Deon, *my maat*, can we have some of that awful coffee of yours?' Some things don't change.

He continued minutes later. 'I've profiled him based on my extensive experience. He's smart, successful and driven. Nothing stands in his way. But he's isolated, no obvious relationships outside of work, particularly romantic ones. He was raised primarily by his father in a strict, authoritarian, emotion-free environment. Life was all about getting ahead, making money, being successful. Women were seen as lesser mortals. Male dominance was paramount and there was definitely a bit of racism thrown in as well. The London jaunt last August shows that he is a serious risk-taker and thrill-seeker. I also called James at Regalbank in London and he put me in touch with two other guys, Zack and QSH. The computer evidence from the hack and the story from the PI in London who tailed him and saw the images on his laptop indicate that he is definitely obsessed with Abby.'

'Does this predispose him to being some sort of sexual predator?'

'That's the obvious question. But the answer is not always what you would expect. To be blunt, it probably doesn't, at least at this stage. My conclusion is that Mark Whyte is lonely, desperately needs a romantic relationship, and is unable to find a girlfriend through normal routes because he is inexperienced in that area. He doesn't understand women, and his ego prevents him from becoming vulnerable with them. So he fixates on the person he sees as the perfect woman, the one of his dreams. He sees Abby as successful and driven, just like he is. He's looking for someone completely out of the ordinary. In summary, he definitely doesn't look like a criminal to me. Just a sad sort of guy.'

'So he fixates on Abby.' It all made sense.

'Exactly. He fantasises about her but, for many reasons, one of which is that she is physically inaccessible for most of the time, he's resorted to having some sort of imaginary, remote, virtual relationship with her.'

'Could this escalate into something serious?'

'In my experience, these situations can escalate but it's not automatic. The perps get more confident and more desperate as they work to make the target increasingly accessible. But it will take time. The fact that he managed to get her into his office to talk to the interns was a major breakthrough for him. It may give him the opening to pursue a normal relationship. Don't ask how I know, but he suggested that they have a coffee date. If she rebuffs him, it could possibly get nasty.'

Natie explained about the security camera footage around the Dennison home. 'One thing we noticed was interesting but, to be honest, it's not incriminating. One of the cars that appeared four times in a week was a Porsche. I checked the licence plate number and it was Whyte's car.'

'Wow, that's something.'

'Maybe, maybe not. Another fun visit I made was to Mark's father who lives in a retirement village. I posed as a journalist.' He grinned and pointed at Deon. 'I learned from you. Cheap clothes, nerdy look, very serious. Anyway, the guy ticks all the boxes: tough, unemotional, ambitious for his son, brought him up mostly alone. But I also got one decent piece of info. They always went to uMhlanga for their holidays. Stayed at the Sands in the same suite every year.'

'Now what?'

'This is my plan. Honestly, I don't think Whyte is a risk to Abby right now, but you never know. If at all, the crunch will come at the R1609 race in Durban in April. I discovered that Whyte has put in for a week's leave around that exact date. He will be in Durban, you can bet on that, probably staying in uMhlanga. I want to go to Durban and keep an eye on him. Just in case it gets nasty with Abby. It may be do-or-die for him there. These people are very volatile.'

He hesitated and Deon waited. 'One more point, and this complicates things. When I visited the dad I found out that his retirement village is close to the Dennison home, which could mean everything or nothing. Mark visits his father every week but varies the day from week to week. No set routine.'

'So his trips in Abby's area could be a coincidence, him just visiting his dad?'

'Yes.'

37

Tuesday, 2 April
Eight days until R1609

ROSEBANK, JOHANNESBURG

Eight weeks later, Deon was sitting at a table in the lobby bar of the Rosebank Hyatt nursing a Windhoek Lager. Abby walked in at two o'clock.

Over those weeks, they'd messaged and had regular phone conversations, Abby usually standing under the macadamia trees, away from the others. Even a casual observer would have noticed that she shared more information than he did. He made no mention of the Mark Whyte probe and mainly let her talk, which is what Abby longed for during those incredibly intense weeks of training. Someone outside of the Team to unload on and to confide in.

He had promised to keep everything she said off the record as no one wanted her training progress splashed all over the news. As far as the world was concerned, Abby Dennison had simply disappeared but, of course, nothing is ever completely secret and a few people had found out where she was and what her programme entailed.

The meeting was her idea. 'As soon as I get back, I want to catch up,' she had said. 'I feel awfully claustrophobic, kind of locked-down out here.'

He watched her cross the room and noticed that the barman and two gents propping up the bar counter stopped what they were doing. Deon wasn't surprised. Long ago he'd learned that pretty much anyone with a pair of eyes would react to her presence.

He was delighted to see her after such a long break, the sudden emotion something new and exciting, a strange warm feeling in his body and a sudden rise in his heart rate. She was no longer just a good friend, he realised, but he had no idea what that meant. He parked the thought.

She looked amazing. A pair of high-heeled sandals added to her height, pushing it to six feet. Her hair had grown since he had last seen her – which was nearly two months earlier – and the unruly blonde curls cascaded to her shoulders. Her dark glasses, as usual, were almost hidden amongst the curls.

She wore a short denim jacket over a pale blue shirt. Her white jeans fitted snugly and reached to her calves, revealing a small gold chain around her left ankle. A broad belt circled her narrow waist and around her neck a long, brightly patterned cotton scarf coiled several times before disappearing down her back. A small, black patent leather bag hung over one shoulder.

She looked slimmer than he remembered, not the emaciated look of the anorexic, but a kind of thinness that was seductive, hinting at athletic musculature that had been honed to perfection on the track and in the gym.

Abby held four Barberton daisies – yellow, white, purple and crimson – the iconic signature flowers of the Lowveld region where White River lies snugly between the hills, valleys and rivers of that lush, tropical and beautiful land.

Clutching the flowers in one hand, she thrust out her arms. 'My favourite reporter!' Her smile was wide and genuinely joyful as she encircled him with a hug that initially forced the breath from his chest. 'You look great,' she continued, now holding him at arm's length and looking him up and down, much like an aunt does to a favourite nephew, not seen for a while. 'Oh, have you put on some weight?' she teased.

Deon had to disentangle himself from her before answering. He had to look slightly upwards and he realised that she was slightly taller than him in her strappy heels.

'Too much beer,' he managed to say. 'And too many birthday festivities. Anyway, what are these?' he asked, pointing to the flowers and deftly changing the subject.

'Barberton daisies. My souvenir to you from White River. I wanted to bring a baboon or a leopard for your birthday, but Dad said no.' She laughed happily.

For a moment, Deon was silent, then he managed a muted, 'Thank you Abby, they're beautiful.'

'I know. That's why I brought them.' She kissed him on the mouth fleetingly then sat. 'Be a honey and get me a Coke Zero.'

They were there for nearly two hours and the conversation alternated between the frivolity and giggles of old friends catching up to heads-down, no-smiling, low-voiced intensity as key information was exchanged.

She told him about the White River compound, the Team's activities, the gym, the forest runs, the local school with its HOD of sport who kept the hordes away as she trained in the pool and on the track. She told him about Bonnie the family dog, the lights in the macadamia trees.

With joy, she related encounters with baboons and vervet monkeys in the nearby fields and forests, sightings of the Lowveld birds: hornbills, kingfishers, starlings, rollers, hamerkops and herons in the rivers, bateleurs and Wahlberg's eagles in the skies, even a martial eagle clutching a leguaan in its massive talons while perched majestically in a tree.

She told him about her training. 'I don't want to bore you with endless details,' she said, 'but it was pretty intense. I just trained, ate and slept. Road work and hill reps, track work, gym, swimming, a bit of cycling. Also lots of physiotherapy, massages and my favourite, aromatherapy. Obviously, for a non-athlete it would seem crazy, that lifestyle, but for me it's normal.'

'How did you cope mentally?'

'I took it one day at a time. Get up, train with JP, work out in the gym with my personal trainer, then physio, then aromatherapy, then sleep. Lots of sleep, up to ten hours a day. I had my schedule and just worked through it. Mentally, you can't think a week ahead, it would be too scary. Bronwyn and I spent an hour or two a day just talking, laughing, walking, looking at birds and flowers. Rest was key and one day in eight I would do nothing except go for a short run. Bron and I would go for drives. Twice we went into Kruger for the day armed with binoculars and cameras and one day we saw a leopard in a tree with an impala kill.'

'That's the power of the Team.'

'Absolutely. Paul is my rock, my inspiration, my manager. JP is my coach and I believe completely in him. Mizadams is like a stand-in mom, a friend and confidante.'

'How were your times in training?'

'To be honest, the best ever. I seem to have reached a new level, just enough to know that I'm in better shape than at the Bannister meeting. In my classic session of fifteen by 400 metres the average was under fifty-nine seconds. Before Bannister, it was over sixty and that's three seconds in a mile race right there.'

Deon said nothing. He knew that achieving these results on a cinder track out in the backwoods of Mpumalanga running alone against the stopwatch was nothing short of amazing. A perfect foundation for R1609.

For a while he talked about his work, pretty mundane stuff in comparison.

Abby stayed with Coke Zero and he switched to lime and soda to keep sharp. They both declared themselves hungry and ordered toasted cheese sandwiches and salads from the kitchen. The bar filled up with late-afternoon drinkers, but the higher noise levels from the people coming in after work failed to disturb their intimate conversation.

Only when several smartly dressed young women came over and asked for a group selfie and autographs did they sit back, smile and greet the people, which resulted in ragged applause and raised glasses from the drinkers.

'What about races, the ones at the end of the training period? You told me that JP had set them up.'

'What fun those were. Have a look.'

She pulled out an iPhone. 'I ran three races. Proper races, with decent competition, officials, timekeepers, about two hundred spectators, the works.'

'But no media.'

'Thank goodness, a media blackout.' She giggled and punched him lightly on the arm. 'No offence, Deon.'

'Of course. What happened?'

'Bronwyn filmed the final two, the 1 500- and 800-metre races and I dumped them onto my phone. The other runners were local men and women with real talent who set the pace and raced hard.'

'Did you treat them as proper races?'

'Absolutely. JP and I did our warm-up routine on a field as if they were the Diamond League, including having my special drinks during the warm-up and just before the start. We even had a call room, which was set up in the women's changing room in the clubhouse. We had race numbers and everything. It was quite funny actually.'

For the next ten minutes Deon stared, fascinated, at races unlike anything he had seen before. Men and women raced together, some of them pacemakers, dropping out after a lap or two, while others jumped in mid-race to keep the tempo going. The stronger men raced as hard as they could to beat Abby. She, in turn, was in full racing mode, wearing her complete racing outfit. She put her heart and soul into the competition as if the million dollars was on the line in Mbombela and not in Durban. Not to be outdone, spectators screamed and jumped up and down while officials punched stopwatches and yelled intermediate splits. It was happy, exhilarating, one-of-a-kind mayhem.

The results reflected the amount of progress she had made, and appeared as a graphic at the end of the video:

RESULTS OF THE 'MBOMBELA CHALLENGE' RACES

Friday, 29 March: 800 metres
1. Abby Dennison   1:55.9
2. Lebohang Phumzela 1:56.0
3. Reggie Boneng   1:56.7

Sunday, 31 March: 1 500 metres
1. Reggie Boneng   3:54.6
2. Abby Dennison   3:55.7
3. Lebohang Phumzela 3:56.1

Deon stared at the phone for a long time, absorbing this information. Eventually Abby said, 'Are you asleep? While you get yourself back onto the planet, I'm off to the ladies' room.'

He stood and said, 'I …' when she returned.

She cut him off. 'I know these are good times. A great time in the eight, and fourth best ever in the fifteen. Yadda yadda. Let's move on. I don't want any *ja, ja*, brilliant, and so on.'

They nursed their drinks and the room filled but they didn't notice the crowd. They were cocooned in a tiny world of a table and two chairs. Deon explained how the R1609 organisation was progressing including construction, technology and other details; he listed some of the VIPs coming, including the World Athletics president, several senior local and regional politicians, some of the directors of Regalbank and a full complement of local and international media.

'This must be costing Regalbank a fortune,' she said. 'How can they justify all this money?'

'In sport, the most important value comes from rights – TV, live streaming and even radio rights. The value of these belongs to whoever owns them.'

'And Regalbank owns all of these rights?'

'Correct. And, given the vast audience across the world for this race, the value is huge, way more than the cost of staging the meeting. There are agencies that measure these things.'

Deon could imagine the wheels turning in her head. She said, 'I get it now. This entire exercise, the whole vastness of the work and the money, it's really all about a single race, the mile race. Wow, that's incredible!'

'Correct again.'

'And if I wasn't in the picture?'

'It would be far less valuable to Regal.'

Abby was silent as she absorbed that. Deon sat back, watching her. She closed her eyes, and he could imagine the pressure she had to be feeling at that moment.

He recalled something a professor of psychology at Rhodes University had once said. 'Often, the most influential people in the world underestimate the value they represent to others, how they lift people's lives, add value and make them happy. On the other hand, many so-called celebrities who are famous just because they are famous completely overestimate their intrinsic value, which is usually zero.'

He said, 'Abby, try to move beyond the pressure and be proud of the fact that you and the Team have risen to a position of prominence and value in athletics through talent and hard work. Internalise that fact and convert it into action and success on the track, just as you've always done. Use your talent to add a little bit of joy to millions of people, like your pastor friend said in London.'

She held his hand tightly and said, 'Thank you, Deon. You are now officially the fifth member of the Team.'

He asked, 'What are your plans?'

'We fly to Durban on Friday, seven days before the race. We're staying at a private house Dad organised in La Lucia, next to the sea and away from the beachfront hotels where everyone else is staying.'

On the sound system, Freddie Mercury launched into 'Don't Stop Me Now', which made them laugh.

Then she became serious. 'Deon, I have to know. Who's running? I can guess most of the people, but can you tell me the full field?'

'There are nine runners. Suzy Marshall is the pacemaker again. We also have Mary McColgan, Elinah Kiptanui, Brigita Karlovic and Jane Beardsley. New faces are the American, Molly Fields, and Ekaterina Vinitskaya from Russia.'

She tapped her fingers, one at a time. 'With me, that's eight. I presume Sarah Moyo is the ninth?'

'Yes.'

38

Tuesday, 2 April

JOHANNESBURG

The same day that Deon and Abby were having their reunion drink in the Hyatt, Mark Whyte sat at a corner table in The Butcher Shop and Grill in Nelson Mandela Square, the towering statue of the great man dominating the square outside. Looking around, he saw with satisfaction that most of the diners wore smart suits, and sat behind laptops or gathered in small groups in what were clearly business breakfast meetings. It was exactly the atmosphere he wanted to create.

Three minutes after the agreed time, Solomon Moyo arrived at the restaurant entrance and scanned the room. Mark had studied his image on several athletics websites, recognised him immediately, stood and waved. Solomon crossed the room and joined him. They shook hands.

Moyo cut an imposing figure. Like his sister, he was not particularly tall, but his clothing was totally different from the rest of the diners. His long-sleeved shirt, hanging loose and reaching below his waist, was decorated with the colourful designs so popular in Africa, with bright red, yellow, green and blue stripes and circles. It had no collar, rather a deep V down the front. His trousers were black and he wore sandals with no socks and a white, cylindrical hat. Mark recalled such a hat would be called a fez in north African countries. He looked like a prosperous businessman from a country in the north of the continent.

He greeted Mark warmly, 'Mister Whyte, so good to meet you at last.' They sat and ordered coffees. 'I avoid heavy breakfasts,' he said with a smile, 'must be my close association with a world-class distance runner. Runs in the family.'

'It's Mark, please. We are just simple athletics fans here. Solomon, let me give you some background, you must be wondering what's going on.'

'Indeed.'

It took ten minutes. Mark had prepared carefully for this part of the discussion. Prabesh's digging had revealed a number of key facts in the Moyo family's history: the siblings' grandparents had struggled to survive under the oppressive Ian Smith regime of Rhodesia in the 1960s. Later, Solomon's father and uncle had fought in the savage bush war that ultimately resulted in their country's liberation, the creation of Zimbabwe and the departure of the despised Smith and the British colonialists. Sadly, the uncle had died after being ambushed in a forest in the Eastern Highlands just a few weeks before a ceasefire was negotiated. This unnecessary death remained a horrible reminder of what could happen as a result of colonialism that had ruled much of Africa for centuries.

After talking about his own privileged upbringing, education and entrepreneurial history, Mark said, 'Let me give you the basic summary. My business involves offering essential life and funeral insurance at low cost online to millions of unbanked South Africans. The model is successful, as you would have seen from our website, and has changed the financial landscape for some of our people. My plans are to expand this offering across southern Africa, including Zimbabwe and other countries, then further into Africa. My international technology partners and I follow athletics passionately, in particular the women's middle-distances, where the emergence of brilliant athletes like Abby, Olga, Elinah and now, Sarah, has captured the world's attention.'

He paused and drained his cup, waved to a waiter and ordered a refill.

'Anyway, you also need to know that a friend of my father's, a man called Simon, was an anti-apartheid activist in the seventies, went into exile and mysteriously disappeared in Mozambique. We believe that he was eliminated by apartheid hitmen. Moving on, I know we live in a different, post-1994 era now, but I still seek out opportunities to help talented and hard-working young African people who may not have grown up in an environment of privilege and wealth.'

'Like Dennison has.'

'Precisely. Where I can, I support young, talented runners. I have nothing against Abby personally, she is a wonderfully talented young woman, a credit to the sport we love, but now my focus is to help your Sarah achieve the same success. And, let me be honest, at the same time build my technology business across Africa. Cutting to the chase, I have assembled a group of international partners who are willing to invest in a substantial sponsorship for Sarah. We're aware of her problems dealing with the media, et cetera, but we see that as manageable. This will be a long process, but can we start the journey, Solomon?'

Solomon looked long and hard at Mark before answering. 'Let me be honest, Mark. I like what I am hearing, but learned long ago never to take things at face value. We need to consider the details, who your partners are, the kind of deal you envisage. Of course, that may change dramatically after R1609, so let's wait for that.'

'Agreed, obviously.'

Mark called a waiter over and ordered a breakfast of muesli, Bulgarian yoghurt and berries. 'Let me ask you one thing, Solomon. If we're going to be partners, I believe we should be talking the same language, have the same attitude to life. I'm pretty ambitious and don't really appreciate competition. I get what I want, in fact, I managed to get into the media centre at Bannister under false pretences. It was fun, but that's another story. I never take prisoners in business. How do you see the modern world of track and field, all that money, the rampant doping, even the diabolical Fedorova incident?'

Solomon looked across the room, pondering how to respond. Then he smiled and said, 'Up in Eldoret, my brother Samson, as well as Sarah's coach, Caihong, and I were having beers one evening. We were discussing R1609 and Caihong said something that changed my way of thinking. He said that, while all the athletes in R1609 look sweet and friendly, all good sportswomen, underneath they are mostly just sharks, willing to do anything to win, set records and take the cash. He said that this is not sport, it's war. I believe he is right.'

'No love for the competitors?'

'No.'

'But Sarah won the Bannister race, has the world record. She's now the world number one. She must be favourite for R1609.'

'No. One person stands in her way.'

'Dennison?'

'Of course.'

'But do you think she can be beaten?'

'Yes. As coach Junren said, this is war. She will be beaten, somehow.'

Afternoon: Zinkwazi, KwaZulu-Natal North Coast
That same afternoon, Sarah and her coach were sitting on the side of a grass athletics track at the local high school outside Zinkwazi, a small coastal town ninety kilometres north of Durban. For six weeks they had been staying in a nearby house, rented through Airbnb and situated on a hill with an excellent view of the Indian Ocean. In the evenings a gentle breeze filled the house with warm air that drifted up from the sea and mingled with the fragrant tropical aromas from the surrounding dense coastal forests.

The beautiful environment was not on their minds at that moment. This was a key training session. Like Abby had done in faraway White River, Sarah had been preparing in a little town, after she returned from Eldoret midway through February. She, too, had been training hard but her programme focused less on pure speed – there was no way she could string together a series of two-hundred metre sprints close to twenty-five seconds as Abby could – and more on what coaches call speed-endurance, the ability to keep running at close to maximum speed for an extended period in a race. Whereas Abby did three one-thousand-metre repetition runs a lot quicker in training, Sarah did as many as six in a session, a total of forty minutes of mentally demanding and physically exhausting exercise. Pure speed-endurance conditioning.

Sarah was in peak condition and had rested up for two days before this ultimate test. Junren spoke quietly to her as the mynah birds squabbled and fluttered in the trees. 'This is a once-off time-trial, 1 200 metres, the same as usual before a big race. It will tell us what sort of shape you're in and I'm confident that you'll do it quicker than before the Bannister race.'

She went through her elaborate warm-up routine, put on her spikes and stood at the start/finish line on the track. There was no one watching.

'I want you to go through the first lap in sixty, drop your pace to sixty-two for the second lap and then go as fast as you can on the third. The best you have ever done is 3:05 and that's a tall order. I will call out your time each lap.'

Sarah Moyo, like the elite East African distance runners, both male and female, was short and thin and seemed to have virtually no body fat at all. She was fifteen centimetres shorter than Abby and weighed in at forty-three kilograms. Her hair was braided and woven close to her scalp and she had an unusually large forehead over a narrow face with high cheekbones. Her arms and legs were skinny and her feet tiny. She looked absolutely nothing like Abby Dennison.

But looks can be deceptive, as a generation of European and American distance runners had learned the hard way. Time and again, the lithe bodies of the Kenyan and Ethiopian distance runners moved effortlessly past when it mattered in World Championship and Olympic finals.

Sarah Moyo was not Kenyan, but she was gifted with a genetic make-up similar to her neighbours in the north. No one knew for certain, but it was likely that some of her forebears had made the short trek southwards from the land of the African Rift Valley to Zimbabwe less than a century earlier. The genes would tell the story.

She was ready to go. Wearing an old T-shirt over black running shorts, she could have been a neighbourhood jogger had it not been for the bright-pink Asics spikes that would have set that same jogger back a few thousand South African rand at the local sports store. And such a purchase would have taken a while to arrive, for such high-tech footwear would have to be imported from Japan.

'Go!' shouted the coach, simultaneously clipping a digital stopwatch.

She ran off into the first bend of the track, her compact body consuming the metres effortlessly with little knee-lift or arm movement, the very essence of minimalistic, energy-efficient running.

The seconds ticked off on Junren's stopwatch. Fifty-eight, fifty-nine. On exactly sixty seconds she flashed past. 'Sixty-one,' he yelled, adding a second to the time. 'Push now!'

The second lap, not surprisingly, was four seconds slower. No runner could sustain a speed so close to their maximum for too long, especially in the mentally challenging environment of a solo time-trial on a grass track with no one else in the race and no spectators.

'2:04.'

Moyo dug deep into her reserves of grit and determination as she willed her body to go faster, faster and then even faster over the final two hundred metres. The watch clipped again as she charged over a crude white line painted on the grass.

All Sarah could think of was getting as much air into her lungs as possible as she bent over, exhausted, twenty metres past the line. Her pulse rate dropped from its maximum of 220 to 180 then 100 then 60 in less than two minutes.

She walked back. 'Coach?' she enquired.

'3:04. Last lap sixty. Very good.'

It was more than very good, it was a personal best. Just before her race in London eight months earlier she had done the same session, in similar conditions, in 3:05.

Neither Junren nor Sarah would ever know but, two weeks later, an official from the North Coast High Schools Sports Association would come to that field to prepare for a big regional interschool athletics meeting. Using a land surveyor's wheel, accurate down to half a metre, he found that the track was exactly three metres longer than the required four hundred. He instructed the groundsman to make the first bend slightly narrower to correct the error.

That meant that Sarah Moyo had run 1 209 metres in 3:05, worth another 1.5 seconds. Her real time was 3:03.5 for the three corrected laps. Not much, but critical.

Tagging on another 409 metres in 65 seconds, to make up the mile distance, would have given her a finishing time of 4:08.5.

And that was out in the boondocks, on a grass track with no competition. In the white-hot atmosphere of a world-class race, on a super-fast track, in front of thousands of screaming fans and watched by millions across the world … who knew how fast she could run? Not to mention the incentive of a million dollars.

After Sarah cooled down, she and her coach sat on the grass under a tree, the mynahs still screaming furiously. A grey vervet monkey darted past and disappeared up a tree, clutching a banana plundered from a nearby kitchen.

'Next week Friday, if you run like that in Durban and tag on another lap of sixty-two, you will run 4:05, 4:06 and win the million. And you will beat Dennison. She cannot run like that.'

Sarah wasn't so sure, but said nothing.

It was fully dark two hours later in Zinkwazi as Sarah lay relaxing in a warm bath, the soapy water enveloping her in a luxurious white cocoon of bubbles that allowed her tortured muscles to relax and eliminate the toxins that extended anaerobic exercise builds up.

Deep down, Sarah didn't share her coach's equanimity. Dennison would not just roll over. Only time would tell.

Evening: Johannesburg

The sun sets on the North Coast of KwaZulu-Natal about twenty minutes earlier than in Johannesburg and, six hundred kilometres to the north-west, it was still twilight in South Africa's biggest city as a car pulled into the parking area of the Town Lodge hotel in Grayston Drive, not far from Mark Whyte's office building. A man climbed out and went directly to room 102, dragging a suitcase on wheels behind him.

The door was opened by another man, who wore a pair of black shorts and a white vest. They high-fived, fist-bumped and man-hugged. Samson Moyo said, 'Hey bro, good to see you. The N4 back from Mbombela was busy and I nearly got a traffic fine near Emalahleni. Man, those speed limits seem to change every few kays.'

He grabbed a beer from the minibar, flopped into a chair and cracked the cap. 'That miserable little rental car couldn't go much over ninety, even on the highway. And hot, I suffered big time, man. The aircon, it just blew out hot air. This beer tastes great.'

'How was your day in Kruger?' enquired Solomon.

'Good thing I took a day off. The whole Mbombela exercise was pretty stressful but worth it in the end. I'll show you now. In Kruger I saw four of the Big Five, but I must say it's not as good as the game reserves in Kenya.'

Then Solomon got serious. 'Give it to me. You said the operation was successful. You know I don't do subtlety. Give me the facts.'

Samson replied rather angrily. 'Of course it was successful. What did you expect? Think I'm some sort of idiot?'

'Show me.'

Opening a small case, Samson withdrew a compact video camera which experts later realised would have had the capabilities of a top-of-the-range Sony Camcorder. 'Look here,' he said quietly to his brother. 'This is what I filmed when Dennison warmed up and raced in Mbombela. I couldn't get into the place on Sunday, but the Friday was easy. No one noticed me on the roof and this camera has a long range. I saw the warm-up and the race.'

For ten minutes Solomon watched the viewfinder. There was no soundtrack. There was no need for one.

'I knew it,' breathed Solomon. 'She has a routine, same as in London. Well done, bro. Don't know how you did it, but the game has changed.'

There was silence, then Solomon slapped his brother on the shoulder. 'There's more. Today I met a guy called Mark Whyte. I checked him out, he owns a successful IT company. His family has a history with apartheid hit squads and now he's an athletics fan and keen to invest in young African running talent, including Sarah. I told him to wait until she's won the R1609.'

'Things are getting better and better. Tell me more about this Whyte guy,' said Samson.

39

Thursday, 4 April

DURBAN

Natie Swanepoel drove his rented Toyota from the top of Durban's Berea down Sandile Thusi Road towards the ocean. He hung a left onto the M4 highway and headed north towards uMhlanga Rocks.

Arriving at the uMhlanga Sands Resort, he parked near the hotel entrance, checked in, dumped his stuff in his room and went downstairs to reception. When he flashed his creds and asked for the duty manager, the desk clerk ushered him into the office of Nelson Pillay, the point man at that hour.

Without preamble, Natie closed the door, handed over a business card and stood over the now-jittery duty manager. 'No need to be nervous, sir, I am just doing a small investigation. What we talk about needs to stay between us, as it is rather sensitive.'

Pillay agreed without hesitation. 'At your service, detective.'

'I believe that you have a guest here, a single man aged about thirty. His name is Mark Whyte.'

Ten minutes later, Natie had all the information he needed. Mark Whyte had arrived the day before and was booked until Tuesday, April 16, the Emperor Suite, paid up front in cash. As security, he had presented a corporate credit card in the name of MileStar Electronics, the card subsequently approved by the bank. He also booked a car into underground parking, a rented Audi A5. Natie wrote everything down in a wirebound A5 notebook.

Twenty minutes after that, he was out on the pool deck, contemplating a generous portion of Cape Malay prawn curry with a large bowl of rice on the side plus an ice-cold Castle Draft, all free thanks to the generosity of the ever-helpful Nelson. He took out his notebook, read through his notes and added a few more.

Then he leaned back in the comfortable chair and looked out over the sea. It was flat and wind-free. Several kids ran around on the beach chasing a brown dog, which scampered away each time one of them got close. Mom and Dad lay on the sand under a striped beach umbrella, the woman reading, the man sipping a cool drink and watching the occasional girl in a bikini walk past.

He took in the peaceful scene of a family enjoying the beauty of a late summer beach holiday, his body and mind relaxed as if a load had been lifted from his shoulders. It was always like this – a tough investigation, high stakes, outcome uncertain, clear thinking needed, resourcefulness, the right people to talk to, the right questions to ask. Answers leading to facts. Complete the puzzle, connect the dots. Bingo.

Natie loved his job, especially when a plan came together. He looked down at the table. The curry was still hot and the beer cold.

In the Dennison home in Johannesburg, Paul and JP were on the outside patio, discussing Abby's final hard training session before R1609, the classic fifteen by 400-metre repeats. 'It was slightly faster than in Loughborough, about half a second on each lap,' reported JP. There was no need for discussion as they both knew what that meant.

Paul's phone buzzed. The call was from James Selfe, and he came straight to the point. 'Paul, I need a favour. There is much more media activity around this race than we'd expected and we're scrambling a bit to cope with it all. You know that some of the other runners in R1609 are doing a media conference on Thursday. This excludes Abby, who will have her own one-on-one with the BBC on Wednesday.'

'Yes ...' replied Paul, guessing that there was more to come.

'Well, I must ask a favour. The media people wanted to chat to Abby but I said no, it would be a total zoo. But we discussed it a bit and I agreed to ask you if the whole Team – you, Bron, JP and Abby – could come on Friday at about noon to the beach outside the media hotel for a photo-op. No questions, just photos. We'll manage it so that it is totally non-intrusive. Just you four, for thirty minutes. Please.'

He sounded a bit desperate and Paul understood that the media would want that. In fact, they had been starved of contact with Abby because of White River. It wasn't much to ask, but still.

'That's race day,' he said. 'We'll all be pretty tense and Abby has a fixed routine. Can't it be Thursday?'

'Not ideal. The media conference will take my team all day to set up. Please, Paul, it will take less than ninety minutes from when you leave the house until you get back.'

Paul said, 'Just accredited media. We'll be there at twelve and leave at twelve-thirty. That way Abby can get back to our house, have her pre-race meal, rest a bit and get to the stadium. The timing will work because Abby and JP get absolutely everything ready early on the morning of a race. They have a checklist and nothing is left till the last minute. If we're out for a while it actually won't be a problem, maybe even take her mind off the race for a while. We leave for the race with our police escort at five-thirty and arrive at Kings Park Athletics Stadium at six. Bronwyn and I will go to the VIP centre while Abby and JP go into the warm-up area. She'll start her warm-up routine at six-thirty in time for her race at eight.'

'Paul, you are a true gentleman. We'll notify the media tomorrow. Thanks.'

40

Friday, 5 April
Seven days to R1609

DURBAN

As it happened, the Team flew to Durban on the same flight as Deon. On arrival, Abby, Paul, JP and Bronwyn were collected by an official event Mercedes and were whisked away to their house in La Lucia, while Deon rented a compact car and went directly to the media hotel.

After unpacking, he called Emily Williams on her cellphone. She was excited to hear from him and they agreed to meet for lunch on the pool deck of the hotel, with its view of the ocean across rolling lawns that ended at a wide beach.

He was enjoying an excellent filter coffee when he heard a voice, 'Deon, Deon!' followed by the sound of footsteps and a bear-hug from behind, arms around his neck. Emily had arrived.

He was genuinely pleased to see her. 'You look fantastic,' he said, and meant it. The demure hotel receptionist-cum-volunteer had metamorphosed into someone far more substantial, impressive and confident in eight months. She wore a pretty pink and blue floral-patterned dress that reached just below her knees. Multicoloured sandals, a gold chain with a dolphin around her neck and an assortment of coloured bangles that decorated both wrists were her African-themed accessories. Dark eyeshadow drew his attention to large green eyes. Her dark brown hair was cut into a fashionable bob that framed her face. She dropped a blue handbag onto the table.

'I have an expense account,' she announced proudly. 'Lunch is on me.'

Deon ordered another coffee and she settled for a pot of tea, ever so British.

She signed the bill to her room. 'Media relations,' she said with a grin.

They chatted like old friends, swopping information rapid-fire style for an hour. He told her about his work and she talked about her new job, 'the chance of a lifetime, especially out here in the sun', progress with the track meeting and details about the media plans.

It was clear from what she said that Selfe's advance party, partnering with the city of Durban, had done everything necessary to convert Kings Park Athletics Stadium into a venue befitting the status of the event.

She explained that on Wednesday there would be a one-on-one BBC interview with Abby at her La Lucia house as part of Paul's deal with James. 'On Thursday, we're having our official media briefing with all the runners, excepting Abby, Suzy Marshall and Sarah Moyo, who doesn't do interviews as you know.'

A waiter came over and they ordered a light lunch. Deon was tired after his early flight and still needed to file his first report later in the afternoon. Emily said, 'Deon, this is really a beautiful spot, the sea, the beach, the warm weather. I love it.'

He smiled. This young woman, through a combination of aptitude and hard work, had secured a plum media job in one of London's biggest banks. 'I'm proud of you,' he said, 'this time last year you were just a student with a part-time job in a hotel. Now you're in South Africa, it's fantastic.'

They were quiet for a while, soaking up the ambience, the peacefulness of everything. The sea was a calm, glassy blue, the waves breaking white on the shore. A breeze, quiet as a whisper, drifted in, cool and fresh. The gentle movement of air ruffled the leaves on the palm trees on the terrace and the salty smell of the ocean evoked images of thousands of kilometres of vastness stretching all the way to Australia.

Just then her phone rang. 'No idea who this is,' she said, 'let me take it.'

Standing, she moved away and spoke for about two minutes. 'Who was that?' asked Deon afterwards. 'A media person I guess.'

'Yes, but not someone I know. It was a guy from Cape Town, editor of the lifestyle section of the *Cape Times*, in town for something other than the track meeting. He wanted to confirm Abby's address in Durban and I remember it being in a place called La Lucia. Homeford Drive, I think it is. He wanted me to organise an interview with Abby but I said that wouldn't be possible. He was a bit insistent, so I told him to call my boss, Gretchen. She will definitely say no, so it won't be a problem. I still have to learn how to politely say no to journalists.'

The call was forgotten as their food arrived with a cheery '*Bon appétit*, folks,' from the waiter.

Two hours later, Deon had fired off his first situation report leading up to Durban's biggest-ever track race, the much-anticipated R1609.

41

Sunday, 7 April
Five days to R1609

HOLIDAY INN, UMHLANGA

It was going to be a busy day for Solomon Moyo. He and Samson had arrived from Johannesburg by air the day before, thanks to the deal he had hammered out with James Selfe. The brothers had joined Sarah and her coach in a hotel up on the hill overlooking the uMhlanga area of Durban. Each had their own room on the sixth floor with wonderful views across the ocean. The previous evening they'd enjoyed a quiet dinner at an African-themed restaurant in uShaka Marine World at the southern end of the Golden Mile, close to the harbour entrance. It had been a time of celebration after a separation of nearly two months since they were last all together in Eldoret.

Solomon elected to take breakfast in his room while Samson, Sarah and Caihong took a drive into the centre of the city to look at Kings Park Stadium using their meeting accreditations, delivered the day before to their hotel, to get past security.

As he sat down in front of his laptop, the room phone rang.

'Hello, this is Solomon.'

'Solomon, my man, this is Wilson Sibanda from the *Harare Sun* newspaper. How are you and our little champion?'

'Hey, Wilson my bra, good to hear your voice. Been a while. I'm happy there's at least one Zimbabwean newspaper here to witness history for our country.'

'Sol, you know that there is only one paper still operating there.' He laughed.

'*Ja, ja,* but hopefully one day we will have a proper country again.'

'Amen to that. Now tell me, what's happening with our lovely Sarah?'

Solomon told him everything and nothing at the same time. Sarah Moyo's elder brother had learned long ago how to give snippets of information about his sister, all wrapped up in lengthy political-speak. He had been an eager observer of Robert Mugabe in his youth. No longer.

The pair chatted amicably for a while about the state of their country, its sky-high inflation rate and the chances of another coup d'état.

'What can you tell me about the media side of this meeting?' asked Solomon. It had been agreed several weeks earlier that Wilson would be Moyo's inside man and feed back to him any information that may be of use to the Moyo camp.

'I know that all they care about is Dennison. She's their golden girl and Regalbank will do anything to make her win the race. It's all about marketing. A quiet black girl from deepest Africa wouldn't fit the bill at all. But Sarah is actually a better runner and deserves the million.'

He continued, 'There's been a change in plan. I guess you know that Dennison and her precious Team are having a photo-op on Friday at twelve. The dad, the aunty, the coach, the runner. On the beach outside the hotel on the Golden Mile. But pictures only, no questions.'

Solomon mulled that over for a while. Then he said, 'Friday at twelve. On the beach in Durban. You going?'

'Wouldn't miss it for the world.' Wilson hesitated then said, 'Hope it doesn't disrupt Dennison's preparations. It's race day, after all.'

Solomon said, 'Thanks, pal. I suppose that means they'll be away from their house for quite a while?'

'Yes, a couple of hours. Are they staying in a house and not the hotel?'

'Apparently.'

For the next three hours, Solomon remained busy and uninterrupted. First he logged on to the web and downloaded the print and television interviews that Regalbank had done with Abby in her build-up to R1609. Then he downloaded the full package of Deon Coetzee's profile pieces from the APN website. One was of particular interest. It was entitled, 'Is Abby Dennison superstitious?'

Next he watched, several times, the three videos filmed by Samson on the Sony Camcorder, two at the Bannister meeting – one at the warm-up track and the other as Abby did her final routine before the start of the race – and the third at the warm-up race in Mbombela ten days earlier.

Then he browsed the websites of Abby's various sponsors, including clothing, shoes, sunglasses and sports-drink partners. Eventually, he found what he was looking for, three advertorial interviews with her, one each for her clothing, shoe and sports drink sponsors. Typically for an advertorial, each interview included several colour images.

After a room service breakfast of savoury omelette, three pieces of buttered toast, fruit salad and cream and two cups of coffee, he logged on to the websites of four well-respected international running magazines. It took a while, but eventually he copied and pasted three more Abby interviews as well as standard print advertisements with her sponsors.

Just before midday, Solomon left the hotel. The rest of the group had returned, so he took their communal rental car and went shopping, visiting a pharmacy, a nearby Sportsmans Warehouse branch, a hardware store and, finally, the local Virgin Active gym.

Later that day, Solomon, Samson, Sarah and Caihong enjoyed tea and scones on the hotel's terrace. Away to the south, the iconic roof of the Moses Mabhida Stadium was clearly visible. Right next to MM was Kings Park, where builders, painters, computer technicians and security people were putting final touches to the infrastructure that would host the most prestigious athletics meeting in Africa's history.

42

Monday, 8 April

UMHLANGA SANDS HOTEL

Mark Whyte was pretty relaxed, all things considered. Business-wise, it had been a good week. The guys from InterTechnologies had set up a Skype meeting with him far from inquisitive ears in the MileStar offices. InterTech had increased its offer to buy his company; not the cash part of the offer, but an additional share-option scheme whereby he could buy 100 000 shares in Intech's listed parent company at fifty per cent of the ruling price at the date of the sale. He would hold them for at least three years before selling. A deal-clincher.

Significantly, they had also agreed that Mark would have a shortened two-month handover period, enough time to train up the new CEO, apparently a young genius of twenty-nine with a doctorate in statistics.

But, as he gazed out over the calm ocean, he was far from sure whether he was ready to cash in his chips and move on. Wealth was one thing, but what would he do all day? Maybe fate would play a role in the next few weeks. He had no idea.

Putting business out of his mind, Mark went onto the small balcony outside his room. It was warm, even early in the day. Durban's notorious humidity, peaking at an insufferable ninety per cent in December and January, was down to a more comfortable sixty per cent. He watched as joggers and walkers criss-crossed the famous boardwalk that goes from La Lucia in the south right up to the uMhlanga Lagoon Nature Reserve in the north.

He smiled at the thought of what would happen if Abby did the same thing, and the hordes of media people and other hangers-on that would crowd around her. Fame, he wondered, is it worth it? What sort of life must she lead, being constantly in the public gaze, never able to escape the cameras and questions of the media? No wonder Paul did what he did, keeping her hidden away.

Personally, he was happy the way things were going Abby-wise. The session with the interns had been a brilliant idea and had opened the door, sort of, to him. At least she knew who he was – a successful and wealthy entrepreneur and not a pesky, rude journalist.

Since then, he had done nothing more about contacting her, realising that her mind was fully focused on the race. He was certain that she would win and possibly break the record, and his decision to buy a regular spectator ticket in the grandstand section of the stadium was the correct one. No more inveigling his way into the media section, that was for sure.

He also pondered the weird meeting with Solomon Moyo. At the time, he was just interested in getting more information about the mysterious Sarah, another of his wild throw-caution-to-the-wind escapades. After the meeting, the more he thought about it, the more it worried him. A nagging, deep-in-the-pit-of-his-stomach sensation remained, impossible to pin down. Something was missing.

His phone rang. Mark stared at the caller identity, not particularly keen to have a conversation. The name that came up was someone he'd not heard from for several weeks. He touched the green icon.

Mark said, 'Hello my friend and loyal partner. How are you doing? Surviving the dreaded regime?'

They laughed and chatted for a while, then he was told, 'I've got something that may be of interest.'

The call lasted another two minutes. Afterwards, Mark stood for a long time on the balcony, his thoughts initially a jumble, but after a while a few things began to make sense.

He went inside and powered up his MacBook. He needed to find out where the Team was staying, knowing now that they would not be at the hotel with the other athletes. Too public, too crowded, too accessible.

But where? Not another hotel, for the same reasons. But close by, for sure.

He logged on to Facebook and went to the Abby Dennison home page. It was no surprise to find nothing helpful there. As he knew from countless visits to the site over the years, her page was filled with pretty pictures, Abby's messages to fans and her comments about everything from plastics in the ocean to the #MeToo movement. All very generic, all very bland and sweet, all profoundly unhelpful.

Mark then googled Paul and JP, neither of whom had a Facebook presence. Then he did something he'd never done before. He googled Bronwyn Adams and, to his surprise, she had a well-constructed Facebook page.

He dug, scrolled, opened and closed things. Then he struck gold. In the photos section, there was an array of images. Tucked away between pictures of elephants in the Kruger Park was a single photograph, taken with a cellphone: a patch of lawn, a low white picket fence, a stretch of beach and, off to the right, a distant line of tall white buildings next to the sea.

Then he saw Bronwyn's caption: 'View from my balcony. Hope the weather stays like this for another week.' There were several little thumbs-up emojis from her 'friends'. The image was a day old.

Mark copied the image onto his hard drive, maximised and studied it, section by section. He knew exactly where it was – next to the beach between uMhlanga Rocks and Virginia Airport. The line of buildings to the south was the famed Durban Golden Mile and its hotels. The photograph had been taken in La Lucia.

Mark concluded that the Team was staying in a house right on the beach somewhere in La Lucia. It made sense – close enough to the stadium but secluded enough to ensure privacy. And no more than three kilometres from where he was sitting.

But his problem remained. The beach adjacent to La Lucia was nearly two kilometres long and the Team's house could be anywhere. It would be like looking for a needle in a haystack, especially from the back, the only access point by road.

He studied the photograph and the caption again. He made short notes. 'Balcony', 'double storey', 'picket fence', 'right on the beach'. Helpful, but not definitive.

He went deeper into the image and scanned across from left to right. Then he noticed, on the extreme left of the frame, a rocky outcrop, right where the waves reached the beach. Across the image to the right, in the direction of Durban, there were no more rocky outcrops.

It was the kind of wave-lashed outcrop of black rocks with little pools that small boys, like himself in his youth, loved to explore, fascinated by numerous tiny fish darting about, ugly black mussels clinging to rocks, shiny crabs with eyes on stalks and fearsome pincers, hermit crabs and sea anemones waving their pink and green arms about under the water.

Bingo. He had a marker to pinpoint the house.

In Google Maps he searched for La Lucia/Durban, and chose satellite mode. The screen came to life, showing real houses, roads and a beach. Scrolling closer and closer in, he could identify individual homes, unpaved walkways from the road to the beach, swimming pools and fences.

He knew that the Google satellite had flown overhead at some point in the past, collecting the images that were now on his screen. But he had no idea when that had happened and, possibly, things could have changed in the interim. Lawns could have been turned into swimming pools, picket fences erected.

But one thing was certain – rock pools had been there for countless millennia and would be there for countless more, long after Abby Dennison, Mark Whyte and Google Maps had moved on to their various eternal destinies.

Then he spotted it – the rock pool, the double-storey house and the white picket fence. He also found a wide access path from the road down to the beach, about fifty metres long. It ran right alongside the house.

Jackpot.

He checked his flourishing three-week-old beard in the mirror, put on his jogging clothes, dark glasses and baseball cap. Then he went for a run, southwards along the beach.

He didn't know it, but at that moment there was an internal phone call to room 1011, where Natie Swanepoel was doing what detectives the world over hated the most about their jobs – waiting. Ever since he'd arrived and discovered that Whyte was already in the hotel, he'd waited. It had been long and boring, but finally, the call had come.

'Mister detective,' a female voice said, 'this is Suraya from reception. Mister Whyte has left the building in his jogging clothes. Looks like he's going for a run. Funny time for a run and it's also pretty hot outside. I guess he has his reasons.'

'Which direction?'

Suraya peered through the high windows and saw a figure disappearing onto the boardwalk, direction south.

'He's on the boardwalk heading towards Durban.'

Natie said, 'Thank you, Suraya, well done. This is very important.' He grabbed his keys and a pair of binoculars, caught the elevator, exited to the outside parking area and drove out, turning left and heading southwards. He drove about two kilometres to the spot where the boardwalk ended and parked. Five minutes later a figure jogged past, looking decidedly hot and bothered.

Natie set off on the beach after him, walking fast, about three hundred metres behind.

After exactly fourteen minutes of running, Mark found what he was looking for, the house in the picture, close to the rock pool. The grassy patch, the balcony, the white picket fence, the works. He stopped and stared at it for a long time.

From his position further up the beach, Natie watched and noted.

Mark turned, ran up a wide, bumpy, unpaved access path onto the road and back to the hotel, where he enjoyed a lazy shower and later a cold beer on the terrace overlooking the crystal-blue Indian Ocean. The surface was dead calm, the gently undulating swells evoking a feeling of peacefulness, sleepiness, the beautiful harmony of nature.

But Mark Whyte knew that things were never what they seemed. Beneath the calm surface of the ocean, he wondered what life-and-death battles were being fought, predators versus prey, eyes probing the sunless depths, tentacles grabbing unsuspecting victims, rows of jagged teeth beneath malevolent, beady eyes. Everything was hunting something. Nothing was safe out there.

He had also learned the hard way that the world of people was the same. Who can you trust? What is truth and what is fiction? When will something jump out of the dark and destroy your dreams, consume you?

He shivered, even though it was warm outside next to the calm and beautiful ocean.

43

Friday, 12 April
R1609 race day

DURBAN BEACHFRONT

The Team left their La Lucia house in a chauffeur-driven Mercedes at 11h18. Fifteen minutes later they passed through a police checkpoint and pulled into a secure parking area on North Beach. It was the only car in the cordoned-off area, and four uniformed security guards escorted them onto the beach.

They walked south along the sand for about a hundred metres, arriving at another cordoned-off area patrolled by more security people. Unlike the one in the parking area, this one was decorated with a number of colourful Regalbank banners that fluttered in the light breeze.

Five Regalbank staff, including James Selfe and Emily Williams, were waiting. A local radio DJ held a microphone connected to an elaborate sound system rigged up in a small marquee. The DJ was the person responsible for directing this crazy circus as best he could.

11h38
Durban's North Beach has a metre-high retaining wall separating it from the walkway, and Abby put her hands over her mouth in amazement when she realised that there was a crowd of at least forty people with cameras standing behind the wall.

'Look at all those people. This is going to be chaos,' she said to Paul.

'No, it's not. James has it under control.' And he did.

11h50

Marshalled by Regalbank's media people and assisted by ten security guards, the photographers were ushered forward in relays, ten at a time, to take the pictures. Mostly they were of Abby alone, looking happy and relaxed in her casual sponsored clothes and shoes. There were also photographs of the whole Team together, plus each member individually.

12h22

The photo session took thirty-two minutes to complete. The Team was ushered back along the beach, into the secure parking area and into their Mercedes. They were driven home and arrived at 12h48. They'd been gone exactly ninety minutes.

'Thank heavens that's over,' muttered Bronwyn, grabbing a bottle of water from the fridge.

'Amen to that,' said JP, the first words he had spoken in over an hour.

But it wasn't over. Not by far.

Later, independent analysts agreed that the photo-op, engineered by James Selfe in yet another effort to squeeze media mileage out of the R1609 event, had been an exercise in organised chaos that did little to endear Selfe to his board of conservative London bankers. Some called it 'undignified', others 'a mess', while others went as far as to say it had been 'an unnecessary intrusion into Abby Dennison's final preparations for the biggest race of her life'.

Everyone, it became apparent much later, had unknowingly completely missed the point. The photo-op on Durban's North Beach that day may or may not have been undignified and a mess, but it added yet another little twist to the ongoing and memorable saga that the track race known as R1609 was turning into.

44

Friday, 12 April
R1609 race day

LA LUCIA

Introduce, for exactly one hour and thirty-five minutes, a parallel universe.

11h15
Natie was in his room, again. Waiting, again. Then a call came, 'Detective, Mister Whyte is leaving by car.'

He had to rush, but his car had been left outside the entrance for just such an eventuality and he pulled out of the hotel driveway into the road a hundred metres behind Mark Whyte's rented Audi. They travelled in convoy through central uMhlanga, taking a few turns and ending up in the centre of La Lucia suburb, about a kilometre south of the end of the boardwalk.

Mark slowed, looking for a particular bumpy, unpaved pathway that led from the road between the houses down to the beach. He stopped, checked something, reversed and parked.

Natie, not wanting to be noticed, had to make a few quick decisions. He realised that Whyte had parked very close to a walkway that led from the road to the beach. But this was no random walkway, it was the one that ran alongside the house where the Team was staying. Natie knew this from information he had obtained from Deon Coetzee and, anyway, it was where he'd seen Whyte stop and leave the beach on his run four days earlier.

What the hell was Whyte up to?

Natie parked well away and decided to go to the beach rather than stay on the road. He sprinted back to the next walkway and ran down to the beach, arriving about a hundred metres north of the Dennison house. He peered onto the beach from behind a wall, as he had no desire to be spotted by Whyte.

11h32

He saw Whyte emerge from the walkway onto the beach, next to the white picket fence. Nothing happened for quite a long time. Natie stayed out of sight more than a hundred metres up the beach while Mark remained outside the house. Whyte sat down on the beach and stared up the walkway as if he was waiting for someone or something.

11h40

The next series of events took less than four minutes. There was the distant sound of a car and Mark jumped up, shouted and ran up the path away from the beach. Natie set off towards him but he was at least a minutes' run away and the sand under his combat boots was soft.

There was shouting, but Natie couldn't see what was happening. This continued until he reached the corner of the property and could see up the walkway. What he saw would be etched in his memory forever.

There was a car parked there, facing away from the sea, driver's door open, engine running. He saw two men – Whyte, and another man – dressed all in black, wearing a hoodie and white surgical gloves and carrying a small bag – who were screaming at each other. Then Whyte charged at the man, tripped over something and fell. Both were on the far side of the car, away from Natie. The second man kicked Mark a few times as he tried to stand.

Natie shouted, 'Police, stop!' and started running up the pathway, pulling out his service pistol as he went. But he was still about forty metres from the men; Mark on the ground, the hooded man standing over him.

The hooded man saw Natie, scrambled away from Mark, dropped what he was carrying in his haste to get away and jumped into his car. Because the engine was still running, he could move forward immediately. By now, Mark was on his feet, but it was too late to evade the now-moving vehicle. The enraged driver drove straight into him. Whyte flew into the air and his head hit the windscreen, which shattered. Mark crashed to the ground, landing awkwardly on his right hip.

Natie ran up to Mark, who was unconscious on the grass next to the white picket fence. He had no chance of chasing the car, which by now had disappeared onto the road. Grabbing his phone, he called an emergency number and squatted down next to Mark, who had blood all over his face, his body lying at an unnatural angle.

Looking around, Natie spotted the small, zipped bag that the fleeing man had dropped. Pulling on a pair of gloves he drew from his pocket, he carefully picked it up, unzipped it, looked inside and saw several items. He zipped it closed.

Waiting anxiously for help, he tried to remember as much detail of the getaway car as possible. Later, all he could recall was that it was a generic black SUV and there was mud smeared all over the number plate.

11h57

An emergency services helicopter and SAPS squad car arrived thirteen minutes later, the chopper landing on the beach. Paramedics quickly assessed Mark's condition, put him in a neck brace, inserted an intravenous drip and loaded him into the helicopter, which took off, clattering its noisy way towards Durban.

The responding police constable asked Natie, 'What the hell happened?'

Natie flashed his WO creds. 'I know that this is a crime scene, but we need to get away. Now.'

The officer looked at him, stunned. This was not normal procedure, far from it. 'But it's an active crime scene.'

'Look, this is Abby Dennison's house and she's probably on her way back here right now. If she sees police here she will freak out and not run her race tonight. You know about the big track meeting in Kings Park?'

The policeman nodded. They were part of the security detail, hence their rapid response to Natie's call.

Natie continued, 'If there's any comeback, I'll take the heat. Let's go.'

The officer looked doubtful, but quickly understood. 'It's your funeral, warrant officer,' he said as he and the other policeman left the scene. Natie jogged away, collected his car and drove back to the hotel, the zipped-up bag safely on the passenger seat.

12h48
The Team arrived back. They'd been gone exactly ninety minutes.

'Thank heavens that's over,' muttered Bronwyn, grabbing a bottle of water from the fridge.

'Amen to that,' said JP, the first words he'd spoken in over an hour.

No one noticed that there were skid marks and blood on the grass out on the walkway next to the house.

45

Friday, 12 April
R1609 race day

KINGS PARK ATHLETICS STADIUM

Deon went to the venue early, his normal routine, to select the best position in the media working area, set up his laptop and generally get the feel of the place and avoid the rush. Have a sandwich and a cool drink with the hospitality folks in the media centre.

For kilometres in every direction, traffic control points had been set up across the city to manage the arrival of thousands of cars. Significantly, a dedicated lane had been created that led from the city centre hotels to a closely guarded parking area just outside the new western entrance to the stadium. This route would give the more than one hundred VIPs, including several heads of state, important local politicians, numerous athletics luminaries and the runners in the R1609 and their coaches, rapid and secure access.

He looked out at the stadium, all shiny and new, the temporary stands forming a semi-circle above the permanent seats on the far side. The capacity of the stadium had been boosted by 15 000, making the total capacity close to 25 000.

There was plenty of colour. Red, gold and black – the corporate colours of Regalbank – dominated the branding. Perimeter advertising boards, mounted on the low fences that separated the track from the spectators, went virtually all round the competition area. Regalbank flags hung limply in the windless air from poles positioned high up in the stands. A two-metre high and at least fifteen-metre wide rectangular board, similarly branded, stood behind the starting line of the one-hundred-metre and high hurdles races.

THE FINAL LAP

People were busy, scurrying around with clipboards, measuring tapes and walkie-talkies. The track and field officials, whose job it was to ensure that races, throws and jumps were run strictly according to international rules, were doing final checks on track markings, stacks of hurdles, high jump equipment, landing mats and, critically, all the electronic paraphernalia needed to record and display times, heights and distances to competitors and spectators.

Deon stood inside the recently revamped media area, high up in the main grandstand opposite the finish line on the track, contemplating what lay ahead. For numerous people: athletes, sponsors, coaches and family members, this day would be important, maybe even life-altering. Business careers, record times and vast financial incentives could change peoples' lives immeasurably in the space of a few hours. For some people, life would change for the better. For others, the opposite.

Who would fall into which category? He had no idea and that, he knew, was the beauty of sport.

It was surprisingly quiet, just the muted sounds of conversation and the white noise of highway traffic. No music played, no public address system blasted messages across the field, and Deon imagined that he could even hear the waves crashing onto Country Club Beach.

He glanced at his watch: 11h50. Eight hours and ten minutes to R1609.

At that moment, the silence was shattered by the screaming sirens of security vehicles – probably the South African police, judging by the volume – moving at speed on the nearby M4 motorway, heading north. Less than a minute later came another sound, the distinctive clatter of a helicopter. He peered out from under the roof and there it was, moving swiftly in the same direction as the cars with the sirens, a yellow and blue SAPS helicopter.

He wondered what all the fuss was about. Then everything went quiet again and he returned to his work.

Seven hours later, seated in his designated media workstation watching the action unfolding on the track, there was a tap on his shoulder. Looking around he saw it was Emily. Gone was the smiling face he knew so well. Instead, she stared at him through wet, tear-stained eyes. 'What's wrong?' he asked, alarmed.

She told him.
'You mean, she's out of the race?'
'Yes.'
'Oh hell, that changes everything,' he said quietly.
'What do you mean?'
He told her.

46

Friday, 12 April
19h45

R1609

Kings Park Stadium was full. Later, the crowd count was reported to be 26 345, well over the stated capacity of 25 000. As Deon reported, 'Had the President of the United States arrived looking for a seat, he would have been turned away by a "House Full" sign on the gate.'

The athletics started quietly at 18h00 and the crowd politely sat through what turned out to be an excellent programme of track and field events, applauding generously as the medallists stood on the podium after their events. Another Coetzee phrase summed it up rather well, 'Everyone was just there for the mile race. The early events, as good as they were, were like the local high school rock band before the arrival of The Rolling Stones.'

If the crowd in the stadium was large, it paled into insignificance compared to the television audience around the world. Accurate viewer statistics provided by Regalbank's audience analysis agency revealed that, at 19h45 South African time, the worldwide television audience was between 200 and 250 million, equivalent to three per cent of the total world population, or about one in every thirty-three people on the planet.

And that was without an estimated seventy million more watching the race on live-streaming platforms in territories where television rights had not been sold, or listening on radio sets in remote areas including the Congo, the Amazon Basin, Central America, several African countries and much of eastern Russia, Ekaterina Vinitskaya's home region.

Before the runners emerged from the call room, it had been agreed that the stadium announcer, a local DJ from a regional radio station who was clearly not overawed by the immense occasion, would provide the crowd with the relevant statistics around records, best times and the incentive.

The DJ had rehearsed and read from a script. 'Ladies and gentlemen, here is what you need to know about the R1609 mile race. The current women's world record for the distance was set up last year by Sarah Moyo of Zimbabwe. Her time in London at the Roger Bannister Memorial Meeting was 4 minutes, 7.25 seconds. Now, let me give you the various statistics around this race tonight. The incentive offered by Regalbank to break this record is one million American dollars.' There was a ripple of conversation as that fact was absorbed by the crowd.

'To achieve this time, the runners need to run at an average speed of 61.5 seconds per lap. To keep the crowd informed, the organisers have set up a digital scoreboard linked to the electronic timing system. It stands in the middle of the field and faces in four directions so that everyone can see it. This scoreboard will show two numbers each time the leader passes the finish line. Based on the required average lap time, this scoreboard will show, first, the time of the just-completed lap, and second, the cumulative time that the runners are ahead of, or behind, the required incentive pace. So, just remember the number 61.5 and look for a minus number, meaning they are ahead of schedule, or a plus number, the number of seconds they have to make up. I hope you've got it.'

Probably about ten per cent of the crowd got it, and the rest nodded as if they had.

What the announcer failed to say was that a second scoreboard would be placed just outside the track on the grass, thirty metres past the finish line on the bend, facing the runners. That way they would also see the race status. It was agreed by the runners, their coaches and the officials that it would be impossible for the incentive to be achieved without the athletes knowing where they were. Intermediate times were crucial.

At that moment, the athletes for the R1609 race were gathered in the call room under the guidance of Kurt Hunsler. As a token of his gratitude for many years of service to athletics in Europe, James Selfe had invited Hunsler to Durban, and the German official was thrilled to bits, this being his first-ever trip to Africa.

Hunsler took the runners through the normal call-room routine, exactly the same as he had done eight months earlier in the Olympic Stadium. But this time there was one significant piece of information. He spoke quietly for less than a minute. There was a stunned silence, then Mary McColgan, her face a mask of shock and surprise, shouted, 'You mean, she's out of the race? She's actually not going to run?'

'Yes.'

They all stared at Hunsler in horror. 'Oh hell, that changes everything,' Mary said quietly.

Ironically, these were the exact words Deon had uttered less than an hour earlier.

Hunsler clapped his hands, moved towards the exit, put on his most authoritative voice and said, 'Ladies, it's time to get out there. Whatever happens, I wish you good luck and enjoy the race.'

After eight months of waiting, the time had finally arrived for arguably the most anticipated middle-distance track race since the Coe–Ovett 800- and 1 500-metre showdowns at the 1980 Moscow Olympics. Hunsler led eight women, their unsmiling faces hinting at a new level of fear and uncertainty, onto the Kings Park track.

The highly experienced official would later say that, in twenty-three years of athletics officialdom, he had never been more aware of the tension, electricity and excitement throbbing like a heartbeat through the stadium. 'I was actually moved to tears when the crowd started chanting her name,' he said.

Most people were. Before the neat line of runners had reached the midway point on the track, it started. Hesitantly at first, on the far side, then growing in volume as the crowds around picked up the refrain, it finally reached its peak as more than twenty thousand voices joined in the chant, 'Ab-by, Ab-by, Ab-by.' Then everyone stood, even the media people drinking beer and the VIPs sipping cocktails. For a full minute the roar swept around the stadium like a tsunami, engulfing everyone in a unique outpouring of admiration, love, hero-worship, whatever.

'Ab-by, Ab-by, Ab-by.'

Kurt Hunsler and his little brood of athletes stopped in the middle of the track in a ragged line. Some runners looked down at the ground, a couple waved weakly and the rest just stared. It was that sort of moment, a mind-numbing, emotional video clip that would stay forever in their collective consciousness. Scott Stewart, directing his many cameras from inside his OB van, had to choose between panning across the screaming, jumping and waving mass of fans, or closing in on the bemused group of runners, or zooming in on Abby herself.

He chose the latter, a wise decision. In a sequence that would define Abby Dennison the person, as opposed to Abby the runner, she briefly gazed around the stadium, smiled and then, as the camera closed in to make her face full-frame, the tears came. She closed her eyes and wept silently.

A minute later it was over. The crowd went silent, Hunsler gathered his little flock around him, said a few quiet words and put them back in line. With Hunsler proudly leading the way, they walked briskly onto the grass infield then onto the track. He gave them another four minutes to do a few strides up and down the straight. Then it was time to get down to business.

The runners peeled off their tracksuits and gave them to their personal assistants. Before handing her small bag over, Abby pulled out her Xtend drink bottle, drained it and put it back in the bag with her clothes. Her trusted ritual.

Exactly four minutes before the scheduled start of the race, the announcer said, 'Ladies and gentlemen, please welcome the runners in the Regalbank Women's Mile Challenge, better known as the R1609!'

The athletes stood side by side on the track ten metres before the start line. The crowd, raucous and boisterous minutes earlier, was now silent, reverent almost. It was like being in a church as the stadium announcer signalled the start of R1609.

'Let me introduce the field for the final event of the evening, the Regalbank Women's Mile Challenge.

'Molly Fields of the United States is the current American 1500 metres champion.

'Ekaterina Vinitskaya holds the Russian record for both the 800 and 1500 metres and is the current European champion over 800.

'Brigita Karlovic of Croatia is the reigning European champion over 1500 metres and last year was ranked fifth in the world with a time of 3:55.

'Mary McColgan of Scotland was third in the Bannister Mile race in 4:10.31 and second in the World Championships over 1500 metres.

'Jane Beardsley is the current world champion over 1500 metres and was fourth in the Bannister Mile. She comes from Birmingham, England.

'Elinah Kiptanui unfortunately could not finish the Bannister Mile race last year, but remained ranked third in the world over 1500 metres at year-end. She comes from a long line of brilliant Kenyan athletes.

'Sarah Moyo of Zimbabwe is currently ranked number one in the world over the mile and set the current world record of 4:07.25 in the Bannister Mile last August.

'Abby Dennison of Johannesburg, South Africa, was second in the Roger Bannister Mile, where she ran 4:08. She recently ran a world-leading but unofficial 3:55.7 at a warm-up meeting in Mbombela, Mpumalanga.'

Although they all looked straight ahead, six of the runners digested this previously unknown and unwelcome fact with surprise. Vinitskaya didn't, as she struggled to follow the English.

There was a pause and then the announcer said, 'Before the race starts, I have to announce a sudden and extremely unfortunate change to the field for R1609. The American athlete who was brought into the race to act as pacemaker, Suzy Marshall of the United States, has had to withdraw.' There was an audible gasp from the crowd. 'Just two hours ago, as Ms Marshall was leaving her hotel to come to the stadium, she was accidentally bumped by a man entering the hotel. She fell down five steps and in the process badly twisted her ankle. So far, security personnel have been unable to trace the man responsible. Nevertheless, the race will continue with the athletes already introduced to you.'

The crowd was silent, trying to absorb this information and what it meant.

Those even remotely in the know realised that, in a moment, the entire complexion of the competition had changed. Without a designated pacemaker, the risk was that the race could turn into a pedestrian affair with just a crazy sprint at the end deciding the winner. In a world-class field such as this, it was possible that no one would step into Marshall's shoes, lead the field at world-record pace and, as a result, probably sacrifice her own race in the process.

People appeared to be frozen like statues. James Selfe stood next to the South African president just inside the glass wall of the VIP centre; Paul had his hand on Bronwyn's shoulder just outside the VIP area; Deon Coetzee sat impassively behind his laptop in the media seating area. He'd heard the news from Emily earlier and understood the impact this could have; JP van Riet stood high up in the open stand on the first bend of the track. He had made sure there was an open passage down to the track so he could quickly go and congratulate Abby when she won. He now had no idea what would happen, but he nevertheless sucked on a large, sticky, brightly coloured and extremely sweet lollipop that he had bought from a vendor earlier in the day.

Every eye in the place was focused on Abby. She stood completely still, in the eighth lane, waiting for the command of 'on your marks'. Her competition clothing had been specially designed for the meeting by her apparel sponsor and consisted of a single item, a body-hugging short-sleeved running vest that merged seamlessly into running tights that stopped centimetres short of her knees.

The design revolved around the South African flag that stretched obliquely from her left shoulder down to her right knee. Across the centre ran the iconic twin green lines that merged at waist-level into a single line. The familiar colours – red, blue, black, white and gold – filled the rest of the outfit, front and back.

She wore a similarly coloured head band and calf-high compression socks. Around her neck was a thin gold chain, at the end of which was the small crucifix she usually wore. Her Maxx branded spikes were shining gold with four bright purple stripes down the sides.

The silence was a thing you could almost touch.

47

Friday, 12 April
20h00

R1609

'On your marks,' said the starter into his microphone. Three seconds later the report from the pistol echoed around Kings Park and was immediately followed by the roar of twenty-six thousand voices.

The eight women charged away from the start line, across the finish line nine metres later and into the first bend. Not surprisingly, the initial pace was quick as they jockeyed for early positions but, fifty metres into the race, the pace dropped noticeably. Without a pacemaker, the eight of them looked confused and rudderless, a tightly bunched group of athletes without a leader.

There was an audible groan from the crowd. This is not what they had come to see.

As the athletes went into the back straight, a voice could be heard from inside the group, loud enough to reach people in the nearby stands. 'I'll do it.' It was Jane Beardsley.

Immediately she accelerated, quickly putting ten metres between herself and the rest. Her move turned out to be a game-changer in terms of the race outcome. Deon later called it 'a heroic act of self-sacrifice'.

JP
Thank goodness for Jane, she's saved the race. I just hope she gets the pace right and doesn't go too fast. But they've already lost a few seconds in that first hundred metres.

She did go too fast. The British runner covered the next 200 metres in under thirty seconds and only Dennison, Moyo, Kiptanui and McColgan kept the pace. It was too radical for the others.

The five of them ran over the finish line in a bunch. The clock stopped on +3.0, taking into account the 109 metres already covered. This meant they were now three seconds off the required world-record pace, thanks to the pedestrian first hundred metres.

Going into the bend, Beardsley's enthusiasm dampened a little and she slowed down fractionally. They swept into the back straight, no more than three metres separating them. Kiptanui and McColgan were in lane one, Dennison and Moyo running slightly wide.

Abby
It's too soon for me to take the lead. I hope Jane can keep going.

Down the back straight, Beardsley's pace slowed again. The world's top-ranked mile runners breathing down her neck was simply too much for her and she moved out into lane three. She had led the race for 500 metres and, for everyone concerned, saved the day. They were back on pace and the chasers swept past, but they had lost a precious three seconds. Beardsley happily slipped in behind them. Now all she could do was hang on for as long as possible.

Deon
What now? With Jane not setting the pace, will it revert to another slowdown?

It didn't. With more than a thousand metres to go, Sarah Moyo moved away from the others.

Sarah
Coach told me to take the lead on lap two. No one else would have taken over. Coach said that I must think about Zinkwazi and run sixty-one-second laps to the finish. That way I can still get the record and the million dollars.

Sarah Moyo may have been nervous in company and socially withdrawn, but many people with Asperger's have been shown to have superior intelligence. In Sarah's case this translated into the ability to seamlessly process numbers rapidly and accurately.

Even though her mathematics was correct in terms of achieving the record, her pace judgement wasn't quite up to par. After racing into the lead, she settled into a pace that was later measured at sixty-two seconds per lap.

Abby
I know what she's doing. A long sprint all the way to the finish, hoping to burn us off. I'll just sit here.

They all sat there, a neat row of four athletes running at close to four-minute mile pace. Only Jane Beardsley could not hold the pace and fell back, with Molly Fields closing the gap on fifth place.

When Moyo reached the finish line with two laps to go, the clock said +3.5.

The crowd groaned again. The record now looked even more remote. They would have to run sub-sixties for two full laps.

Sarah
I have to run two minutes for eight hundred metres. I can do it. Remember Zinkwazi, remember Zinkwazi.
Mary and Elinah
This is anybody's race. The record, I'm not so sure. Just go for the win, be smart here.
Abby
If Sarah slows at all, it will be a huge battle and anyone can win. I must wait as long as possible before my final sprint.
Deon, JP
Anyone can win this thing. Incredible race.

Sarah Moyo stayed in front all the way through lap three. Kiptanui was just behind her with McColgan and Dennison side by side a metre back. You could have thrown a blanket over the four of them.

Twenty-six thousand people in Kings Park watched the infield scoreboard as Moyo reached the end of lap three. As the official rang his bell, the numbers flashed around the world: +3.0.

Abby, Deon, JP, Paul, Bronwyn
The final lap.

The first runner to lose contact was Mary McColgan, the plucky Scot, who simply could not hold the pace. The gap grew rapidly, two metres, then three, then five. Realising that her podium challenge was gone, she glanced over her shoulder, a clear signal to the runners behind that she was ripe for the picking. Beardsley and Fields gave chase.

At the 200-metre-to-go mark, Abby made her move. Going wide, she surprised Sarah by moving up on her outside. They were both going at sub-sixty pace, but the Zimbabwean refused to surrender her lead and increased her pace, forcing Abby to run wide all the way round the bend. Two metres behind the leaders, Elinah was still there.

As the trio hit the final straight, everyone in the stadium was on their feet. The noise was deafening as thousands of people joined in the thrill of the final sprint, their shouts coalescing into a wall of sound that drowned out even the announcer.

Abby was in full sprinting mode now, the colours of her running outfit flashing, her arms high, her powerful legs driving her forward in the classic middle-distance runner's charge for victory. With sixty metres to go, she pulled level with Sarah and started to inch ahead, the Zimbabwean athlete unable to sustain her killing pace. With forty metres to go, Abby was clear of Sarah by a crucial, race-winning metre.

It was game over, thought several hundred million people.

Except it wasn't.

While the vicious battle between Abby and Sarah was playing out, tiny, almost-invisible Elinah Kiptanui, dressed all in black, was biding her time. With Abby no more than thirty metres from the line, Elinah found another gear and slipped past, her arms raised in victory as she won the R1609 race by half a metre, an agonising seven one-hundredths of a second. She had led the race for less than five seconds. It was a classic, brilliant victory.

And Abby had finished second once again. The crowd was suddenly quiet. This was not what they had come to see – Abby Dennison losing and no world record. They were collectively stunned.

The runners huddled forty metres after the finish line, arms around one another's shoulders, heads bowed, chests heaving. They knew that they had shared a little piece of history. There had been no record but, without a pacemaker, theirs was a race of classic proportions, an epic. But for only one runner, small, quiet Elinah Kiptanui, had come victory. Once again, the power and skill of an East African middle-distance runner had grabbed the biggest prize. The athletes set off on the post-race victory lap, each clad in their respective national flags, handed out by specially designated officials. The now-standing crowd roared its congratulations once again in a noisy finale that lasted for more than seven minutes.

Then everyone, including the runners, went silent and stood watching as the large scoreboard flashed the results of the Regalbank Women's Mile Challenge, the now-famous R1609. The same graphic appeared simultaneously on millions of TV screens across the world.

1. Elinah Kiptanui (KEN)   4:09.12
2. Abby Dennison (RSA)   4:09.82
3. Sarah Moyo (ZIM)   4:10.88
4. Molly Fields (USA)   4:12.50
5. Mary McColgan (SCO)   4:13.00
6. Jane Beardsley (GBR)   4:14.04
7. Ekaterina Vinitskaya (RUS) 4:17.33
8. Brigita Karlovic (CRO)   4:20.45

R1609 went into the history books. It was over.

PART III

48

Tuesday, 16 April

DENNISON FAMILY HOME

JOHANNESBURG

The call had come on the Saturday, less than twenty-four hours after the race. Deon's mind was still trying to process everything that had happened and his level of alertness was not improved by the fact that he'd joined Emily Williams and other Regalbank people at a post-event celebration until something after four o'clock in the morning. Had it been mid-summer, it would almost have been dawn.

He was at King Shaka International Airport, about to board the plane for his flight home when his phone rang. 'We Are the Champions' sounded.

It was Natie. 'Howzit my mate, sorry to bother. How cool was that race? I couldn't believe she was pipped at the post like that.' He sounded a long way from happy and was clearly skirting around something.

'What's up, Natie? Why the call?' Deon was suddenly wide awake, his journalistic instincts on full alert.

'Listen my buddy, something's come up, a bit of a problem, like a pin inflating a balloon. Know what I mean?'

Deon had no idea. 'Natie, tell me.'

'Listen, we have some decisions to make. Long, long story. Can we meet tomorrow at your office, say at about ten o'clock?'

'*Ja*, but …'

'Please, can you wait? Tomorrow everything will be clear.'

'Okay.' What more could he say?

The meeting took place the next day and Deon just sat there, numbed by what Natie told him, first because of the catastrophic injuries to Mark, and second because what could have ensued, but didn't.

At the end, Natie asked, 'Do we tell Abby and the Team? What about the media?'

Deon thought about that. 'Yes and no. Yes, we have to tell the family and no, absolutely no, we do not tell the media. It will be a circus and will add unbelievable pressure to Abby. This needs to be on a need-to-know basis. As few people as possible in the loop.'

'I agree one hundred per cent. Will you set up the meeting with Paul and company?'

'Tuesday at nine unless you hear from me.'

'Thanks my mate. You are a pillar of strength.'

Deon felt sick as he walked into the Dennison home that Tuesday. Literally nauseous. Abby met him at the door so he did his best to smile, straightened his back and went inside. She asked, 'Are you okay? You look terrible.'

'Not great, to be honest.' She stared at him. This definitely wasn't the Deon she knew. A feeling of uncertainty came over her mood like a dark cloud. This sudden meeting without any warning …

A car pulled into the driveway. 'That will be Natie,' said Deon.

'Who?'

'You'll see.'

After a round of introductions, six people were seated at the big table on the patio: four extremely confused and nervous Team members plus Natie and Deon. Even though the atmosphere was relaxed and friendly, with bottled water, orange juice and a selection of Woolies cakes and muffins on offer, there was a clear undercurrent of tension, thanks to the presence of Natie in his full SAPS uniform, warrant officer badge and all. He carried a small zipped-up bag. In any society, South Africa in particular, the unexpected arrival of a uniformed police officer does little to lower tension levels.

Deon had made the call on Monday requesting the meeting, what he termed 'a post-R1609 debrief'. Paul had initially balked at the idea. 'Honestly, Deon, haven't we had enough talk about that race? Can't we wait until we've settled back into normal life? We only got home two days ago. Abby is still unhappy about everything. Blames herself for using poor tactics. She's even more depressed than after the Bannister race.' He sounded pretty upset, as only Paul could.

'This has little to do with the race. It's something else. Quite a long story, actually. You guys need to know.'

'Need to know … that sounds like spy stuff from the movies.'

'It's weirder than that,' he replied, which didn't help at all.

Deon dressed quite smartly for the occasion, by his standards. He wore a shirt with a collar – he only possessed five such shirts – with dark blue chinos and Hush Puppies. Paul looked like a businessman going to an important meeting, with an open-necked, button-down, long-sleeved shirt under a navy-blue jacket with smart grey trousers and shiny brown leather shoes. Later, Deon learned that he was 'going to an important meeting with my brother. We're looking at some investment opportunities.' Interesting.

JP, as always, wore his trademark tracksuit, training shoes and branded cap. Bronwyn looked smart in a dark grey suit over a white shirt. Her usual string of pearls hung around her neck. She looked the picture of elegance, her shiny light brown hair cut short above her ears. She was going with Paul to the lunch meeting.

Although she looked good in a denim shirt under a thick green jersey and Levi's, Abby's mood clearly didn't match the brightness of her outfit. 'I'm tired,' she announced after shaking hands formally with Natie. 'Honestly, can't you do this without me? My feet are sore after my run today.'

She took off her shoes and put her feet up on a low wall around the patio, her long legs stretched out elegantly. They were the legs of an athlete-goddess, fit for the legs hall of fame. Perhaps that was why she did it, or maybe not. Anyway, her feet looked fine to Deon.

Bronwyn ruffled Abby's hair. She smiled and said, 'Sorry, that was rude. You guys came here for a reason.'

The small talk was over and Deon got down to business. 'Thanks for your time, everyone. And let me say at the outset, this is not a pretty story. In fact, it's quite ugly, as you will see. Today, Natie and I will be giving you some simple facts. I'm not sure, but I guess that, as you process what you're going to hear and discuss everything amongst yourselves, you will want to speak with people outside this little circle, people skilled in helping you understand how the world works and how we are continually surprised and even shattered by what we learn about others.'

The silence was complete. It seemed that even the birds had gone quiet.

Natie continued. 'I have to stress now that what we'll be telling you today is highly confidential. Only twenty-seven people outside of this group know the full story, including the South African president and the ministers of sport and police. The president, in particular, wanted the details because, as he put it, "we must look after our national treasures, which include Abby". This cannot get to the media or the general public. In fact, as you will see, it's part of an ongoing criminal investigation which could be compromised. It was only Deon's insistence that we have this meeting at all. But I trust you, as does Deon.' He smiled.

'Holy hell,' exclaimed Paul, 'what on earth is going on?' He'd suddenly gone pale and sweat beaded his brow.

Deon said, 'What Natie will now tell you summarises what we know. The investigation, as he mentioned, is ongoing. But there's enough here to inform you of what happened at the Bannister meeting and now at R1609.'

Autumn in Johannesburg can be beautiful. Cool day temperatures convert into chilly evenings where a warm coat, fluffy slippers and a thick scarf work well. But chill is not always in the temperature. It can be felt in the atmosphere of a room when there is a sudden shift in the general mood. Laughter gives way to frowns; no one speaks; eyes cast to the floor or out the window, seeking something beautiful or even normal to distract from the tension.

Natie felt truly sorry for the little group of people at the table. Imperceptibly, they had moved closer together. Bronwyn's hand was on Abby's knee. In the face of an unknown threat, such as really bad news, blood pressures rise and people sweat. Fear is a tangible thing. But Natie had done this hundreds of times before – given awful news to innocent people. Part of his job description.

Deon moved on swiftly. 'Let me start by saying that none of this is a risk to you now. It's about you and the whole Bannister, R1609 thing, but you guys are not at fault in any way. It happened around you, not to you.'

'Let's hear what you have to say,' said Abby calmly.

For the next fifteen minutes Natie told the story of how Mark Whyte got himself accredited as a media person at the Bannister meeting.

'One week before Bannister last year, the media department in London received an application for accreditation from a South African journalist called Mark Whyte from an athletics website, MileStar. No one had heard of him or his website but, because World Athletics wants to spread the sport to African countries, he was accredited and arrived in London. James Selfe and Simon Hardy did some digging because they weren't happy with the whole MileStar thing. On the surface, the actual website looked fine, but then Regalbank found that there were a suspiciously large number of images of Abby on Whyte's computers and that the website was almost certainly fake.'

Paul said, 'We know this guy. In fact, Abby spent time at his company with some interns before R1609. He seemed legit then. You mean the guys in London hacked his computers?'

Natie continued, 'Your words, not mine. Anyway, the investigation led to an IT company called MileStar Electronics, which, as you know, has its offices on Rivonia Road, less than five kays from where we are now, as it happens. It's owned by Whyte. James Selfe was concerned that there may be some sort of risk to Abby and got his friend, a guy known as QSH in the spy business, to have Whyte followed while he was in England. Then it got comical. Whyte managed to disappear after attending the Bannister meeting as a fully accredited media person by changing his flight and going home via Paris.' He smiled. 'Off the record, the Metropolitan Police are not what they are cracked up to be, it seems.'

Bronwyn said, 'So Whyte must have been tipped off?'

'Yes,' said Natie. 'The hack into his MileStar computers, when they found all the Abby images, was detected back in Joburg. Mark got the hell out of there. I would also have done that, to be honest.'

'Stop right there,' said Abby, raising her hand like a traffic cop, angry now. 'What the heck is going on? Who is this guy, what's he up to? At his office that day with the interns he seemed fine, friendly. Now he's got photos of me on his computer and the London police are tracking him? What sort of photos? Has he been peeping through my window? What happens if they end up on the internet? Is he some sort of risk, like a rapist?'

There was silence and everyone looked at her. They realised that her questions were valid, the kind that any South African woman would ask, given that gender-based violence was endemic in the country.

Natie stepped in. 'Abby, let me assure you that all these photos are benign. It was the first thing I asked QSH. Whyte obviously took most of them himself, you in the shops, running on the track, that kind of thing. Some are downloaded from websites. Nothing dodgy.'

'Okay, that's something, I suppose. But still, why the London police, for heaven's sake? They must have thought he was a criminal.' She paused, then said, 'Wait a minute. Is he a stalker?'

Her body language changed. From being wide-eyed, aggressive, chin thrust out and speaking loudly, she slumped down into her chair. 'I must be naïve, a baby, completely out of touch with reality. I guess women like me must be a target for weird men. But I don't understand the psychology. Someone please explain it to me.'

Then she started crying, gentle sobs and tears, her head down in her hands, body shaking gently. 'It's all too much, this running thing,' she said. It was a pivotal moment, everyone realised.

Bronwyn spoke. It was the voice of reason, compassion and experience. 'Here are my answers to your questions. I don't have the full picture, but this is my analysis and advice to you and it's based on personal experience. Without too much detail, let me say that I, like numerous women, have had my own share of abuse. It happened when I was young, still a teenager, and it coloured my view of men in general for years. I'm single, say no more. Then I dug into the whole stalking issue when I was studying psychology, got help from my professors, read a lot and came to several conclusions. Basically, stalking is pretty common, especially for high-profile, attractive and successful women. It's a fact, happens across the world. Occasionally it turns nasty, especially when the stalker has a close relationship with the victim. Now I'm not saying that Whyte is a classic stalker; he may just be a sad, confused young guy. But the problem needs to be addressed and, in this case, not by me or Paul, but by you, Abby. We need to plan this carefully, but you have to sit face to face with Mark, ask him about the pictures, the fake website, the possible car-following scenario, which you mentioned to me occasionally. He needs to know that you know.'

Abby said, 'I agree. And if I find out that he is actually a bad guy and not just a confused fan, I want him punished in some way.'

'Personally, I'd like to kill the bastard,' said Paul grimly.

Natie patted Paul on the shoulder and smiled. 'Actually, you might not when you hear the full story. I also did some digging and have some experience as well. I spoke to Mark's father before R1609, part of my background research. Here we have a case of a lonely young guy, very successful in business and very rich. He started his own IT company which took up all his energy, leaving him no time for relationships. In any case he had a fractured relationship with his mother and a very pushy father. He became more and more scared of relationships and at the same time was obsessed with the whole idea of Abby, her success, her looks, her mystery, sort of.'

'That's true,' said Bronwyn. 'Sad, really.'

'In this case, profoundly sad, as you will see.'

Abby said, 'He should still be punished somehow. Even if he is a sad, confused guy with fractured relationships and a pushy father. He can't just walk away.'

Deon spoke. 'Guys, let's stop right there with this talk of punishment. What follows now is the real story, why we are actually here. I don't know about all of you, but I need a beer. Abby tells me you have a decent stock somewhere.'

That eased the tension in the room and Abby disappeared into the kitchen and returned with a green bottle, cold and dripping condensation, and a glass. 'Windhoek. Your favourite.' She gave him a brush-kiss on the cheek and a quick hug. He blushed.

Natie stood, which made everyone go silent.

'Even though there was a possibility that Whyte was potentially harmless, we didn't want a repeat of the Bannister episode at R1609, so Deon asked me to keep an eye on him, should he go to Durban. A brilliant move, as it turned out. After digging around how he spent his youth, his formative years, I knew that the family always went to uMhlanga Rocks for their holidays. Sure enough, he was booked into the Sands Resort exactly during the R1609 period. I also checked in there. Coincidentally, it's less than three kilometres from your house in La Lucia.'

Deon added, 'Natie wanted to see what Mark did. Basically if he was any sort of threat to Abby.'

'I watched him, day and night pretty much, for four days. He also asked the hotel to get him a regular ticket to watch the track meeting. This time he was going as a spectator, not a journo. He'd learned his lesson, it seems. He did nothing but stay in his room and go for a few runs on the beach.'

Abby got the picture immediately. 'Northwards or southwards?' she asked.

'Mostly northwards, but twice before race day he ran southwards towards Durban. Past your house in La Lucia. Even now I have no idea how he figured out where you were staying. But he's a smart operator. I tailed him but he just ran past your place on the beach, turned around a few minutes later and went up to the road behind the house. The beach is quiet in that area, as you know.'

'Then what?' asked Bronwyn, in a way that suggested she had no desire to hear the answer.

Deon said, 'Okay guys, this is the crunch. Please let Natie finish. It's not a pretty story, but it's true. It also says a lot about the evil that can inhabit people, the power of unbridled greed, the lengths to which criminals will go. Can we take a minute? This whole thing makes me sad and angry at the same time.' Without waiting for an answer, he left the patio and walked around the pool. He could feel tears welling up but gathered himself and sat.

There was silence again and then Natie spoke. 'The day of R1609, only last Friday would you believe, I was in the hotel where Whyte was staying. This was key as it was race day and if something was going to happen, it was then or never. From Deon, I knew that the Team was going to this beach photo-op thing at midday and that you would be away from the house for a couple of hours from just after eleven. To this day I have no idea how Whyte also knew this, but at exactly 11h15 he left the hotel in his car and went south towards the house. I followed. He parked in the road.'

Natie then told the Team the whole story of the attempted break-in, starting with, 'for a while, nothing happened, then ...'

When Natie finished, Abby grabbed Deon's hand and clutched it as if she was drowning in a turbulent sea.

'Where is he now?' she asked, pale as a ghost.

'They stabilised Whyte and took him straight to Entabeni Hospital where they treated his broken ankle, but the problem was his head injuries. To get the best neurosurgeons, he was airlifted by helicopter to Hillside Clinic here in Joburg that same night, still unconscious. He has plenty bucks, so expense was no problem.'

'How's he now?' asked Paul. He looked broken.

'They thought he might need brain surgery, but that's apparently not necessary. They put him into an induced coma because there was swelling on his brain. They said it was touch and go but that was Saturday, since then I've not had an update.' It was all he could say. It was the truth.

Abby looked grim. Gone was the happy Oxford girl. 'Who was the guy in the car? Did you catch him?'

Natie shook his head. 'We have no idea. He was gone before I could get a good look at him. The car was a generic black SUV, maybe a Kia or a Honda. I had no time to catch the details. I do remember that the licence plate was covered with mud. It's gone, and with it our best lead.'

Even the normally unflappable JP looked grim. He asked, 'What did you recover from the scene? What the hell was this guy doing there? You said he dropped a bag.'

Natie put a dirty zip-up leather bag on the table. Everyone stared as if it carried the plague.

'We found a full set of master keys to the La Lucia house, the kind burglars use to break into homes. The alarm was set off but he took the chance of only being inside for a few minutes. Too short for the security guys to arrive. Then we found this.'

He reached into the leather bag and put an Xtend bottle on the table. It was identical to the one Abby took to races.

Abby screamed.

It took a while for Deon to say, 'He was going to go inside, find your regular bottle somewhere, swop it and get the hell out of there. He knew that you always set up your tog bag the day before. You mentioned that in one of your interviews. You wouldn't have taken it to the photoshoot. There was a good chance you wouldn't notice the new bottle. It was exactly the same.'

'Why the hell would he do that?' asked Abby, now recovered and hyper-alert.

JP said, 'I know. He planned to ruin your life, totally and completely. To take away the glory of you possibly winning the race, setting the world record and collecting the million dollars. To open the way for other runners to dominate middle-distance track athletics. To show you just how much he hated you.'

There was silence for at least a minute as everyone digested that. Paul, Abby and Bronwyn stared at JP, confusion and fear competing for dominance in their minds.

Eventually, Abby asked, 'Some sort of poison, to stop me running?'

JP said, 'I'm pretty certain I know, but I need Deon to confirm my fears.'

Deon answered, 'Not poison. In fact the worst possible scenario short of attacking you physically. In that bottle was your regular Xtend sports drink. It was diluted exactly as you would have done it. You wouldn't have noticed a change in taste because the amount of stuff in there was tiny and formulated so that the taste would be the same, but with just enough extra ingredients to achieve his goal.'

'What the hell was in there?' asked Paul.

Natie replied, 'The lab result came back yesterday. In the drink were traces of stanozolol, a banned anabolic steroid, and fencamfamine, a banned stimulant.'

The Team absorbed this information and slowly everything made sense.

Abby was ashen. 'If I'd taken that, it would have been absorbed into my system by the time of the post-race dope test. I would have crashed the test, been guilty of both stimulant and steroid use, disqualified, stripped of both my Bannister and R1609 results, received no prize money, been disgraced forever, banned for at least four years and lost my sponsors. And, by the way, become the laughing stock of the world, ruined the lives of Dad, Mizadams and JP, disappointed millions of fans, and sent the sport of athletics firmly into the dope-addled universe of cycling and other suspect sports. Holy shit.'

'Exactly,' said JP, 'a genuine doomsday scenario.'

Abby looked around, eyes wide in horror, fear and anger. Everyone waited for her response. In doping situations, it's always the athlete on the line, not the coach, parent or partner. No avoiding culpability. Subconsciously, they all knew that, so they waited, hardly breathing.

Eventually she spoke. 'Guys, I need to process this carefully. To be honest, all this information has shaken my world. Natie, thanks for everything you've done. Honestly, without your incredible dedication and skill, my life would have been ruined. Now I want my Team and Deon to sit down and sort all of this out, where we go from here.'

She hugged Natie for a long time, her eyes wet with tears of genuine gratitude. He looked embarrassed but still managed to say, 'Just doing my job, folks.' It was time for him to go and, after a round of handshakes, he left the house.

The five of them sat for an hour, Bronwyn gently driving the discussion. It was intense, emotional and ultimately liberating.

Eventually, she summed up the discussion. 'The attempted doping was a crime, pure and simple. Thanks to a set of circumstances, it didn't have the desired result. But we need to learn from that and move on, sadder but wiser. The outcome is out of our control. Natie and the athletics authorities will do what they have to do.'

'Okay, so we move on,' said Paul, 'to the inevitable issue of Mark the potential stalker. We dare not forget that or it will haunt Abby for ever. Bron, what do we do?'

The teacher looked at her young friend. 'Now it's all about Abby, her career, her life.' She put her hand on Abby's shoulder. 'What do you want to do?'

Deon looked at his friend, recalling the girl from their schooldays. He could have been mistaken, but he sensed a new resolve in her body language, an almost-smile on her face, a confident look as her eyes swept across the table. She was in charge now, he realised with a burst of pride.

She said, 'Mark prevented the doping thing from happening and now he could die. He literally saved my career, my life almost. But he also could be some sort of stalker. It's a weird combination of factors and the only way that I can possibly move through this mess is to go face to face with him. Put it all on the table, both my deep gratitude for him risking his life, and my fear of being stalked. I want to see him. I don't care what state he's in, induced coma or no induced coma. Deon, you're coming with me. As soon as possible. Please will you set it up?'

49

Thursday, 18 April

SANDTON, JOHANNESBURG

Hillside Clinic is situated in the central business district of Sandton. Because of its location close to some of Johannesburg's wealthiest residential areas, it attracts upmarket clientele with deep pockets and substantial medical insurance cover. It is generally accepted that the level of care ranks among the best in the world.

Like on any mid-morning Thursday, the place was busy, with visitors, patients and doctors passing through its wide doors.

Just after 10h00, a car pulled into the parking lot and Abby and Deon climbed out. Her eyes were hidden behind dark glasses. They went through the lobby to the elevators and exited on the third floor, which was quiet and smelled of floor polish and disinfectant. On their right was a set of double doors with a sign that read 'Surgical Ward'. Abby was surprisingly calm as she stood outside the doors. Deon was considerably less calm but he realised that, for Abby, this was rather like going onto the track before a big race: the mind takes over and creates calmness in the face of intense pressure and profoundly uncertain outcomes.

Deon rang a bell, and the doors were opened by a tall man in his fifties, wearing a white coat. He looked stressed and uncertain about how to respond to one of the most recognisable women in the country. He nodded curtly and said, 'Welcome, I'm Mark's neurosurgeon, Doctor Eric Wasserman.'

They shook hands formally and he continued, 'Deon, thank you for your call requesting this visit, but I have to say that I have limited the number of visitors to this patient to immediate family members, of which there is actually only one, his father. No friends, no work colleagues. I have no idea why you wish to see Mister Whyte, Miss Dennison, but given your profile, I suspect there must be a very good reason. Can you give me some idea of what it is?'

Abby took off her dark glasses and said, 'Doctor, I appreciate your position and I thank you sincerely for even considering our request. At this time I can't give you any more details about why we're here, as these are confidential. However, I can say this and I hope that it will mean something. I will be in that room for less than two minutes, just myself. Mister Coetzee will wait outside. Based on absolutely no evidence at all, I hope – no, I actually believe – that what I plan to say to the patient may be helpful in his recovery, and my own, for that matter. I'm no doctor and no expert on the human brain – not yet – but I read somewhere that people in comas can register what someone says to them. And what I plan to say may just, somehow, help this man.'

Before they moved down the passage, Deon asked, 'What are his chances, Doc?'

'To be honest, I can't give you a definite prognosis. There was severe head trauma but I honestly believe that this patient, young and strong, has more than an even chance of making a full recovery. We'll know in a few days, one way or the other.'

'How important was the initial treatment?' asked Deon.

'It saved his life. I have to say that the paramedics and surgeons in Durban were excellent, even though they're Sharks fans.' He smiled weakly.

Abby asked, 'Can I see him now?'

Most people, from politicians and sponsors to business executives, media people and athletes, look at Abby Dennison and see what they expect to see: a tall woman, famous athlete, world champion, media darling. Eric Wasserman had done this when he'd opened the ward doors.

But of those thousands of people who had interacted with Abby the athlete, very, very few understood that her public persona was only part of the full picture. Under the very real physical presence and sporting success was a person with significant understanding, real courage and deep empathy. In just a few minutes, Eric Wasserman joined that select few. He was no fool.

'Come inside, Miss Dennison,' he said. They went in and closed the door.

Inside the private ward at the end of a passage, the scene was like something out of a medical television series: a man on a bed, perfectly still, eyes closed peacefully. He had a breathing tube down his throat and several needles in his arms, taped down. There were connections everywhere: a pipe from the breathing tube led to a ventilator; tubes snaked upwards to large and small plastic intravenous drip bags hanging on steel poles, the large bags pumping balanced fluids and essential nutrients, the small bags delivering life-saving antibiotics.

A plastic SATS monitor on his left index finger, looking rather like a clothes-peg, connected to a machine that flashed his blood oxygen levels in red numbers on a screen. Six electrodes stuck onto his chest each had a wire that led to a heart machine, its perpetually moving orange ECG patterns pulsing as they moved across a screen at a steady seventy beats per minute. Another tube snaked from under the blankets to a half-full urine drainage bag hanging from the bed frame.

In the quietness, the various monitors beeped and pulsed with a life of their own, while the ventilator membranes opened and closed, hissing and sighing as the machine breathed for him.

His head was swathed in white bandages.

All the typical, frightening images and sounds of desperation, dread and lurking death.

Abby responded with a sharp intake of breath. She had never seen anything like it in her life. As she stared at the serene face, she immediately recognised him from the day with the interns. But now he looked years older, his skin a sallow yellow, his lips drained of colour, cheeks sunken, scraggly beard unkempt and not at all fashionable.

She noticed that one ankle was encased in plaster of Paris.

Eric Wasserman stood silently as she spoke and he noticed a hint of moisture in her eyes. Her tone was gentle, soothing. 'Mark, I'm here to give you a message from my heart. I want to thank you for your bravery. I don't understand why you took so many risks for me, but in the end you effectively saved my life. Now yours hangs in the balance. I want you to recover completely and get your life back. I also want to understand you better and help you to see yourself as a person with much to offer. When you recover, as you will, you must find your true self, your true destiny and your true love.'

She stood with her eyes closed for a few seconds, then glanced at the heart monitor standing on a table. She noticed with a shock that his heart rate had accelerated to over ninety. What was going on? He was in a coma and comatose patients don't hear things. Or do they? She had no idea.

Four minutes later Abby and Deon exited the parking area of the clinic and turned left towards Bryanston.

50

Sunday, 21 April

BRYANSTON, JOHANNESBURG

A cellphone bleep signalled an incoming WhatsApp message. It was an unfamiliar number.

'Can you come to the hospital as soon as possible? There has been a development.'

The man lifted himself slowly out of a deep chair in the residents' lounge, moved to the reception area and spoke to the receptionist on duty. She looked at him with sympathetic eyes, for he'd aged visibly in the past two weeks. His face seemed to have deep lines added around the mouth and the skin under his eyes was puffy from lack of sleep. He had lost weight and his trousers hung below his waistline. The buttons on his shirt were incorrectly done up.

The night staff had reported seeing him sitting out in the garden at two in the morning in his pyjamas on several occasions. Everyone was worried.

Five minutes later, he was in a branded minibus with a driver and after fifteen minutes they walked into the reception of Hillside Clinic. 'Doctor Wasserman, please,' he asked the lady behind the welcome desk. She made a call and the neurosurgeon appeared in his white coat and took the man up to the third floor to a private ward with a view over the parking lot.

The man stopped outside the door, seeming to gather himself for what he would see inside. But what he was actually doing was listening. Listening for the characteristic and truly awful hissing and wheezing of a ventilator.

He heard nothing, which could only mean one of two things.

He hesitated, knowing that the next few seconds would be critical, possibly life-altering.

'Please come in,' said the neurosurgeon, taking him by the arm.

They went inside.

A man lay on the bed with several needles in his arms. These were connected to tubes that emerged from plastic bags on a drip-stand. But there was no cardiac monitor and no SATS machine.

No wheezing, whispering, sighing ventilator.

The patient slowly opened his eyes. 'Hello, Dad,' said Mark Whyte, 'It's good to see you.'

51

Saturday, 4 May

GRACEMOUNT HOTEL, MAGALIESBERG

After living in Johannesburg her whole life, Abby knew that there was a shortage of really beautiful places to escape to when life became hectic and stressful. The nearest ocean was nearly six hundred kilometres away and the Vaal River, while wide and impressive, was a boring, dirty brown colour. There were no mountains close by to interrupt the bland, flat landscape of the Highveld. Waterfalls, lakes, beaches? Forget it.

But she did know that there were little gems hidden away that offered the stressed-out city dweller a haven of pampered luxury that could be reached in less than two hours' drive from the metropolis. Classy, but pricey.

Such a place was Gracemount, a country hotel of epic quality tucked away at the end of a winding road in a densely wooded region of the Magaliesberg hills to the north-west of the city.

It was to Gracemount that she escaped that particular Saturday. She'd discussed the trip with no one, including the family and Deon. Truth be known, in the weeks since R1609, Abby's day-to-day life had changed. She still followed JP's training programme and consulted the Team on occasional media interviews, sponsor meetings and invitations to talk to various groups. But in other areas she had been privately questioning what she was doing with her life. Everyone realised just how damaging the second consecutive loss in a major race had been, but even Bronwyn had decided to let her deal with the situation in her own way.

The revelations about the potential doping and Mark Whyte's suspicious behaviour only added to her general discomfort.

She had become introspective, remote from people. She spent hours online in her bedroom. Everyone pretty much left her alone.

Critically, the Team had avoided the topic of racing after she'd blurted out back in April, after Paul suggested they sit down and plan the summer racing season, 'Guys, give me a few weeks. I don't want to even think about racing yet. I'll carry on with JP's winter programme but can we hold off on the planning for a bit? Please?'

Abby had been in contact with Dr Wasserman and knew that Mark had recovered. 'It was as close to a miracle as I've ever seen,' said the neurosurgeon. 'But he still needs several weeks of recuperation to regain his strength, preferably away from the pressures of work. I recommended the Gracemount.'

Abby had also enjoyed a number of lengthy coffee sessions with Deon in the week after their visit to Hillside Clinic. Naturally, the subject of Mark was at the top of both of their minds. 'I think I want to visit him. I need answers and I want to know how he's recovering.'

Deon said, 'Do you really want to see him? Do you feel safe enough? I'm also pretty sure he knows nothing about the attempted doping story. It's been kept completely under wraps. If you do go, will you tell him?'

'I don't know. Maybe, maybe not. But I also need to understand him better, especially his obsession with me. I may even have to confront him about that. He needs to know it wasn't okay.'

Deon responded, 'Mark, impetuous, brilliant, tortured, sad Mark. He's the kind of guy who's always been in control of what he does, but his judgement is often poor, particularly when he makes bad decisions on issues around emotions, where he lacks common sense. People even say he has a mental illness, obsessive-compulsive disorder, that he's narcissistic. I believe that his random, erratic behaviour happens mainly because he has no one to modify him, advise him. There is no governor on his accelerator pedal. He just presses it down and goes faster and faster. He gets a thrill out of the sheer speed of his life, the risk of disaster at any moment.'

Abby recalled what Wasserman had said and phoned the hotel, confirming that a Mr M Whyte was in residence. 'Can I direct your call to him?'

'No. Just make sure you tell him that someone will be visiting him tomorrow at ten and that this will be an interesting visit.' She was banking on his natural curiosity to overcome the desire to be left alone. People normally cannot resist a surprise.

At exactly ten o'clock she walked into the hotel's sumptuous lobby and headed for the front desk. Halfway across the room she noticed a man easing himself out of a chair. He stood, then stopped. No part of him moved, arms remaining in a walking position, head turned towards her, eyes wide. He looked like a person frozen in time, like something you see in a waxworks.

Mark didn't look at all like she'd expected. He was thin, his hair long and uncombed. He wore a long-sleeved T-shirt that hung below his waist, baggy, oversized tracksuit pants and slip-slops without socks.

After a few seconds he said one word, 'Abby.'

'Hello Mark.' She thrust out her hand and, as if by instinct, he shook it. He looked like he'd seen some sort of ghost.

'What are you doing here?' he asked lamely. By now, they'd caught the attention of the people in the room and she heard the inevitable whispered words. 'Look, that's Abby Dennison, the runner!'

'Mark, let's go somewhere less public.' She took his arm and moved in a direction that she hoped would lead to somewhere with fewer gawkers, but still within shouting distance, should she need help. She waved to the people in the reception area. 'Cheers folks, have a nice day!' and noticed a few of them reaching for their phones.

Mark followed her down a passage where, mercifully, there was a small lounge area with large, deep chairs. A waiter appeared and Abby said, 'I would like a pot of rooibos tea, a small jug of milk and two of your famous choc-chip muffins with cream. And you?' She waved casually at Mark.

'The same, please,' he said, meekly.

She looked around. So this was how the wealthy escaped the city. The room was small and comfortable. Soft choral music filtered gently from a hidden sound system and she recognised the joyful excitement of the 'Hallelujah' chorus from Handel's *Messiah*. Classical pieces from Verdi's *Requiem* and Bach's *Magnificat* followed as the morning progressed.

Clusters of genuine leather chairs nestled on the dark red, deep-pile carpet.

Two of the walls were wood panelled and one had rows of bookshelves crowded with volumes that ranged from *The Complete Works of William Shakespeare* and Jane Austen to Danielle Steel and Wilbur Smith. Evidently, wealthy people had eclectic tastes in literature. There were no self-help books – the Gracemount clientele apparently had no use for them.

On two walls, dark blue, double-width, hand-pleated curtains were drawn, cutting out the light and darkening the room, giving it a midnight feel. Without three elaborate chandeliers that hung low from the ceiling, glittering weakly, and several standard lamps with gold lampshades, they would have been in darkness.

There were no other hotel guests in the room, but staff did occasionally wander through. The intimacy of the setting was somewhat unsettling and the silence awkward. Then their teas arrived, changing the mood. When she gave the waiter a generous tip he said, 'Thank you ma'am, but an autograph would be wonderful.' A pen and paper appeared from somewhere and she signed.

Mark looked directly at her. 'Seriously, Abby, why are you here? I mean, it's miles out in the country. I haven't seen you since the session with the interns.'

'This is a long story. There are a couple of very good reasons for this visit. There are two things I want to say. Actually, one of them is a question and the other is a deep, profound thank you from the bottom of my heart. But first the question, then the thank you. Tell me about your trip to London, the fake website, the photos on your computer. You can't be surprised that I know about that. I just need to understand why.'

Mark looked at her, considering how to frame his response. He was calm, measured and in control. He decided that it was time for honesty, no more bluffing, pretending and lying.

'I'll begin at the end. Today, I'm sitting here the survivor of a near-death experience. No one knows how that feels until it happens to you. It changes your entire view of life. But please tell me, how did you know about the MileStar website and my computer's hard drive? You must realise how embarrassing that is for me.'

'I do, seriously. But it's all part of the longer story I mentioned earlier. I have no intention of coming all this way to punish you in some way. I just need to understand. To put it bluntly, were you stalking me?'

For the first time, Mark looked uncomfortable under her direct, watchful gaze. She just sat there, waiting. He took a long time before answering.

'I definitely, absolutely meant you no harm. All my life I have admired a few people whom I saw as driven, motivated and super successful. Mainly entrepreneurs who built business empires from nothing. You know the kind of people I mean, Steve Jobs, Richard Branson, the local guy Adrian Gore. I read their biographies, studied their methods and somehow wanted to emulate them. None of them were women. Then you came along, completely unlike my other heroes. Firstly, you were a woman; secondly an athlete, not a business leader.'

He paused, planning how to phrase the rest of the story. 'Everything changed in my mind and I began to shift my focus to this new person. You were close by, accessible. You radiated beauty as well as success. I guess I was kind-of infatuated and I wanted to get closer to you but I had no idea how to do that so I did follow you occasionally, usually in my car but also to training sessions. I took photos, downloaded images and looked at them regularly. It was a poor substitute for actually meeting you. Then the Bannister meeting came along and I was determined to be there, in the media, where I could actually interact with you. Do you understand?'

She thought for a while then said, 'Yes, I suppose so. But did you ever think it might be negative for me? What would happen if I found out – as I did – and thought that you may be stalking me and that I may be in danger – as I did?'

'No, it didn't enter my mind, and for that I am profoundly sorry. I know I can be impetuous and sometimes rush into things. It was selfish and stupid. I apologise unreservedly.'

'Mark, we all gain wisdom and insight as we get older. I'm a different person after Bannister and R1609, and I hope you are as well. I do accept your apology but you need to know the negative impact it had on my life and even the lives of my family. End of discussion. Let's go for a walk.'

She led him out into the sunshine where they found a pair of chairs under a wide umbrella. She said, 'I want to get your story, how your family operated when you were growing up, how you built your business and created a successful company. What drives you, how you negotiate and manage employees, get important people to do what you want them to do.'

Mark perked up and became more animated, telling her about raising funding from venture capitalists, borrowing until he feared his company would go under, then deals selling 'the crazy new technologies my tech geniuses created'. Also about marketing insurance products under white labels through existing insurance companies. The millions that rolled in, the bonuses to his staff, his precious Porsche, the penthouse apartment in the middle of Sandton.

Golden-boy-entrepreneur-tech-genius stuff.

They talked for an hour then enjoyed Gracemount's classic buffet lunch. Abby had salads, smoked salmon, a selection of sushi, a small portion of hot chicken curry with fragrant chutney and a papadam, then a seldom-enjoyed treat, ice cream with hot choc sauce. Mark piled his plate with several types of red meat carved on site. Carnivore, she thought.

They returned to their seats outside in the sunshine. Now's the time to move on, she thought, to the real reason for my visit. She said, 'I heard about your accident and the hospital stuff and the danger. I was worried.'

He smiled. 'No problem. It's just such a surprise and I had no idea you knew about my so-called accident. Of course I heard about the race, how exciting it was. Pity about poor old Suzy, that certainly upset the whole applecart.'

Then it suddenly dawned on her – he had no idea what had happened out there in La Lucia, the spiked drink, the incredible, unthinkable consequences if he hadn't arrived at that precise moment. No one had told him because of the secrecy around the case, and after ten days in hospital he had been discharged and had gone directly to Gracemount.

She gazed at him. What she saw was a dishevelled, thin, nervous man somewhat overwhelmed by everything that had happened, including her sudden visit.

She decided to hold back on telling him the full story. 'I really want to know – what now for you?' she asked.

He looked straight at her, the hang-dog, unkempt, sad Mark now gone, in its place a half-smile and eyes that seemed to penetrate her very soul. 'No,' he said, 'that will come later. What I want to know is what comes next for you. I know about the Fedorova incident in London, the reason for you not winning that race. Getting beaten in the last few metres by Elinah in Durban. How do you feel after that? What are *your* plans?'

She gazed at the sky, thinking about her reply. 'Honestly, I don't know. I've asked my people to hold back on plans to race. I'm not even sure whether I want to race again. There seems to be too much stacked against me, call it fate or whatever. I'm really not sure.'

His eyes narrowed and he leaned forward in his chair and stared directly at her. 'I have no right to say this, but I'm going to say it anyway. It's your life, your career, your decision. But I have a simple message for you. Outside the house in La Lucia on that fateful day, I encountered a criminal. Even now I don't know exactly what he was doing there, but he was definitely up to no good. I'd been tipped off. Then it got ugly and I came off second best. The doctors told me it was a kind of miracle. Now, here's the thing: I survived, partly because of excellent medical treatment but mostly, I believe, by the power of my mind, my spirit, my will to succeed no matter what. It's part of my DNA. As are my other problems, which, hopefully, are a thing of the past.'

He stopped speaking and stared at her. She was taken aback by the power of his words and the depth of his self-belief.

He continued, 'Now this is my message to you, Abby Dennison: make up your mind to continue racing. Decide to get that world record you deserve. Decide that no one, neither Mark Whyte nor anyone else, will stop you. Literally, do what I did: survive and succeed!' The final words were said with such emphasis and power that she just stared. Then he smiled and said almost in a whisper, 'I hope that helps you.'

'You have no idea,' she said.

She gazed at the forest, the distant hilltops and high wispy clouds. She could smell jasmine and hear the sunbirds in the bushes, their calls high-pitched and just within an audible range.

The time had come. She said, 'Let me tell you a story. It's a sad, crazy, evil and ultimately liberating story. And it's the other reason I'm here.'

She told him about the spiked drink, the planned break-in and how everything had worked out the way it had. How he had saved her career while nearly losing his life.

He stared, wide-eyed, open-mouthed, saying nothing for a long time as he absorbed what she'd told him. 'You mean?' he began.

'If you hadn't rocked up at that very moment, in that exact place, I would have drunk that spiked drink. It looked and tasted exactly like my normal one. Those people knew what they were doing, how the bottle looked, how the drink was mixed, where I would be at that time, everything. It's terrifying. Imagine for a minute what would have happened. I would have been caught for doping and my life, not only as an athlete but as a person, would have been destroyed. And you stopped it. You … stopped all that from happening.'

He looked at her in silence, his mind absorbing the enormity of what she had just told him.

He said, 'But I have a question, an obvious one. You were never going to be culpable. Couldn't you have explained that you were set up, ambushed?'

'No. The rules are clear in doping. No matter what happens, the athlete is responsible. You cannot blame your coach, other athletes, the pharmacist who sold you the stuff, the manufacturer who made it. No one. It's your job to keep drugs out of your body, end of story.'

'Wow. I never knew that.'

'It's the law. The immutable law of doping in athletics. It has to be like that, otherwise there would be chaos. Doping is a huge problem as it is and giving the athlete a chance to duck out of culpability would make the problem much bigger.'

He absorbed that slowly and his eyes widened as the horrible reality of that Friday afternoon registered.

She said, 'I came here today to confront you, to face my own fear and anger about possibly being stalked. But I've realised that I should also thank you. Mark, I will never forget what you did.'

The sun was below the tops of the trees by now and the air was cooler. It was time to go. But there was one final question. 'Why on earth were you outside my La Lucia house at exactly the right time? I've thought about that a lot. Why then?'

'All I can say is this. It was no accident, no trick of fate. It started with a particular meeting I set up with a guy in Nelson Mandela Square in January. No details, but this meeting got me thinking. I had a feeling deep down, a kind of premonition, I suppose. Based on this weird, unformed feeling, I got hold of a good friend, someone I trust implicitly. I won't tell you his name but he lives in Zimbabwe and, as many people in that unfortunate country do, he works two jobs. Most of the time he is my agent in Zim, selling my tech products to anyone who can pay for them. Then there's his other job. He's the sports correspondent for the only independent newspaper remaining in Zimbabwe.'

She had no idea what he was talking about.

'He was in Durban, an accredited member of the media at R1609. A few days before the race he called me suddenly with some information he thought I might find important. About a particular photoshoot on the beach. He told me that certain other people also knew about it and had been unusually interested. He found that suspicious and thought I should know. He was very insistent.'

That was it. No more details, just a lingering mystery, hanging in the air like a faint mist.

Her brain a confused jumble of images, impressions and facts, she left Mark Whyte at the entrance to Gracemount. In the car park, she could not stop the flow of silent tears. Then she calmed down and her mind clicked into overdrive and she joined a couple of previously unjoined dots. Call it an epiphany, call it genius, call it anything you like.

She understood what had happened out there next to the house in La Lucia, the one with the grassy patch and the picket fence, the one close to the rock pool. She knew everything.

Abby spoke out loud in the car. 'This changes everything. For the second time in my life I get it, the profound evil that can take over a person's life. Last time I was just a young girl, now I'm a woman with my own mind.'

A couple walked past her open window and stared in as she told them, 'Mark is right. He's saving himself, and now I must do the same. I am going to get that record.'

The couple stopped and a pen and paper appeared. The woman smiled. 'You are Abby, aren't you? My daughter is a big fan. Please sign this for me?'

Abby grinned. 'A pleasure, what's her name?'

'Olivia.'

She wrote: 'To Olivia, good luck and best wishes from Abby Dennison, future world-record holder.'

52

Monday, 6 May
10h00

APN CONFERENCE ROOM

Even before what became known in the athletics business as the Dennison/Moyo Summer, APN was the biggest independent news agency on the continent, covering business, crime, politics, travel, culture and entertainment, as well as sport. Each of these seven departments, or desks, had a senior editor, one of whom was the ageing Charlie Savage in sport.

In a remarkable surge of worldwide interest in the Women's Mile stories, APN's already high ratings, as measured by a sophisticated and complex combination of metrics that included advertising revenue, page impressions, downloads, syndicated purchases and international reach, had increased by exactly 15.6 per cent during the six-month period September to February compared with the previous half-year. And that was across all the various desks, not only sport. The Dennison/Moyo Summer had accounted for a large portion of the increase. It was unprecedented.

By May, of course, the story had died down, as stories always do, even one as big as this. There was plenty of other news to report on.

APN had a conference venue consisting of a low stage up front and two hundred seats. It was used regularly for media briefings, sponsor road-shows and rented by advertising clients for events ranging from investor presentations to fashion shows. Today, it was the venue of a much-publicised and eagerly awaited in-house announcement.

There were seventy-two people in the room. The editor-in-chief, the hugely respected Margery Harrison, had invited the seven desk editors and senior advertising, distribution, technical, financial and administrative staff. In addition, selected reporters from the various desks were there, including everyone from the sports desk.

There was one outsider present, at the specific request of Deon Coetzee.

On the stage were a microphone on a stand and three chairs behind a small table, on which stood an impressive arrangement of Barberton daisies. The audience was excited about the pending announcement and they sat comfortably, having polished off a dozen platters of Margery Harrison's trademark *Panforte di Siena*, specially ordered from an Italian patisserie in Melville.

Margery Harrison, Charlie Savage and Deon Coetzee emerged from the wings and took their seats at the table. The audience applauded politely, not only because it was politically correct corporate behaviour to do so, but also out of genuine respect, not only for their leader, but also for the incredible work done by the sports desk, in particular the young Coetzee. Even the cynical old hacks who had been on the beat for more than thirty years secretly admired the efforts of the sports reporter, even though they wouldn't freely admit it.

Gone were Deon's grubby T-shirts, running shoes and faded jeans. In their place was a blue and white striped Country Road shirt under a dark blue blazer. Grey trousers and shiny brown leather shoes completed the outfit.

'You need a makeover,' Abby had insisted the previous day after they had enjoyed lunch in an intimate bistro in Nelson Mandela Square. 'We're off to Woolies.'

'I can't afford fancy clothes,' he'd protested.

'I'm paid in dollars, I'll pay. I recently had a raise from my boss.' That got a laugh from Deon and it was game over.

The trio took their seats and the crowd hushed in expectant silence. Harrison normally summoned the senior staff on special occasions, including when the news was not good. Everyone expected that today would be the opposite.

It was. The editor-in-chief began with a general review of the past year, highlighting the progress in the metrics of the business and in particular the contribution made by the sports department, 'even though you had fantastic material to work with, Miss Dennison being a local lass and all that'.

Few in the room would have argued with that and they all smiled politely. Most, however, realised that great subject matter is only half the problem solved. The other half is critical investigation, wise analysis and superb, fearless writing.

Margery concluded her presentation with a smile. 'Now I would like to introduce our longest-standing desk editor, none other than Mister Charlie Savage.'

The old man stood and again the room erupted in applause that lasted a full minute. Everyone loved and respected the old rogue, who had dominated the local sports journalism scene for more than three decades.

'Thanks folks,' he said gently. The crowd was completely silent. This was a new Charlie Savage – unusually introspective and gentle, not the blustering, take-no-prisoners, typewriter-wielding demon of his days as a reporter out on the beat.

Deon looked up at his boss, certain that he could detect a hint of moisture in the old man's eyes. 'I've had fun,' Savage said, 'sport and sports people have been my life ever since, as a kid in the fifties, I lay in front of an ancient radiogram on a Saturday afternoon listening to the sports reports coming from all over the world on good old-fashioned radio. I listened to Charles Fortune on cricket, Gerhard Viviers on rugby and a host of brilliant BBC men talking about soccer. As a journalist I went to Kinshasa to watch Muhammad Ali in the Rumble in the Jungle, saw flour-bombs coming out of the sky on the Springbok rugby tour of New Zealand in eighty-one. I was the first writer to interview Francois Pienaar the day after he lifted the world cup in Ellis Park. I saw Penny Heyns and Josia Thugwane win gold at the Olympics; I savoured Jonty, Jacques and AB on the cricket field, Masinga and Tovey in Bafana jerseys, Ernie on the golf course.'

There was a ripple of conversation as it dawned on everyone what was coming. After all, they were reporters with noses trained to detect the very hint of a story, much like the way a trained dog can follow a scent.

'So here I am, seventy-one years old, with dodgy lungs and a body allegedly destined for a heart attack.' He hesitated, placing a hand on Margery's shoulder, 'So, it's time to go. Ladies and gents, at the end of June I will, finally and irrevocably, retire. I'll be out of here.'

Then two things happened. Charlie Savage actually burst into tears and the audience stood in spontaneous applause. It was the end of an era.

Then Margery stood. 'Thank you, Charlie, my friend. Ladies and gentlemen, I must tell you that we refuse to let Charlie Savage depart the South African sports scene like this. As he said, he has just over two months to go and, together with several big federations and a whole queue of sponsors who have been clamouring to get involved, there will be a grand farewell function in a month's time. Details to follow.'

Savage grabbed the microphone. 'I just hope my heart can stand all the pressure,' he shouted above the clamour, grinning.

The editor-in-chief continued, 'There remains one more task for me today. Obviously, the board of APN has been looking carefully at how we should replace the irreplaceable. We need a new sports editor. And, as you may have guessed, the new sports editor at APN, effective next week, is Deon Coetzee.'

This time the applause was even louder. Michelle Flanagan, the department's sub-editor, was the first person to stand, and she was followed by the rest of the sports department, then the two people on the stage. In less than half a minute, everyone in the room was on their feet, clapping, shouting and whistling. It was a scene of unbridled joy and genuine congratulations.

Margery managed to calm everyone down with a wave. 'As a matter of interest, at just twenty-eight Deon is our youngest-ever sports editor. In the years since APN was founded, no one under thirty years of age has become the head of any of our desks.'

Deon stood and gestured for silence. There were a few whistles before silence eventually descended. 'Thank you, madam editor-in-chief, thank you, boss and thank you to everyone for this amazing vote of confidence. I really don't want to bore you with a long speech. You know I talk through the stories that I tell, good and bad, about the wonderful world of sport. However, I must pay tribute to my dear friend and father figure, Mister Charlie Savage, who taught me everything I know about journalism. Sadly, he couldn't teach

THE FINAL LAP

me everything *he* knows, that would take a lifetime.'

He hesitated. 'How do I feel? How am I going to approach my job? In a sentence – the way Charlie Savage did. Find the truth, analyse the truth, tell the truth and take no prisoners. Now, if you'll excuse me for a minute.'

Deon went backstage and returned carrying a large box, which he placed on the table. 'In this box is something I will keep in my office to remind me of who I am following. Like any good sportsperson, I got this sponsored,' he paused for a rattle of laughter, 'by none other than Nike.'

He tore the wrapping off the box, opened it and took out a massive pair of running shoes, Nike-branded. The shoes were made of plastic and were at least half a metre long. Deon held them up to peals of laughter.

'I'm sure you get it, everyone. These are the shoes I am going to fill. They are Charlie Savage's shoes and, boy, are they big!'

The room erupted into laughter, which eventually died down when it was clear that Deon had more to say.

Now he was more subdued and his face had turned serious. 'One more thing, please. There is one person in this room who doesn't work for APN. And if anyone has had a major influence on my career other than Mister Savage, it's her. As a writer, two things are essential: skill, dedication and hard work on one hand, and brilliant subject matter on the other. Please welcome the world's best distance runner and someone I am proud to call my best friend, Abby Dennison.'

In the back row, Abby took off her dark glasses and cap and, with a small wave, stood up. Everyone looked around and, once again, there was lengthy applause. There were also plenty of smiles when she blew Deon a kiss across the room.

Later, it emerged that not even the sharpest photographer in the room had been fast enough to capture that particular moment on camera. It was a pity, everyone agreed.

53

Tuesday, 7 May

JOHANNESBURG AND MONACO

Two important meetings took place that morning. They were worlds apart geographically, but both concerned the incident that took place in La Lucia almost a month earlier.

09h35, Johannesburg
Natie Swanepoel was on the patio outside the Dennison home with Deon, Paul, Bronwyn, Abby and JP. Once again, the mood was subdued and everyone was nervous.

The meeting only lasted twenty minutes. Natie quickly got to the point, 'I have the outcome of the La Lucia investigation. My team was thorough, we've pieced together what happened and we know who the perpetrators are. The story goes right back to the Bannister meeting last year. And, like most successful police investigations, this one involved three things: a careful study of the details, anticipation of what could happen and pure luck.'

The others sat silently. To Paul, it seemed like they were watching one of those Agatha Christie crime movies, where the detective explains everything to the people involved, ultimately identifying the culprit among them. Only this time, the perpetrator was not in the room.

Natie continued, 'Deon told me about your planned training stint in Mbombela and I was worried about potential security issues around Abby, so I called an old buddy of mine, a detective who relocated to the area two years ago and was working for the Mbombela detective branch. Apparently he's a bird fanatic and spends his down-time looking for rare species in the Kruger

Park, a bit like tracking down criminals, he says. Anyway, after Abby's race he called me with a tip.

'It happened like this: the day after the 1 500-metre race there, the organisers called the Mbombela police. Because the spectator limit at the race was full, a friend of the club chairman was allowed to watch from the balcony of the clubhouse, which is quite high up, and he took pictures of everything with a decent camera. Before and during the race, he noticed a guy sitting on the roof of an adjacent building and filming everything with a high-powered video camera. He took a few images of the guy using his long lens and later told his friend the chairman about it. He in turn reported it to the Mbombela police and my friend called me.'

'I guess that's when you looked back to the Bannister meeting,' said Deon, his mind piecing together the narrative.

'Exactly. I got QSH to find any available security footage from around the Bannister meeting. If any country has cameras everywhere, it's England. Sure enough, they found footage of Abby and JP at the warm-up track and a man videotaping their every move. He wore a coach's accreditation tag. I sent the images of the guy in Mbombela to QSH and he compared it with accreditation photos of all the coaches at Bannister. And guess what – that person was none other than Samson Moyo, Sarah's brother. Bingo!'

Slowly, everyone got the full picture. Faces registered first amazement, then anger.

JP was the first to join the dots. 'They filmed Abby and me at both the Bannister and Mbombela races. That would have shown her taking her next-to-last Xtend drink during the warm-up. They would also have seen her taking her final drink just before the start of the race and decided to spike her Xtend bottle at R1609. Diabolical!'

'Now we know who tried to dope Abby. It was Sarah's family. I can't believe it. What the hell next?' exclaimed Paul, his face reddening and his arms waving in the air.

JP echoed these sentiments, 'That means that one of the Moyo brothers was outside the La Lucia house and nearly killed Mark Whyte while trying to destroy Abby's career? I can't believe that someone so involved in athletics could do something like that. It goes against every principle of sportsmanship. Are you sure?'

Natie was grim-faced. 'Yes. In Durban, Solomon got into action. We now know that he'd called Emily Williams, posing as a reporter from a Cape Town newspaper, and she told him where you guys were staying. By the way, she was severely reprimanded as a result of that classic error. Anyway, Solomon's big chance came when he heard about the photoshoot on the beachfront. On the Sunday before the race, he managed to obtain the steroids from a dealer at a local gym. They're available if you know where to look. The stimulant fencamfamine was available with a prescription, which he obtained from the doctor serving their hotel. I checked that as well. He also bought various items of hardware to break into the house, surgical gloves and a face mask. Presumably sourcing information available in the public domain about your specific Xtend drink formulation and your regular movements on race day, particularly just before the race, plus confirmation from the video footage, he knew exactly what he had to do. He prepared the spiked drink and took it to your house, knowing that no one would be there. To be safe, he covered the number plates of his rented Kia with mud. You know the rest. Next morning he dumped the rented car, with its smashed windscreen, in the long-term parking at King Shaka International, flew his family and Sarah's coach to OR Tambo International and took a flight to Harare that afternoon. Then Sarah and her coach travelled from Harare to Eldoret in Kenya, their default bolt-hole. The car rental company confirmed it was him, and forensic evidence, fingerprints and blood on the windscreen showed that Solomon was the driver and Mark the victim. Just over twenty-four hours after nearly killing Mark Whyte, they were gone.'

After another stunned silence, Paul asked, 'What do you think he would have done if there'd been no photoshoot? If we'd been in the house right up until race time?'

'Good question, and one I asked myself. This took a lot of time, but I think I've figured it out. Off the record, I went back to the hacker guy at Regalbank and he looked into the Moyo emails. Remember, folks, that nothing, and I mean nothing, is perfectly hidden on the internet. He found a certain message from Solomon to Sarah's coach, Junren, sent the following week.'

Natie took a small piece of paper out of his pocket and read, 'Hey bra, pity it didn't work out the way we planned. Some guy got in the way. Maybe we should have gone with plan B from the beginning. We could have got the coach away from the bag while she was warming up. Would have been easy with the fake-paparazzi idea and I could have quickly swopped bottles. You know the warm-up area at Kings Park was just a nearby field, dark and with little security. But there's always another time. We'll get her eventually. Go well my brother.'

Everyone just stared straight ahead. The revelation that it was the Moyo brothers and Sarah's coach who were culpable hung in the air like a bad smell. It was a weird, incomprehensible outcome. One by one, they realised that it was true.

Then Abby stuck up her hand like a kid in school. 'What about the Suzy Marshall thing, the way she was injured just before the meeting? Was that also part of their plan?'

'I think I know how that happened,' said JP. 'On balance, removing Marshall from the race would have helped Sarah more than Abby. No one would have taken the lead, especially not Abby. It would have been slow to start with and that would have allowed Sarah to take the lead with three laps to go, kicking into her traditional long sprint. She would have wound it up steadily and by the final lap she would still be able to drop in a sixty- or sixty-one second circuit. Not even Abby could live with that. Abby needs a steady sixty-three second pace, then hits the front with three hundred metres to go and runs a last lap of fifty-seven. I would guess that the Moyos somehow organised that Suzy Marshall thing as well. Obviously a slow start would have destroyed the chance of a record but, for them, a Sarah win in a slowish time was a better option than losing to Abby in a record time. As it happened, that didn't work out either because Elinah upset everyone with her strength and, of course, Jane stepped in to set the pace.'

Natie said, 'Oh boy, this running stuff is complicated. I'll just stick to catching criminals. Anyway, they never found the guy who pushed her. It was well planned. I saw the surveillance footage and no way was that an accident.'

They all sat, absorbing this series of revelations, then Natie said, 'What I don't know about the La Lucia thing is this – how did Solomon get the exact details of the photoshoot?'

'I know,' said Abby.

They all stared at her. 'One day I'll tell you how I know, it's quite a long story. But right now, it doesn't matter. What does matter is this. I've listened to Natie's explanation of what happened and I am as shocked and amazed as you guys. It's sad, totally unsporting and could have had dire consequences for both me and Mark.' No one knew Abby better than Bronwyn. Maybe it was a woman's intuition or possibly an undeclared natural motherly love, but the older woman sensed a change in Abby, a shifting of mood, of confidence and determination.

'Tell us what's on your mind,' she said.

Abby did. It was the product of a radically changed set of circumstances, not least of which was her visit to Gracemount. As she spoke, they all realised that this was a different Abby, confident, assured and somehow even a little mysterious.

She said, 'You're looking at a new Abby, a grown-up, mature Abby, worldly-wise if you like, ready to take on whatever the universe throws at me. This is what JP and I propose, and I want you all to consider it carefully before we do the detailed planning.'

Bronwyn smiled. 'I love it, the new Abby. My dream happening right here.'

Abby gave her a brief shoulder-squeeze then continued, 'JP and I have been looking at a bunch of options. But the main decision is this: I am going to run the Bannister Mile in August. I simply have to. But before that, I want to run the 1500 at the Paris Diamond League meeting at the end of June and another fifteen in mid-July at the Bauhaus-Galan in Stockholm. But those races are long before Bannister, so JP has found a small meeting in Gateshead ten days before the big race. He knows the meet organiser and we'll ask for a top-class 800-metre race there. That will confirm my fitness. JP and I want to go to Loughborough again, eight weeks before the Bannister race. But just the two of us, no need for everyone to be there. Hope that's okay?'

Five heads swung towards Paul. He hesitated for a few seconds then said, 'I'm happy with this. JP and I will sit down and plan all the details. If this is what you guys want, then I'm all for it. I'm delighted that you are aiming for Bannister. It's perfect for us. Well done, both of you. In any case, Bronwyn and I are looking at some options around getting my construction business with my brother back on track. As you know, it's been underperforming for a few years. I guessed you would run Bannister again, so we plan to spend more time in the business while you train in Loughborough.'

Abby continued, 'Dad, that's such good news. But I'm not done yet. Understand that I'm going for that world record. No Solomon, Olga or any other criminal is going to get in my way. And here's the fun part. I want you all in London for the big race. My precious Team, Dad, Mizadams, JP and, of course, Deon. But please, not wearing a journalist's hat. You are now a full member of our Team. Dad, can you call James and confirm? JP, let's work on my programme. Deon, hold my hand and be my support. Mizadams, keep my mind focused. That's nearly all for now, folks.'

Deon grinned and Natie slapped him on the back. 'Go, my china,' he said happily.

Bronwyn asked Abby, 'There's more?'

'Yes. I also want Natie to be my guest in London, right up there in the VIP section with all those lords and ladies and maybe even the Lord Mayor. You are the reason I avoided the hell of being caught doping. But please, please, don't wear that ugly belt or those camouflage clothes. The Brits simply wouldn't understand.'

Natie was silent, stunned, speechless. Eventually he said, 'This is fantastic. Going to London has always been on my basket list.' Everyone smiled.

It was done.

11h00, Monaco

The headquarters of World Athletics is situated in the Principality of Monaco. If the entrance, at 6–8, Quai Antoine 1er on Port Hercules, looks understated, being small and hidden away under wide arches alongside the busy road, the facilities inside are anything but.

The main boardroom, appropriate for one of the world's major sporting federations, is a sight to behold. On this particular day, however, the five people in the room had matters on their minds other than valuable artworks on walls and rare sculptures on tables.

The WA president, who was resident in Monaco, was joined by four of his closest friends and advisors, who had arrived the previous evening from London on the federation's private jet. One lived in London while the others had come from New York, Nairobi and Tokyo.

Three men and two women were seated when the president spoke. 'This is a private meeting and is not being recorded, nor will minutes be taken. I have invited you because I trust your judgement and your confidentiality.'

He continued, 'A week ago I received a phone call out of the blue from a detective working for the police services in South Africa, a man called Natie. I had his background checked and my people told me that he's genuine. I called him back and he told me a story, the likes of which I have, honestly, never heard before in all my years in athletics. He thought I needed to know. Now, we as a group need to agree on how to move forward. Natie emphasised that the people in the know in South Africa are few and include the country's president, would you believe. He also promised that this story will never reach the media.'

The four people sat open-mouthed as the president gave them the raw details. He concluded, 'I have my own ideas about how to move forward, but we need consensus. If this story hits the media, it would be an international scandal that would hurt our sport for years. Just look at cycling.'

'Anything around Abby Dennison is big news. Even if she takes her dog for a walk the paparazzi are there,' said the man from New York, himself a former New York City Marathon winner.

The WA president neatly summed up the dilemma they faced. 'The South African police people, in particular this Natie, were outstanding and uncovered a lot of information that is, frankly, damning. Then the police in London, through a man called QSH, added a few more pieces. We are now certain that the perpetrators, who nearly killed a man called Mark Whyte, who happened to be on the scene and tried to stop the unthinkable, were Sarah Moyo's brothers, Solomon and Samson. Given her mental status, we are reasonably sure that the athlete herself had no idea this was happening. Can we sanction her? Especially without clear evidence? I think not. There is in addition zero likelihood of any criminal prosecution taking place against the brothers, unless they return to South Africa, which they won't. Natie said a charge of attempted murder is waiting for them there.'

They debated for an hour.

The president concluded, 'Ladies and gentlemen, this is what we have agreed. Firstly, we say nothing to anyone outside this room. Secondly, we say nothing to the major meeting directors around the world other than the following: when Sarah Moyo is invited to their races, as she most certainly will be, they politely and very quietly suggest to their governments that visas for her two brothers be denied. We agree that, at this stage, to deprive Sarah of her coach as well would result in irreparable harm. So, for now, he can travel with her. That will send a clear and unambiguous message to the brothers. They need to know that we know.'

There was more discussion and the president continued, 'We also agree that the president of African Athletics,' pointing to the lady from Kenya, 'will set up an immediate meeting with Solomon Moyo and explain the findings of the South African authorities, and our recommendation that only Sarah and her coach be invited to countries where there are key track meetings. Obviously, there are other countries where we cannot exert pressure on governments. Solomon will then face a dilemma. Sarah is their route to wealth, fame and the trappings of success. He will want that to continue at all costs. It will therefore be up to him and his fellow conspirators to decide what to do. It's clear that World Athletics faces an impossible situation here. On the one hand we have a brilliant athlete, a once-in-a-generation runner with certain handicaps, and on the other hand a management team who will stop at nothing, including serious criminal activity, to destroy the careers and very lives of her rivals. Dennison was the first, meaning that there could be more. They have to be stopped, and it would be remiss of us to allow them to continue as before. Who knows what they would do? The meeting with Solomon Moyo needs to send a clear message: Sarah is welcome but you aren't. So you need to make a plan.'

They all agreed. After all, the sport had to come first.

54

Thursday, 9 May

LONDON

James Selfe sat with Simon Hardy and Mary Southgate in his office, with its view of the Shard and the Tower. He was brief. 'On Tuesday, Paul Dennison called me to say that Abby will be running the Bannister Mile. Far from being demoralised by the Fedorova incident last year and the loss to Kiptanui in Durban, he says she is more determined than ever to break the record and regain her number one status. Since Durban, a group of our bank's directors, including the chairperson and myself, have been toying with the idea of upping the ante this year in London. We were just waiting for the Dennison confirmation, which we now have. Here's what we've decided: the world record is around 4:07 right now. At Bannister this year we are offering an increased financial incentive. I want you to get your team to prepare a media release and set up an international online media conference for next Tuesday. We are going big here, seriously big. Hold onto your hats.'

Hardy asked in a quiet voice, 'What is the time target and what is the incentive?'

'Wait for it: 4:06 and six million dollars. The biggest prize ever, by far, in the history of the sport. And also a likely first-ever sub-3:50 time for a woman in the 1 500 metres. A possible double-whammy of two world records in a single race, both the mile and the metric mile. Never done before. It will be spectacular.'

Twenty minutes later, Selfe was on the phone to Paul Dennison. They swopped small talk, how are you? How's Abby? Delighted that she will be in London again this year. Hopefully no chaos this time. Et cetera, et cetera.

Paul realised there was more to come.

James said, 'I'm telling you this in the strictest confidence. Embargoed, as they say in media lingo. This stays inside the Team please, including Deon. I trust him. Yesterday the Regalbank board had a meeting and approved the incentives for Bannister. Next week this will go out internationally, but I wanted Abby to know now. Between us, had she not signed up for the Bannister race, this would never have happened.'

'James, give me the details.'

He did.

55

Friday, 10 May

THE WESTCLIFF, JOHANNESBURG

Deon knew a lot about sport, its rules, history and current champions. Its competitions, traditions and amazing performances. Sport was his domain, the place where he was most comfortable. In the press box, on the golf course, behind his computer.

Human relationships? Not so much.

Marriage, the whole 'unto death do us part' thing, was a topic that had never been high on his list of priorities. His experience of marriage, he reluctantly admitted to himself, was more about 'until booze or adultery or abuse or poverty or boredom do us part'.

Looking at his own family's sad history, he'd be forgiven if he was put off relationships for life. So far, bachelorhood had worked just fine.

Or so he believed. But life has a habit of switching lanes when least expected. Nothing ever stays the same forever.

All his notions of relationships changed when he asked Abby out on a date.

It wasn't some sort of drawn-out strategy, days and weeks of planning, getting advice, figuring out how, when and where. Scraping up courage, sweating, stressing. No, he just called her on a Tuesday afternoon and said, 'Abby, you're my best friend, so will you go out on a date with me? I was thinking high tea at The Westcliff. Friday afternoon when you don't have a track session planned?'

'A date. Like, a *date*. An *actual date*?'

'Yes.'

'A boyfriend, girlfriend kind of date?'

THE FINAL LAP

'That's pushing it a bit, but yes. Sort of. You have to understand, dating is not something I've done a lot, so I need help here. I don't want to screw it up, especially not with you.'

'And you think I'm the dating expert? The last proper date I had was with Roly Anderson three years out of school.'

'Roly? You're kidding! All that guy had to offer was a big stomach and an Alfa Romeo.'

'And restless hands.'

He laughed. Roly was at least eight centimetres shorter and twenty kilograms heavier than Abby. 'I hope you smacked him.'

'No. I jumped out of his fancy car and ran home. It was actually quite a good training session. Good thing I was wearing running shoes.'

'I assure you, I have neither an Alfa nor restless hands.'

'Okay, I accept. Friday. I expect nothing less than flowers as well. And you pay, The Westcliff is crazy expensive. What time will you collect me?'

'Three o'clock sharp. You can tell Paul and Bronwyn but not JP. He probably wouldn't understand what a date is.'

'See you then. A date? I can't believe it!'

Predictably, he brought Barberton daisies, four of them, red, yellow, purple and blue. They arrived at The Westcliff, an exclusive, rambling hotel set high on a hillside in Joburg's posh Westcliff suburb, overlooking the green expanse of the city's zoo and its vast surrounding gardens. It is said, probably inaccurately, that Johannesburg has the greatest number of trees of any comparable city in the world, but as they sat outside, the expanse of endless green carpet below lent credence to the claim.

The Westcliff offered a legendary and extremely pricey high tea. Good thing he was now sports editor and not a poor reporter.

Far from being uncomfortable, the atmosphere in the car was relaxed and in a strange, unexpected way, joyful. It was as if some sort of tension had been released, the previously taboo subject of an actual relationship between Abby Dennison and Deon Coetzee now on the table, even if somewhat precarious and without any sort of structure. After all, they'd been acquaintances since she was in grade ten at school, about ten years. A shift to a romantic relationship was therefore strange and pretty much unthinkable, like dating a cousin.

Deon was certain that neither of them had given the matter serious thought until now. At least he hadn't.

They arrived and were taken to a corner table with a view across the suburbs. The room was lavishly decorated, the scenery relaxing and the quietness of the room a welcome escape from Johannesburg's normal frenetic pace.

A waitress presented them each with a menu, detailing the vast variety of drinks and cakes that formed the basis of the hotel's famous afternoon tea.

'Let's have a look,' said Deon, and they scanned the menus.

'Wow, I'll have to do a few extra training sessions after this,' said Abby, laughing.

After some discussion, they settled on two different teas, jasmine, and apple and pear. For cakes they decided to try raspberry and poached pear chocolate tarts, homemade pecan praline scones, and apple cinnamon cheesecake.

The afternoon soon became a gentle to-and-fro of discussion, punctuated by the arrival of the first tea and, one by one, the various cakes. The two of them sat lost in a tiny bubble of intimacy, the outside world, for once, absent. The subject of their date never came up. They simply spent a pleasant hour reminiscing about schooldays, the ups and downs of matric exams, his time at Rhodes University, her first tentative steps onto the world stage, the inclusion of Bronwyn and JP into the family and the impact this had on her career.

They also discussed the Bannister meeting, R1609 and the incident outside the La Lucia house. He asked her, 'Honestly, how do you feel about that now?'

She was quiet for a while, considering her answer. 'It was a giant shock. I can understand the Fedorova tripping plan because she just wanted to destroy my race as a last-ditch thing in her career. She knew it would finish her. But La Lucia was different. It was so premeditated, so evil, so unsporting. So cowardly, I suppose. I guess it was God who was out there protecting me. The only real emotion I have is for poor Mark, who ended up in a coma, for heaven's sake.'

'What about the perps?'

He was surprised at her response. 'We know who it was. But that's not my issue now, the police and World Athletics must deal with it. One day I'll read about it in the media, or not. But one thing is certain, what goes around comes around. And this thing will come back to bite the people who did it. Now, please can we move on?'

They did and he asked, 'After the latest Regalbank announcement, tell me how you feel about potentially being a multi-millionaire?' This was one of the questions he'd wanted to ask. But on a date? Was it a risk?

She thought for a moment, then said it was difficult to get her head around all that money. 'To me, it's a bit ridiculous, winning so much for running a race. I know millions of dollars is the norm in sports like golf, tennis and soccer and I've often wondered about the morality of that. Kicking or hitting a ball earning you a fortune? Crazy. All those people out there homeless and someone gets a few million dollars for running fast round and round a track. I am seriously not comfortable with that. Deon, I haven't even trained for the race, let alone won it in a record time. The whole thing is too far-fetched, too remote, too ridiculous.'

He interrupted. 'Hang on, Abby. Take a break. Come with me.'

He stood and gently took her hand. They walked outside towards the edge of the garden and she put her arm around his waist. For the first time Deon sensed a shift in their relationship, a warm feeling that drifted up from his feet and settled somewhere in his stomach. A tingling. Her body was warm against his, her hand pulling him closer, her eyes looking up at his face.

They were standing right at the end of the garden, next to a low stone wall, and the view was spectacular. Jan Smuts Avenue was buzzing with traffic far below and the green canopy of trees stretched to the horizon. On the hill to their right the huge, grey concrete block of Charlotte Maxeke Hospital stood on a ridge, row upon row of windows hinting at healing inside bleak walls, dedicated doctors and nurses working twenty-four seven to help the vast number of people reliant on state, as opposed to private, healthcare. Care that was available in places like Hillside Clinic, provided you could afford it.

A different world.

The afternoon drifted on and the autumn air cooled, hinting at winter just weeks away. Abby shivered in her sleeveless blouse and snuggled up to Deon, her arm still tight around his waist. 'I'm cold,' she said, 'but not only from the temperature. I'm a bit scared, to be honest.'

'I get it. You're not a little girl anymore,' he said, almost in a whisper. 'And the world is a big, intimidating place.'

'I know. La Lucia changed me. It opened my eyes to unpleasant, sad things that I suppressed ever since Mom was killed. It was a reality check.'

They were silent for a while then she pointed and said, 'Look at the huge hospital up there. People sick and dying, terrified and in pain, alone. And here I am, complaining about a bad training session. I am so out of touch with the real world.'

'What do you want to do? What do you need?'

'Dad and the others are really just a trio of parents, to be honest. I need to grow up, become independent, make my own decisions. Obviously Dad will remain at the centre of my universe, but I need to spread my wings, so to speak. But I can't suddenly take on the world, branch out as a real adult, on my own. I need someone to share everything with, my running, my hopes and plans. Even my fears. That's what's missing, a partner, for want of a better word.'

This time the shift was more tangible. The physical intimacy of the occasion out there in the garden reinforced the emotional power of the need she radiated. He smiled at her and she gazed back. The unspoken agenda was clear. He pulled her closer and she responded immediately.

For a long time neither of them said anything. They walked, hand in hand, through the expanse of the garden as the sun disappeared behind Westcliff hill. She took a thick, long-sleeved tracksuit top out of her bag and put it on, pulling the hood over her head. Deon felt its warmth and softness as she stood touching him when they stopped at the far end of the garden.

'This is so lovely, this closeness,' she said softly. 'I feel safe here, with you. Somehow, you've always been this strong male figure in my life, mostly out of sight but seldom out of mind. A kind-of rock.' Then, 'Deon, I have to know. What do you say? How do you respond to that?' she asked, her stare level, her eyes wide.

He felt a surge of affection for this person, unlike anything he had previously allowed into his head, a sudden uncertainty, driven by the need to reciprocate her brutal honesty. What should he say? It felt like they had reached some sort of fork in the road. No going back.

'For my whole adult life I've avoided emotional involvement, mainly because it scared me. I was aloof, joking with women rather than seeing them as potential lovers or partners or even marriage material. I fiddled around with dates and tried a couple of relationships, but nothing stuck. Maybe I also need to grow up a bit.'

She said, 'Be honest now. I've known you all my adult life and still have no idea how you actually see me as a person.'

He hesitated, sorting out his thoughts. How did he see Abby Dennison? Runner, champion, icon? Schoolgirl? Best friend? Potential girlfriend? Life partner?

'Abby, I remember you as a girl in grade ten, all ponytail and long legs, running around the school track. Then I became the reporter, all statistics and interviews and photographs and profile pieces and trips to Oxford. In the past few months that image changed again, to Abby the beautiful, successful, driven woman with the world at her feet. Then today. What can I say about today? Even this past hour. Gone is the brilliant runner, the icon. Now I see a person setting out on a new, exciting journey, reinventing herself, brave, determined, yet nervous, vulnerable, even a little scared.'

'And how do you, as Deon, respond? Still the head boy, the reporter, the sports editor? I honestly hope not.'

'Not for a millisecond. I want to be involved with you on a deeper, personal level, with Abby the woman, not Abby the runner. A brand-new, exciting, wonderful journey. Like a dream come true.'

He kissed her then, full on the lips, long and deep. She responded with a little cry that seemed to come from somewhere deep in her soul. For both of them it was like a revelation, the opening of a previously closed book. The kiss had a certain inevitability about it, as if it were predestined but hitherto not understood. It was exciting, euphoric, sensual. The ultimate freedom.

For a long time they stood like that between the roses, clivias, jasmine and azaleas. Neither wanted to pull away.

Eventually they went silently hand-in-hand back to their table. No words were necessary. They realised that high tea had some way to go. The waiter came over, hesitantly, as if unwilling to break some sort of spell. 'Can I bring the jasmine tea now? And how about our strawberry and pistachio pastries, or our speciality, pink French macarons?'

They laughed. 'Bring the lot,' said Abby, 'this is a special day!'

He did, and it was.

On their way back to the car, she asked, 'Deon, the London thing, the Bannister race. You will be there but not as a reporter, rather my partner, friend, supporter?'

'Wouldn't miss it for the world.'

56

Wednesday, 19 June

JOHANNESBURG

The afternoon that Abby and Deon spent at The Westcliff marked exactly fourteen weeks before the Roger Bannister Memorial Mile. As Johannesburg hunkered down into its winter season of bare trees, freezing mornings, anaemic midday sun, brown grass in the parks, indoor heaters and layers of warm clothing, Abby and JP did what they had always done in the build-up to a series of important races: they trained. Like in White River, Abby's days consisted almost entirely of the sweat and toil of training: distance runs on the golf course, speed and speed-endurance work on the track at the Wanderers Club, hill sprints on one of the steep hills near her home, strength, cross-training and leisurely swimming sessions in the local Virgin Active gym. There were regular appointments with Janine, her personal physiotherapist, plus her favourites, the sauna and aromatherapy sessions after a long day's workout.

After just three weeks into her programme, JP noticed that Abby was training with a kind of pioneer spirit that he'd not experienced before. Her determination had ratcheted up and the pure effort she put into every session was clearly evident. He thought about it carefully and his logical, scientific mind slowly unravelled the apparent mystery of her mindset. Looking back, he understood that she'd subtly changed the day that Natie had told them about Solomon Moyo's culpability. It was then that she'd spoken excitedly about her determination to break the record at Bannister. Something had happened around that time to reignite her motivation and determination levels, but he had no idea what it was. He decided to find out, somehow.

Several other things changed in her routine compared with previous years. Abby's relationship with Deon blossomed like early spring flowers. They met regularly for quick coffee sessions, intimate dinners once a week and, when they could fit them in, walks, hand-in-hand, through the city's beautiful green belts on winding paths in the shade of giant bluegum trees.

The change in Abby was obvious. She looked relaxed and happy, even in the midst of intense and demanding training. While Paul and JP took note of her new and deeper relationship with Deon but said little, it was Bronwyn, predictably, who spoke to her about it. Abby happily shared details of their walks and dinners, and Bronwyn gladly entered into the joy of Abby's first real boyfriend.

Abby also managed to find about twenty hours a week to sit behind her computer. Everyone wondered what that was about.

May had slipped into June, and one day, out of the blue, Abby got a WhatsApp from Mark Whyte: 'Hi, apologies for intruding on your training for London, but I have some interesting news to share. Can you and Deon find an hour to pop into my offices? Any time that suits you both. Send a reply and I'll be here. Regards.'

She called Deon straight away and told him. Predictably, he wasn't too keen. 'What now?' he asked, 'I know the guy is some sort of hero, but maybe his news should wait until after Bannister.' Smiling, Abby thought that he was ever so slightly jealous, but said nothing.

'Well, no, I owe him and I'd like to know what he has to say to us. Please come with me.'

How could he refuse? 'Sure,' he said.

Two days later, in the afternoon after Abby's track session, they were ushered into Mark's corner office, the one with the splendid eastward view across the city.

He immediately cut to the chase. 'Thanks for coming in. I know you're both busy. But first, Deon, I'm pleased to eventually meet you formally.'

They shook hands and Deon said, 'Likewise. Obviously I was horrified to hear about the chaos in La Lucia and I really want to thank you for stopping the unthinkable. What you did was life-altering for all of us, particularly you. We will always be grateful.'

Mark nodded. 'Of course. But now I want to share a couple of things with you. Firstly, there are probably fewer than fifty people in Joburg who don't know that you two guys are, what shall I call it? An item? Anyway, congrats, I am genuinely happy for you. It's a perfect match, but one that has saddened probably about five million eligible and hopeful young male athletics fans across the world.'

'Yourself included?' Abby asked cheekily, smiling widely.

'Of course. Now, moving swiftly on. After the chaos in Durban, I took a hard look at my life and I've decided not to sell MileStar but rather focus on building it further. The business is helping many thousands of unbanked South Africans achieve some sort of financial security and that's important to me. Now I want to add another product, disability insurance, to the range and also expand into neighbouring territories including Namibia and Zimbabwe, where I already have a small presence. But here's the punchline, the main reason for this meeting. Look over there.' He beckoned Abby and Deon across to the floor-to-ceiling window on the east side. 'What do you see?'

'Lots of tall buildings,' said Abby.

'And what do those buildings represent?'

'Enormous wealth, huge economic power, billions of rands turning over every day,' Deon said thoughtfully.

'Exactly. But look further, about three kilometres. What's over there?'

'Smoke,' said Abby, 'and no tall buildings.'

'Exactly. That's Alexandra township, a.k.a. Alex to everyone. No tall buildings, no wealth, just half a million people living in poverty with an excellent view of the tall buildings and the billions of rands across the M1 highway.'

'Point taken,' said Deon as they sat. 'I suspect there's something coming.'

'There is. I have a number of big-business partners, men and women with their companies operating in those tall buildings. Every day they look across at the smoke, as Abby correctly calls it. Several of these guys have been meeting with me and I have decided to lead a consortium to create a massive new

NGO in Alex, funded by MileStar and my partners. We're working with local structures in Alex, the municipality, civil society groups and churches. A decent-sized piece of vacant land close to the N3 highway has been donated, and over the next year we're going to build a new centre focusing initially on offering abused women and abandoned, orphaned and vulnerable children a safe place to live and get their lives back. Then we plan to start a skills development programme for potential entrepreneurs.'

There was silence, then Abby said, 'That's incredible. Everyone knows that gender-based violence is like a pandemic in South Africa. And thousands of kids are orphaned or live in desperate circumstances.'

'And after that?' asked Deon.

'Who knows, maybe a Saturday school for primary school kids. Alex schools aren't great. We'll see where it takes us.'

They spoke for a while, Mark giving more details about the plans, partners, budgets, the lot. It would be up and running within a year.

It was fully dark outside and Deon said, 'That's really great, Mark, but why this meeting? Why are you telling us all this stuff?'

'Because I have a request. But before responding, I'd like you to take your time, ask questions, think and consult. No rush. I'm confident that our new NGO in Alex is going to be a ray of hope and light in a dark place where there is smoke and no tall buildings, just across the highway from the biggest economic hub in Africa. Now here's the crunch. My partners and I have one request: we would like Abby Dennison to be our patron, our figurehead, our role model.'

He hesitated, nervous now. Then he smiled and looked at her directly. 'Abby, what do you say?'

57

Wednesday, 24 July

JOHANNESBURG

Deon was at his desk – not in the cramped cubicle of his days as a reporter, but in the spacious corner office of APN's sports editor, with its view across the plush suburbs of Melrose and Houghton. Charlie Savage's domain for more than a decade.

Truth be known, Deon felt vaguely uncomfortable in his new surroundings, like he was somehow intruding into the old man's private space.

He was reading through a report he had written, to be issued later that day.

> With the much-awaited Roger Bannister Mile for Women less than a month away, the contenders for the unprecedented $6-million incentive are running races across Europe, fine-tuning their preparations and posting times that they hope will put fear and trembling in the hearts and minds of their rivals.
>
> Never before in the history of the sport has so much money been on the table and they all know it.
>
> First to reveal their form were British friends and training partners Mary McColgan and Jane Beardsley, who ran a low-key 1 500-metre race in Zürich. With a local Swiss pacemaker taking them through 1 100 metres at 3:55 pace, Jane surprisingly outsprinted Mary by just a tenth of a second to win in 3:54.11, the quickest time in the world up until then.
>
> It didn't last long.
>
> Although her time was a comparatively slowish 3:58.20, thanks to the absence of a pacemaker, Elinah Kiptanui managed to put forty metres between herself and her rivals in the 1 500-metre race at the Emil Zatopek Memorial Meeting in Prague.

What is important here is that the Kenyan's final lap was timed at an eye-watering 56.3 seconds, a reminder to her rivals of the deadly sprint that took her to victory earlier this year in the now-famous R1609 mile in Durban.

Sarah Moyo, winner in London last year and the current world-record holder in the mile, elected to go for a longer distance in Nairobi last weekend, not far from her training base in Eldoret. In a 3 000-metre race where she basically ran a time-trial against the clock, Moyo managed to beat the African record for the distance, winning in 8:19.34. Interesting were her splits: Moyo ran the first 1 500 in 4:14.34 and the second half of the race in exactly 4:05, remarkable in what was essentially a solo performance. She ended with her signature fast two-lap sprint at the end, which took her just five seconds over two minutes to complete. Another big warning to the others.

Of interest is the fact that the Zimbabwean runner now has a pair of new coaches, German Hans Schreiber and his wife, Heike, after she fired her former Chinese coach, Caihong Junren, for undisclosed reasons. The trio now travel together to the various track meetings.

Finally, we have South Africa's Abby Dennison, winner of neither the Bannister Mile last year nor R1609. The former world number one cannot wait to get onto the track in London on August 16 and set the record straight with a world record and a massively improved bank balance.

Dennison has run two races in the past two weeks. The first was in Paris on June 30 where, with experienced pacemaker Suzy Marshall taking her through three laps at a decent pace, Dennison found a 57.5 second final lap to stop the clocks at 3:55.09.

But better things were to come in Stockholm on July 14, a month before the Bannister showdown. With Marshall again doing the hard yards, Dennison upped the ante for London by popping a final lap of just under 57 seconds to stop the clocks at 3:52.79, a personal best and the fastest time in the world for three years. Converting that into the mile distance would have given the South African 4:09. Can she find another 3 seconds in London and grab the $6 million in the white-hot atmosphere of the Bannister Mile? Probably.

Let the fun and games begin.

Just then there was a knock on the door and Deon's sub-editor, Michelle Flanagan, entered the office. She was holding a bunch of flowers set securely in colourful wrapping paper, with a large card emerging from the blooms.

'These came for you from NetFlorist,' she said, 'they're beautiful.'

'Barberton daisies,' he said, smiling.

'How did you know that?'

'Oh, I've seen them before. Pretty special, aren't they?'

He hesitated, realising who had sent them. The knowledge caused him to blink, stand and pull a handkerchief out of his pocket without Michelle noticing.

'Open the card,' she said, not moving away.

He did. Staring at it for a minute, he wiped his eyes and said, 'Look.'

Taking the card hesitantly, reverently almost, she read the message.

'Dearest D ... I told you this was not the beginning of the end, it's the end of the beginning. I thought that the jigsaw puzzle of my life was complete until Westcliff. That day I realised that a piece had been missing all the time, right in the centre. Now that you are in my life, that gap is no longer there. The puzzle is complete. See you in London. I love you ... A.'

Michelle burst into tears, causing the normally noisy newsroom outside to go quiet and heads to turn.

Deon, Paul and Bronwyn were at OR Tambo International Airport with Natie. The policeman was super excited at the prospect of his first-ever trip to England. He'd taken three weeks' leave, hooked up with QSH ('my brand-new British china') and was about to check in at the British Airways counter.

They shook hands, hugged and wished him bon voyage. 'Thank you so much, *okes*, this is like a dream come true. I feel like Alex going into Wonderland,' he announced as he moved into the departure area.

'He'll never make a journalist,' quipped Deon. 'Too many mixed metaphors.'

58

Friday, 16 August

LONDON OLYMPIC STADIUM

James Selfe and Simon Hardy were sitting in the VIP boardroom as dozens of volunteers, officials and workers scurried about, putting the final touches to the stadium and the VIP and media centres. It was Roger Bannister Memorial Athletics Meeting day.

Both men were satisfied that everything was going according to plan and, after the success of the previous year, they knew they had a winning formula.

Selfe looked at his watch and smiled. 'Simon, there is something I need to tell you. Pretty confidential and all that, so keep it under your hat.'

Ten minutes later, there was a soft knock at the door. 'Can I come in?' enquired Deon Coetzee.

'Of course, we're expecting you.'

'Hello, James, Simon. It's good to see you both.'

James thrust out his hand. 'Deon, great to see you too. Welcome to our humble track meeting.'

After chatting for a while, Deon looked enquiringly at James.

'It's all sorted,' said the meeting director.

19h46

Paul, Bronwyn, Deon and Natie stood just outside the VIP centre. The policeman had a beer in one hand and a salmon sandwich in the other. 'I can't believe what I'm seeing,' he said, gazing across the vast stadium, 'it's like Loftus Versfeld on steroids.'

The place was throbbing with excitement as the seventy-thousand-strong

THE FINAL LAP

crowd waved flags and took endless photos on their phones. The big screen was showing crowd close-ups and people jumped up and waved as their excited faces appeared, several metres high, on the screen. On the far side of the stadium a group of discus throwers had gathered on the grass after their event, waiting for the final race to start. Officials in their smart Regalbank uniforms stood expectantly around the arena. The BBC's tracking motorcycle was waiting in the outside lane after the first bend. Its team of driver and cameraman were hoping that they would not play any sort of starring role this time around. Four digital signboards stood in their positions, one next to the finish line on the infield, the second in the middle of the arena, facing in all four directions, the third on the first bend outside the track, and the fourth on the infield ten metres beyond the 1 500-metre mark, just before the final bend, 109 metres from the end of the mile race. The numbers on the signboards were counting down the minutes and seconds to the start of the race: 12:57, 12:56, 12:55 ...

'I've watched hundreds of sports events on TV,' said Natie, 'but I never knew what being inside a massive stadium was like. It's amazing, all those people, the crowd has its own life, like a massive herd of wildebeest in Kruger.'

'Cells in a body, bricks in a wall,' said Bronwyn softly.

Natie looked at her. 'Exactly, they're like a single organism,' he said.

Deon added, 'And about two hundred million more out there watching on TV. The power of sport. No wonder there's six million dollars on the line.'

'Where's JP?' asked Natie.

'He always sits in the crowd on the first bend. That way Abby can go directly to him after the race. It's their ritual,' said Bronwyn.

They stood quietly for a minute, then Paul said, 'Here they come.'

An orderly row of nine people emerged from a door at the far end of the stadium and walked towards the start line. Kurt Hunsler was followed in lane order by Mary McColgan, Elinah Kiptanui, Sarah Moyo, Molly Fields, Jane Beardsley, Ekaterina Vinitskaya, Abby Dennison and Suzy Marshall. A minute later they arrived at the start area, met their assistants, discarded their tracksuits, put on their spikes and started their final warm-up routines.

No one smiled and no words were exchanged between the runners. Even the crowd was silent as everyone realised that the eagerly anticipated race was about to start. It was the culmination of four months of intense speculation, driven by the massive Regalbank media machine and underpinned by the unprecedented incentive. By now the athletes were household names: Abby Dennison, the flamboyant South African who was unable to win either of the two previous mile races; Sarah Moyo, the silent Zimbabwean and the current world-record holder in the mile; Elinah Kiptanui, denied a possible victory through cheating in the last Bannister race but who'd bounced back with a famous win over Dennison in Durban; and the British pair of McColgan and Beardsley, the crowd favourites and both overdue for a podium finish. Fields, the American champion, and Vinitskaya from far-eastern Russia.

Mouth-watering didn't come close to describing the race. History-in-the-making was probably more appropriate.

Six million dollars was available for the first time in the sport, should the winner achieve the near-impossible target time of 4:06. If the time was slower than that, of course, it would signal one of the great anticlimaxes in the history of athletics. Such is the human mind: 'It's all or nothing', 'Go big or go home'. And none were more aware of this than the eight runners.

The sixteenth of August also marked Donna Gray's twenty-ninth birthday, and Donna was celebrating by sitting high up in the media area opposite the finish line. She had with her three things: her trusty laptop, a digital stopwatch and a pair of high-powered binoculars. An honours graduate in English literature and classics from Cambridge University and the holder of a pair of British Championship long jump titles, including a personal best of 7.17 metres, Donna had retired from the sport at twenty-seven to pursue a career in journalism. She was now considered to be Britain's foremost athletics correspondent, a rare feat for someone so young. Her regular day job was with the *Daily Mail*, one of the country's biggest daily newspapers, but on this occasion James Selfe had approached an old school friend, now sports editor of that same newspaper, to 'lend me your young star writer for one night'. The friend had agreed provided he, his wife and teenage daughter were given VIP accreditation.

THE FINAL LAP

Donna's task was simple: write the official race report on the Bannister Mile for Regalbank's media people, no more than fifteen hundred words, to be issued after the meeting to a news-hungry world.

She started writing her report at 20h10 London time and completed the first part of the task ten minutes later, before the post-race media conference. This described in clinical detail the race itself. The second part of the full report, including the post-race media conference, was added later. In the days to come, this entire story would become one of the most downloaded and widely distributed news items of the year. In the first part of the report, Donna Gray described the second Roger Bannister Memorial Mile for Women:

> The start was orderly, thanks to Marshall, who sprinted over the finish line, stayed wide into the bend and immediately settled into perfect record-breaking pace, around 61 seconds per lap. McColgan and Beardsley followed the leader, with Kiptanui in fourth spot. Dennison tracked the Kenyan, a tactic that was clearly the core of the South African's strategy throughout the race. Moyo, Fields and Vinitskaya followed in a line. Even though the pace was quick, it was clear from the word go that the runners were going to stay in touch for as long as they could, not surprising given the fact that these were the best mile athletes in the world. No more than seven metres separated first from last.
>
> The clock at the first checkpoint – after 309 metres – stopped at 47 seconds, and Marshall even gave a brief thumbs-up signal to the followers. But they had all seen the time and knew that they were on record pace.
>
> Marshall led them through the finish line – 409 metres gone, three laps to go – in 63.5 seconds and the others followed. Not much was going to happen, given that they were on the right pace.
>
> Fireworks were certain to happen later.
>
> Everything changed at the end of the second lap. As the clock showed 2:04.9 – the last 400 metres completed in a swift 61.4 seconds – Marshall stepped off the track and McColgan, with Beardsley in tow, surged into the lead. Then Sarah Moyo ran around Dennison and Kiptanui into third place.
>
> The message was clear: the British women and the Zimbabwean world-record

holder were determined to show the favourites, Kiptanui and Dennison, that they had a battle on their hands.

The Scot's lead didn't last long, less than 200 metres in fact. Down the back straight for the third time Moyo put in her signature surge, powering past the two Britons into the lead. So strong was this surge that by the end of the straight she was eight metres clear of McColgan.

The expected response from Kiptanui, and therefore Dennison, didn't materialise. To the surprise of everyone, the pair remained in Beardsley's slipstream, a full 10 metres behind Moyo. They flashed past the clock at the 1 500-metre mark, which showed 60.3 seconds for the previous lap. But that time, of course, was not Moyo's as she had been, at the start of that lap, at least a second behind Marshall. Moyo had therefore run sub-60!

Down the finish straight for the penultimate time, Kiptanui, with her faithful follower, Dennison, eased past the British pair and by the time they reached the bell, the Kenyan was second and Dennison third, now 12 metres adrift of Moyo.

The clock stopped at 3:06.2. There was an audible gasp from the crowd as the realisation dawned that Moyo would have to find 59.7 seconds on the final lap to beat 4:06. Kiptanui/Dennison, on the other hand, needed a seemingly impossible sub-58. After a race where the average lap speed was around 62.5 seconds, this was a seriously tall order.

The world waited with bated breath in front of television sets, the crowd was strangely quiet and even the stadium announcer said nothing. It was the sort of moment where anything could happen.

Pause here for an instant. What exactly was happening? Why did the two favourites not respond earlier to Moyo's surge? Why did the Zimbabwean play her standard, predictable 'long sprint' card once again? Was it possible for either Kiptanui or Dennison to make up a deficit of more than 12 metres? Everyone waited for answers.

Down the back straight, Kiptanui picked up the pace. It was gentle, but obvious. Moyo, of course, had no idea what was happening behind her – the curse of being the race leader. Dennison continued to breathe down the Kenyan's neck. The gap shortened achingly slowly, twelve metres, then ten then eight, then six. Moyo's face was a picture of pain – she was desperately going as fast as her legs could carry

THE FINAL LAP

her, knowing with deadly certainty that the gap was closing behind her. Six million was an astronomical number and she could feel it slipping away. Keep going, keep sprinting, they must also be tired, she would have told herself.

The inevitable happened on the final bend with 170 metres to go. Kiptanui drove forward, arms pumping, legs driving, the hint of a smile on her face. With Dennison still a metre behind, she went past Moyo and into the lead. By the time they reached the key line on the track denoting the end of 1 500 metres, Moyo was two metres behind Dennison.

The clock stopped at 3:49.11, a new world record for the women's 1 500 metres. But hardly anyone noticed. The next fifteen seconds would decide the fate of the mile record plus the destination of the almost mythical six million dollars. The record was there for the taking, but whose record would it be?

The crowd, by now, was on its feet. The sound was deafening, the stadium announcer inaudible, the roar reverberating across London, the tension almost unbearable.

What would happen? At no stage had Dennison attempted to take the lead, she had simply opted to let Kiptanui do the work of winning. They both knew what Moyo would do. After all, she had to go early because she could not outkick the other two in a final-straight dogfight. Dennison also knew that Kiptanui would leave it to the very end, as she'd done in the R1609 in Durban. But this time Dennison was the hunter, not the hunted.

In the end, Abby Dennison rolled out her secret weapon – the precious Final Lap.

With 60 metres to go, she shifted into the second lane and, with the hint of a smile on her face, kicked into sprint mode. Kiptanui had no answer to the South African's raw power and by the end all she could do was stare in wonder at the back of Abby's vest, the image of the South African flag seared into her memory.

Abby Dennison won the Roger Bannister Memorial Mile for Women in a new world record of 4:05.20. Her final lap had taken just 57 seconds and the last hundred metres a staggering 13.1. She would take home to South Africa the six million dollars, less taxes of course, but still a fortune in South African rand terms.

Elinah Kiptanui finished in 4:06.10, Sarah Moyo in 4:08.99, Mary McColgan in 4:11.22, Jane Beardsley in 4:11.54 and the final pair, Molly Fields and Ekaterina Vinitskaya in 4:13.10 and 4:14.09 respectively.

Kiptanui, of course, was rewarded with a new world record for the 1 500 metres – corrected later to 3:49.10 – with Dennison also breaking the 3:50 barrier with 3:49.89. Everyone in the field broke 3:57 for the 1 500 metres, the first time ever.

It was the greatest women's middle-distance race in the history of the sport, emulating Roger Bannister's classic effort on a gravel track at Iffley Road, Oxford on 6 May 1954. Had he been in this race, he would have been a mere 40 metres ahead of Abby.

20h20

Donna Gray sat back in her seat in the media centre. That was pretty special, she told herself with a smile. What an evening!

She had no idea.

In the stadium, the crowd remained in their seats. Hardly anyone had left. The runners were still out there and everyone wanted the magic to continue.

It was all over, the race, the two results announcements, the two world records, the lap of honour around the stadium by the eight athletes, draped in their respective national flags. The roaring and cheering, the flashing cameras, the tears, the arms raised in celebration and the millions of people still staring at their television screens in wonder at what they had just witnessed.

But it wasn't over.

The announcer called for silence and the crowd eventually obeyed. What now?

A little girl, carrying a small bunch of flowers, emerged from the tunnel next to the finish line and walked slowly towards the first bend. She moved onto the grassy area outside the track and carefully went up three steps onto a raised platform exactly ten metres square, a platform that hardly anyone had noticed before.

It was Mary-Jane Selfe, the eleven-year-old niece of the meeting director and the little girl who had burst into tears a year earlier when she couldn't hand her flowers to Sarah Moyo, the winner of the race that year. This time there would be no mistake, no disappointment, a classic tradition across the world in elite athletics meetings. She would hand over the flowers this time, that was for sure.

She stood on the stage as the crowd fell silent. The stadium lights dimmed

THE FINAL LAP

until only the stage, Mary-Jane and the surrounding grassy area remained brightly lit. She smiled at the Steadicam resting on the shoulder of a camera operator a few metres away. Millions of people watched on television, mesmerised. She looked beautiful in a long white dress with frilly sleeves, a mass of yellow flowers decorating her blonde hair. The atmosphere was filled with tension, anticipation and mystery. Seventy thousand people fell silent.

A second spotlight lit up the same tunnel as a tall man emerged carrying two microphones, linked remotely to the central sound system. The TV cameras tracked him. It was Marcus Findlay, stadium announcer and popular morning show host on a local radio station.

He climbed the steps, gave Mary-Jane a quick hug and stood next to her. The crowd waited in nervous, confused anticipation. It was weirdly quiet.

Marshalled by Simon Hardy and Kurt Hunsler, the eight athletes from the mile race came from where they had been sitting on the grass nearby and formed a line in front of the stage. Ten carefully selected photographers and three more cameramen came with them and took up positions around the stage.

The spotlights remained on the stage and the people around it as Findlay said, 'I would now like to invite Abby Dennison to join me.' There was a brief hesitation as the cameras sought out Abby, who stood in the middle of the line next to Suzy Marshall. She didn't move and gazed around her, eyes wide, like the proverbial deer in the headlights.

'Abby, please join me up here,' Findlay said again, grinning. Suzy Marshall gave Abby a shove from behind and she slowly climbed the stairs, moving next to Mary-Jane as if seeking company. She had absolutely no idea what was happening.

During this time, a man had been walking, unnoticed in the dark, out of the same tunnel, down the track and onto the grass. He joined the others on the brightly lit stage.

There was a lengthy pause as the crowd absorbed the tableau, four people on a low stage in the glare of the spotlights, the rest of the giant stadium in near darkness. Abby's face filled the big screen, then the focus widened to include the others on the stage. The tension was something you could reach out and touch.

Findlay said, 'It is now my pleasure to introduce something historic. And it will become your privilege as well.' He stood back and handed the second microphone to the man, who took the flowers from Mary-Jane. Only a handful of people in the stadium recognised Barberton daisies from White River, Mpumalanga, South Africa. Red, yellow, white and purple.

The man gazed around the vast stadium in apparent wonder, then said, 'Ladies and gentlemen in the stadium here and around the world, I am not going to say much. In fact, I have just seventeen words to say.'

Moving forward, he stood in front of Abby and held out the flowers. She took them.

'My name is Deon Coetzee and I am a humble sportswriter.'

A long, extremely pregnant pause, then, 'Abby Dennison, will you marry me?'

Her eyes widened, she stood apparently frozen, then threw her arms around his neck. In the roar that followed, Findlay had to shout into his microphone. 'Abby, what's your answer?'

She stood back, took the microphone, stared at Deon for many seconds, smiled and said, 'No world record, no millions of dollars, no titles can compare with how I feel now. Deon Coetzee, I love you and I will definitely, without any hesitation, marry you.'

Seventy thousand people in the stadium and millions more across the world watching and listening experienced a sudden, unexpected intake of breath. Within seconds, a large percentage of them had tears in their eyes.

For the second time that night, the roar was deafening.

The second Roger Bannister Memorial Athletics Meeting ended in a way that no one in their wildest dreams could have imagined, in a way that no one would ever forget. The crowd started to leave the stadium. It had been a night to remember in so many ways.

In a super-anticlimactic end to the proceedings, eight athletes, each accompanied by a personal doping-control official, trooped off to a small changing room deep in the stands, the one with the black door and several toilet cubicles.

'Please urinate into this bottle, Miss Dennison.'

The rules, even on this amazing occasion, had to be observed.

59

Friday, 16 August

ATHLETES' HOTEL, LONDON

Abby was alone in her room on the twelfth floor of the athletes' hotel, sitting on her bed. The events of the day swirled around her brain in a rush of colour, noise and images. Much of it was a blur – the gun, the fierce race, the incredible power of the other runners, the tension, the fear and then, as if by the hand of God, the Final Lap.

Then she remembered a particular moment and everything else left her mind. For the umpteenth time that day, her pulse quickened and a frown appeared on her face. She reached into the pocket of her tracksuit and there it was, a small envelope, crumpled and smeared with sweat and dirt.

In the pandemonium that followed the race and the few quiet moments as they all stood in front of the stage, the runner next to her had pressed something into her hand. 'This is for you,' she said quietly, her eyes on the ground.

Abby had thought no more about it until now. She stared at the crumpled, dirty paper. On the front of the envelope was written in black ballpoint pen, 'Abby Dennison. Private.'

She opened it and inside she found a small piece of paper. On it she saw the following, written in the same handwriting and with the same black ballpoint pen:

'I'm sorry. I didn't know. It wasn't my idea. Please forgive me.'

EPILOGUE

Monday, 21 October

JOHANNESBURG

The Charlotte Maxeke Johannesburg Academic Hospital is little more than a massive concrete block of a building on one of the city's ridges, its prominent position making it a very visible, but not particularly beautiful, landmark in the city.

CMJAH is not the biggest hospital in the region – that honour belongs to the massive, sprawling complex of buildings in Soweto known across the world as Chris Hani Baragwanath – but its importance lies in the fact that it is adjacent to the medical school of the University of the Witwatersrand, an academic institution with a long history of producing fine doctors and brilliant academics, including the 2002 Nobel Prize winner for medicine.

The medical school is less imposing, consisting of a few buildings tucked behind the giant hospital edifice and linked to it via a series of passages.

It was in that very medical school on a bright spring morning that Abby Dennison was led by a smartly dressed woman to the end of a passage on the third floor. They stopped outside a door, and the woman said, 'Good luck, Abby!' and left.

There was a sign on the door that read, 'Professor Rufus Holmsworth, Dean of Medicine'.

Abby hesitated, then knocked firmly three times. 'Come in,' boomed a voice.

She entered a room that was the epitome of an academic man-cave. It had a faint, musty smell mixed with a whiff of floor polish, which made her nose wrinkle. Bookshelves covered two of the walls, while on the third were numerous framed degrees, membership certificates to all sorts of societies, and photographs of the professor with everyone from Nelson Mandela and Chris Barnard, to Francois Pienaar and Trevor Noah. Next to the Pienaar photo was a space where another image could be added, when the time was right.

The professor's desk, crafted from dark teak, was massive and remarkably neat for an academic's work surface. There were, however, piles of medical journals on a side table. A laptop computer was open. Two visitors' chairs stood next to the desk, but the room's occupant directed Abby to the far corner of the room, where there were three easy chairs around a low coffee table.

The professor was short and slim with a neatly trimmed ginger beard and rimless glasses. He wore a shabby corduroy jacket, his tie loosely knotted and decorated with images of microscopes and syringes. His trousers looked several sizes too big, seemingly only kept in place by a sturdy leather belt. His brown leather shoes were badly scuffed and in desperate need of a polish.

'Please have a seat,' he said, pointing to one of the chairs. 'I must say that I am finally pleased to make your acquaintance after communicating for so long via email.'

'Me too, Professor.'

'I see that you wrote the Cambridge International A Levels. Let me start by saying that your results were outstanding. Chemistry, physics and mathematics, all in the ninetieth percentile. And you even did a fourth subject, biology, where you scored a distinction. You know that only three subjects are required?'

'My matric results were below par, Professor. I wanted to make sure.'

'Very good. With ninety-one per cent in maths you could have become a data scientist. Less messy, more money apparently.'

She smiled enigmatically. 'I would hate to spend any more time behind my computer, Professor. Other people need to become data scientists.'

'How did you manage such fine results doing the courses online?'

'Well, over the past year and a bit I've had plenty of free time and, when it comes to important stuff, I'm pretty focused and determined.'

'Indeed. Some tea, perhaps?'

Without waiting for an answer, Holmsworth moved to a corner of the room where a kettle was bubbling, the steam fogging up a nearby window. Three minutes later he returned, holding a tray with two full cups, a sugar bowl, a milk jug, two teaspoons and four biscuits on a plate.

'My favourite morning break, rooibos tea and shortbread biscuits.'

They sipped and nibbled politely.

Then he said, 'Let's get down to business. You must be excited.'

'I guess I am. This is something that I've been working towards for nearly a year.'

'Only a year?' He sounded surprised.

'Yes. Everything changed for me about this time last year.'

'Well, let's cut to the chase. You know that Wits only admits a hundred and fifty new undergraduate medical students each year straight from school and another fifty from our Graduate Entry Programme. And we have to balance our intake in terms of gender and racial equity. This is South Africa, after all.'

She smiled. 'I knew that, and that's why I did the A-Level exams. At least I score on the gender requirement.' She saw his frown. 'Oh no, please don't tell me that men are now the endangered species?'

They both laughed.

His face became serious. 'I don't always enjoy this particular exercise, one which I am forced to do every year. Over four hundred people make it onto the shortlist. It's hard to tell wonderful, passionate, smart young people that they haven't made the grade.'

She stared at him and her heart sank. 'Please tell me I'm not one of those, Professor. Please.'

He smiled. 'Not a chance. I am delighted to confirm that you have been accepted into the first year of study at this very medical school. In six years' time, if you work hard, you will be a doctor.'

There was silence, then she said, 'Thank you, Prof. I had no idea whether I would make the grade. Honestly, I can't say that being a doctor has been a lifelong dream. The opposite, in fact. I only decided to aim for medical school about twelve months ago. But now that you have confirmed my acceptance, the weight is finally off my mind. Can I give you a hug, Prof?' She grinned.

The old man went red but stood, his arms wide. They hugged.

'Welcome to Wits University medical school. May I call you Abby?'

'Of course, Prof, everyone does.'

For both, it was a special moment.

Then he looked down, fumbled in his pocket and pulled out a phone. 'One last thing, Abby. Can I have a selfie? For my grandchildren, of course.'

'Of course, Professor, for your grandchildren.'

Some things never change, she thought.

As she turned to leave, he said, 'I look forward to working with you, Mrs Coetzee.'

AUTHOR'S NOTE

This story is mainly, but not entirely, fiction.

The characters in the story – Abby, Deon, Bronwyn, JP, Mark, James, Emily, Natie, Abby's competitors and the others – do not exist in real life. They were created to populate the pages of this book and make it real. Similarly, many of the events and organisations are also not real: the Bannister Memorial Athletics Meeting, R1609, Maxx, Xtend, Regalbank, APN. But many of the athletes, events and places mentioned in the story are real. So, too, are existing world track records at the time of writing. Records are regularly broken, as we saw in the story.

The way the Regalbank track meetings are organised also broadly reflects reality, although different meetings may have different structures. Intermediate times, the use of pacemakers, call rooms and warm-up areas are normally part of such events.

In middle-distance races beyond eight hundred metres, the tactics employed by athletes are critical. Every runner goes into the race with a broad strategy (such as Abby's plan to sit behind Elinah in the second Bannister race), but things can change rapidly in the competition, where life is on a knife-edge and a single split-second decision is often the key to success, or not. It isn't a matter of going round and round a track until someone wins. The mile races reveal how a skilled coach, a good tactical plan and correct decisions taken during a race, often unconsciously, are essential to success.

One of the core themes of the book is the incredible sacrifice elite individual athletes and the small group of people around them have to make in terms of lifestyle. Constant travelling is necessary and only a few months of the year are spent at home. The athlete is always surrounded by the same small group of people, which can be difficult at times.

Hard physical work, hours a day, weeks on end, is essential to success. The intensity of the way elite athletes train and prepare for competitions is extreme in anyone's book.

Understanding the complexities of the science of exercise physiology and staying abreast of developments in training methods means that a skilled coach is essential. JP's crucial role in Abby's success cannot be underestimated.

Mental preparation is also critical, hence Bronwyn's key role in the Team. When everything else is equal – ability, preparation, tactics – it comes down to the strange magic of Big Match Temperament, where the athlete with the strongest mind wins the race.

There are major risks that athletes face on a daily basis, all of which could spell disaster and the premature end of a career.

The constant risk of injury means that there is a fine line athletes walk between peak fitness and physical breakdown. Injury prevention – a science all on its own – is far better than injury cure.

Doping in athletics is a fundamental, if unsavoury, part of the sport. The authorities, including the World Anti-Doping Agency, do their best to eliminate it, but success is not easily achieved as the science of doping always seems to be one step ahead of the enforcers. And the rules as they pertain to the athlete are unforgiving and rigidly enforced. No matter the circumstances, the athlete is always considered to be guilty if caught.

Another risk, often overlooked but nevertheless real, is the threat of criminality. Stalking, kidnapping, extortion, even violence, are fellow travellers of fame. Numerous famous women and men – actors, sportspeople, politicians, rock stars and others – have had their lives impacted, ruined and even lost through criminal activity. Think John Lennon. The initial nervousness around the motives of Mark Whyte in *The Final Lap* is a result of this reality.

Finally on the risk front, and given their very public personas, sports heroines like Abby have to fiercely guard their privacy and avoid any hint of impropriety. Every angry word, unwise text message, improper image, racist, homophobic or sexist remark will inevitably be repeated a million times on social media.

The Final Lap also enters the debate around the huge amounts of money available to elite performers in various high-profile sports. Top sportsmen and women earn vast, some would say obscene, amounts of money. The reasons for this are complex but are generally linked to the power of television, the media in general, and the strength of brands such as Manchester United, Real Madrid and other football clubs plus numerous sponsors such as Nike, Adidas, Red Bull and others.

Athletics has generally offered only small fractions of the amounts earned in other sports, and the idea of a six-million-dollar payday seems outlandish by current standards. But, given the power of an international icon such as Abby and a smart, adventurous sponsor such as Regalbank, such amounts are possible in the future.

Louis Sachar wrote, 'They called her "a genius". And even though it really didn't explain anything, everybody considered it a satisfactory explanation. And that way, nobody had to try to understand.'

In this book, much is made of the fact that Abby is 'unique', 'once-in-a-generation', and 'a genius'. This is by no means unusual. All aspects of human endeavour – sport, art, music, mathematics, literature, business and any other field of activity – occasionally produce a person who is truly unique, a game-changer. This is what Abby is, an athlete possessing the perfect genetic and physical make-up, the brain, mental toughness and the ideal environment in which to flourish. There were 'genius' athletes before her and there will be more to come.

On a philosophical level, consider the discussion between James and Bronwyn just before the first Bannister Mile when they spoke about the possibility of people like Abby being viewed as more than just an athlete. Do people out there see them as someone to be worshipped? Whether this is true or not, and the implications for society, is a debate for another time. For this author, though, the idea of an ordinary person being elevated to some sort of deity is disturbing, to say the least. But, sadly, it's reality.

Finally, consider this: why did Abby, a world-record holder with the athletics world at her feet, retire from the sport at just twenty-five? Was it the restricted lifestyle, the boredom, the sense that she was unidimensional and not exploring her other talents? Was it the risk of danger or injury? The fear of unknowingly been caught for doping? The possibility that she had achieved all that she had set out to do? Ticked all the boxes?

The book leaves the answer to this question open-ended. It could have been none, some or maybe all of those reasons.

In the end *The Final Lap* is, essentially, about change. Most people – famous or not – will one day take a long, hard look at themselves and decide if what they are doing is still appropriate. It's one thing that makes us human.

They all did that: Abby decided to become a doctor, Mark re-evaluated his moral compass and his worldview. JP, Bronwyn and Paul had to change how they lived when Abby became a medical student. Inevitably, this takes courage. It's not easy to shift your life out of a safe, comfortable and predictable environment into something fundamentally new.

My precious characters in this story all changed. Let's hope for their sakes that these changes resulted in happier, more productive lives.

Only time will tell.

ACKNOWLEDGEMENTS

Firstly, there are the two special and amazing women to whom this book is dedicated. As I mentioned, you know who you are. For everyone else, they are Sonja and Kim, my precious family.

Many wonderful, dedicated and skilled people played roles in the process of producing this book.

Tom Cottrell, my long-time friend, collaborator in many projects related to the written word and now my publisher, rescued me from a dismal fate involving printing a few hundred copies and begging everyone I know to buy one. Thanks, Tom, let this not be the last time we collaborate.

Tom also introduced me to my editor, Russell Clarke. Having one's first novel read by an experienced editor is not for the fainthearted. For me, that first call, email or even WhatsApp message from Russell after he had read my first draft was rather like waiting for my final-year exam results to be posted on the Wits University noticeboard: excitement, nervousness and uncertainty all mixed up together. Thankfully, Russell gave me a clear thumbs-up. Since then he has proved to be skilled, helpful and wonderfully supportive of this project.

Thank you, Tom and Russell.

Finally, there are many key people who supported me through many years as an international athletics journalist and commentator. Without their counsel and unstinting support, this book would not have seen the light of day. From a long list, let me mention specifically Stewart Banner, Greg Upton, Daan van den Berg, Scott Seward, Robin Kempthorne, Melinda Lombard,

Gert Ungerer, Aubrey Coetzee, Bruce Davidson, Helen Mittwoch and David van der Sandt.

To fellow athletics journalists, my sincere thanks for being fine colleagues: Gerald de Kock, Steve Britten, Arnie Geerdts, Vaylen Kirtley, Mark Etheridge, Tony Frost, Michael Finch, Helen Lucre and Bruce Fordyce. Finally, to the late Zithulele Sinqe and Lindsay Weight, now sadly departed the commentary box, you are not forgotten.

Dear patient reader, thank you for reaching the end. I hope the journey has been a pleasant and useful one. All of us – writer, readers, precious characters – will meet again sometime, God willing.

IAN LAXTON